THE MEDALLIO...
OF ALL THEIR PROBLEMS, AND BOY, DID THEY HAVE PROBLEMS!

Laly sat on the edge of the bed next to her friend Sugar. "The first chance I get, I'm going to steal that medallion from the captain of this ship—and I don't care what I have to do to get it," she said.

Sugar sighed and closed her eyes to her friend's plan, which was really no plan at all. "Laly, if you'd just be a little patient, we might be able to get it without having to steal it."

"Do you think the man is just going to hand it over if I ask him nicely?" Laly asked sarcastically.

"Of course not, but I don't think you need to start thinking about taking drastic measures just yet." Sugar was worried that Laly's penchant for the dramatic would get them into even more trouble than they were already in.

"Sugar, we're more than three hundred years in the past, sitting in the captain's cabin on an English warship, and we're believed to be mermaids. When exactly do you suggest I start taking drastic measures?"

"I guess . . . Laly, I just don't want things to get worse."

"And how could they possibly get any worse?"

Sugar sat bolt upright on the bed. "In case you haven't noticed, we *are* sitting in the captain's cabin and wearing his warm, dry clothing, not shivering in the ship's hold, wet with salt water and at the mercy of the crew. I think you'll agree that things could indeed be worse!"

*　　*　　*

Praise for this author's previous work

"Sure to please . . . grabs the reader's attention from the first page, gallops along at a breakneck pace, and doesn't let up until the last word."

—*Romantic Times* on *Rosebud*

ALANE FAY
MERMAID'S DREAM

PINNACLE BOOKS
KENSINGTON PUBLISHING CORP.

PINNACLE BOOKS are published by

Kensington Publishing Corp.
850 Third Avenue
New York, NY 10022

The P logo Reg U.S. Pat. & TM Off. Pinnacle is a trademark
of Kensington Publishing Corp.

First Printing: June, 1995

Printed in the United States of America

*This book is dedicated to my mother,
the anonymous star.*

One

"Help me with this fresh tank, Jim," Laly asked one of her students as she pulled a heavier weight belt around her hips and strapped it tightly.

"Let me do it." Sugar Stephens took the heavy tank from the young man and headed toward her friend and associate Dr. Lorraine Lawrence, known as "Laly." "Are you really going through with this?" She looked behind her to where the anthropology students where standing in a group, whispering among themselves. "You preach to everyone about the necessity for safe diving, then you go off on this wild-goose chase."

Laly just looked squarely at her friend and frowned. This wasn't a wild-goose chase. She was certain she'd found a beam, or what was left of a beam, on her last dive. If it hadn't been for an uncomfortable lack of air, she'd still be forty feet down, surveying the area for the possibility of it being a shipwreck. "I'm going down, Sugar."

"Alone?"

"Yes, alone. With this storm front moving in, I need you topside to help get these students ready to get the hell out of here as soon as I get back."

Both women looked toward the northeasterly horizon. The black storm had appeared out of nowhere and was descending on them with uncanny speed. Sugar turned back to her friend. "I don't like it one bit. You know better than this."

Laly smiled an appeasing smile at her best buddy. "Of course I do. But when has that ever stopped me?" She hefted the weight of the BC onto her back. "Come on, Sugar, chill. If I don't go back down now, the storm could move the bottom sand so much that I'd never find the wreck again."

"Assuming it is a wreck."

"Okay, so I'm assuming a lot. But I've got a funny feeling about this. I don't know why, but I think I'm on the verge of something really big."

"I've got a feeling about this, too, and I don't like it." Sugar looked once more at the rapidly advancing storm front and was sure she'd seen a bolt of lightning. "Oh, hell. Well, if you're determined to do this stupid thing, get going. Just hurry. I don't like the looks of this storm."

Laly gave her friend the thumbs-up sign and pulled her mask up over her eyes and nose. Fins in hand, she made her way down the ladder in the center of the thirty-five-foot catamaran they'd hired for this expedition to the Bahamas. As she entered the water, she glanced at the storm. She would indeed have to hurry if she wanted to beat the fury of the wind, rain, and lightning headed their way.

Just three feet beneath the surface of the water,

she was no longer thinking about the storm. She was thinking of her find. The beam. It had to be the mast of a ship, sunken, possibly centuries ago. If she could find more debris, cannon, cannonballs, the anchor . . . treasure—and could identify her find—she'd have achieved her lifelong dream. To uncover a piece of as-yet unknown history.

History—anthropology, to be exact—was what she taught at the university. All winter long she would plan these expeditions, recruit competent students interested in furthering their education, and with the college's blessing and their money, spend her summers searching the ocean bottom for buried treasure. The monetary gratification went to the college, the glory to her.

She was just about where she'd been when she'd seen the beam, so she slowed her movements. Any unnecessary motion could raise a cloud of sand and obscure her vision to the point of making it impossible for her to see something right in front of her. Gliding along the underwater ridge, she descended at a rapid rate. Nearing forty feet when she saw it, she felt the excitement leap in her chest. There was no mistaking that it was manmade and embedded in the coral reef just under the sand. Allowing herself to float downward until she could reach the beam, she stretched her gloved hand forward, almost afraid to touch it.

She pulled her hand back at the last moment. She wanted to touch it with her fingers, not the rubber of her gloves. Quickly she pulled off her right glove, then her left, and stuck them under her weight belt. Then she reached for the beam again. She was so excited, she had to force herself to breathe more slowly. The rough surface of the wood was cool and solid, but as she placed both hands flat against it she could have sworn she felt a warmth from it.

She jerked her hands back and waited a moment. Was she so excited that she was imagining things? She'd told Sugar that she had a funny feeling about this. She still did, only now it was stronger. She looked around her. She was, of course, still alone. Why was she feeling this way? Although she knew the dangers of diving alone, as did all divers, she had to admit that she usually enjoyed the solitude she found alone below the ocean's surface.

She mentally shook herself. She was being ridiculous. She reached for the beam again. It's just wood, she told herself. This time that's all she felt, wood. She was glad her silliness was passing, and decided to follow the beam to its other end, needing to determine its length to identify it. Slowly she swam along, searching for any other signs of ship's wreckage.

On the surface, Sugar watched the storm bearing down on them and couldn't help but worry about Laly. She was always in search of high adventure, and this time Sugar was afraid Laly might have bitten off more than she could chew. "Damn it," she muttered under her breath.

"Dr. Stephens?"

Sugar jumped, startled that someone had heard her oath. She turned to see a pretty young woman watching her with concern. "Yes, Julie?"

"I was just wondering if Dr. Lawrence will be all right."

"Of course she will. Now, you go help Chad strap down the empty tanks. We'll need to be ready when

Dr. Lawrence gets back." Sugar watched as the student shrugged and returned to help the others, who looked just as worried as she did. "Damn you, Laly," she muttered again. "Why did you have to go off like this now?" She glanced once more at the angry black clouds and felt the first raindrops hit her skin.

Sugar looked at her watch and determined the length of time Laly had left on her tank. It had been too long. She'd never get back before this storm hit full force. The weather reports they'd received that morning had said nothing about a storm front, but in tropical waters a storm could blow up very unexpectedly. Apparently this was the case today. She gritted her teeth and pushed an angry hand through the damp tangle of long black curls that the wind seemed determined to keep in her face. Laly was always causing her trouble.

Sugar and Laly had met while they were both students at the university where they now taught. It seemed destiny that their lives, running so parallel to that point, had finally brought them together. They'd both come from single-parent families, lived on the California coast, learned to dive at an early age, and been interested in the same subjects at the university. Yet no two people could have been more different in temperament.

Sarah Stephens had received her nickname, Sugar, from a great-uncle because she was so sweet, generally even-tempered, soft-spoken and levelheaded. A "rule follower," Laly had called her once, making it sound like an insult.

Laly, on the other hand, was always looking for trouble, invented it when there was none to find, and seemed to enjoy the discomfort she caused Sugar throughout their college days. Lorraine, as she'd

Alane Fay

been christened, was a driven soul, certain that life was holding tightly to a secret that she had to uncover before she could rest.

This was what bothered Sugar now, with the storm fast approaching and Laly's need to test the limits, to push her luck beyond reasonable bounds. Laly'd said she had a funny feeling about this find. Sometimes feelings were warnings, only Sugar was sure Laly wouldn't recognize them as such. She reached for her dive gear. She had to get to Laly quickly.

"Dr. Stephens, what are you doing?" Sugar heard Julie's voice behind her again.

"I'm going down for Dr. Lawrence. I'm sure she doesn't realize the storm is moving so swiftly." She looked past the girl and raised her voice to be heard by everyone. "You all be ready to go. Keep the nose of the catamaran pointed into the storm and wait. I'll be back before you know it." She tried to sound reassuring, but the worried expressions facing her told her she'd failed. Sighing, she finished putting on her gear and headed toward the ladder. Once more, before she put in her mouthpiece, she muttered, "Damn you, Laly."

Laly's heart was in her throat. She'd almost glided past the object without seeing it, then something had told her to look closer. That feeling again? Whatever, she turned slightly and saw it wedged under the edge of the beam. Pulling it gently from the sand had been easy. Now she held it in her hand. Whatever it was, it was heavy, nearly five pounds was her guess. She turned it over in her hand. It was some kind of metal disk or medallion covered by black corrosion. It covered the palm of her hand and seemed to have some kind of markings.

She pulled her knife from its sheath on her left forearm and turned it over in her hand to hit the object with the handle. She struck it several times before a chunk of the corrosion broke away, revealing the shine of metal underneath. In the turquoise depths of the ocean water colors couldn't be distinguished without a flashlight, and she cursed not having one with her. She couldn't tell what metal the object was made of. By its weight it could be solid gold, but she wouldn't allow herself such wishful thinking. It was more likely a primitive mixture of lead and iron. She continued to chip away at the corrosion, forgetting completely the importance of time.

Sugar descended as quickly as was safe. She was an experienced diver and could usually clear the pressure in her ears simply by swallowing at the necessary times, but if she dropped too rapidly, there was the danger of bursting an eardrum. She'd done that once as a child and could still remember the excruciating pain that had immobilized her for several minutes, and worse, curtailed her diving for several weeks while it healed.

She scanned the area where she knew Laly should be and looked for her bubbles, the easiest way to find a diver. As she swam toward the shadows ahead of her, she noticed the color of the water changing. It was getting a whole lot darker down here. She clenched her fists at her sides as she swam. That storm was nearly on top of them.

Laly continued working on the object. She had been able to knock away most of the corrosion and found a small hole on one edge, probably for a chain or cord to suspend it. She felt it was too heavy for a necklace but couldn't think of another use for it yet.

Then she noticed the darkness. Very suddenly the waters around her had filled with gray shadows. A chill went down her back as she looked around her. The storm? It hadn't looked like it was moving so quickly, but in the Bahamas, in any tropical area, for that matter, storms were a tricky business. She realized that it was time to get out of here, and fast. She only hoped the storm wouldn't disturb the bottom so badly that she'd be unable to find the beam again after it passed. Sometimes storms would churn up the ocean floor to the point that objects on the bottom were moved miles away from their origin.

Laly looked around her once more. She wished she could shake these eerie feelings she was having. Putting her knife back in its sheath, she unzipped the front of her wetsuit and slipped the medallion inside to sit against the front of her bathing suit top. She zipped up the wetsuit and was turning back toward the catamaran when she felt something grab her arm. She let out a yelp into her mouthpiece just as she recognized Sugar at her side.

Sugar almost laughed at Laly's reaction but was too concerned about the color of the water. They were now in nearly total darkness. She was about to signal to surface when they both felt the water begin to heave. The looks they exchanged from behind their masks were of sheer terror. Tidal wave!

All Laly could remember about that moment was the way she and Sugar clutched each other's hands in fear. "Death grip" was a good description of the way they held on. It seemed they both knew that to be separated could mean death for either one, and being together meant possible death for both.

The ocean seemed to rise up like a huge sledgehammer and aim itself directly at them. The force of the wave moved them swiftly forward across the bottom. Over and over they rolled, disoriented, beaten and bruised, but still holding onto each other. As they fell to the harsh sandy bottom again and again Laly and Sugar watched to make sure that each was still alive, breathing from her mouthpiece, not just floating limply, injured. Neither could have stood the loss of her best friend.

The humming started with the light. It sliced through the water like lightning from above, and the women watched with horror as the strange glow drove toward them. Suddenly, they were held captive in the turmoil by the tingling, nerve-jarring light that seemed to be the center of the storm. Seconds passed slowly as the painful brightness churned the water and twisted them in its grasp. Then they were free, the water merely rolling with its normal, almost restful rush.

Laly was the first to test her limbs. She was already stiff and feeling some soreness in her lower back, but could tell she'd made it through the battering with little damage. She looked to Sugar, who was now also gingerly turning her arms and legs, checking for serious injuries. She gave the thumbs-up sign when she found none. Laly returned the gesture and grinned with her eyes behind her mask.

They both thought of the catamaran at the same moment and started their ascent. The students topside, although most were advanced divers, were probably not capable of handling the catamaran through the kind of storm that had just passed. Laly and Sugar prayed in unison that they'd find the catamaran and students intact, safe and sound.

Following one of the most steadfast rules of diving, not to beat your bubbles to the surface, Laly and Sugar rose at a sure rate, watching their speed. Sugar frowned when she realized they'd been taken much deeper during the storm. She made a mental note to ask Laly about it when they surfaced. The time it was taking them to surface told her that they were more than lucky neither one had suffered severe pressure damage during their pummeling by the storm.

As they neared the surface, Laly thought she heard something. It sounded like thunder, but they were still too deep to be able to hear what was left of the storm. She slowed and touched Sugar's arm to stop her also. They hung there suspended in the water and Laly motioned for Sugar to listen.

Sugar's eyes glanced first in one direction, then another, as she tried to identify the sound she was hearing through the water. She shrugged her confusion at Laly then turned in a full circle, searching the surface directly above for the shadow of the double-hulled catamaran. Laly did the same. When they once again faced each other it was with brave expressions, each trying to reassure the other.

Then the sound vibrated through the water to them again. What was it? They were now sure it wasn't thunder and continued their ascent.

Laly reached the surface just seconds before Sugar and pulled her mask down to rest loosely around her neck. She took her mouthpiece away and gulped the fresh air around her, thankful they'd made it through the storm alive. She faced her friend.

"Well, we made it, Sugar." Laly grinned.

An explosion that would have made the thunder sound quiet shocked them both into sucking water. "J. H. Christ! What was that?" Laly sputtered, choking.

Sugar looked around them, wiping water from her face, and was certain she was dreaming. "What the . . ."

Laly's eyes followed where Sugar's led and she, too, was dumbfounded. There, a distance away, were two vessels, mint-condition replicas of seventeenth-century fighting ships. And they were in battle! Laly tried to focus, sure she was seeing things, but couldn't blink the sight away. Just then, another volley of burning cannon fire flew over their heads. "Oh my God, *dive*!"

They dived in unison, pulling up their masks and inserting their mouthpieces by instinct. Just ten feet below the surface they stopped and stared at one another. Unable to communicate under water, other than with a few signals, they just waited. The thunder—no, cannon fire—continued as the battle raged on over their heads.

Laly knew that Sugar was probably wondering the same thing she was: how had they spent the past week on New Providence Island, in the Plantation Hotel in Nassau, and not heard about a historic battle reenactment set for today? And what battle would it be?

She knew from her research of the area that during the 1600s Spanish, and sometimes French, piracy in the area had been rampant and that King Charles II had tried to end it by sending English ships to the area. But she knew of no one battle that would have been worthy of reenactment.

The abundance of sunken Spanish pirate ships was what had caused her to choose this particular place for her studies. It was also what had convinced Sugar to join her on this expedition. Sugar's recent studies, the effect piracy had on colonization and genealogy in the region, coincided with this trip perfectly. Now here they were, two college professors, hanging ten feet below the surface of the ocean, knowing nothing about a battle reenactment taking place over their very heads. Another explosion, much closer this time, sent them to the surface once more.

The ships had moved nearer to them and they could see that one of them was on fire. Men scrambled across her decks, hauling wooden buckets of water from the sea on long ropes to fight the flames. Laly looked at Sugar in disbelief. "They can't mean to destroy these beautiful replicas, can they?"

"Looks that way. I just don't understand this. They're using real ammunition. Oh, my Lord." Sugar pointed to the side of the ship not burning, where men stood with old-fashioned muskets, firing at the other ship. "Look at the flags, Laly." The ship's colors had caught her eye.

Laly looked to the ships' mainmasts. One showed English colors, the other Spanish. She shook her head and examined the costumes of the actors more closely. She was amazed at the authenticity of the designs.

Another volley of cannon fire whizzed past their heads and landed, steaming, in the water just behind them and too close for comfort. "Laly, they're not playing around. This may have started out as a reenactment, but these fools have gone way beyond that. They're trying to blow each other out of the water. And we're in the way!"

Laly looked from one ship to the other. Smoke darkened the sky from the now-smoldering fire on board the Spanish ship. The shouts and cries of the men coming across the water were authentic, all right. The explosion of gunfire once again took her attention and she was horrified to see a man fall overboard, a dark red stain of blood covering his chest.

Sugar grabbed Laly's arm as she, too, watched the man fall to his death and sink below the surface of the water. "Laly, we've got to do something. These men are insane," she whispered.

Laly couldn't think, couldn't speak. She'd never seen a person murdered before. She tried to swallow the bile that rose in her throat. A few moments later she looked back at Sugar. She could see her friend was shaking, horribly affected by what they'd just witnessed. She knew they had to get out of the water. What they'd just been through in the storm, and now the horror of what they'd seen, was causing both of them to feel shocky.

Just then a thought occurred to Laly. If this was a staged battle, or if it had started out that way, there would be spectators. She looked around them. There had to be small boats observing what was taking place. But try as she might, she could find no such craft. They were out here alone. Alone, except for the maniacs on the two ships.

More cannon fire burning overhead caused Laly to pull Sugar abruptly under the surface. They resurfaced seconds later, choking on the salty water. Sugar continued to shiver, but tried to be brave. "I'm f-fine, r-really," she tried to assure Laly.

"Yeah, I can tell how fine you are." She was now getting angry. This was ridiculous. No matter how this whole show had gotten out of hand—the understatement of the century—it had to stop. She and Sugar had to get out of the water, and the only place to do that was on board one of those ships. "Come on, Sugar. We're going to get someone's attention."

"Okay." Sugar wasn't sure that was such a good idea. After all, they'd just witnessed a murder. But she swam after Laly toward the ships.

"Hello!" Laly called, angry that the battle raged on overhead and she and Sugar were now in more danger than ever and she couldn't get anyone to notice them. "Damn it! You big dumb jerks! Look down for Christ's sake!"

"Ahoy!" Sugar joined in the shouting.

"Ahoy? Where did you get that?" Laly asked incredulously.

"Well, they're t-taking this s-sailor thing p-pretty seriously. It doesn't sound so s-stupid if y-you think about it," Sugar answered, her teeth chattering violently.

Laly supposed she shouldn't be surprised by anything, after what this day had brought so far. "Okay, I'll bite. *Ahoy*!" she screamed at the top of her lungs.

Slowly at first, the gunfire from the English ship seemed to abate somewhat. Then Laly and Sugar watched in amazement as the battle came to a screeching halt. Crew members on both ships crowded the sides and gaped in what could only be described as awe as they watched the women swimming between the ships.

"I g-guess they're s-surprised to see us," observed Sugar.

"Well, I don't think they were expecting to have two women interrupt their battle." She looked from one ship to the other. A commotion was beginning on both ships, and she guessed it had something to do with them.

Men were scurrying around, shouting to others.

Laly noticed that the crew of the Spanish ship was indeed speaking Spanish. What authenticity! She then began to wonder about the man they'd seen killed. If pains were taken even to see to the language spoken on board these ships, then it was more than explainable how they'd made the man's death seem so real. She found herself feeling foolish about the whole thing.

Another thought had occurred to her. The audience she'd expected to see watching from a distance in small craft was probably on board the two ships. What better way to get the full impact of the battle? She found herself wondering what a seat at this kind of show would cost. She was sure it was worth every cent.

Laly felt Sugar shivering beside her and wished someone would hurry and do something about getting them out of the water. So far, the men were still gaping and gesturing like idiots. What was taking them so long? Was the confusion so great because the show had been stopped? Whatever the reason, there was no excuse for this wait. Couldn't someone on one of the ships send down a ladder or dinghy?

Captain Devon Bradley had been sent by King Charles himself to see to the pirate problem in the West Indies. New Providence Island settlers were being harassed regularly by the overrun of the Spanish and French pirates floating off their shores. The blackguards had even had the audacity to come ashore and pillage the settlements almost nightly.

The waterfront had become a pirate's den of murder and mayhem, the only control being the twisted honor of the pirates themselves, which, in most cases, turned out to be no honor at all, just the ability of one man to better the other, usually leaving a man with a knife in his stomach or back. They weren't too particular.

So far on this tour he'd found several Spanish and French ships, had run them down and boarded them, only to find their holds empty of booty. The arrogance of the bounders when he had to let them go still burned in his belly. But today was different. This ship hadn't merely turned and run, leading him on a useless chase. She'd fought. And he could see by her watermark that she was full of loot. This ship was the *Puta*, captained by Raul Rodriguez, a man Bradley had a personal hatred for.

He'd met Rodriguez on the waterfront when he'd first arrived on New Providence. He'd been scouting for information about the pirating and had followed a lead into the Blue Parrot, a bar known to cater to the worst of humanity.

As he'd sat drinking, pretending a drunk he didn't feel, he'd listened to the whispered conversations around him. He'd managed to pick up some facts concerning a valuable shipment of cedar and silverwood, due to sail on the *Flower* the following morning, when he'd noticed a sailor in the corner opposite him pulling on the arm of a young woman.

"Owww, matey. Let go o' me arm. Ye're goin' ta break it," the girl whined.

Bradley noticed she looked to be no more than thirteen, though she'd dressed herself to look older. He shook his head. It was sad to see a girl needing to pander herself in order to eat, but he'd seen it often enough on the waterfronts, both in England and here, to know that such was the lot of many.

He continued to watch with some interest as the sailor refused to release the skinny creature.

"Sit here, Niña," the sailor insisted, indicating the front of his dirty trousers.

"No, I want none o' ye," the girl whined again. "Last time, ye beat me raw. Now let go o' me arm." She pulled hard, only to be jerked roughly to the man's lap in obvious pain as he twisted her arm behind her.

This was enough for Bradley. Buying the child's services, immoral as it was, was one thing; injuring her to accomplish a seduction was another. He stood and crossed the room, stopping at the stranger's table. "I believe the girl has other plans for the evening." His voice was quiet. He didn't need to draw attention to himself in a place like this. All it could get him was trouble.

Rodriguez looked up from his chair. *"Que?"*

Bradley sighed. "I believe the child has other plans for this evening. If you would be so kind as to let her go?"

Rodriguez knew a challenge when he heard one. This Englishman seemed to want this little whore. He looked the girl over. She was young and had dirty hair and almost no breasts and smelled bad. But she had a good mouth. She'd proved that to him several nights earlier, when she'd made him forget his troubles with that mouth. Still, why would this Englishman be willing to die in a fight over a young whore?

"I said release her." Bradley's voice was still quiet, but now it carried a menacing tone that few men disregarded.

Rodriguez waited only a moment before striking. The girl fell to the floor with a scream as the knife flashed past her and sliced along the cheekbone of the Englishman.

Bradley was startled by the Spaniard's quickness but was able to move in time to keep the knife from going through his eye, its intended mark. With lightning speed he grabbed the wrist of his attacker and jerked him forward as he crashed his knee upward between the man's bent legs. The feel of the man's testicles being crushed against the bones of his knee gave him great satisfaction as he felt blood running from the deep cut on his face.

Rodriguez slumped to the floor in agony, sure he would never again feel the rush of fluid from his loins. "I will kill you Englishman," he hissed to the departing back of the stranger. "I will find you and destroy you."

Bradley didn't hear Rodriguez's threat but carried the burden of tremendous guilt when he learned later that the man had unleashed some of his anger on the poor girl he'd believed to be the cause of his troubles. Her body had been found behind the Blue Parrot, slashed from gullet to bowels.

Now Bradley had his chance. The *Puta* was in his grasp. Before long, Raul Rodriguez would be swinging from the yard, along with any of his crew who refused to swear allegiance to King Charles.

Two

When the guns stopped firing, Captain Bradley was at the stern of his ship, the *Vengeance*, conferring with his first officer, Charles Wainwright, on their next course of action. "We must get Rodriguez in our first attempt at boarding the *Puta* or we may fail." He looked up at the silence. "What's happened? Have they surrendered?" He couldn't believe this to be so. He'd been certain that Rodriguez would fight to the death.

"Captain, it's mermaids!" A crew member came running to the stern, his eyes so wide he looked like they'd pop from his head. The man danced from foot to foot with excitement.

"Calm down, man. What's this tale? Has the *Puta* surrendered?"

"What? No, Captain. It's mermaids!"

"Have you gone daft, man?" he demanded, looking past the man to where his entire crew had assembled at the port casemate. Had they *all* gone daft?

"No, Captain. We've found mermaids, or they've found us. Come look, Captain. You'll see for yourself. You'll see old Joe's not crazy." The man began pulling on Bradley's sleeve.

As Captain Bradley made his way to the side of the *Vengeance* he became aware that the *Puta* was no longer firing either. Instead of cannon balls and musket fire, the air was full of shouts and prayers. Bradley was beginning to believe that the crews of both ships had come down with the same kind of insanity at the same moment. Then he looked over the side.

"Laly, w-what are th-they w-waiting f-for?" Sugar continued to shiver.

"I don't know. You'd think they'd never seen women before." She held tightly to Sugar's forearm as they floated between the ships. Laly had convinced Sugar that this was still a staged performance, but she continued to worry about her friend. She knew from experience that if the shivers weren't stopped, the person suffering would continue to lose body heat. Even in tropical waters this was dangerous.

She looked upward to the English ship. "Come on, guys. Send down a ladder!" She glanced at Sugar and doubted her ability to climb. "Or better yet, a couple of you big guys, come down here and give us a hand!" she shouted. She knew she was being heard. She just couldn't figure out why her requests were being ignored. She even noticed several of the men cross themselves when she spoke. With her long white-blond hair plastered to her head, and maybe a few bruises from the storm, she probably didn't look her best, but she doubted she looked frightening.

Then she saw the captain. He had to be the captain. His manner spoke of authority. His costume of the day was tight black breeches, thigh high black leather boots, and a loose-fitting white shirt. Over this he wore a long blue coat with gold braid trim. She couldn't help noticing that this actor looked magnificent. "Wow, Sugar. Check out the captain."

Sugar looked in the direction Laly indicated and could see that the actor playing the part of the captain was exactly her friend's type. Tall, dark, and handsome was just what made Laly's heart sing. And this guy had it all. The way he towered over the other actors, he had to be several inches over six feet. Broad shoulders and muscular thighs filled his costume to perfection, and she knew she'd be hearing about his thick, wavy black hair before this day turned into night. He even carried a scar along one strong cheekbone, although that was probably fake. *"Dreammmy,"* she agreed, then, "He's p-probably g-gay."

"Sugar!" Laly spat at her friend.

"Sorry. B-But the w-way this d-day has g-gone I w-wouldn't b-be s-surprised."

Laly started pulling Sugar toward the English ship. She knew who she wanted to be rescued by.

The captain watched with disbelief. Never in his life would he have dreamed he'd see real mermaids. He'd heard all the tales of mermaids rescuing fishermen and luring sailors to sea, but never in his wildest imagination could he have pictured a day when two of them would interrupt an important battle.

Raul Rodriguez also watched the progress the mermaids were making toward the English ship. He'd not believed his men when they'd started screaming and praying at the side of the ship, but it was true. Two mermaids swam below him, their blue and green skins reflecting the sunlight, their long hair floating fanlike around them. He looked across the water to where he could see Captain Bradley standing, waiting for the mermaids to near his ship. His heart burned with the rage he still felt for the man. While everyone watched the mermaids, he slowly drew his pistol, took aim, and fired.

The explosion of gunpowder nearly caused Laly to jump out of the water. "What the hell?" She looked around and could see all eyes were turned toward the captain of the English ship. He stood defiantly, staring directly at the man who had fired the shot. Laly's eyes grew wider when she noticed a streak of red darkening the sleeve of the English captain's coat.

"What's going on?" questioned Sugar.

"I'm not sure. Maybe . . . I don't know. The show must go on?" she remarked feebly. This was all too real to be comfortable.

Raul could hear the grumbling of the men from both ships. They were afraid of the mermaids and didn't want to anger the mystical creatures. No one knew what they were capable of, so his attempt at killing Bradley had not been looked upon with good favor. He scowled and cursed as his desire to murder Bradley was thwarted.

Bradley knew the wound was not bad. His upper arm burned but it only gave him fuel for his hatred. He wanted to return Rodriguez's fire, to see his musket ball shatter the man's face, but right now he needed to see to the mermaids. What was he supposed to do? Why were they here?

Raul could see that the mermaids were swimming toward the English ship. If he could not kill Bradley today, he would at least take the mermaids. They could bring him good luck, and a goodly fortune.

His greedy heart nearly burst at the thought of how much gold he would be paid at the slave market for real mermaids. Rubbing his hands over the stubble of his unshaven jaws, he looked to his men with half-closed eyes. "You—and you," he pointed to two of his crewmen he knew to swim strongly, "into the water with you. Bring me those mermaids!" He wouldn't let the English have them.

Bradley saw immediately what Rodriguez was up to when the ropes fell over the side of the *Puta*. Although the mermaids were closer to the *Vengeance*, they'd never board without assistance. "Lower the ropes. Some of you, get into the water to help them." His voice boomed across the expanse of ocean between the ships.

Laly watched as ropes and men from both ships now fell to the water for their aid. She didn't know what had prodded everyone to action now, she was only grateful they were finally doing something. She raised her arm to the English captain. "Thanks, Mate!" she shouted. When the captain's dark eyes fastened on her, she felt a jolt of awareness. Chagrined about her sodden appearance, but more concerned about Sugar, she continued, "You wouldn't happen to have a doctor on board, would you?"

Bradley didn't answer. He could think of no reason mermaids would need a doctor, and right at the moment he was more interested in getting them on board the *Vengeance* before Rodriguez's men got to them. He could only imagine what heinous things a man like Rodriguez would do to them. He remembered again the poor girl the man had murdered and shuddered. It was becoming more important by the second that he be the possessor of the mermaids.

"Hurry, men. You've got to get them on board!" he shouted to the men now swimming toward the mermaids.

Sugar was having a hard time keeping track of her surroundings. She knew she needed to get out of the water, and she didn't particularly care if it was Spanish actors who saved her or English. The first man that reached her touched her fearfully on the arm. "Help me, please," she asked him. Just then the mouthpiece on her diving gear turned over in the water and began to sputter.

"Help, Captain! There's a monster got her!" the man shouted. "And the other one, too!" He began to swim away.

Sugar and Laly looked after the man helplessly as he, and now the others, swam farther from them. "No, please help us," Laly begged. She too was starting to feel the exhaustion from their ordeal. She'd thought she was moments from rescue and had started to relax. Now her rescue party was headed in the other direction. "Sugar, what are they shouting about?"

Sugar just shook her head weakly and shrugged.

"Please, help us," Laly repeated, seeing that all the actors were treading water some distance away, seemingly afraid to approach them. What was wrong with these people?

Captain Bradley looked closely at the mermaids when his crewman had shouted about a monster. True enough, the mermaids were being held from behind by strangely-colored, large-shelled creatures with black tentacles. The dark haired mermaid seemed to be floundering. "Men, do what you must to help them," he shouted down to them. Something told him it was vitally important to help these crea-

tures. He threw off his topcoat, ignoring the burn of
the recent wound on his arm, and moved to where
the mermaids were treading water next to his ship.
Looking directly down on them, he removed his
boots, ready to jump in to assist the men in their
rescue.

Rodriguez's men had shied away from the mermaids at the warning of a monster and no amount
of shouting from him was making them continue
their attempt at capture. "Bastards, take them!" he
ordered. With a black scowl, he watched as Bradley's
men began to swim toward the mermaids again and
his men continued to keep their distance.

Rubbing his whiskers, he watched angrily as Bradley
and his crew gave their whole attention to capturing
the mermaids. Suddenly he realized this would be
the perfect opportunity to leave the area. He'd been
willing to fight Bradley over his cargo, had relished
the idea that he would kill the English captain slowly
if given the chance, but he had to admit that the
tide of the battle had begun to turn just when the
mermaids had appeared. He'd started to lose. Perhaps that was why the mermaids had arrived when
they did. Did they wish him, Rodriguez, to escape?
Could this be so? "We go!" he shouted to his crew,
the decision made quickly.

Laly and Sugar could see that the Spanish actors
had begun swimming back to their ship. "Apparently,
the Englishmen are going to be our heroes," Laly
told Sugar, trying to keep an up note in her voice.

"Mmmm, j-just so s-somebody is," Sugar whispered
through chattering teeth.

Bradley watched as the *Puta*'s sails caught the wind
and she began to move away. He was angry that he
was losing the chance to take Rodriguez, but the

mermaids' appearance must be dealt with. He was certain that he would get another chance at Rodriguez.

He looked back to see his men approaching the mermaids slowly. He couldn't say he blamed them. These creatures were mythical beings. At least, he'd always believed so. Now here were not one, but two of them. And they carried some sort of monsters on their backs, monsters which seemed to be sapping their strength. He stepped up on the casemate and dived head first into the water near the imperiled mermaids.

Laly watched in amazement as the actor playing the part of the captain dived the tremendous distance from the ship to the water. "This guy must be an Olympic diver," she whispered.

"What?" Sugar asked.

"Nothing really, I just said . . ."

"Sharks! Sharks! Captain, get out of the water quickly!"

Laly's heart lurched to her throat as she heard the cries of the English crew. She looked around for the large shadows that the sharks would be underwater. Contrary to television movies, sharks rarely swim along the surface, their fins erect, before striking. They usually come from below and bump their intended victim, sort of checking it out. Laly and Sugar both knew this, but the fear of sharks never quite diminishes, no matter how much knowledge one possesses. Laly felt the grip of Sugar's hand become tighter on her arm and looked into the frightened eyes of her friend. How much more must they endure this day?

The captain had surfaced and was swimming the short distance to the mermaids with strong strokes.

"Damn," he cursed. He'd heard the men's shouts of sharks. It was usual during a battle for the big maneaters to circle in hopes of a meal. He just didn't want to become one. "Hurry. Help me get them quickly," he ordered the men still in the water with him. He could see the fear on their faces and hoped they remained to assist him. Fortunately, he had a loyal crew and they swam to help.

He and the men reached the mermaids at nearly the same moment. "Quickly, now! Cut away the monsters and get the mermaids on board!"

"The what?" Laly tried to ask as large, strong male hands turned her in the water. "What are you doing back there?" she asked as she felt the captain turning her tank. "Sugar, are you all right?" she asked when she could no longer see her friend.

"Yes. What are th-they doing? Hey! S-stop that! Laly?" Sugar felt the blade of a knife against her back.

Laly could hear Sugar struggling and tried to turn to see what was happening but was being held fast by the captain. "Let go of me!" she demanded. "What are you doing to her?" She could feel the captain behind her, then heard the pressure of air being released in a rush. "What have you done?" She started to fight in earnest. These men were crazy after all.

Bradley felt he had just about conquered the monster on his mermaid's back when she started to fight him. She was only making things more difficult. "Hold still. I've just about got you free."

"Free of what?"

"This monster." He pushed his knife up between the mermaid and the monster and cut deeply.

Laly felt the back of her BC giving way and couldn't figure out what on earth this idiot was doing. "Wait a minute. This is very expensive equipment." Then the BC was stripped from her back and she heard a cheer go up from the ship. Next, she watched as her mask floated underwater out of sight. "Are you mad?"

"Come, we must get aboard the *Vengeance*. Didn't you hear the men shouting about the sharks? Move quickly, Mermaid," he ordered.

Laly couldn't believe what was happening. This idiot, handsome as he was, had just cut a two-thousand-dollar piece of equipment to shreds and let it sink to the bottom of the ocean, and he was calling her "Mermaid." She could hear Sugar exclaiming behind her, although weakly, that the two sailors sent to help her had done the same. "I hope you realize that I expect to be compensated for the destruction of my equipment. I'll be reporting this to your superior as soon as I get back to New Providence!" Laly threatened.

Bradley pulled the arguing mermaid to the side of the ship and grabbed the bottom rung of the wood and rope ladder his crew had thrown down to him. "Hurry . . . Miss." How did one address a mermaid? He then noticed the silver-gray shadow of a giant shark just below them. "Shark!" he growled. "Men, quickly. Get on board!"

"Captain, look out!" Wainwright's voice rang out over the murmuring of the crew, then taking careful aim with his pistol, he fired at the circling shark. A cloud of dark red blood billowed from beneath the water and the crew's murmuring turned joyous.

The explosion from the gun, and turmoil in the water as other sharks attacked the injured one, frightened Laly nearly to tears, her anger forgotten. "Hurry, get Sugar on board first. She's chilled." Her turquoise eyes met the dark brown of the captain's with the plea.

Captain Bradley felt as though he'd been touched to his soul. The strange blue of the mermaid's eyes held him prisoner for precious seconds. Was it the luring magic of the mermaid?

"Captain?" A voice behind him broke the spell.

"Yes, yes. Carry them up. Hurry." He ordered gruffly.

Laly watched as the two men lifted Sugar from the water, then felt the captain wrap his arm around her waist and begin to carry her up the ladder. She heard a hushed whisper pass through the crowd of men on board as they were brought up out of the water.

"They've got two fins instead of one." "Look, one's blue and the other's green." "They've got scales up to their necks, not just to the waist, like in the stories I've heard."

Laly listened in amazement to the odd remarks she heard as she neared the deck. The captain lifted her over the railing on the side of the ship and let her drop to the deck to sit next to Sugar. "Are you all right?" she whispered.

Sugar just shrugged. She'd stopped trusting her judgment long before this. She was cold, could tell she was in shock, and wasn't altogether certain she hadn't died and gone to hell.

Laly looked around for the audience she was sure she'd see once on board. None of the men on the deck before her looked like spectators. First of all, they were all men. Not one woman graced this ship. She supposed the reenactment was authentic but it would have been nice to see a little of the nineties' equality in evidence, even if the female actors had to dress as men for the parts.

The more she looked around her, though, the more uncomfortable she became. There were no spectators of any kind. These men looked like hard-worn seamen. The captain had climbed aboard and was now staring at her and Sugar just as curiously as the others. Now what, she wondered. "Are you all going to stand around here staring at us all day? Would one of you get us some dry towels and some fresh water? My friend isn't feeling well." She reached to her hips and let her weight belt drop to the deck with a thud. She felt slightly guilty that she'd let the captain carry her on board with the heavy thing still on, but it was too late to worry about it now. She turned to Sugar and released hers also.

The men continued to stand and stare. A few glanced to the captain for guidance, but none moved to do her bidding.

"Are you all deaf? Someone please get us some dry towels." Laly's tone was becoming increasingly impatient. She looked at Sugar and could see how pale she was. "Oh dear. Sugar?" She knew that they needed to get out of their wet suits and into some dry clothes. She reached for the zipper at the neck of Sugar's suit and began to unzip it.

"Lord, Captain. She's taking her skin off!"

Laly heard the exclamation behind her and turned to find the idiot trying to be funny. This was a very serious situation to her, not something to be made fun of. Anger burned in her chest. Tears filled her eyes as she jumped clumbsily to her feet, still wearing her fins, but ready to fight the whole lot of them. "How dare you make fun of us at a time like this!" she fumed. "My friend is ill and all you can do is make jokes? Well, it's not funny, not one little bit. If any of you was even half the man your silly macho costumes profess you to be, you'd be giving us some kind of assistance now, not standing around cracking asinine jokes about our wet suits!'' She turned to the actor playing the captain's role. "And you! You seem to be the leader here. Why don't you do something, instead of standing around like the rest of these idiots?"

Bradley had never had a woman talk to him in this fashion, and whether this was a mermaid or not, it was female. "Control yourself, Miss. I will not be spoken to in this manner." His dark eyes had narrowed. "You are a mystery to me and my crew, therefore you will accept our curiosity with some understanding." His eyes roamed over her from top to bottom. "Now explain yourselves."

Laly looked up at the dark countenance of her rescuer and for just a moment felt a frisson of fear skim down her back. This man, though a consummate actor, had no right to take this kind of attitude with her. She and Sugar were the injured parties here. Yes, he'd rescued them from the ocean, and possibly from the jaws of death—she felt herself shiver with the memory of the sharks—but he had no right to now expect her to stand around and give him some lengthy explanation of how they happened to interrupt his performance—not with Sugar looking worse every minute. "Look, Mister, I don't have time to play your little ego games right now. I want to see the person who's really in charge here. Do you have a director or producer on this stupid ship? And a doctor, if there's one around." She turned her back on the tall antagonist and knelt back down to tend to Sugar. She'd used her most authoritative tone and she expected to be obeyed. She was, after all, a college professor, and used to being taken seriously.

Bradley could hear the curious murmuring of his crew behind him. He watched as the blond mermaid went back to her dark-haired friend. She had asked to see a "director" or "producer?" What was she talking about? She had such a strange manner of speaking. And she had asked for a doctor. He had to admit that the one mermaid didn't look very well, but what could the ship's doctor do for a sea creature? Still, he supposed he should do what he could. "Wainwright, tell Doctor Wells to come to the front."

"Aye, Captain."

Very soon, Wainwright was pushing an old man forward through the crowd. "I don't know anything 'bout mermaids. I don't want to know anything 'bout 'em!" he sputtered, as he tried to remain behind the front row of sailors circling the two creatures.

Captain Bradley nearly laughed at the man's arguments. He'd been certain that this would be Wells's reaction. He wasn't known for his bravery, but he was a fairly good ship's doctor, setting bones and bleeding the ill when necessary.

"The blond mermaid has demanded your services," Bradley informed him. "It seems she thinks you can do something for her friend."

Laly looked behind her expecting to see a competent doctor. The little man, dressed in tattered pants and shirt, and fighting to get away from them, was not what she'd hoped for. "You've got to be joking." She addressed the captain.

"This is the ship's doctor," he told her, rubbing his chin as he watched her reaction.

Laly shook her head. "I think I can do better myself." Her voice held a note of disbelief. This little man showed no signs of being a doctor. He was dirty and unshaven. His teeth, the few that remained, were discolored and rotting from his gums, and the dimness of one eye told her he was in bad need of a thorough checkup himself. She reached once more for Sugar's zipper. They had indeed fallen in with a shipload of fools. Only the actor playing the captain seemed somewhat normal, and even he was rather frightening, with his air of superiority, as though he believed the part he was playing. "Would someone please get us some dry towels or blankets?" If she was going to take care of Sugar, she might as well get started. "And some aspirin, if you've got it."

Captain Bradley didn't know what "aspirin" was, but he could supply the blankets. Then, before he could give the order to oblige the mermaid, he was left speechless while he watched the skin on the dark-haired mermaid's body being opened down the front. It seemed she was able to peel her blue scales away to reveal the white flesh of a normal woman. He was amazed as the blonde assisted in this feat. Under the blue skin it looked as though there was another sort of suit that covered very little flesh.

"The blankets?" Laly demanded.

"Yes . . . yes, of course." Bradley motioned to several crew members to get what the mermaid requested, then continued to watch as they pulled off their fins to reveal feet! This was all too amazing. Were all mermaids able to accomplish this? Did mermaids walk among men when they chose to?

He allowed his eyes to explore the figure of the dark-haired woman now sitting shivering on the deck. She was rather pretty, though a little shallow of figure for his taste. She was wearing a small blue cloth garment of some kind that covered her only from breast to hip, and he could see the leers of his crew as she transformed before their eyes from mermaid to woman.

He noticed that one of his men had brought the blankets. Crossing to where the man stood, he took the blankets from him, wanting to get closer to the mermaids to see the texture of their skin. Was it possible to tell a mermaid from a real woman up close?

Laly finally had Sugar's wetsuit off and could tell that in itself had helped her some. The hot tropical sun was already doing its magic, warming her.

She looked up to see the captain standing over them with the blankets. "It's about time," she stated, as she reached to take them from his grasp.

"Allow me." Bradley leaned over the dark-haired mermaid and laid a blanket across her shoulders. He could detect no difference between her flesh and that of a human woman.

"Thank you, Captain," Sugar said softly, grateful for the feeling of dry cloth around her.

"You are welcome, Miss." He then turned to the blond mermaid. "One for you?" He held out another blanket, wondering if this mermaid would remove her outer skin also, and curious about her figure underneath.

"Thanks." Laly grabbed it from his hand, feeling like it took altogether too much time to receive this response to her request.

Bradley straightened. This mermaid did try his patience with her brisk manner.

"Is there something you want?" Laly asked, when she noticed the captain staring down at her.

"No . . . yes, just an explanation."

Laly sighed. He wasn't going to rest until she explained how they interrupted his stupid battle. "All right, already." She glanced at Sugar and, satisfied that she seemed to be coming out of her groggy state, stood once again to address the captain. "Sugar and I had taken our students out in search of shipwrecks. I had just found something, possibly the mast of a ship, when we were caught in the storm." She watched his face and saw not a whit of understanding. "Well, anyway. I was only about forty feet down, but Sugar was worried about me because the storm looked so violent. She came down to get me, but we were too late. When the storm passed we surfaced and found that the students and catamaran were gone, though I can't say I blame them. You can well imagine our surprise to surface right in the middle of your reenactment of . . . what battle were you doing, anyway? I hadn't heard about it on New Providence, and we've been there for a week."

Bradley listened to the mermaid's strange story and could understand very little. The fact that she claimed to teach other mermaids was almost believable. If one was forced to believe in mermaids, one must assume they be taught something by someone. Her babbling about a storm in the area didn't make much sense, as the skies had been clear for more than a week, but the part of her story that bothered him was her reference to not hearing about this battle while on New Providence. Why would a mermaid expect to hear about a battle before it took place? Had Rodriguez expected to meet him at sea? His eyes narrowed as he examined the female before him. Was it possible she was a spy? Could Rodriguez have initiated the aid of mermaids? His common sense rebelled wholly against such a preposterous idea, but today much of what he believed in had been shaken. A myth come to life was, in fact, standing before his very eyes.

"Well?"

"Miss?" He raised one thick black brow.

"Are you going to tell me what battle you were reenacting or not?"

This question was puzzling to him. She kept asking about the battle as though it should have a name. "I do not understand."

Laly was having a hard time controlling her temper again. Yet the look on his face . . . no, he was just being deliberately obtuse. "Sir, if it is so difficult for you to answer a simple question, just never mind. I'll ask the desk clerk when I get back to the hotel. What time does this ship dock at New Providence?"

"What time?"

"Jesus H. Christ! Have you made it your mission in life to make me crazy?" Laly demanded. "Why can't you just answer one question when I ask it? Would that be so difficult?" Angrily, she began to unzip her wetsuit. As she pulled the zipper down across her chest, the medallion she'd all but forgotten slipped to the deck at her feet. "Damn," she cursed, as she reached for it. The hard brown fingers of the captain closed over her wrist before she could touch it.

"Hey!"

Captain Bradley recognized the gold medallion even before it hit the deck. He stopped the mermaid from picking it up and reached for it himself. The King's Medallion had been pirated more than a year ago from under the governor's very roof. It had been made by the hands of local natives, with the markings of their tribal gods, commissioned by the governor to be sent to King Charles as a gift. Before it could even be shipped, it had turned up stolen. Now, here it was, falling from between the breasts of a mermaid.

Laly straightened and tried to jerk free of the captain's viselike grasp. "Ouch, what's the matter with you—and give me that."

Bradley held her with little effort and examined the medallion in his hand. It was worth a fortune and proved to him that these mermaids were indeed spies.

"Silence!" he ordered loudly, and pulled her against his chest, pinning her arm behind her back. "Where did you get this?" he demanded.

Laly was stunned speechless. She was being held flush with the captain's strong body, feeling the heat from his muscles burning her through the rubber of her wetsuit. She looked up into his dark eyes, demanding an answer from her, and couldn't speak. The blood was rushing through her body at an alarming rate, causing all sorts of responses she thought she'd never feel again, hadn't felt since before her divorce two years earlier.

Captain Bradley jerked the mermaid even harder against him. "I asked where you got this, mermaid. Answer me." He looked hard into the turquoise eyes of the mermaid and realized too late his mistake in holding her so close. He felt his body springing to life and was startled that he could feel so strong a reaction to a sea creature.

Laly's eyes widened when she felt the stiffening of the captain's body against her's. "Captain, I . . ." Her breathing was erratic and her heart hammered against her chest.

"Laly? Captain, let go of her!" Sugar demanded from the deck. She'd seen the man drag Laly against him and would fight to the death to help her, even in her own weakened condition. "Release her!" she shouted again, trying to stand.

"Captain?" Wainwright questioned. He'd seen something fall from the flesh of the mermaid, but he wasn't close enough to identify it. It was obvious from the captain's reaction that it was something important, but what? Now he watched as the dark-haired mermaid moved toward the captain on very wobbly legs. Stepping in front of her, he caught her as she began to fall.

Three

"Laly!" Sugar called, as she fell into the young officer's arms.

Wainwright stumbled backward with the weight of the mermaid, tripping over the heavy belts they'd dropped from their waists. "Captain?"

Laly felt the bodies hit her from behind and was pushed even harder into the captain's body. "Sugar, are you all right?" She tried to turn around and see what was going on, but she was too close to the captain. This had gone far enough. She wouldn't allow herself and Sugar to fall prey to the manhandling these Neanderthals seemed to think was necessary.

Bradley dropped the medallion and held the weight of the falling bodies against him but was unprepared for the knife the blond mermaid pulled from the band on her arm. Without any warning, the sharp silver edge of a four-inch blade was being held against his throat.

"Let us go," hissed Laly threateningly. She felt for

sure footing and untangled herself from the captain's grasp, slipping from between him and the other officer while keeping the blade in place. "Sugar, can you move away from him?" she asked, not taking her eyes from the captain's.

"Yes, I think so." Sugar couldn't believe what Laly was doing. This was getting totally out of hand, but why had the captain grabbed her the way he'd done? Had it something to do with the medallion that fell from Laly's suit? Sugar pulled back from the officer very slowly and half crawled back to where she'd been sitting before.

Laly watched Sugar's progress from the corner of her eye. "Now, then, Captain, it's your turn to do some explaining."

Bradley could see his men, including his first officer, readying themselves to grab the mermaid from behind. The evil intent in their eyes showed they'd have no mercy for one who threatened their captain. With the twitch of an eye, he signaled them to wait. He knew he could disarm this creature with the wave of one hand but wanted to see what her intentions were while she thought she had the upper hand. Many was the time a criminal had undone himself by his own words while thinking to hold a captive secure.

"What would you have me explain, Mermaid?"

Laly continued to hold her knife to the captain's throat. "First of all, why the hell do you keep referring to me as mermaid? Do you think it's cute?"

Bradley looked her over. Her long white-blond hair reached nearly to her hips and the opening in the front of her green mermaid skin revealed the lush, ripe curves of a delicious woman, truly the temptation of a siren. And there was the fact that he'd just pulled her from the middle of the ocean. Still, if she wanted him to explain the obvious, he would. "You have the eyes of a witch, the body of a sea goddess, and come from the deep to tempt me. What would you have me call you?" his voice rasped softly from between firm lips.

Laly looked at him startled. The brown of his eyes had darkened as he spoke and the timbre of his voice vibrated through her nerves. She thought she heard the chuckle of soft laughter behind her. Had these men heard what he'd just said to her? She felt herself blushing from the tips of her toes to the top of her head. How dared he make fun of her this way? She had the blade of her knife against his jugular. Didn't he feel in the least threatened? "I would have you call me by my name," she informed him stiffly.

"Your name?" Bradley felt a little foolish. It hadn't occurred to him to ask the creatures' names, although he'd heard them refer to one another.

"Yes, my name. I am Doctor Lorraine Lawrence. My friend is Doctor Sarah Stephens. We teach at the same university."

"If you're both doctors, why did you demand the services of ours?" His voice held a tone of sarcasm that couldn't be missed.

"We're not those kinds of doctors," she told him, frowning, becoming more irritated by his attitude every minute. "Now, what's your name?" she demanded.

Raising one brow, he looked down on her from his superior height. "I am Devon Bradley, captain of this vessel, the *Vengeance*."

"Right. But what's your real name?"

Bradley decided at that moment that this farce had gone on long enough. He was getting tired of standing still so this mermaid could keep her blade at his throat. Swiftly, without blinking an eye, he reached between them and flipped the knife to the deck. "My name is Captain Bradley." He straightened to his full height and once again pulled the startled mermaid to his body. This time he wasn't surprised by his body's strong reaction.

"Let go of me, you big jerk." Laly couldn't believe how easily the captain had freed the knife from her hand and realized that he'd only let her hold him that way while it suited his purpose. Why he'd allowed it, she'd never guess, but finding herself once again feeling the hardness of his body pressing into hers caused her heart to beat wildly in her chest. This guy had some very odd ideas about how to handle a woman in public.

In public? She looked around her once more and had a very terrifying thought: maybe these men were criminals of some kind. Modern-day pirates, perhaps. The way they acted was certainly very strange. The captain seemed to believe he really was a captain and the men around her treated him as such. Did pirates exist today? What would they do to her and Sugar?

She looked up at the handsome but frightening face of her captor. The scar that crossed his cheek was new and the thought of how he'd obtained it caused a shiver to ripple along her spine. Feeling the arousal of his body against her she could only imagine what he intended. He wouldn't harm her in front of all these men, would he? He wouldn't . . .

"So, my little mermaid. What else do you want me to explain?" Bradley had watched the play of emotions cross the creature's face. He couldn't tell if she was truly frightened or just acting for his benefit.

He looked to where the other mermaid sat staring at him with genuine fear in her eyes.

Sugar prayed that Laly wouldn't do anything else stupid. During the last few minutes she'd come to realize that their rescuers were probably very dangerous men. Why else would they have been in a battle? She was certain now that it had been an actual battle, not a reenactment. The man they'd seen shot had really died before their eyes. And the wound on the captain's arm had been put there by a bullet from an ancient pistol. She couldn't explain why all this had happened, she only knew that it did. It was real. It was continuing. And her suspicions were scaring the hell out of her.

"So, Mermaid," Bradley repeated "what would you have me explain further?" He wanted to catch her in her own trap, to trip her up with one of her own questions. All she had to do was inquire about his activities against Rodriguez and he would have her caught in her own web of deception.

Laly didn't know what to say or ask. She now knew that threatening the captain with her knife had been a really foolish move. She was sure she'd hear how foolish from Sugar if they both lived long enough to discuss it. Right now she didn't know what to make of this whole situation. She glanced to see Sugar sitting near the side of the ship with the other officer watching over her. They were really in a mess this time and it was her fault. She was usually to blame for their adventures gone awry, only this time she felt they were in way over their heads. She had to think of something. Letting out her breath slowly, she relaxed her shoulders and looked up at the captain's dark eyes. "I would like you to explain why you feel

the need to handle me in this fashion. I find it very
. . . very chauvinistic,'' she said as calmly as she could
and waited for him to become embarrassed and
release her.

She hadn't used the word "chauvinistic" in years,
but it was definitely appropriate. These men, with
their macho costumes, their ridiculous battle, and
the obscene chuckles and leers she was receiving at
the treatment of the captain, were beneath even the
typical lowbrow locker-room mentality.

Bradley's brows raised curiously but he continued
to stare down at the face of his mermaid. "I don't
understand this word you use. Chauvinis . . .?"

"Very funny. You know damn well what it means.
Now, let me go." She pushed against his arms.

"It means to let you go?"

"Laly?" Sugar's voice came softly across the deck.

Laly tried to turn in the captain's arms to see her
friend. "Are you all right?" she asked, concerned
that Sugar might be feeling worse.

"Your friend is fine," Bradley told the mermaid.
"Now, what is this chauvinistic?"

Laly sighed. How could she hope to get anywhere
arguing with a man who wouldn't even acknowledge
the words she used?

"Laly, tell him what it means." Sugar had begun
to experience a feeling of horror. Everything had
started to make sense to her in a very frightening
way. She was certain she had to be wrong. No one
in their right mind could believe what she'd started
to suspect. That was why she asked Laly to explain
the word to the captain. She needed to be proved
wrong—that she was, in essence, out of her mind.
She would feel much better when she knew for a

fact that she was temporarily insane. Her train of thought was so ridiculous that she even giggled.

"Sugar?" Laly was worried about her.

Bradley looked to where the dark-haired mermaid sat with her hand over her mouth to cover her laughter.

"I said tell him what 'chauvinistic' means," Sugar said, from behind her fingers.

"Tell him . . .?" Laly didn't understand. She knew this man was just being an ass.

"Tell him!" Sugar was insistent. "Tell him exactly what it means."

Laly looked over her shoulder at Sugar, then back at the Captain. Sugar had something she was trying to find out or prove, and though Laly didn't know what Sugar's reason was, she decided to take her very seriously. "All right. 'Chauvinistic' means to be fanatically loyal to a team or a ruler, or in your case and the case of these other jerks, loyal to your gender. Even to the point of being prejudiced against women."

"More, Laly. Tell him more." Sugar waited, holding her breath.

Laly frowned, not knowing what Sugar meant for a moment, then remembered. "The word comes from the name 'Nicolas Chauvin.' He was a pompous soldier of Napoleon I, Emperor of France, who wouldn't accept the demise of the imperial cause." She couldn't think of anything else and wondered why Sugar would want her to give such a definition.

"Who is this Napoleon you speak of?" Bradley asked suspiciously. Was something going on in France he should know about?

"Oh, get real. Every schoolchild has heard of Napoleon."

"Laly, tell him." Sugar's voice was once again insistent.

Laly frowned up at the curious face of the Captain. "Napoleon I was the Emperor of France during the early 1800s. Like you don't already know that."

Bradley listened to the story this "Laly" was telling and could think of no reason she would have for making up such a tale. He raised his gaze from her face and looked at his crew. In a strong voice he spoke. "Tell this mermaid what year it is and what king sits the throne of France."

Almost in unison the crew shouted. "It is 1678, and Louis XIV is king."

Laly heard Sugar's gasp behind her. *They're all mad,* she thought, but her worry was for Sugar. Finding the captain had loosened his hold on her, she turned a little to look at her friend. Sugar was pale, more pale than she'd been earlier. Laly looked up at the captain. "Please let me go to her; she's ill."

The plea in the mermaid's eyes touched his heart. "All right, go to your friend." He reluctantly took his hands from around her waist and watched her walk to Sugar. Even if she was a spy, she wasn't going anywhere right now.

Sugar reached frantically for Laly's hand when she neared and pulled her down to sit with her. "Laly, did you hear them? Did you?" Sugar questioned urgently.

"Of course I heard them. They're all nuts," she stated flatly. She turned to glance at the captain. He had pulled on his boots and was now picking up her knife. "Oh, hell," she muttered, "I'll probably never get that back."

"Laly, don't you get it?" Sugar's voice was a distraught whisper. She took Laly's face in her hands and forced her to look into her eyes. "Laly, what year is this?"

"Come on, Sugar. Don't let these guys get to you." She put the back of her hand on Sugar's forehead to feel for fever.

"Damn it, Laly!" Sugar hissed. "What year do you think this is?"

"Well, it's not 1678!"

"Are you so sure?"

Laly tried to see any sign of concussion in Sugar's eyes. Maybe she'd hit her head during the storm. "Don't worry, Sugar. I'll take care of you. I'll get you back to a doctor in Nassau as soon as I can get these goons to take us there." She now let her eyes find the captain again. He had the medallion in his hand and was talking quietly to the officer called Wainwright. They both looked her way periodically so she knew what their topic of conversation was.

Sugar watched the captain, too. He was an intelligent man, but would he let himself believe that she and Laly were from more than three hundred years into the future? Hell, could she even make Laly believe it? Did she herself believe it? Yes, she did. She didn't know how it had happened, sometime during the storm, she guessed, and she couldn't begin to figure out why, but she knew it happened. She and Laly had been transported into the past.

She watched the captain turning the medallion over in his hands and wondered if that piece of metal had something to do with it. Oh God, who knew? Who could figure it out? Maybe there was no reason behind it at all. Maybe it was just a freak accident and would never happen again. But no, she wouldn't let herself think that. She and Laly had to get back to their own time. They didn't belong here. Their presence here could mess up history, perhaps already had. The battle they'd interrupted may have been important. Her mind reeled with the possibilities she imagined. "Laly, I have to tell you something."

Laly looked back to her friend. "Yes, do you need something?"

"No, I have to make you understand something." She stopped, not sure how to proceed. "It's something you're not going to believe, but it's true. I know it is."

The urgency in Sugar's voice was frightening. "What is it, Sugar?" Laly stared at her friend, not sure what to expect.

"Laly . . ." Sugar took a breath. "Laly . . . we're in the past."

Laly's heart was breaking. Her best friend in the world was seriously ill and they were miles and hours from help. The sting of threatening tears caused her to blink. "You'll be all right, Sugar. I promise."

Sugar could see the complete disbelief on Laly's face. She knew this wasn't going to be easy. "I'm already all right, Laly. Really, I am. I don't know how or why it happened, but we are now in 1678." She could see Laly begin to protest and put her fingertips over her mouth. "Laly, I know this sounds crazy. It *is* crazy, but it's *true.* Just look around you. Can you explain it?"

Laly looked at the ship and then at the men still watching their every move. The ship was perfect. The costumes were perfect. But it was all just a wonderful job of reproduction. People didn't just go back in time. "Sugar, I think you're just a little off kilter yet. You'll feel better after you get some rest and food."

"Why do they think we're mermaids?"

"What?"

"Laly, these men really believe we're mermaids. I'll bet if you jumped up and told them you were going to call on Neptune to destroy this ship, every one of them would be on his hands and knees praying to you to be merciful."

Laly almost laughed. "Sugar, you've got one hell of an imagination. What ever it was that hit you must have packed a wallop . . ."

"I call on mighty Neptune to seek out this ship!" Sugar's voice raised above the murmurings of the crew.

"Sugar, what are you doing? Are you nuts?" Laly couldn't believe her friend's actions.

"If I'm nuts, this will prove it. If I'm not, I'll prove my point. Now, shut up," she whispered. *"I call on Neptune to seek out this ship!"* she called out again in a booming voice.

If Laly hadn't been so concerned about her friend's health, she'd have exploded in a fit of giggles. This was more her kind of stunt, not Sugar's. Then she noticed the crew. Every man on board the ship was getting very nervous. Their eyes were wide and watching.

Bradley didn't know what the mermaid was up to, but he didn't like it. He could see how she frightened the men and took a step forward, her eyes narrowed. "What are you doing?" he demanded.

"I call on my father to help me," she answered sternly.

Laly watched in amazement.

Bradley didn't know what to think. He'd only just had the existence of mermaids proved to him; he wasn't ready to believe in a giant God rising from the ocean's depths to smite him. In fact, he wasn't sure he believed in the mermaids. Yes, he had pulled them from the ocean himself. And yes, they wore the costumes of fish, but something bothered him about them. It was perhaps the way Laly had felt against him, the way her eyes had darkened when she'd felt his desire pressed firmly to her abdomen. His natural suspicion had kept a small doubt in his mind. Could a mermaid respond to a mortal man as she had? "I would have you stop. You are upsetting my men." His tone held no room for argument.

Sugar continued. *"Oh, mighty neptune . . ."*

Three of the crew members fell to their knees praying at that moment. "Do I need to go further?" Sugar turned to Laly and asked.

"I said stop!" ordered Bradley.

"Yes, Captain." Sugar smiled at him and then back at Laly, who sat staring wide-eyed at the crew. "Do you believe me now?"

Laly just shook her head. This couldn't be possible. None of it could. Her mind was racing with a thousand questions and none of them answerable. She looked at Sugar and opened her mouth, but no words would come to her lips.

"I know how you feel," said Sugar.

Laly just sat speechless for several minutes. What were they going to do? They had to get back to their own time, but how? "The storm," she blurted.

"Probably," agreed Sugar. "So?"

Laly just shrugged. She looked around her at the crew and the captain again. No wonder they all acted like such jerks. How would she act if she were confronted with a real live mermaid? Probably exactly the same way.

"So, what do I do with you?" The captain's voice broke into her thoughts. What indeed, she mused.

She looked to Sugar for ideas but only saw her blank smile.

"I suppose you could show us to a cabin. I'd like to get out of my wetsuit and into a hot shower." Sugar's nudge made her realize how strange that request probably sounded. "I . . . ah, some dry clothes would be nice. We can't wear these blankets forever." Laly looked at the captain in a different light now. He was still gorgeous, but now he wasn't the "idiot with a big ego" she'd thought him to be. In fact, considering what he'd had to deal with today, he'd managed remarkably well.

Bradley thought for a minute. He had no women's clothing on board, wasn't sure what mermaids required in the way of fashion. The small blue garment Sugar wore was perhaps an undergarment? He found his eyes searching the opening of Laly's green skin. Her breasts were full and held by a brightly colored cloth of some kind. He wished she'd remove the rest of her mermaid's costume to let him see the curved secrets of her body. "I have no silks or satins on board."

"We don't need silk, for goodness' sake. Just some jeans and T-shirts will do," Laly said before she realized once again she was talking to a man who didn't know what a zipper was. The look on his face caused her to explain. "Some trousers, pants? You know, like you have on." She pointed to his legs. "And some shirts?" She then pointed to his chest, hoping he would understand.

"You wish to wear my clothing?"

"Not yours specifically, just *like* yours."

Bradley's brows knitted together across his forehead. He couldn't imagine a woman in men's clothing, but these were not normal women. He signaled

Wainwright. "Take them to my cabin and let them
have what they need to cover themselves."

Wainwright stepped closer to the captain and spoke
softly. "What if they try to escape before we get back
to New Providence?"

"Could you stop them if they dived off the ship?"
Bradley answered.

"No, sir. But shouldn't we tie them up?"

Bradley had already thought of that course and
dismissed it. These creatures had come to them of
their own free will and didn't seem to have any intention of leaving. Their reasons for being here, he felt
sure, would be discovered sooner if he allowed them
to remain free. If it turned out that his suspicions
were correct, that they were spies, he would deal with
them when the time came, including turning them
over to the authorities in Charles Towne.

Later, in the captain's cabin, Laly helped Sugar
wash up and settled her on the bunk to rest. She sat
next to her and looked around at their surroundings.
The cabin was small, with a desk in one corner, an
armoire in another. "So, what now?" she asked, not
really expecting an answer.

Sugar lifted her shoulders and watched the gentle
swing of a lantern that hung from the cabin ceiling.
"I want to go home." It was a simple statement but
carried the weight of their predicatment. Tears began
sliding down her cheeks, though she blinked rapidly
to staunch their flow. "Damn it, Laly. What happened?" She brought up her hand to swipe angrily
at her dripping nose. "How did we get here?"

"I don't know. I don't understand it any more than
you do. Maybe we're dead. Maybe we're in limbo.

Maybe we're in hell!'' She unzipped her wetsuit and pulled it down forcefully, fighting the tears that threatened to fall from her own fluttering lashes. "I do know that I've got to find something dry to put on." She kicked the wetsuit away from her feet and walked to the washbasin. She took a deep breath and swallowed, refusing to give in to the fear and dread that clutched at her heart. She had to keep her spirits up for Sugar's sake. Had to keep going to find a way out of this nightmare. "I'll find us both something to wear. You'll feel better when you're dressed," she said, after she rinsed the salt water away as best she could.

She threw open the doors of the armoire and began going through the captain's clothing. Shirts, pants, coats—all a hundred sizes too large—hung before her. And all carried the captain's scent. Laly found her senses reeling, remembering the strong length of his body next to hers. She muttered an oath and shook her head. It wouldn't do her any good to be attracted to a man in this century. If . . . *when* she and Sugar were able to get back to their own time, she didn't need any romantic entanglements complicating things.

"Is there anything we can wear?" Sugar asked from the bunk. She had managed to stop her tears, determined to be stronger for Laly's sake. She sat up, and though her head still reeled a bit and her stomach churned a little, she looked over the garments Laly held before her. "Lovely."

"Do you want blue or black?"

"Which is my best color?" Sugar tried to joke, as she answered lightly.

Laly tossed her friend the black pants and then a white shirt. "Black has always been too harsh for me," she answered, grinning. She looked down at the brightly colored bikini she was wearing and wondered if she should remove it or leave it on as an undergarment, then decided that it was still too wet with salt water to leave on. She peeled the suit off and suppressed the warm feelings she experienced as she pulled the captain's pants up over her bare bottom. Several deep breaths later, she tied a length of scarf she'd found around her waist to keep the pants from falling back down again. The shirt she tugged on was even larger and of a gauzelike fabric. No matter how she tried to secure it, it remained loose and billowed around her. "Oh, well, so I don't make a fashion statement." She shrugged and turned to face Sugar.

Sugar sat on the bunk, once again fighting the nausea that roiled in her middle. She'd managed to get dressed and was grateful for the dry clothing, but couldn't seem to shake the waves of illness that washed over her. "I'll be all right," she answered the look of concern in Laly's eyes.

"Of course you will. We've been through a lot today." Laly shook her head and fought against the hysteria that threatened at the understatement in her words. Laughter of a crazy nature bubbled just under the surface as she sank down next to Sugar on the bunk. Leaning forward, resting her head in her hands, she tried to calm the fears she felt. "I guess this is a little more of a fix than when I got us locked in the men's dorm all night."

"Yeah, I guess so." Sugar remembered how frightened she'd been then and wished with all her heart she was back there now, afraid of discovery and expulsion. Such small worries compared to what they now faced. "We'll get out of this, too," she assured her friend quietly, not at all sure of their future.

Laly sat up straight again. "Yes, we will. We know that the storm had something to do with sending us here."

"We think it did," Sugar corrected.

"Okay, we think it did. But why here and now?" Laly's eyes narrowed as she thought. "The medallion?" She looked to see the confirmation on Sugar's face. They'd both come to the same conclusion. The medallion had something to do with all of this, and right now the captain had it and didn't seem likely to let it go.

"Captain, are you sure it's a good idea to leave them alone in your cabin?" Wainwright questioned. He wasn't afraid of the mermaids, not really. He just didn't like having them on board the *Vengeance.*

Bradley looked at his first officer, then lowered his gaze to the medallion in his hand. "I'm not sure about anything. Not even that they are mermaids."

"But, Sir—you saw them come from the ocean yourself."

"Yes, that is true. But how did they get there?"

"Why, I suppose . . ." Wainwright sputtered.

"You suppose, like everyone else on this ship, that they came from the depths of the ocean. What if they came from the *Puta*?"

"Sir?" Wainwright removed his tricorn and frowned his confusion.

"Could they not have come from *Rodriguez*'s ship?"

"I don't see how it would have been possible, Sir. We were in the midst of a bloody battle."

"What better time for two women, dressed as mermaids, to drop into the ocean on the far side of the *Puta* and swim between us, stopping the very battle that allowed the deception?" Bradley straightened from his leaning position against the casemate and looked out to the open sea.

"Well, Sir, I suppose it's possible." Wainwright's tone of voice allowed that he didn't think it possible at all.

Bradley smiled at his first officer. "You would rather believe in mermaids?"

"I . . . Sir . . . I . . ." Wainwright's face beat a vibrate red with his pulse. "Sir, I assure you . . ."

"Never mind, Wainwright. Mermaids or not, I will know why they are here." He put a hand on the back of the younger man and continued to smile. "It may prove to be an extremely interesting puzzle."

Wainwright smothered the impulse to sputter further and found himself grinning at the captain. When the dark mermaid had fallen into his arms, he'd been pleasantly surprised by the soft curves of her slender body. "Yes, Sir, I agree. I will assist you in any way I can."

"I'm sure you will. Now, if you will excuse me, my own clothing is drying to a salty crust. I think I'll go see if the mermaids have left me anything at all to change into."

Four

"I still don't agree with you, Laly. It's too dangerous."

"What else are we supposed to do, just let Captain Bradley keep the medallion and blow the slim chance we might have of it getting us home again?" Laly sat on the edge of the bunk next to Sugar and fought with the Captain's comb as she tried to pull it through the tangles in her hair. She rubbed her hands together and grimaced at the gritty feel of salt that clung to her white-blond tresses. "The first chance I get, I'm going to steal it from him—and I don't care what I have to do to get it."

Sugar sighed and closed her eyes to her friend's plan, which was really no plan at all. "Laly, if you'd just be a little patient, we might be able to get it without your having to steal it."

"Do you think he's just going to hand it over if I ask him nicely?" Laly asked sarcastically.

"Of course not, but I don't think you need to start thinking about taking drastic measures just yet."

Sugar was worried that Laly's penchant for the dramatic would get them into even more trouble, if that were possible.

"Sugar, we're more than three hundred years in the past, sitting in the captain's cabin on an English warship, and believed to be mermaids. When exactly do you suggest I start taking drastic measures?" She stopped combing her hair and looked directly at her friend.

"I guess . . . Laly, I just don't want things to get worse."

"How could they possibly get any worse?"

Sugar sat bolt upright on the bunk and fought a wave of nausea that accompanied her sudden movement. "In case you haven't noticed, we are sitting in the Captain's cabin and wearing his warm, dry clothing, not shivering in some ship's hold, wet with salt water and at the mercy of his crew. I think you'll agree with me when I say that things could indeed be worse!" She let herself fall back onto the bunk.

"I'm sorry, Sugar." Laly studied the pale face of her friend. "You're right. But I can't help but believe that it's imperative we get that medallion back as soon as possible—no matter what. What if the storm came through again and we weren't ready? We might be stuck here forever."

Sugar realized she was right. She just didn't want to have to think about the danger Laly might put herself in, or what the captain would do if he caught her stealing the medallion from him. "What can I do to help?"

"I'm not sure yet. I may just need you to cover for me, to distract the captain. We don't even know if he's going to have it with him all the time or put it somewhere for safekeeping. We'll have to play things by ear for a while." A knock at the door startled them into silence.

"Excuse me, ladies," Bradley announced, as he walked into the cabin. He saw that the mermaids had changed into his clothing and was disappointed that the blonde was so well covered by his shirt. He'd wanted a better look at her figure without the benefit of the thick green skin which now lay folded on the floor of his cabin. "I see you found garments that suited you."

"Yes, Captain," Laly answered sweetly. "Thank you."

Bradley narrowed one eye as he looked at her. What game was this one playing now? She'd replaced her brazen behavior of a short time ago with the softness of a meadowlark and he knew by instinct the falseness of her demeanor. "You're very welcome— Laly, is it?"

"Yes, Captain. That's correct." Laly noticed the way his large, muscular frame filled the small cabin. "Sugar and I are most grateful for your hospitality."

He bowed slightly in the cramped quarters. "It's my pleasure, ladies." He looked from one to the other. "If I might inquire, how long will you be my guests?"

Laly glanced hurriedly at Sugar. If only they knew. The storm could return any minute, or not for days. "We're not certain, Captain. You see, we got lost in the storm. Perhaps we'll find our way home when it returns."

Bradley listened to her explanation. She'd mentioned a storm once before, and it still made no sense. There hadn't been a storm of any importance for over a week. Was she trying to make him believe they'd been adrift for that length of time?

"We would be forever in your debt, Captain, if you'll allow us to remain here on your ship for a short while," Laly continued.

The more he watched her, the more he was convinced she was no mermaid, but he found himself reluctant to believe she worked for Rodriguez. There was a softness about her, despite her anger and the knife wielding of before, that caused him to doubt an affiliation with the likes of the murderer. Still, where else could she have come from? And if it was proved that she and her dark friend were indeed the accomplices of his hated foe, the best place for them to be was under his very nose, where he could keep an eye on them. "You may stay as long as you feel it is necessary. But I must get some of my belongings." He turned and pulled several garments from the armoire, then paused at the desk to pick up some maps.

"Captain, you don't mean to give us your cabin?" Sugar asked.

"Yes, Miss. I do."

"But Captain, where will you sleep?" Laly inquired.

"With my crew." Bradley turned to face her. "Excuse me now while I go change my clothes and put a few things away. You will both join me and my officers for dinner?" His gaze left Laly's face and followed the curve of her throat downward to the enticing swell of her breasts. A flame lit the darkness of his eyes when he saw the crimson color of twin crests beneath the white fabric of the shirt she wore.

Laly felt the heat of his perusal and blushed uncomfortably as she realized what was causing so bold a stare. Flustered, and suddenly anxious to see him on his way, she responded, "Yes, of course, we'd be delighted to eat with you, Captain."

Bradley forced his gaze once again to meet the turquoise depths of the lovely eyes before him. "Very well, then. Until later, ladies." Bowing slightly, he allowed himself one more sweeping inspection of Laly's form beneath the garment, then made his exit.

After the door was shut firmly behind him, Laly sank down to the bunk again. She let her breath out slowly, only then realizing she held it. Her skin felt warm where his gaze had traveled and she shook herself to be rid of the unnerving sensation.

"Laly, if I eat, I'll puke." Sugar groaned.

Laly felt Sugar's forehead again and was relieved to find it cool, but not clammy. Sugar might have been suffering from mild shock, and perhaps even a bit of seasickness, but Laly felt certain she would be fine very soon. "You stay here and rest while I go eat with the captain. I might find out where he's keeping the medallion. After dinner, I'll bring you some bread and maybe some broth of some kind."

Sugar looked anxiously at her friend. "Don't do anything stupid, Laly."

"I'm only going to eat with him. And you heard him—his other officers will be there. I hardly think I'll get the opportunity to do anything tonight but eat." She took Sugar's hand in hers. "What do you think they're serving?"

Dinner proved to be better fare than Laly expected. After she'd explained Sugar's absence, the roasted pork, fresh vegetables, rolls, and wine caused her mouth to water furiously, making her realize she was more hungry than she'd imagined. "Captain, everything is delicious," she told him between bites.

He smiled at her, perplexed by her open display of a healthy appetite. She obviously wasn't concerned by the present opinion that ladies never ate more than a bite in front of a gentleman. "I'm glad to see you're enjoying the meal," He waved at the cook to bring her another helping of the vegetables and reached to fill her wineglass.

"Mmmm, it's wonderful." She sipped her wine. "I have to say I'm surprised. I've read that the meals on board old vessels were lacking any fresh meats or vegetables."

"The *Vengeance* is hardly old. It was commissioned only last year," he stated, frowning curiously.

Laly stopped her wineglass in mid air. "I, ah, of course, Captain. How stupid of me. I didn't mean to slight your ship." She looked at the faces of the other men seated at the table. They watched her closely, cautiously, disapprovingly. Uncomfortable, she noticed that they'd all finished eating and put her fork down to rest on her plate.

When she'd entered the dining room she hadn't been surprised to see the young man the captain referred to as Wainwright in attendance. He'd bowed over her hand at their formal introduction and then assisted in the further introductions of the other officers. Laly had made a mental note of each name as she'd heard it. Being friendly with the crew certainly couldn't hurt her and Sugar's position here. Now, they watched her with raised brows at her strange and somewhat insulting remark. How long was it going to take her to remember to think about everything she was going to say before she said it? "Gentlemen, please allow me to apologize for my ignorance. I'm not used to being on board a ship such as this." Definitely not a lie, she thought.

A smothered chuckle from Wainwright seemed to break the tension and was followed by more nervous laughter from the others. Laly looked from face to face. The red jowls of the man introduced as Harvey Lawson fairly shook with his mirth, and the somewhat stern visage of a tall, thin man called Spears seemed to crack a little. She suddenly realized that they still believed her to be a sea creature, a mermaid, and therefore her statement about not being used to being on a ship was most amusing to them. She found herself grinning back at them and, picking up her wineglass, raised it in salute.

"Very good," laughed Lawson. "Very good, indeed." He raised his glass to her and the others followed suit.

Laly smiled at each man, letting her gaze travel from one to the other. The only man not smiling in return was the captain. When her eyes met his, he raised his glass and slowly placed it against his lips. Her breath caught in her throat as she watched him taste the liquid and once again lower the glass. He watched her too intently for comfort, and even though she'd put her bathing suit top back on under the shirt she wore, she felt he was seeing her nude form beneath the filmy fabric. "Sir?" Her voice came out a hoarse whisper.

"Yes, Laly?"

"I thought you were going to say something. Never mind." She lowered her glass to the cloth-covered table and sighed, not knowing where to put her hands, now that she'd finished eating.

These gentlemen were very formal in their gold-buttoned blue uniforms and she'd noticed through-out the meal that their manners matched the formal-ity of their attire. Each had devoured the food with relish, but none had allowed his elbows to rest on the table or failed to use the cloth napkins provided. She couldn't help but wonder what they'd think if they saw her eating pizza on the floor of her apart-ment in front of a San Diego football game on TV. "Times have changed," she whispered, and looked down at her fidgeting fingers.

Bradley watched Laly with a keen eye. He'd noticed the brightly colored garment she wore under his shirt the moment she'd entered the dining room. He'd kept his smile to himself, approving of her modesty and at the same time feeling disappointed that the view he'd so enjoyed in his cabin was now concealed from his vision. Now and then he could still see the smooth curve of feminine breast as she moved, but for the most part, his shirt did an excellent job hiding those portions of her he'd most like to see.

Placing his elbows on the arms of his chair, he touched his fingertips together and rested his chin on them. Still he studied her and waited . . . waited for her to reveal the meaning of her visit to his ship. Did she think she could sit with his officers, partake of their food, sleep in his cabin, and not explain herself? Did she think that it was usual for the crew of the *Vengeance* to pluck beautiful women from the ocean and not question the course they took in arriv-ing there? He could be a patient man, but even his patience had its limits. He sat forward abruptly. "There has been no storm in this area for nearly a fortnight," he stated bluntly.

Laly started at his directness. The other gentlemen

stopped talking and turned their eyes to her, waiting for her to make some kind of rebuttal to the captain's statement. She looked into the dark eyes that examined her so carefully. How could she make him understand? She was a mermaid to him, a myth come to life. At least a mermaid was something written about in books and song. Crazy as it sounded, a mermaid was more believable than a woman come back from over three hundred years in the future. Hell, the truth of it was that, given a choice, she herself would believe in mermaids before she'd believe in the possibility of time travel. Yet here she was, sitting on board an English ship in 1678 with the captain breathing down her neck about where she'd come from because he was having a hard time with the mermaid idea. He'd never believe the truth. Not even if she took three hundred years to explain it.

Sighing, she rubbed a hand over her eyes. "Captain, I can assure you that Sugar and I were caught in a storm. I can't explain how we ended up here. Please believe me when I tell you we had no intention of intruding on you or interrupting your battle today." She paused. "It was a most unusual storm."

"Unusual, you say? How?" Wainwright questioned.

Laly looked at the young officer. "It came out of nowhere with a surprising force—and light."

"Light?" Bradley asked.

Laly looked back at the Captain. "Yes, light. We were in the water when the storm hit"—she didn't add that they were forty feet beneath the surface—"and a light surrounded and held us trapped for quite some time."

Bradley half closed one eye, lowering his brow skeptically. "A light held you trapped?"

"I know it sounds strange. It frightened the hell out of us," she heard a slight gasp by one of the officers at her curse, "and when we were released, we were here with you." She didn't know how else to explain it so they would have any chance of believing her. "Captain, I'm telling the truth." She placed her hands flat on the table before him in a pleading gesture. She could see the lack of trust in his dark eyes but had to continue if she ever hoped to escape this time. "And there's one more thing: the medallion. I've got to have it if I ever want to get home."

Bradley hid the emotions that churned in his stomach at her revelation. She had finally let some of the truth be known. She hoped to get the medallion back and seemed willing to play upon his sympathy and concoct wild tales of mystery storms to do so. "So, Miss. You think I should give you the King's Medallion?"

"King's Medallion?"

He watched her arrange her expression into one of innocence. She didn't really think she'd make him believe her feigned ignorance of the piece, did she? "Yes, Laly. You're not aware of its origins?" he asked her, softening his tone to snare her further.

"No, Captain. I know nothing of the medallion, except that I believe it had something to do with my and Sugar's arrival here. I had just found it when the storm hit."

Bradley stood quickly, scraping his chair roughly back across the floor beneath him. He saw the startled expressions on the faces of his officers and turned his back on the table before he let his temper get the better of him. This woman must think him an imbecile to tell him such a tale. He turned back toward her and rested his hands on the table. "Laly, I do not believe even one word of your story. There have been no storms near here anytime of late, and the King's Medallion was stolen from the governor's mansion over a year ago. It is a most famous trinket, worth a fortune, and would be recognized by nearly anyone who saw it."

"But Captain . . ." Laly protested.

"I have wondered whether Rodriguez gave you the medallion in payment of some service, but I do not believe he would part with a treasure of such worth. Therefore, I must assume you had it on your person before you boarded the *Puta*, although I find that a very foolish move considering the man's immense greed, and his lack of qualms about murder."

"Captain, really! If you'll just let me talk . . ."

"Yes, Laly?" Bradley stood straight again and looked down on her from his towering height.

Laly was determined not to be intimidated by this man. She stood to her height—full five feet seven inches—and tried to meet his level gaze. "Captain Bradley, I don't know who this Rodriguez is and I really don't give a damn whether you believe me or not. I know I'm telling the truth, and that's all that really matters." The captain's black scowl and the astonished expressions of the other gentlemen reminded her of her precarious position in this time period. "I only mean . . . I'm not telling you lies, Captain, gentlemen." She turned her plea to the other faces in the room. "Don't you see? I'm as confused by all this as you are. I don't know why Sugar and I were brought here. I only know, or think I know, that the medallion has something to do with it.'' She sank back down to the chair and lowered her face to her hands, as close to crying as she'd been in the last several years. Her eyes stung and her throat felt tight as she fought back the sobs that threatened to overtake her. Refusing to give in to the desire to bawl, she flung a heavy swath of blond hair over her shoulder as she raised her head to once more face the captain.

Lawson cleared his throat before anyone else could speak. "Perhaps, Captain, there is some truth in the mermaid's words?''

Bradley looked surprised at his officer. Lawson was a loyal man, not usually given to belief in fairy tales, which is what he felt Laly was asking of them. "You think she and her friend were adrift for more than a week? Did you see any salt sores on their bodies? Were they near death from lack of food or water?''

"Well, Sir . . . I,'' Lawson stammered.

Bradley gestured toward Laly. "I ask you gentlemen: do you see any evidence of hardship on the body of this woman?''

Laly felt all eyes on her and tried to take their inspection casually though her heartbeat increased with her nervousness.

"Well, gentlemen? Have not one of you an opinion on how she and her friend could accomplish such a feat?''

Spears's voice was soft when he spoke. "Perhaps mermaids don't feel the affects of the salt water as humans do?''

Bradley crossed his arms in front of him. "So you still believe she and her friend are mermaids. Gentlemen, please, doesn't it make more sense to believe that they were on board the *Puta*? Wouldn't it have been easy for them to slip into the water to divert our attention from Rodriguez's escape, to make that escape possible?''

Lawson pursed his too-full lips and looked Laly over before speaking. "I must admit it is difficult to really believe this lovely woman is a mermaid, but I find it equally difficult to believe that she and her friend are working for the likes of Rodriguez."

Bradley once again let his gaze rest on Laly's face. He found that he also doubted she was an accomplice of the notorious pirate. Still, where she and Sugar had come from was a great mystery to him. None of the solutions he'd come up with were very satisfying. Mermaids or pirates, neither answer pleased him. "You see, Laly, I am in a very awkward position. By my crew's words, you are unexplainable. Although you possessed the King's Medallion, I have no evidence to prove you stole it. You claim to have found it. You could be lying, probably are, but without evidence I cannot, in good conscience, treat you as a criminal. Until we reach Charles Towne, you will have the freedom of the ship. Once in port, you will be put ashore. The King's Medallion will be given back to the governor and whatever course you take will be up to you. I suggest you make wise choices and stay away from Rodriguez." He raised his hand to silence her when she moved to interrupt. "Don't bother to protest, Laly. I am merely giving advice, not accusing. Now, if you will excuse us, my crew and I would like a few moments alone. I'm sure you'd like to check on your friend now, anyway. I believe the cook has a tray of food ready to take to her."

Laly was stunned by her dismissal. This arrogant man had judged her to be a liar, perhaps even a pirate, and though she had the freedom of the ship, she was being ordered from the room.

Frustration burned in her chest as she stood to leave. She was no closer to the medallion now than before she'd sat down to eat; in fact, she was now very certain she'd have to steal it. How she would accomplish this was still a question for her. She had no idea where it was, and as she thought about it more, she knew she would be the prime suspect should it be discovered missing before they docked at New Providence. "Very well, Captain. I'll leave you to discuss me further in private," she goaded, and noticed the red faces of Lawson and Wainwright. The Captain, however, just stared darkly at her as she left.

Once outside the closed door of the dining room, she was met by the cook with a tray of succulent food. Even after the large meal she'd consumed, the aromas from the tray tantalized her senses. "I always do have a big appetite at sea," she whispered. Then the words of the captain hit her with their full force, almost causing her to drop the tray. They were to be put ashore in Charles Towne. In Charles Towne? "Oh, my God!" she hissed, and hurried to the captain's cabin and Sugar.

"Sugar, wake up. Please wake up!" She'd set the tray on the desk and was now shaking her friend from the deep sleep she'd so desperately needed.

"Laly?" Sugar had fallen into a dream state unlike anything she'd ever known. She imagined she and Laly had gone back in time and were on an English ship captained by a dark man named Devon Bradley. It was all so real. She even felt the gentle roll of waves beneath the ship.

"Come on, Sugar. Wake up. I've got to talk to you," Laly persisted.

"No, Laly. Let me sleep. I'm having the most incredible dream," Sugar mumbled into the pillow.

"But the captain is going to put us ashore in Charles Towne!" She shook her friend's shoulder. "Did you hear me? I said we're being put ashore in *Charles Towne!*"

Laly's words finally got through to Sugar's exhausted brain. She cringed against the reality of waking up. It was all a dream; it had to be. She opened one eye and looked up at Laly. Behind her she could see the swaying lamp of the cabin and the captain's desk. "No!" she wailed. "I thought it was a dream, but it's a nightmare."

"You don't know how close you are to the truth. Captain Bradley and his crew think we may be pirates, or at least, working for a pirate named Rodriguez."

Sugar slowly pulled herself up to lean against the wall. "Rodriguez? Why would they think that? I thought they were convinced we were mermaids."

"The question is still in the air. But because the captain isn't convinced, he's come up with another theory. This Rodriguez thing."

"Who is Rodriguez?"

"Apparently he's the captain of the other ship in today's battle."

"Why would Captain Bradley think we would have anything to do with a pirate?"

"I suppose it's easier for him to believe in female pirates than in mermaids," Laly said, lowering herself to sit beside Sugar on the bunk.

"Great." Sugar grimaced. "Any luck with the medallion?" Laly shook her head. "I don't have any idea where it is. And the captain sure isn't going to hand it over to us. Apparently the governor had it made as a gift for the king. It was stolen before he got a chance to send it. The captain's planning on sending it back to the governor's mansion as soon as we dock." Laly then looked up into Sugar's brown eyes. "We're to be put ashore."

Sugar stared at her friend as she digested what she'd been told. New Providence in 1678 was not what it was today, or would be in three hundred years, she corrected her self. She wracked her brain for historical information about the area. The governor's mansion was on a hill overlooking the town. The population was made up of English settlers, many of them involved in the export of the valuable woods of the islands. And the waterfront was a dirty, rough place where two women could fall easy prey to the most vile of the island's pirates, rapists, and murderers. "What are we going to do?" she asked in a breathless voice.

"We're going to get the medallion back so we can get out of here," Laly answered, with a conviction she didn't quite feel.

"How?"

"I don't know yet, but we'll think of something. Right now we've got to get your strength up. Are you hungry yet? I brought you some dinner." She stood and crossed the short distance to the desk, bringing back the tray.

Sugar felt her stomach growl at the thought of food. "I guess I am." She realized she was feeling much better. "Is it edible?"

"Judge for yourself." Laly lifted the cloth covering the food and watched the surprised expression cross Sugar's face. "A whole lot better than we expected.

Must be the close proximity to the islands that allows such a menu. Well, dig in," she prodded, when Sugar just stared at the tray.

Several hours later, Laly lay awake in the bunk next to Sugar. They'd found that by putting their heads at opposite ends, they could sleep fairly comfortably. At least, Sugar was enjoying a restful slumber; Laly lay awake with eyes that refused to close. The slow rocking of the ship had relaxed her at first, then she'd started thinking about their situation and begun counting the times the lamp swung back and forth. Instead of being hypnotizing, the motion became nerve-wracking, and she was soon so tense she wanted to scream.

Carefully, she slid off the bunk and looked at Sugar's sleeping face. "At least one of us will be refreshed in the morning," she whispered. Sugar could fall asleep anywhere, anytime, and under any circumstances, a trait that had driven Laly crazy during their college years. No matter how nervous they were about final exams, Sugar would drift off as though she had not a care in the world, while Laly paced the floor for hours, fighting the urge to stuff herself with junk food. Shrugging, she mouthed, "Some things never change."

Outside the cabin door, she wondered where she should go. She had the need to take a walk but wasn't sure about exploring the ship in the middle of the night. If only I knew where the medallion was . . . she thought, then remembered she needed to be patient. Finding the whereabouts of the medallion was important, but not taking it until they were almost in port was mandatory.

Deciding that some fresh air would make her sleepy, she headed down the narrow corridor toward the stairs to the deck. If she ran across one of the officers she'd met at dinner she might be able to coax him into revealing where the captain was keeping the medallion. She hoped Lawson had night duty. He seemed the most likely candidate to fall prey to some feminine wiles. She smiled at her thoughts and wondered if she knew how to use feminine wiles, if she even had any.

The 1990s had produced strong, independent, intelligent women, capable of competing with men in every field. She and Sugar had each received tenure with their university at young ages and were considered very successful in their own right. Dinner with the ship's officers, their shocked reactions to her swearing and outburst at the captain, had shown her that in 1678 she'd have to use more feminine means to achieve her goals. She only hoped she'd be able to cope with the rules here.

The light breeze blowing across the deck felt wonderful on her skin as she crossed to stand near a railing and look at the moon shining a silver path across the surface of the ocean. The brilliant glint, like a hundred coins shimmering and dipping with the waves, caused her to stand still and enjoy the beauty. No matter what century, she loved the ocean. The thought of how wonderful it would be to sail on a ship such as this forever brought a smile to her face.

Something inside her ached dully. It was a feeling she was familiar with, a feeling she'd grown up with. Whenever she gazed out over the seemingly never-ending waters of an ocean, or watched a gull fly into view from a distant shore, she would experience a sense of longing, a happy melancholy that she never quite understood but felt comfortable with. She continued to smile as the breeze took hold of her hair and whipped a piece of it around to cover her face. She pulled it down and sighed. "Oh to sail tall ships . . ." Her voice was lost in the billowing of the sails.

Five

Bradley had been standing on the upper deck, thinking about the women in his cabin, when he saw Laly come from below. He watched as she stood in the moonlight and wondered what she saw as she looked out to sea. Her back was to him so he couldn't read her face, but his breath caught in his throat when the cool breeze lifted the fabric of her shirt, revealing the alluring curves of her woman's body. This, he was sure, was no mermaid. This was a woman, warm-blooded, with a fiery temper and turquoise eyes that even now haunted his vision.

He waited to see what she would do. What had brought her to the deck at this late hour? The wind caught her hair and as she pulled the offending tresses from her face she turned her head slightly, giving him a view of the soft planes of her face. She smiled, and the distant look in her eyes puzzled him. What was she thinking? She looked as though she'd lost something, or perhaps waited for something, someone. He quietly made his way down the steps to the lower deck, needing to be nearer to her to read her expression more clearly.

Laly didn't hear the captain behind her but knew when he stood just inches away. "Hello, Captain," her voice came soft in the breeze.

Bradley took another step closer. He could almost feel the warmth from her body. "Good evening, Laly. Or should I say, Good morn?"

"Is it that late?"

"Aye."

Laly felt the timbre of his voice in the air between them. "Then good morn," she returned.

"Why are you here?" Bradley asked her softly.

Laly thought she read something in his question beyond the obvious. She tried to find an answer he could accept. She found none.

Bradley stepped to her side and looked into her face. Something there concerned him. She met his gaze directly, not hiding secrets or deceit. He struggled with himself and the position she'd put him in. She was in all probability a spy, yet he couldn't totally distrust her. "You will not tell me your business here?"

"I have no business here. I only wish to get home."

"And you need the medallion to get there," he repeated her story and sighed.

She looked downward. "Yes, Captain." She'd had time since dinner to realize that the captain was only doing his duty in deciding to put her and Sugar ashore. These were different times. He couldn't just call the authorities on ship-to-shore to corroborate her story. He had only his experience and knowledge to depend on in his decision making. It didn't make the idea of the Charles Towne waterfront any less frightening, but it took the edge off her anger with the man responsible.

She'd also had to admit that he couldn't really help his attitude toward her. The arrogance he'd displayed in dismissing her from the dining room was natural in this year, although she felt it was possible to work on this aspect of his personality. Too bad I won't be around long enough to make some changes in him, she thought, surprising herself.

Bradley looked down at the blond hair that seemed to glow with the brilliance of the moon. The turquoise of Laly's eyes was hidden beneath black lashes and he frowned with curiosity at her coloring. If he weren't a realistic man he might have been tempted to believe she was a mermaid. Here in the moonlight she possessed the beauty that could indeed bewitch the heart of a sailor. But no matter how beautiful she was, his duty was clear. "You understand I am unable to give you the medallion."

"I know that, Captain." She raised her eyes to his and felt sorry that she must be his adversary. She had to get the medallion and he was determined to see it safely back in the hands of the governor.

The breeze became stronger around them and Laly stood transfixed, the darkness of his eyes holding her captive. She shuddered.

"Are you chilled?" he asked.

"No."

"Do you wish to go below?"

"No." Her answer was no more than a murmur. As she stood gazing up into his eyes, she felt a desire burn deeply within her—not the desire made up of lust, but of longing. She barely knew this man, but something about him tugged at her. Something in the depths of his eyes reached her soul and caused her to dream of impossible things. Of lying in his arms as the sun rose like a fiery sword over the ocean, slicing its way through a tiny window to illuminate the strong length of his body over hers. Of nights such as this and kisses that branded her his from the beginning of time.

She took a deep breath and tried to stop the emotions she was feeling. This was crazy. It was just the moonlight, the breeze, the gentle rocking of the ship. She tried to tell herself it was just the magic of the night weaving its web around her, and yet . . .

Bradley was held spellbound by her eyes. Only hours ago she didn't exist for him, and now he could feel her heartbeat, though she stood inches away. It seemed she was a part of him, her pulse his, her warmth his own. The palms of his hands tingled with the need to touch her, to know the weight of her breasts, the curve of her stomach, the secrets of her body. A blazing heat coiled deep within his middle and spread downward to his loins, a heat he knew only she could cool.

What was this magic he felt? She was a stranger to him. Perhaps the night wind had brought with it a drugging scent to cloud his thinking. It was the sway of the ship teasing his senses, the moonlight blinding him to reality, and yet . . .

Laly saw the captain's dark head lower and felt the heated touch of his lips. A stabbing jolt shot through her at his gentle pressure. Softly, his tender lips moved over hers in question, then she felt the tip of his tongue trace the curve of her mouth. Leaning slightly forward, she opened her lips and allowed her tongue to meet his. She tasted the heady maleness of him in his kiss. Her heart beat violently in her chest, feeling every bit as though it would burst as it pounded wildly

within her. She opened her mouth further and
allowed the exploration to grow. Moaning softly as
she swayed ever closer, she felt the strength in his
arms as he pulled her to him. The astonishing arousal
she felt when her body melded with his took her
breath away.

Bradley was lost in her kiss. He let his tongue
explore the soft, heated regions of her sweet mouth
and was unprepared for her responding curiosity as
her tongue darted to meet his. He had to feel her
against him. He pulled her closer and was nearly
undone by the feel of firm breasts against his chest.
The blood pounded in his manhood as he pressed
himself against her. He needed release as he'd never
needed it before. He moved rhythmically against her,
ready to explode with his desire. His mouth left hers
and trailed a burning path to her throat. He hadn't
touched her breasts or let his hand roam to that warm
place between her thighs, and yet he knew it would
take only the merest stroke to undo him completely.
How could this woman cause such a fire to rage in
him?

Laly gasped for air when his mouth left hers to
roam with gentle kisses down her throat. The rhythm
he'd begun between them she answered with the
rocking of her own body. His huge desire pressing
into her abdomen, the rock hardness of his thighs
as he moved himself up and down against her, sent
the demand through her to respond, a demand she
could not ignore. The hard peaks of her breasts ached
with the need to be suckled. The moistness of her
woman's core longed to be filled. Leaning her head
back against his arm, she raised her hand to her breast
and lifted it to him in a plea. Her request was answered
when his mouth closed over the ripe peak, his tongue

teasing, his teeth gently biting as she desired. Even through the fabric that separated them, she could feel the passion growing out of control.

The hard bud of Laly's breast pushed against the cloth of the garments she wore. He could taste her through the fabric and longed for the slick feel of her skin on his tongue. He raised a hand to unfasten the shirt and pulled it aside; then, kissing the swell of breast above the bright top she wore underneath, he tugged the cup down over the ripened hardness of her nipple. His mouth covered it hungrily, sucking it wholly into his mouth, biting down tenderly as he heard her gasp. His own heat was growing ever tighter and the need for release so great he had to stop his movements for a moment and stand perfectly still against her. Another moment and he would be undone. "Laly," he breathed her name over her breast. "What have you done to me?"

Laly heard her name in the hot breath on her breast. She'd felt him shudder against her as he'd stilled his movements. So close, they were so close. She understood his need to stop and waited for him to slow his breathing. His tongue still flicked gently over her nipple, sending shards of electricity shooting through her nerves. She needed to touch him. The pulsing manhood against her abdomen drew her hand. She heard him moan as her fingers found the head of his passion through the tightness of his pants. Slowly she followed its length to between his legs where she cupped that softest part of him.

Laly's hand fondled him gently and stopped his heart. If he moved at all, he knew he would embarrass himself as though he were an inexperienced youth, anxious to release his fluids and not caring how. He couldn't breath as she continued her exploration of his lower body. The sweet torture she exacted sent waves of painlike ecstasy throughout his nervous system. He stood stiffly against her onslaught, rigidly fighting for his control. When her fingers raised to his waistband, he knew he must stop her. If the heat of her soft skin touched the flame that burned between his legs he would burst in her hand. "Laly, no," he whispered, as his lips once again claimed hers. He took her hand and held it flat against him, then moved it slowly up and down along his body, creating his own torture now.

Laly found the rhythm he created and continued it as his hand left hers and went back to her breasts. He released the other from its binding then circled the heated tip with his tongue before he rolled it between his lips. His mouth continued to suckle and tease as his hand slid gently down her side and behind her to hold the swell of her buttocks in his palm. He stroked her boldly, pulling her closer to him, pushing his manhood deeper into her exploring fingers. Then he reached between them and cupped the mound of her womanhood in his hand.

Her breath came in ragged gasps as he rubbed the heel of his hand against that part of her that stood erect to his touch. Her own hands stopped moving in the paralyzing ecstasy she felt. The world spun around her as she neared the brink of the spiraling release he promised. His palm was replaced by his teasing fingertips, tickling then pushing against the fabric that sheathed the silken secrets of her body. Her head fell back, her hair a silver waterfall across his arm. "Captain," she groaned. "Please . . ." Please what, she wondered. Did she want him to stop, or to throw her to the deck and open his trousers, releasing his large promise of fulfillment, and plunge deeply within her, letting her scream her delight into the darkness?

Bradley barely heard her speak. The throbbing of his passion, the taste of her full, ripe breasts, the feel of his hand against the moist heat of her womanhood had drugged him as no wine or woman before her had ever done. He ached and burned for her. The blood in his temples pounded in a primitive rhythm that refused to go unanswered. He needed to bury himself deep within her, to feel her close tightly around his heated shaft and move with him in the dance of lovers. Her body was made for him, her rhythm his own. He knew their passion would be the echoing perfection of twin mountain peaks, soaring high above the clouds to find the heavens together. He pulled her downward, heedless of their surroundings, silently lowering her to the cool wood of the deck. His hands ran feverishly along her body, loosening the scarf that held her pants, tugging her shirt further away from her breasts. He let his mouth follow where his hands led, tasting the sweetness of her flesh.

Laly felt Bradley pulling her downward. Her heart beat loudly in her ears as she felt the wood of the deck beneath her back. The coiling heat in her throbbing center craved the release only his body could give her. She reached out to touch once more the evidence of his passion, the strong length of it promising so much. She rubbed her hand over the head of this promise and felt him shudder against her touch. Her fingers found the fastenings of his pants and she began to release him, anxious to touch the silken skin of that which was so desired.

The startled gasp and sound of someone walking quickly away broke through the passion fog that surrounded them. Laly looked up through glazed eyes into the dark face of the captain. His lids were heavy with desire, but she could also see confusion.—confusion at what they'd just done, or almost done. His hands still covered her breasts and she couldn't help the feelings she suffered at his touch, but she was horrified at being discovered this way by someone. Her own fingers were still tangled in the fastening of his pants; her wrist lay touching the heat of his desire. She jerked her hands back and tried to sit up. "Oh, Lord," she mumbled.

"Laly . . . I'm sorry." Bradley wondered what had possessed him. He couldn't imagine which of his crew had discovered him in such a compromising position and cringed at the sight he'd presented. Never in his career had he shown such a lack of professionalism. "My God," he whispered. Sitting upright, he reached to assist Laly in straightening her clothing. *How* could he have let this happen?

Laly pulled her bathing suit top back up over the breasts and felt the heated blush that covered her body. The captain's hands were warm where he touched her in his attempt to help her cover herself. The breeze that blew her hair around her was warm, but she shivered as she stood. She had to get back to her cabin. She couldn't meet the captain's eyes and wished the sea would swallow her whole. She wanted to disappear from his sight. "Goodnight, Captain," she said softly, as she moved to leave.

"Good morn, Laly," he whispered.

Her eyes darted upward to meet his for the briefest moment, then down again to the planks of the deck beneath her feet. She quickly left his side and headed down the stairs.

Bradley watched her go and couldn't help but feel the coolness of her departure. Part of him recoiled at his lack of discretion, but deep within his soul beat the truth that what they'd begun here would be completed sometime soon. A fire that blazed so brilliantly couldn't be doused with the splash of cool water. Indeed, he felt himself growing stiff again at the mere thought of her body.

He wondered at the strength of his reaction. Was she truly a creature of the sea, sent to bewitch him? He remembered the warmth of her skin beneath his touch and smiled at his foolish thoughts. This was no creature of the deep. Laly was a woman of flesh and blood, bone and sinew, warmth and passion. Whatever her reason for being here, he would discover it. He would uncover her mystery and perhaps convince her to go where her desires led. Now that he'd found this woman who matched his need so perfectly, he had no intention of letting her slip away. He would follow her when they reached Charles Towne.

Laly made her way down the corridor to her cabin. Her blood pounded in her temples and she knew she hadn't stopped blushing since she'd left the captain standing on the deck. How could she have been so stupid as to allow herself to respond to him as she had? She pulled her shirt tighter around her and shuddered with the memory of being discovered in such a manner. "Damn, damn, damn," she cursed under her breath, wondering which of the crew had found them. Which man's eyes would gleam with the knowledge when he looked at her? How could she ever live through the humiliation? And how could she ever face the captain again?

The captain. His tall visage floated before her when she thought of him. Broad shoulders, strong chest and arms, narrow waist, and his . . . "Oh, my Lord,"

Alane Fay

she groaned at the memories. She realized that there was no way she could have resisted the attraction she felt for him. He was her perfect match. The foil to her sheath, the hand to fit her glove. Why on earth would she meet him here, now? Was it to be a cruel joke of fate that she meet the man of her dreams in a time and place she didn't belong, would soon leave?

She neared the cabin door with a sob on her breath. She swallowed the sound and squared her shoulders, knowing she must face what ever the future—or past—had to offer, no matter how painful. She paused a moment in the corridor to calm her breathing before going in. As she turned the handle she wondered again who it was that had seen her with the captain. The still shocked expression and crimson color of Sugar's face as Laly entered the cabin answered her question for her. She dropped her face to her hands in humiliation. "Oh no, it was you!"

Six

"I never thought you'd go so far," whispered Sugar. "I never expected it of you."

Laly blinked unsurely at Sugar, then the understanding hit her: her friend thought she'd tried to seduce the captain to gain access to the medallion. She walked further into the room and sat on the edge of the bed. "What you saw had nothing to do with the medallion," she confessed miserably.

"But . . ."

Laly lowered her eyes. "Sugar, I don't know how to make any sense out of it. You know me well enough to know I would do just about anything to get the medallion back, but just now, in his arms," she blushed scarlet with the memory, "the medallion was the furthest thing from my mind." She looked up at her friend once more. "Being with him felt . . . right. Am I a little crazy?"

Sugar scooted closer to Laly and put a comforting arm across her shoulder. She'd been shocked to walk up on the Captain and Laly in such a compromising position, she'd immediately thought Laly had gone too far in her antics, but the misery in her friend's eyes now brought sympathy welling through her. "I don't think you're crazy. This day is crazy. What's happened is crazy. And I think we're in for a lot more craziness before this is through. But I don't think you're crazy."

Laly shook her head. "I've only just met him. And by the time we get back home, he'll have been dead three hundred years." She shook her head again. "Do you know I haven't so much as let another man kiss me goodnight in months, and here I am, practically screwing a perfect stranger on the deck of a ship—in plain view of anyone who happened by! God, if I'm not crazy, I'm pretty damned close."

Sugar patted Laly's shoulder. "Don't be so hard on yourself. The captain is one of the best-looking guys I've ever seen. He's strong and seems intelligent. He couldn't be more your type if he tried. And look at the bright side. There's no such thing as AIDS in this century."

Laly rolled her eyes. "I appreciate you trying to cheer me up, but do you realize we're no closer to the medallion now than we were before I made a fool of myself with the captain?"

"So he didn't have it on him, then?" Sugar teased.

Laly smirked. "Nope, and believe me, I would have felt it if he had. He had nothing on him that size."

"Nothing that big?"

"Nothing that small!" Laly grinned wickedly at the memory, sending Sugar into a fit of purely female laughter.

"Oh Lord, I can't believe we're still able to laugh

after everything that's happened," Laly said as she joined Sugar in her mirth.

"We'd better be able to laugh. If we let ourselves get too serious, or too down, we *will* go crazy."

Laly sobered a bit and sighed. "Damn, you're good for me. If I had to be sent back in time over three hundred years, I'm glad it was with you."

Sugar smiled at her friend. "Well, if I'd been given a choice, I think I'd have chosen to stay behind this time. Your adventures in the twentieth century were enough for me."

"Not really," Laly feigned surprise.

"Remember poor old Mrs. Melton, our freshman biology professor? You had that woman doubting the laws of nature by the end of the term."

"I hated the way she'd answer every question I asked with the same response."

Both women tilted their heads back, looked down their noses, and said in unison, "For every riddle in nature, there is an answer. One just has to look for it, Miss Lawrence."

"The trouble with her was that she had no imagination," said Laly, chuckling.

"And you did your best to give her one. My mother still mentions the phone call she received from the dean when we were caught feeding the deprivation rats in the lab in the middle of the night."

"We couldn't very well let the poor little things starve to death because Mrs. Melton was doing some cruel experiment, could we?" Laly asked.

"That's the same argument you used to convince me to participate in the first place. I didn't believe your motives then, and I don't now. You were just trying to gaslight Mrs. Melton," Sugar accused.

Laly shrugged. "But you helped anyway." She grinned at her partner in crime.

"Yes, and I paid the price after getting caught with you, too."

"It was worth it. Remember? We couldn't wait for her to check those rats every morning. I wanted so badly to tell her it was just one of nature's riddles waiting to be answered, but I knew she'd get suspicious of us if I did."

Sugar let her gaze drop to the bed, suddenly remembering the trouble they were in. "She was a pain, all right. But I hope she was right about nature's riddles . . . about finding the answer if you look for it."

Laly clasped Sugar's hand. "Don't worry, we'll get out of here. We'll get the medallion back—even if I *do* have to sleep with the captain," she said in a martyred tone.

"That would be such a hardship," Sugar stated sarcastically.

Laly tipped her head back and threw her forearm dramatically across her brow as she spoke. "If I must, I must." She straightened again. "Now, let's get some sleep. We'll think of a way to get the medallion back in the morning."

A few moments later, once again lying with their heads at opposite ends of the bed, Laly wondered how they would get to the medallion. The captain didn't carry it on his person, she knew that for a fact, and the ship was a big place to hide such a small article. She knew it would take both her and Sugar to accomplish retrieving it.

"Laly?" Sugar whispered in the now darkened cabin. "What about the captain, seriously?" she asked.

"I don't know. I guess I'll have to figure it out as I go. I know I'm attracted to him, and he seems to be attracted to me, but I can't let myself fall for a man I have no future with," Laly whispered back.

A few minutes of silence passed, then Sugar spoke again. "Is he really . . . you know?" she whispered.

"Does the term 'racehorse' mean anything to you?" Laly asked.

"Oh, my God," Sugar breathed loudly.

"You said a mouthful," Laly chuckled, then, thinking about what she'd just said, "Hmmm, interesting idea."

"Laly, you're awful!" Sugar pretended shock.

"Damn, she's bewitched me," Bradley cursed into the night.

"Sir?" Wainwright asked, when he heard the captain's voice.

"Sorry, Wainwright. Go back to sleep." He spoke softly, turning slightly in the hammock he'd hung in his first officer's cabin. He tried to adjust his uncomfortable bulk to a more relaxing position. He barely fit in a bloody hammock, let alone fit comfortably. Sighing, he gave up and let himself fall back to the continuously bent formation the hammock insisted upon and admitted he wouldn't sleep that night anyway, even if he were floating on a feather mattress.

All he could think about was Laly, her turquoise eyes burning him with their desire, the silken tresses of her moon-colored hair wrapping around him, the softness of her fingertips as she caressed his body, the hardened peaks of her full, firm breasts beneath his touch. He groaned from the torturing toll these thoughts were taking on his most male parts. His loins ached with a fire he knew would be put out only when he could pour his desire deeply within her. "God's teeth," he cursed again.

"Sir?"

"Nothing, Wainwright. I'm sorry to have awakened you."

"You didn't wake me, Sir. I, too, am having trouble finding dreams this night."

"You are?"

"Yes, Sir. It's the mermaids, Sir. I can't stop thinking about them. I daresay, most of the men on this ship are probably thinking about them instead of getting their rest."

"I believe you're correct, Wainwright." But not every man on this ship has nearly made love to one of them, he added to himself. "You still believe them to be mermaids? Even after having eaten with one of them, after having spoken with her?" he asked his young officer.

"Well, sir . . . I don't . . . I can't . . ."

"Yes?" Bradley raised one brow, waiting for Wainwright's response.

"I have a hard time believing they're working for the likes of Rodriquez."

"Aye. I do, too. But mermaids?" His pulse once again beat erratically with the memory of what a warm-blooded woman Laly had proved to be.

"What other explanation could there be, Sir? They certainly didn't just appear before us from nowhere."

"No, that is true. They had to come from somewhere. And though we've been left with two choices, either to believe they're spies for Rodriguez, or mermaids, I find neither possibility very acceptable." He twisted in the hammock once again, turning to face Wainwright in the dark. "Their story about getting caught in a strange storm was interesting. Too bad there haven't been any storms recently."

"Yes, Sir."

As he settled back down into the hammock, Bradley let his mind wander once again over the memory of Laly as she stood on deck, gazing off across the sea. Her unusual turquoise eyes had held a look of longing, a look that had touched him. "What is your secret, Laly?" he mouthed silently.

The tramping of running footfalls, shouts and curses overhead woke Laly and Sugar the next morning. Sitting up quickly, both women stared hard at each other. "What's going on up there?" wondered Sugar aloud.

Laly leaned across the bed to look out one of the portholes. "I don't see anything here. Let's go topside and see for ourselves."

"Do you think we should?"

"Why not? The captain didn't confine us to his cabin. Come on." She was already up and running the captain's brush through her hair.

"All right," Sugar agreed reluctantly, sliding from the bed.

Laly watched her friend while dipping a cloth into the water basin. "Are you feeling better this morning?"

"Much. I'm getting my sea legs." Sugar took a few steps toward Laly and grinned. "See, good as new."

"Great. Then hurry. I want to get up on deck and see what all the commotion's about." She used a corner of the cloth to brush her teeth, then hurriedly hung it over a hook. She paced while Sugar followed a similar routine.

The noises on deck were getting louder, the shouts more frantic, and though she could identify no particular voices, she knew that somewhere up there was the captain. Laly could barely contain the emotions that roiled through her at the thought of facing him after what they'd shared the night before. She remembered his kisses, the hard feel of his body. She nearly groaned out loud at the memories. Part of her wanted to stay hidden in his cabin forever, and part of her couldn't wait to see him again.

"Okay, I'm ready," Sugar announced. "Let's go."

As Laly led the way up the stairs to the deck, they could hear more of the conversations being yelled between the men.

"They've spotted a ship," Laly said as she reached the top step, pausing to survey the scene on deck.

"Is it the same one they were fighting yesterday?" worried Sugar.

"I don't think so." She scanned the crew quickly, recognizing some of the men from the day before. It took her only seconds to find the tall, muscular form of the captain. He stood on the raised bow of the ship. "There he is," she hissed to Sugar, pointing in his direction. Her color rose as she saw him glance at her just before he raised his arm and gave a signal.

The explosions that followed sent Laly and Sugar jumping for cover in the stairwell.

"Damn it, do they do this every day?" Laly complained.

Sugar shrugged as she crouched next to Laly, her hands over her ears.

Bradley had seen Laly as soon as she'd emerged from below deck, or rather, he'd felt her. His eyes merely followed where his senses told him she was. A surge of acute awareness shot through him at her presence, and a second later, after he'd given the order to fire the cannon, he was relieved to see she'd had the common sense to get back below deck to safety. Besides being concerned for her safety, he was glad she was out of his sight and could not distract him from his duty—a thing she would surely do if she remained where he could see her.

During the next half hour, smoke and the acrid smell of gunpowder and sulfur filled the air. Men shouted and bellowed at one another, and the very timbers of the ship shook from the violent explosions of the cannon. Laly and Sugar huddled in the stairwell, wishing the battle would end. Then, without warning, all was quiet.

Laly raised her head and peeked out across the deck.

"What is it?" asked Sugar. "What's happening?"

"I don't know. Most of the men are lined up along the side of the ship." Laly stood slowly, letting her eyes scan the crew for the captain. "I'm going out there."

Sugar grabbed Laly's arm. "You can't be serious. You don't know what might happen to you out there."

"I doubt anything will happen. They've stopped firing. The battle must be over." She pulled away from Sugar's protective grip and stepped up onto the deck.

Sugar sighed with resignation. She knew there was no stopping Laly, so she took the last step onto the deck and waited, keeping an eye out, should Laly need her assistance.

Laly walked slowly and quietly along the line of crewmen at the ship's side. No one noticed her as their attention was toward a small ship they were pulling along side. She looked for the captain and quickly found him at the bow, giving orders to the crewmen working the ship's rigging.

Bradley saw Laly making her way toward him and scowled, his dark brows forming a black wing over his eyes. Had she lost her senses? Did she want to catch a stray shot? They were about to board an enemy ship, for God's sake. "What are you doing here? I thought you had sense enough to stay below," he barked, when she was close enough to hear.

Laly started at the tone in the captain's voice. The sensual man of the night before was gone completely. Pulling herself up straight, she met his glower with one of her own. "I came to see what's going on."

"I thought it was most clear. We have encountered a pirate vessel. I would have you go below at once," he ordered.

Laly's temper flared. "And I would have you mind your own business," she challenged loudly. She could hear several of the crewmen close by murmur disapproving remarks, and she was certain Sugar moaned behind her, but, damn it, she wasn't going to let the captain talk to her as though she was an idiot. "I will satisfy my curiosity, then I'll go below."

Bradley couldn't believe the woman's gall. She'd been warm and sweet last night in the moonlight. She'd responded with a passion like none he'd ever known, yet today she defied him in front of his crew, and at a most inopportune moment. "Wainwright!" he called across the deck. "Wainwright, get this woman off my deck!"

"Aye, Sir."

Laly heard Wainwright behind her. She also heard the crew's whispered approval of the captain's decision. "I will not be treated like chattel," she threatened.

Bradley quickly looked to the French vessel they were nearing with every passing second. In moments they would be boarding her. He didn't have time to argue with this woman. "Put her below," he stated bluntly, ignoring her expression of anger and horror as Wainwright grabbed her from behind and began hauling her back toward the stairwell.

Laly began to struggle, only to be released as a shot rang out and all hell broke loose around her.

"To the ropes, men! Quickly! The bloody bastards have decided not to give up so easily!" Bradley shouted, as the French began to defend their ship.

Laly watched in horror as several men fell writhing to the deck, holes ripped through their bodies.

"Laly!" screamed Sugar. "Laly, get down!" She yelled again as she fell to her knees on the stairs.

Laly turned to see her friend crouching in the relative safety of the stairwell and ran to join her. Dodging musket blasts and fallen men bleeding at her feet, Laly leaped and jumped to get off the deck. "Oh, my Lord, I can't believe this. I thought the fighting was over when the cannon fire stopped."

"I told you not to go out there. And the captain told you to get below, but would you listen to either one of us? No, you just have to go off . . . oh, God, you're hurt," Sugar exclaimed.

"What?" Laly didn't know what she was talking about.

"You're arm." Sugar reached forward and touched Laly's upper right arm. "Does it hurt? Let me see."

Laly flinched as Sugar touched a wound she hadn't even known she'd received. Paling visibly, she let Sugar pull the captain's huge shirt from her shoulder. She sighed a breath of relief when she saw the wound wasn't much more than a deep scratch.

"Thank God you're okay," Sugar shouted above the din of battle. "You could have gotten killed."

The next several minutes passed quickly but felt like an eternity. Laly and Sugar watched the crew of the *Vengeance* and their captain swing from ropes to board the pirate vessel. The sound of clashing swords, musket and pistol shots, and screams of agony from the other ship gave proof of the torture and murder happening only yards away. In moments, it ended as abruptly at it had begun.

"Do you think it's over?" whispered Sugar.

Laly just shrugged. This latest display of barbarism had caused her to realize how precarious their position was at this time. The captain ordering Wainwright to put her below deck was nothing in this violent male-dominated society. He could just as easily have told him to throw her to the sharks, or hang her from the yard arm, and while it was unlikely he would do so, especially after their encounter last night, the fact was, he could do with her and Sugar as he chose, and no one would argue their point, or even think any less of him for his actions. She shuddered slightly with this realization and felt some anger with herself for not seeing it sooner.

"Are you all right?" asked Sugar, a frisson of concern passing through her at Laly's expression.

"Yes. I was just thinking," she waved a hand, indicating their surroundings, "about all this, and what it means to us."

"Oh?"

"Remember last night, when I joked about sleeping with the captain to get the medallion?"

"Yes," Sugar answered suspiciously.

"I would."

"Laly, you would not."

"Sugar, it just hit me how much danger we're really in," Laly insisted. "I'll do anything to get that medallion."

"You're not the kind of person who could have sex with a man without feeling something for him," Sugar argued. "You wouldn't prostitute yourself for . . ."

"I'll do anything to get us out of here and back to our own time," Laly cut her off.

Sugar could see the determination in Laly's eyes and shuddered with worry. She, too, knew the danger they were in, had probably realized it long before Laly, given her bent for adventure, but she wasn't ready to say she'd do "anything" to get back to the twentieth century. "Anything" encompassed too much, and Laly sleeping with the captain was the least of her worries.

The thud of the two ships colliding softly caught their attention. Raising slightly, they peered out of the stairwell to see what horror awaited them next. Ropes flew from both ships to secure their hold together, and men began climbing from the pirate ship back onto the *Vengeance*. Laly held her breath until she recognized several faces, assuring her that it was the crew of the *Vengeance* that had come out victorious in the battle. Although she wasn't sure why it would make much difference.

"Now what?" Sugar asked quietly.

Laly raised her shoulders in answer. She noticed several of the wounded had been propped up against the side of the ship, and that the feeble Dr. Wells was doing little to ease their pain or mend their wounds. "I suppose we could help him." She pointed at the doctor. "Our twentieth century basic first aid knowledge is probably more extensive than his medical training."

Nodding, Sugar agreed. "I'm game." She followed Laly out onto the deck and knelt beside a man who'd been shot through the shoulder. "It's not bleeding too badly. Must have missed the arteries. What are we going to use to pack and immobilize the wound?" she asked.

Laly looked around her. Nothing on deck was remotely sterile. "Here, we'll use this." She pulled the edge of her shirt up and found the seam. Ripping the gauzy fabric was easy, once she got it started.

While they moved from man to man, doing what they could for each, they were met with wary acceptance. It seemed their help was appreciated but feared somewhat, and after Dr. Wells's initial disgruntled looks, he ignored them, afraid to incur their wrath, the Neptune thing not completely forgotten.

"Did you see the captain come back aboard?" Laly asked Sugar, as she tied off a bandage over a head wound.

Sugar was examining a broken finger and didn't look up. "No. I think he's still on the other ship."

Laly glanced over the side of the *Vengeance* to the smaller vessel floating at their side. "I wish I knew where he'd moved his things. Now would be the perfect time to go look for the ou-yay ow-knay at-whay."

Sugar looked at her perplexed for a split second, then nodded.

"Maybe I should go oop-snay around-ay?"

"O-nay!" Sugar snapped at her. "Let's wait until we know where the ou-yay ow-knay at-whay is, okay?"

Laly looked down at the confused and frightened face of the man they were aiding and grinned.

"Okay." She couldn't help but keep looking for the captain, though. Somehow, she had to make him tell her where he'd hidden the medallion.

"There's Wainwright," Sugar directed.

Laly turned and saw the young man climbing aboard the *Vengeance*. She stood and blocked his way as he started to pass them. "Sir? May I speak with you a moment?"

"Captain Bradley has sent me for the doctrine of allegiance. I must get back to him quickly."

"The doctrine of allegiance?"

"Yes, ma'am. So the Frenchies can swear allegiance to the King of England."

"They want to do that?" Laly inquired, surprised.

"Of course not, ma'am. But the captain told them it's the only way they'll keep their lives."

Laly's stomach did a sickening flip. "I see. When will the captain be available to speak to me?"

"Not for some time, I'd say. He'll be bringing the prisoners aboard the *Vengeance* soon. And there's the matter of the pirate's stolen cargo, and all."

Laly let her gaze fall to the deck. "I see. Thank you." She sank once more to kneel beside Sugar. "Did you hear that?"

Sugar nodded.

"He's going to kill anyone who doesn't swear allegiance to England." She sighed, wondering how she could have been attracted to such a coldhearted killer. He just hadn't seemed so bloodthirsty. And he certainly had been anything but coldblooded when he'd held her in his arms in the moonlight. Maybe the passage through time had muddled her senses.

* * *

Bradley waited while the French officers signed the doctrine of allegiance. He was pleased with the success they'd had in taking the French brigan. It was a small ship, but the hold was full of booty, everything from fine woods to native art, silver goblets to silk and satin gowns, the latter he'd mentally put upon Laly's voluptuous figure.

"There, Monsieur. You have our allegiance and our cargo. You will let us go now, no?" the French captain, Pinot, inquired.

"No." Bradley spoke the word with finality. He'd been standing in a relaxed pose in front of the table, watching the Frenchmen signing their names with a flourish. He now straightened to his full height and looked down on the much smaller men. "You will be taken back to New Providence to stand trial for your crimes."

"But Monsieur, you said . . ." Pinot sputtered. "What of my ship?"

"Your ship will be burned." Bradley stated flatly.

"No! Monsieur . . . please . . ."

"Not to burn the ship," an officer pleaded.

Bradley swept the doctrine from the table and turned from Pinot and his officers, ignoring their continuing protests. "Wainwright, see to the burning after I take these men to the *Vengeance*."

"Aye, Captain."

"Monsieur, you can not mean to destroy my ship! She is a fine vessel, a proud ship. You cannot . . ."

Bradley turned abruptly to face Pinot. He spoke softly through clenched teeth. "This ship was used in crimes against the English Crown. It will be destroyed." The threat in his voice quieted the French protests. "Now, come with me." He turned

and led the way from the cabin to the top deck.
Moments later they were boarding the *Vengeance*.

Pinot seethed as he followed Bradley. His ship was
everything to him, and this English scum had no
right to destroy it. He knew he would take the first
opportunity to kill this man. Besides, it would be
better to die quickly at the hands of his crew than to
wait for the hangman's noose in Charles Towne.

"Look at this, Sugar." Laly held up a pistol she'd
found on the deck behind the last of the wounded
men.

"Put that down. It might go off," hissed Sugar.

"It does look like it's ready to shoot. Look, it's
primed and cocked."

"I don't want to look. Put it down," Sugar insisted.

Laly continued to admire the pistol which would
be a rare treasure in her time. "This weapon looks
just like the one in the museum in Nassau, remember?
Though three hundred years newer," she grinned.

"Laly, please." Sugar sat leaning against a cannon
mount. She and Laly had finished with the wounded
and she was tired, and she realized, hungry. "Do you
know we never had breakfast?"

Laly kept looking at the gun in her hand. "This
could come in handy. I just wish I knew how to load
it properly."

"Do you think anyone on this ship is going to stand
still and let you shoot them?"

"Of course not. But we don't know what we'll
encounter in Charles Towne after the captain dumps
us there. We may need some kind of weapon to
defend ourselves." She turned the pistol over in her
hand. "I doubt if one shot would do us much good
in a really serious situation, though, and after the

load is discharged, this weapon will be useless. Boy, what I wouldn't give for a .38 special.''

"You wouldn't know how to use that gun, either,'' Sugar goaded.

"No, but I think I could figure it out a lot easier than I can this thing.'' She held up the pistol as she spoke.

"Maybe, but we'll never know because you're going to put that gun down before you hurt yourself with it,'' Sugar said pointedly.

Bradley surveyed the deck as he led his prisoners on board. Lawson and several other crewmen brought up the rear, guarding the prisoners, their pistols at the ready. "Take these men to the brig, then meet me in the chart room.''

"Aye, Sir,'' Lawson agreed.

Pinot watched the movements of the English crew as he boarded behind the hated captain. All eyes were on him and his compatriots. If he made a move now and pulled the poignard from his boot, he'd never have a chance. He prayed something would happen to divert their attention before he was put into the brig. Once there his luck would be spent.

Bradley could not help letting his eyes search out Laly. She sat not far from the stairwell, her back toward him, conversing with her friend. Turning slightly, he glanced back toward Pinot and his officers for a moment, then once again focused on the moon-gold hair that fell warmly to Laly's hips. As she spoke to Sugar it became apparent she held something in her hand. A bare moment later he realized it was a pistol. "Laly!'' he shouted, taking a step toward her.

Laly jumped at the sound of the captain's voice.

Turning quickly, she hid the pistol behind her as she stood.

"I told you to get rid of that thing," admonished Sugar behind her.

Bradley took another step toward Laly. She held the weapon behind her, half hidden. "Laly, I suggest you rid yourself of the pistol," he said with grim authority.

Pinot thanked God the moment his prayers were answered. He knew he would die, but he would take the bastard captain with him.

Laly watched in horror as the prisoner just behind the captain reached to his boot, and with a slyness born of desperation, pulled out a deadly stiletto, aiming it at Bradley's back.

Bradley saw the expression of fear on Laly's face and couldn't fathom why she'd be so terrified of him. He'd given her no reason to fear him. "Laly, put down the weapon and come here."

"Laly?" Sugar asked incredulously, certain her friend had lost her mind.

Laly watched the prisoner raise his arm. She saw that the crew's attention was on her instead of on the dangerous man. Without thinking, she began to raise the pistol.

Bradley couldn't believe she meant to shoot him, yet her aim was deadly. He stood stock-still as she leveled the gun on him, waiting for her to fire, not believing she could.

"Noooo!" Laly screamed, as her finger squeezed the trigger. The resounding explosion sent a violent kick up her arm and blew burning smoke into her face and eyes, choking her enough to send her into a coughing fit.

Bradley jumped back in surprise as the pistol went off. She'd actually fired!

At the explosion, everyone leaped into action at once as though time had stopped for the brief second before she'd fired, and then began again afterward. Two crewmen jumped to grab her by the arms. Several others trained their muskets on her. One man even drew his sword in her direction.

"No, Laly!" shouted Sugar, and jumped into the fray with both fists, only to be held fast by several crewmen.

It took Bradley only a second to realize she'd missed him. "Release her!" he ordered. "I will see to her myself."

Laly shook her head, gasping, trying to see through burning eyes if she'd stopped the man from assaulting the captain. "Let go of me, you fools! Did I hit him?" she asked. "Is the captain all right?" Wiping at the tears filling her eyes, she called out loudly, "Captain! Oh Lord, Captain, are you all right?"

Bradley took a step forward, his blood burning with rage.

"Captain, wait!" shouted Lawson above the angry voices of the crew and the cries of protest from the French prisoners. "Wait, Sir!"

Bradley heard Lawson, but didn't stop.

Laly managed to blink away some of the smoke and looked up to see Bradley advancing with murder in his dark eyes. Had he gone daft? Why was he angry with her?

"Sir, she's killed the Frenchman!" shouted Lawson. "Look here, Captain!"

Bradley reached Laly and looked down into her turquoise eyes, eyes that angered him further because of their power over him. "I should let the men have you," he threatened so only she could hear. Grasping her arm violently, he jerked her against him, enjoying the look of shock that crossed her face.

Laly flinched as Bradley gripped her arm where she'd been wounded, but the fierce expression in his eyes made her wonder at his sanity.

"Let her go, you bastard!" shouted Sugar, struggling to free herself from the strong hands of two crewmen. She tried to kick at them, but only caused them to tighten their hold on her, nearly cutting off the circulation to her hands. "Damn you!" she hissed.

"Captain! She's killed the Frenchman!" Lawson tried again, pushing his way through the crowd. "Look, Sir!"

Bradley heard Lawson's words, and it was unfortunate Laly's shot had taken the life of the prisoner, but the fact that she'd fired at him made her poor aim inconsequential. He tightened he grasp on her arm and noticed the way she clenched her teeth. He was glad his grip gave her pain. He was suffering his own pain standing so near to her. Anger increased in his soul. He had to fight the spell she'd cast over him. Even now, after she'd nearly murdered him in front of his whole crew, he wanted to pull her to the deck and bury himself in her.

"Sir." Lawson finally reached his Captain. Touching Bradley on the shoulder, he tried to get his attention. "Look here, Sir. She saved you. The bloody Frenchman had a knife, and an ugly bugger it is, Sir. See? He meant to stick you through." He tugged Bradley's shoulder. "Sir?"

Bradley wasn't sure he heard right, his blood pounded so loudly in his ears. "What? What's that?"

"She wasn't trying to kill you, Sir. She saved you."

Bradley turned slightly and looked hard at Lawson.

The man held a long, narrow knife in his hand, a knife that still carried the dried blood of its last victim. "She what?"

"She saved you, Sir."

Bradley loosened his grip on Laly's arm as he looked at her once more. Then he noticed the blood on her arm beneath his fingers.

Laly jerked her arm free of Bradley's loose hold. She cradled her arm against her and looked briefly, accusingly up into his dark eyes.

Murmurs from the crew grew to a loud buzz as they parted behind Bradley, giving a clear view of Pinot's body. Letting herself scan the deck beyond the captain, Laly saw for the first time what she'd done. Sprawled over a low step was the dead body of the French captain. A crimson smear covered his chest and a hole the size of a small fist was centered over his heart. Laly felt the world begin to spin as waves of nausea washed over her. "Captain . . . I need . . ." she gulped. "I'm going to . . ."

Bradley saw Laly's knees begin to buckle and grabbed her before she fell. Helping her to the side, he experienced tremendous guilt as she heaved, her small body wracked with the shuddering spasms of her retching.

Sugar jerked free of the crewmen, and racing to Laly's side, pulled her hair from her face. She held it to the side for her while she was ill.

Laly vomited again and again. Each time she envisioned the horrible sight of the Frenchman's body she would feel her stomach revolt violently. After what felt like eons, she had nothing left to heave, but still she gagged. Tears streamed down her face as she sobbed in horror. "Sugar," she wept, "I've murdered a man." She felt the desire to vomit welling up inside her again, but the spasms seemed to be subsiding somewhat, as she only leaned weakly over the side, shivering with emotion.

Sugar looked into the captain's eyes over Laly's back. She accused him silently, angry he'd misunderstood.

Bradley dropped his gaze to Laly's trembling form. She'd actually killed a man to protect him. If not for her intervention, he might be lying dead on the deck now instead of Pinot. He brushed a stray tendril of moonlit hair from her cheek with his fingertips and felt the softness of her skin against his hand. He owed her his life, this bewitching woman from the sea.

Seven

Laly lay on the captain's bed, a cool cloth over her eyes.

"Thank you." Bradley spoke softly, watching the slow rise and fall of her breasts as she breathed shallowly, finally free of the violent illness brought on by her murder of the Frenchman. "Do you hear me?" he whispered.

Laly felt more than heard the deep resonance of the captain's voice so close to her. He sat next to her on the narrow bed, had ministered over her for nearly an hour, replacing the cool cloth with a fresh one when it warmed, and had been trying to talk to her for the past several minutes. "I hear you, Captain. I'm just having a difficult time accepting the fact that I'm a murderer." Her chin quivered slightly at the memory.

"But you did it to save my life." Bradley could still scarcely believe she'd killed for him. "You were justified in your actions."

Laly pulled the cloth from her eyes and stared hard into his dark gaze. "I shot a man in cold blood, Captain."

"You shot a man who was about to kill me. That's hardly cold blood."

Laly shook her head. "I've been trying to understand my actions. I know I'd kill to protect my mother. And I know I'd kill to protect Sugar. But they are people I love." She paused there for a moment. "I barely know you, Captain Bradley," she murmured. And yet he was the man she'd responded to so freely the night before, she remembered. Why did he have such a strong power over her? "No matter how I choose to look at it, I'm responsible for taking a man's life."

"And saving another's—mine," he urged quietly.

Laly lowered her eyes. He was right, of course, but she couldn't help feeling ill whenever she remembered the way the Frenchman's body lay lifeless on the deck, blood congealing in the open wound over his heart. "Yes," she whispered, her voice shaking slightly.

Bradley took her hand in his. He turned it over and lowered his head to kiss her palm gently.

Laly's breath caught in her throat when his lips touched her skin. He kissed her softly, cupping her hand over his mouth, cradling it in the strength of his long fingers. Shivers skittered over her nerve endings, sending electrifying messages through her body. "Captain?"

"Mmmm?" He continued to nibble on her palm, tasting her flesh with the tip of his tongue.

"Why?" Her question encompassed so much and she hoped he understood.

Bradley heard the uncertainty in her voice and

looked up into her turquoise eyes. Rising, he sighed. "I don't know, Laly. I know I've wanted you since I met you. Last night on deck, when you gave of yourself so willingly to me, it felt right. Then, today, though you say you barely know me, you killed to save me. And now, just touching your hand makes me want to lock the door against Sugar's return and make you mine the only way I know how. I don't know, Laly. I only know these things are true."

Laly listened while he spoke and watched the strong emotions that accompanied his words mirrored in his dark eyes. She couldn't deny the feelings she had for him. She couldn't fight the attraction that drew her to him, nor could she doubt she'd kill again to protect him. Yet she was leaving as soon as possible. And once back in her own time, he'd be little more than a ghost from three hundred years in the past. Tears began to sting her eyes and she blinked to stop their flow.

"What is it, Laly?" Bradley asked. "The Frenchman?"

She shook her head. "No, it's you."

"Me?"

Tears slipped from the corners of her eyes. "Yes, you." She wiped at the wet trails on her cheeks.

"What about me? I'm sorry if my words upset you."

Laly shook her head again, this time from the futility of her situation. "Your words don't upset me. It's this," she swung her arm to indicate their surroundings, "all this."

Bradley lowered his brows in confusion. "The ship?"

"Yes . . . and no. Oh, Captain, I don't know how to explain it! I *can't* explain it. Even if I tried, you'd think I'd lost my mind."

Bradley eyed her agitated state. She was probably

still overwrought from the incident with the Frenchman. "You don't have to explain, Laly. I think I understand," he said softly.

Laly almost laughed out loud at his remark. "Ha. If you only knew the truth!" She lowered her face to her hands and said again, "If you only knew the truth."

Bradley closed his eyes slightly in speculation. If he only knew the truth? What truth was she referring to? Was she about to reveal the truth about where she and her friend had really come from? His heart beat rapidly in his chest as he waited, and he found himself hoping she wouldn't confess to an alliance with Rodriguez. He was surprised to realize he wanted her to keep up the mermaid story. "What truth, Laly?" he urged quietly.

Laly raised her eyes to his. The dark touch of his gaze warmed her to her soul and made her feel she could trust him, but there was no way he'd believe she and Sugar had floated up from the future.

"The truth, Laly. I want to hear the truth."

Laly swallowed, then tugged her lower lip between her teeth. She couldn't possibly be thinking about telling him the truth! But what could it hurt? "Sugar and I came from . . . another place," she said hesitantly.

"Another place?"

Laly looked around her as though searching for the correct words to use. "Well, not exactly a different place. It's actually the same place." She paused again, knowing how crazy she was going to sound.

Bradley could feel her nervousness, could sense her uncertainty. "Yes?"

"It's the same place, just a different time," she said hurriedly.

Bradley waited for more. What she'd said made no sense at all.

Laly could see the patience on Bradley's face. He was ready to hear more. And it was obvious he had no clue what she was even talking about. "It's the same place, Captain. It's just a different time. We're from a different time. Not this time. Do you understand? We came here from the future—over three hundred years in the future."

Bradley heard her words and did understand. She now expected him to believe she was of a different time. "The mermaid story was better," he said bluntly.

"But Captain, I'm telling the truth. And if you'll think about it, Sugar and I never said we were mermaids. You and your crew surmised it because you found us in the water."

"Sugar called on her father, Neptune, if I recall correctly," he said sardonically.

"That was to convince me, not you," she explained.

Bradley straightened. He was disappointed she'd decided to come up with a ridiculous tale instead of telling him the truth. "She had to convince you you were a mermaid?" he continued the sarcasm.

"No, of course not. She was trying to convince me we'd traveled back to a time when men really believed in mermaids. You see, she figured out what had happened to us before I did."

"You didn't know you'd traveled back in time," he stated flatly.

"No, Captain. It had to be the storm, the one we told you about, that brought us here. I've never seen anything like it before. We were caught by a light in the middle of the storm, and when it released us we were here."

"The storm again." He sighed wearily.

"Yes, the storm. And the medallion," she added.

One dark brow shot up. So she was getting around to the medallion. "The medallion brought you here from the future," he stated.

"Yes."

"Where did you get it?"

"The ocean floor. I was about forty feet under when I found a shipwreck. Under what looked like a mainmast, I found the medallion. It was then that the storm hit."

Bradley stood and paced away from her. Her insistence that she'd found the medallion was the same, but now she'd added this time-travel tale to her story. Still, everything she said led back to the medallion. His disappointment grew to a large weight in his chest. He turned to face her. "So you think the medallion had something to do with you being here?"

Laly looked at him in surprise. Was there a chance he believed her? "Yes. I think the combination of the storm and the medallion did bring us here. What other explanation could there be?"

Bradley walked to the side of the bed and leaned over from the waist, resting his fists next to her on the mattress. "I think you'd say or do anything, including make up this wild story, to get the medallion back. I think it was your payment for some service you rendered Rodriguez. And I think you're upset you've lost your treasure."

Laly's heart sank. For just a moment she'd thought he almost believed her. Laying back against the pillows, she sighed, putting the cool cloth over her eyes once more. "I guess it was too much to hope for," she breathed.

"Yes." Bradley stated abruptly. "It was too much

to hope for. I am not a fool, Laly. I am a reasonably intelligent man, and I like to think I'm capable of deducing the difference between the truth and a pre-fabrication when I hear it. Now, if you'd admitted you were working for Rodriguez, had even said you regretted the decision, I might be willing to help you in some way, but to keep going on with these ridiculous stories . . .'' He rubbed his hand over his eyes. "We'll be in Charles Towne by morning. You'll be put ashore there.''

Laly sat bolt upright, jerking the cloth from her eyes. "In the morning?''

"Yes.'' Bradley looked at her beautiful face and felt a tug at his heart. Why couldn't he have met her under different circumstances?

"What about the medallion, Captain? I need to know where it is,'' she said urgently.

"The medallion will be sent to the governor.''

"But . . .''

Bradley raised his hand to cut her off. "Laly, please don't make this worse. I'm already going against my better judgment by letting you go once we dock. I should, by rights, send you to the governor as well. There is the question of how you came by the medal-lion in the first place. It is, after all, stolen merchan-dise.''

"I told you I found it,'' Laly argued.

"And I am choosing to believe you.''

"Which means you don't.'' She slouched a bit. "I suppose I can't blame you.''

A soft knock on the door preceded Sugar's entrance. She carried a tray with a bowl of broth and a chunk of bread. "Laly, are you feeling better? I had a time getting the cook to warm this for you. You'd think it was every day a woman saved his captain's life." Sugar stopped when she saw the look on Laly's face.

"I'm fine, Sugar. The captain was just leaving," she said pointedly.

Bradley surveyed the two women. They were, indeed, nothing like any women he'd ever known, but they were flesh and blood—in Laly's case, very warm blood, his memory of her kisses heating his loins. They were not mermaids, and they were not from the future, the idea was preposterous; but Laly's refusal to confide in him made him all the more curious about them. His earlier decision to follow them after they left the ship was reinforced in his mind. "If you ladies will excuse me." He made a slight bow and turned toward the door. Just before he slipped through the portal he glanced back at Laly. "If you're feeling up to it later, I'll return to escort you to dinner."

Laly just nodded and watched him leave.

"What was that all about?" Sugar asked as soon as the door closed behind his broad back.

"I told him."

"You told him what?" Sugar placed the tray on the foot of the bed.

"I told him the truth, that we're from the future."

"You what? What did he say?"

"He didn't believe me, of course. I don't even know why I told him. I just thought . . . for a moment . . ."

"What?"

"I don't know. I think I must still be a little shocky over the Frenchman."

Sugar nodded and sank down to sit beside Laly. "You should try to eat this." She indicated the food.

"Mmmm. I guess so." She reached for the bread and broke it in half, handing a portion of it to Sugar. "We're docking in Charles Towne in the morning."

Sugar's eyes opened wide with apprehension.

"We're being put ashore, and the medallion is to be sent to the governor." She took a bite of the bread, then dipped an edge of it in the broth. "Tonight is our only chance to get it before it's too late."

"What are you planning?" Sugar inquired.

"I'm not sure. But I won't let any opportunity pass, and I may need your help."

Bradley paced the small space he now shared with Wainwright. He flexed his muscular shoulders and arched his back in frustration.

"She actually said she and Miss Sugar were from the future, Sir?" Wainwright asked disbelieving. "What year?"

"I didn't ask her. It was just another ploy to get the medallion," Bradley answered shortly.

"I'm sorry, Sir. I suppose you're right."

Bradley dropped to the end of the bed only to stand immediately back up and begin his pacing all over again. "Tonight's the night," he announced.

"Sir?"

"I told her we're docking in Charles Towne by morning, so she'll make her move tonight."

"What do you think she'll do?"

"Whatever it takes to get the medallion. I may need your help in distracting Sugar."

"Yes, Sir. What are you going to do?"

"I'll start by sending the ladies gowns so that they might dress for dinner."

"Sir?"

Bradley smiled at his first officer. "You'll see. You may enjoy this game of espionage, Wainwright."

Laly sat on the bed looking out the porthole at the night sky. The day had passed slowly, each hour crawling by with the dispassionate resemblance to the hour before. Finally, sunset exploded across the sky with brilliant lines of orange and purple, and then the darkness of night claimed the heavens. With the night came their chance to find the medallion.

Sugar stood up as a knock sounded lightly against the door. "The captain already?" she asked Laly.

Laly shrugged. "I think it's too early, unless he needs something from his armoire or desk."

Sugar opened the door, and both women were astounded to see Wainwright standing in the companionway with his arms full of satin and lace. "Wainwright?" Sugar inquired. "Laly, look at this."

Laly stepped from the bed. "I'm looking. What is this?"

"A gift from the captain, ladies. He thought you might like to dress for dinner." With that he maneuvered his way through the door with his enormous load and dumped the lot on the bed. He then hurriedly bowed and made his exit.

Laly and Sugar stood staring at the heap of shiny fabrics before them. "What's he up to?" Laly wondered out loud.

Sugar fingered a rose colored satin and shrugged. "I don't know, but it might be fun to try these on."

"I don't trust his motives."

"He may have no motive other than wanting to see you in something feminine before we leave tomorrow," Sugar offered.

"I doubt it. I'm sure there's more to it than that, but these costumes just might give us an advantage he wasn't planning on." she eyed the pile. "I wonder which one's for me."

Sugar pulled a brilliant turquoise satin from beneath the rose. "Do you really have to ask?"

A warm little frisson passed up her arm as Laly touched the dress. The turquoise was the exact shade of her eyes. She grinned. "I guess you're right."

In minutes they'd stripped down and had donned chemises and pantaloons and were tugging corsets tightly around them. "Oh, God, I can't believe women really wore these things all the time," groaned Laly. "Do you think I could get into the dress without it?"

"Did you see the size of the waist in that dress?" Sugar raised her eyebrows. "Besides, it's not the waistline in that dress that concerns me. It's the bodice. With a neckline that low, and with the size of your breasts, you'll be lucky if you don't fall out with your first breath."

"Maybe that's what he's got in mind, keeping me so busy trying to maintain my virtue that I won't have time to look for the medallion."

"Humph. I doubt that's what he had in mind when he picked that particular dress for you."

Half an hour later Laly smiled at her friend. They'd managed to don the dresses and fasten each other tightly. "Now what?" Sugar asked.

"We've got to do something with our hair. Yours will be no problem, with all that natural curl I hate you for, but I don't know what to do with mine."

"Let me try something," Sugar offered.

Laly lowered to sit on the edge of the bed and let Sugar attempt to put a style in her straight hair. Several minutes and a few curses later, Sugar groaned. "I can't make it do anything I want it to."

"It's okay. You tried," Laly consoled. "I'll just leave it down."

"Let's at least put a ribbon in it," suggested Sugar.

"From where?" There were no ribbons with their gowns.

Sugar pulled up her skirt and began to tear a strip of lace from her slip. "Right here."

"Aren't you becoming ingenious?" Laly laughed.

A few minutes later they were ready. Laly's long hair was pulled slightly away from her face with the lace ribbon, and Sugar's dark curls swirled around her head beautifully, held in place with another piece of slip.

A tap at the door caused them both to jump, instantly self conscious in their costumes. "I guess we're ready," Laly whispered to Sugar. "Let him in."

Sugar, standing next to the door, grasped the knob, and turned it, swinging it in as she took a deep breath.

Bradley stood just outside the door, and as his eyes met Laly's, she nearly stopped breathing herself. Never before had she felt so vulnerable, so feminine. The long sweeping gaze he allowed himself touched her everywhere, from the tips of her toes peeking from beneath the long skirt in the kid slippers he'd provided, to the swell of her breasts where they threatened to spill from the low décolleté of her gown. She swallowed under his perusal and felt her heart begin a rapid beat against her ribs.

Bradley could scarce believe his eyes at the transformation in Laly. He'd never before seen a woman so beautiful. His pulse quickened in his veins, surging through him to heat and raise his manhood beneath his breeches. He had to fight the urge to walk forward and crush her in his arms. "You look . . . lovely. Both of you." He tore his eyes from Laly and included Sugar in his compliment.

Sugar smiled a knowing smile and bowed her thanks. "And you're looking quite dashing yourself, Captain."

Laly agreed silently. Bradley wore his usual tight trousers and thigh-high boots, but over his white shirt he wore a crisp uniform coat, double-breasted, with gold buttons glistening across his broad chest. His hair was still damp from a recent shampooing and was tied back with a black string.

"Ladies, shall we?" He turned and extended his arms to them.

Laly took the captain's arm and felt the muscles rippling under his coat. Closing her eyes briefly, she told herself she wouldn't allow her attraction to this man keep her from her objective.

As they walked along the companionway toward the dining room, Bradley couldn't help but stare at Laly. His eyes strayed from her moonlit hair to her beautiful face to the alluring mounds of her breasts displayed so attractively in the gown he'd provided. Once he'd seen the color of the dress, there had been no other choice for her, but he couldn't have imagined she would look so bewitching in it.

"Here we are, ladies." He stopped in front of the dining room door and swung it open for them. He then stood back to allow them to precede him into the room.

Laly looked quickly around her as she entered the familiar room where she'd eaten the night before. The difference this evening was that the table was set for only four, with candles illuminating the white tablecloth, their flickering reflection dancing over the silver utensils and warming the smoky glass wine goblets. "Captain, everything looks beautiful. What's the occasion?" She turned to face Bradley where he stood just inside the door.

"My lovely guests are leaving in the morning," he bowed slightly, "so this is a farewell dinner."

Laly let her gaze dart to meet Sugar's briefly before returning to meet Bradley's. "Then let's make the most of our last night together, shall we?" She dropped her chin ever so little and looked at him through the thick black of her lashes.

Bradley raised one thick brow at her obvious flirtation. "By all means," he agreed.

Sugar stifled a grin at Laly's actions and turned her attention to the table in fear she'd giggle out loud if she watched her friend much longer. "I see the table is set for four, Captain. Who else will be joining us?"

"My first officer. Wainwright. I hope that meets with your approval. He's quite taken with you ladies."

Laly smiled, pleased. If Wainwright were kept occupied she'd have a better chance of searching his room for the medallion. But how to rid herself of the captain long enough to do so? "Who runs the ship when you and Officer Wainwright are occupied?" she asked innocently.

Bradley turned his attention toward Laly. "My crew is very adept at handling the ship without constant supervision. And if there's ever a problem, I can be summoned in seconds."

"But don't you ever get curious? I think that if I were in command of such a ship I'd have to check to make sure things were running smoothly at least once a night, perhaps even several times," she added.

Bradley smiled down at her. "Years of practice

make a crew nearly perfect, but if you're concerned about the running of the *Vengeance*, you might like to accompany me later for a stroll around the deck. I'm sure you'll see for yourself how smoothly things run when I am otherwise occupied."

Laly smiled back at the captain but grimaced inwardly. Damn, she fumed. She'd been hoping to initiate a trip topside for the captain, not for herself as well. "I'd like that, Captain," she lied.

"Then we'll plan on it," Bradley assured her, nodding. "Ah, Wainwright, come in," he called toward the door as a light knock was heard.

Wainwright entered the room and stopped. He couldn't believe how beautiful the women were in their satins. "Sir, I . . . ladies, you're lovely," he stammered.

Sugar extended her hand. "Why thank you, Sir."

Laly watched Wainwright bend over to kiss her friend's hand and winked conspiratorially at her as he did. "How gentlemanly," she said pointedly.

"Have I been remiss in my manners?" Bradley apologized. "Please forgive me. I was so dazzled by your beauty in the gown I chose for you that I forgot the niceties." Bending low, he took Laly's hand and let his lips caress the back gently. He then turned it over to kiss her palm. Parting his lips, he flicked her sensitive skin with his tongue just once, sending her a distinctive message.

Laly's heartbeat raced at Bradley's touch, then doubled when the heated tip of his tongue teased her briefly. Taking a deep breath was nearly impossible in the tight corset she wore, and as she struggled for air to calm the commotion started by the captain's kiss, she had a hard time keeping her breasts from popping out of the bodice of the dress as Sugar had predicted. "About this dress, Captain."

"Yes? I chose it because the color matched your eyes so perfectly." And I knew what it would do to your figure, he added to himself.

"Yes, and it's truly lovely. But don't you think it's a bit too revealing?" She looked up into the enigmatic darkness of his eyes. "For mixed company, I mean."

"Mixed company?" Bradley asked.

"Yes, men and women."

Bradley pondered her meaning for a moment. "Women dress for men, so all clothing is for 'mixed company,' as you call it. Wouldn't you agree, Wainwright?"

Wainwright was still letting his gaze rest on Sugar's lovely features. Ever since he'd entered the room and seen her slender body encased in the shining satin, he'd wanted to pull the lace from her hair and let it fall loosely around her bare shoulders. Her figure was not a voluptuous copy of Laly's, and it suited him fine. He preferred a more delicate woman, and Sugar fit the bill perfectly. Swallowing hard, he turned to the captain. "What's that, Sir?"

"We were discussing the appropriateness of female attire."

"Sir?" He was having difficulty catching up.

"Do you approve of the ladies' dresses?"

"Oh, yes, Sir," he agreed emphatically.

"That's not exactly what were discussing," interrupted Laly. "I was concerned about the amount of bosom my dress reveals, and whether it should be considered proper."

A giggle escaped Sugar's lips at the shocked look on Wainwright's face. The captain's eyes glowed with mischief, showing he enjoyed Laly's bold conversation, but poor Wainwright wasn't used to such forthright speech from a woman. "You have to excuse her, Sir," she leaned to whisper in his ear. "She sometimes gets carried away with her topics."

Wainwright swallowed again. "It's quite all right, Miss. I'm sure where you come from her speech is very much accepted."

Sugar laughed again. "Not always."

"So what I want to know, Captain," Laly continued, "is, did you chose this dress because of the color, or because you thought it would reveal my . . . assets."

Bradley threw back his head and laughed out loud at her assessment of his decision about the dress. "Never have I met so enchanting a woman, Laly. And I will confess, because I'm so obviously caught redhanded, that I did, indeed, choose your dress because I'd hoped for a certain effect." He let his gaze drop to her exposed cleavage. "And I will add that I've not been disappointed," he said, letting his voice drop a seductive note.

Laly felt herself blush at his perusal and hoped against hope he couldn't see her nipples harden under his stare. "My, it's warm in here. May I ask for a cool drink?" she changed the subject.

"Of course." Bradley stepped back toward the table. "How remiss of me not to offer sooner. I can only say your loveliness is my distraction." Reaching for a wine bottle chilling in a silver bucket, he filled the goblets, then handed them each their drinks. "May I make the first toast?"

Laly let her eyes meet his in agreement. The others nodded.

"I toast the ladies, Sugar and Laly." He stared directly into the turquoise depths of Laly's eyes. "The most beautiful and . . . interesting women to ever grace the *Vengeance*. May this last night aboard her be memorable."

"Here, here," chimed Wainwright before he drank.

Laly sipped slowly, tasting the rich wine filling the goblet. She watched Bradley take some of the fluid into his mouth and hold it there, savoring its essence. He would be the same kind of lover, one who savored and enjoyed each touch and texture, each sound and nuance of the love act. Laly felt her chest heave with the breath she tried to take to clear her thoughts. This man filled her senses in a way that made him very dangerous. Dangerous to her emotions, and dangerous to her mission of finding the medallion and escaping back to her own time.

Eight

"So, how is the dessert?" Bradley asked softly over Laly's shoulder.

"Delicious, as was everything else," she answered, the sweet flavor of cinnamon and rum mingled with cream still on her lips. Letting the tip of her tongue clean her upper lip, she enjoyed the aftertaste of the sumptuous dessert. "Is this dish native to the islands, or something you brought with you from England, Captain?"

"I have to give credit to the cook. He experiments with the native cuisine wherever we put into port. Here, let me fill your glass again," he insisted, as he raised the rum bottle and tipped it over her glass.

Laly felt the room take a slight dip and wasn't sure it was the swell of the ocean. From the wine before dinner, they'd drunk their way through each course of a six-course meal. Now, with dessert, Bradley was pressing her to consume more rum than she'd ever had in her life. "Thank you, Captain, but I've really had enough."

"Nonsense. This is an occasion." He leaned closer to her. "We must make the most of life's opportunities."

She looked to where Sugar was smiling languidly up at a very smitten Wainwright, then back to the captain. She wanted to make the most of her opportunities, all right. And the opportunity she was waiting for was just within her grasp. If only she could ditch the captain long enough to do a thorough search of Wainwright's cabin, she was sure she'd find the medallion. "Perhaps you should fill your glass, Captain. I would like to toast you and your wonderful hospitality."

Bradley grinned inwardly. Did she think she could get him drunk? She herself was already so tipsy she'd nearly spilled her dessert twice. "Certainly, but only if you join me." He tipped the bottle over her glass once more.

Laly smiled weakly. She'd only drunk rum once before, at a friend's wedding, and she remembered it tasted wonderful. But one tropical drink with a tiny pink umbrella didn't make her an authority on the effects of the potent brew. Blinking twice, she raised her glass and tried to remember what it was she was going to say, but all she could do was stare into the dark eyes of the captain as they sparkled over her.

"Yes, Laly?" Bradley inquired.

"Yes," she cleared her throat. "I wanted to propose a toast." She paused a moment. "To you, Captain. And to your crew. And to your hospitality." There, she'd done it. Tipping her head, she sipped the rum.

Bradley drank from his glass while watching Laly. Her mouth was moist from the rum and his heart skipped a beat as her tongue darted to wipe the liquid from her lips. He could almost feel her tongue on him if he let himself imagine. Taking an exceptionally large drink, he steeled himself for whatever she had planned. This was her last chance at the medallion before she and Sugar were put ashore in the morning.

Laly glanced around the dining room. There was nothing in here that would give her an excuse to leave without the captain following. Even if she begged for privacy, the need for the chamberpot coming to mind, he'd be sure to escort her to her cabin and probably wait for her. Sighing, she glanced again at Sugar and Wainwright. There was no doubt the two would be happily sitting together until morning if not disturbed, so it was only the captain she needed to worry about.

"Laly?"

"Yes, Captain?" She swung her gaze once more to the man in question.

"You sighed heavily. Am I boring you, dear lady?"

Laly's eyes parted, surprised. "You could never bore me, Captain," she blurted before she could stop herself, the rum loosening her tongue. Blushing a deep crimson, she closed her eyes, embarrassed by her admission. "I'm sorry," she murmured.

Bradley's heart swelled in his chest and he moved to sit closer to her. "Don't apologize, Laly. I'm flattered such a beautiful, intelligent woman finds me interesting."

"Captain?"

"Please, under the circumstances I would have you call me Devon."

"Devon?"

"My given name." He spoke softly, his breath ruffling her hair.

"Devon," she repeated. "It suits you."

"My father would argue that. It means 'poet,' and since he was an English professor, my choice of going to sea was a disappointment to him," he confided.

"Sailors are poets," Laly spoke. "They ride the waves between earth and stars, belonging to neither world, only yearning for the endless beauty of the sea."

Bradley was struck by her words. She understood. She felt the pull of the waves, the night sky, the fury of the wind, the torment of the tides. It was what he'd seen in her eyes the night before as she watched the moonbeams dancing over the water. "How do you know?" he whispered almost silently.

Laly let her eyes meet his. "I just know."

"You're a woman."

"Do you think only a man can feel the passion of the sea? Why do you think I became a diver? I'm most happy when I'm under the ocean. Sometimes, when I'm diving alone, I inflate my BC and hang just above the ocean floor watching my bubbles float to the surface. I can look up and see the sky beyond the water and I wish I never had to go up again. I love the way the tide pulls me from side to side. It makes me feel alive. I leave my sliding glass doors open most nights so I can hear the waves breaking over the sand on the beach near my apartment. And during a storm I walk the shoreline, letting the wind pound me like the surf pounds the ocean floor."

"But it's not enough," Bradley added for her. He didn't understand some of what she'd said, but he could feel her conviction.

Laly was startled he understood. "No, it's not enough. If I don't live to be an old woman, I hope it's the sea that takes me. I want to die in its arms."

"Or these." He looked down to his own arms.

Laly stopped thinking for a moment and let herself look along the length of his muscled arms stretched out to her. Yes, she thought, I could die in your arms. But she wouldn't say what she was thinking. "Captain, may we take that walk now?"

"Devon," he insisted, allowing her to change the subject for now.

Laly looked to his eyes once more. "Devon, our walk?"

Devon stood and reached to take her arm. "Of course."

Laly pushed away from the table and began to stand. It was then she realized how strongly the rum had affected her. "Oh my," she murmured. Her legs felt like rubber and her head began to spin. "Captain? Devon?" she breathed.

Devon saw her dilemma and smiled. So the little mermaid couldn't hold her rum. "Let me assist you," he offered. Placing one arm around her waist and holding onto her hand, he led her slowly from the dining room.

Once they were on deck, the night air began to revive Laly. She breathed as deeply as her corset would allow of the cool breeze that wafted over the ship and billowed gracefully in the sails.

"Better?" Devon asked.

"Yes, Capt . . . Devon. Thank you." They were standing at the rail, looking out over a tranquil ocean. Moonlight shone across the water much as it had the night before, and Laly couldn't help but be entranced by the beauty. She leaned her head back and let the sea air wash over her.

Devon watched the way she enjoyed the moment, but he wondered how long it would take her to attempt to get the medallion from him. And how would she do it? A seduction, perhaps? Looking at her in the moonlight, he could think of nothing he'd like more. "You're a very beautiful woman, Laly."

Laly heard the sensual timbre of his voice and felt shivers over her skin. She'd been called beautiful before, but she'd always thought it part of a routine, or a line some guy was using to get her in the sack. "Thank you, Devon," she answered. For some reason she believed him to be sincere. Perhaps it was because she felt beautiful, truly beautiful. She smiled. It was probably the rum making her feel this way. It was as if she was caught in a dream. Maybe this whole time-travel thing was a dream, and Captain Devon Bradley was a figment of her subconscious . . . the perfect man come to life for her. She opened her eyes and looked at him. "You're beautiful, too."

Devon's eyes opened with surprise at her words. "You, my lady, are tipsy." He smiled down at her.

"I, your lordship, am drunk," she responded, giggling deeply within her chest.

Devon grinned. "I believe you are. Shall we walk a bit?"

"Mmmm. I think that's a good idea." Laly let him lead her from the rail toward the bow of the ship. If she ever hoped to get to the medallion she was going to have to get her wits about her. Sugar was keeping Wainwright busy below. It was her job to get rid of the captain and find the medallion. She looked up at his dark silhouette and wondered how.

Bradley felt her perusal, and slowing, he faced her.

Laly looked into his eyes and wished things could be different. Once she had the medallion, she was certain she and Sugar would find a way home, but then she'd never see the captain again. Studying his appearance, she wondered about him. She wanted to ask him about his life, his family. He'd mentioned his father. Was his mother living? Did he have brothers and sisters? She raised one finger to the scar on his cheekbone. "How did you get this?"

Devon thought about Rodriguez and a cold shaft shot through him. Looking at Laly's beautiful features he could hardly believe she would work for the filthy pirate, but so far, no other plausible explanation had been put before him. She was no mermaid, and he certainly didn't believe she was from the future. "Rodriguez tried to kill me by putting a knife through my eye. Fortunately, I was able to deflect the blow," he said bluntly.

Laly sucked a breath of air at his words. Rodriguez was the pirate Devon had been fighting the day before. Their battle was the one she and Sugar had interrupted. "No wonder you hate him so." She paused a moment when she remembered he thought she and Sugar might be working for Rodriguez. "I've never met him, Captain. I wouldn't know him if I saw him."

"It's Captain again?"

"Devon," she offered. "I don't know Rodriguez, I swear."

Devon wanted to believe her. He wanted to believe she was the beautiful innocent who'd wretched so violently at the sight of death earlier that day, but the evidence was against her. She'd come from somewhere. And it wasn't the ocean's depths, nor the future. "Very well," he said without conviction.

Laly's heart sank at his tone of voice. It mattered very much what he thought of her, even though she would soon be leaving him. Her gaze fell as tears filled her eyes. "I'm sorry you think so little of me," she murmured.

Devon's heart wrenched at the sight of her sadness. She was probably only acting, pretending to care, but he couldn't help wanting to comfort her. Stepping forward, he folded her in his arms. "I'm sorry, my sweet mermaid."

Laly let herself lean into his embrace. His strong arms encircled her, making her feel safe and protected. "Oh, Devon," she breathed against his chest.

Devon felt her speak his name. He felt the full mounds of her breasts being crushed against him. He felt the softness of her skin beneath his touch. He wanted to taste her also. Touching her chin with his fingertip, he lifted her face to his. Lowering to meet her, he let his lips touch hers gently at first, savoring the moment of union.

Laly felt as though she were floating when he kissed her. Her heart fluttered rapidly in her chest and her blood turned to quicksilver in her veins. "Devon," she whispered against his kiss.

Devon felt his name on her lips and wanted to possess her body and soul. His blood beat wildly through his body, bringing to life his desire. Moving ever closer to her, he deepened the kiss, parting her lips and delving into her sweetness with his tongue.

Laly tasted Devon as a starving woman tastes food, as one who might never eat again. There was an urgency in her response to him, a passion that needed desperately to be slaked. She opened her mouth to him, inviting his invasion, answering his aggression with aggression of her own.

Devon was lost in Laly's kiss, but needed more. His body was rigid with desire, ready to consummate what they'd started. Pushing his desire against her, he made known what he wanted and needed. Reaching between them, he found the curved mound of one breast. Cupping it gently, he teased the hardened nipple pressing tightly against the satin bodice of her gown. "Laly, Laly," he chanted into her mouth, over her lips, across her face. "I need you."

Laly felt as though there was no end to her body or beginning to his. They were one. Where he touched her, she joined with him. When he breathed, she took in his air. Arching her back, she allowed him freer access to her breasts, wishing no fabric impeded his exploration.

Devon tugged gently on the satin covering the smooth globe of Laly's breast. Instantly the nipple was free to his view. Trailing his kisses from her mouth to her neck, he nibbled and tasted his way to the swell of curved womanhood and to the hardened peak that waited for his lips. When he closed his mouth over the ripened bud he heard her gasp with pleasure and felt an answering surge in his loins. "Laly, you're so beautiful," he said against her flesh. "I want to . . ."

"Yes," she breathed. Laly's head was back and she realized they'd somehow managed to lean against one of the ship's masts. Looking around her, she hoped for a private spot where she could finally make love to Devon the way she wanted to. Next to the mast was a huge coil of oiled rope and just behind that a secluded area away from prying eyes. It was just too dark to see the area completely. "Here, Devon. Come with me," she urged. Reaching overhead, she took an oil lamp from a peg on the mast. "Light this, please."

Devon looked down on her through passion-clouded eyes. His hand still fondled her breast and his manhood throbbed inside his breeches. When he looked around and realized what she wanted the lamp for, he agreed. Moments later they were inspecting the small area together. "Are you sure you don't want to go back to the cabin?" he asked, concerned for her comfort and privacy.

"No. Sugar might be there." Laly looked at his handsome face and wanted him all the more. Somehow, before this night was over, she had to deceive and betray this man, but for now she just wanted to love him.

"Very well. Put the lamp down and come lie beside me."

Laly looked around her. Reaching overhead, she balanced the lamp on the rope coil, then lowered herself to her knees.

Devon lay back against the planks of the deck. The wood was cool and hard, and surprisingly, felt wonderful to his heated body. Taking Laly's hand, he pulled her downward to lay across him.

Laly smiled as Devon attempted to lead her to him. The passion in his dark eyes glowed warmly and the evidence of his tremendous desire was visible beneath his trousers. Her heart skipped beats in anticipation of their lovemaking.

As she bent to join him, she discovered this place she'd chosen for their tryst wasn't nearly as spacious as it had appeared before the captain's large, muscular frame lay at its center. "It's a tight fit," she whispered, as she tried to adjust the great billowing fabric of her gown.

Devon grinned at her attempts to join him while

trying to control the cloth around her. "Let's get rid of this, shall we?" he suggested huskily, fingering the fabric of her dress.

"Yes," she agreed. Turning her back to him, she held her hair up and waited while he released the tight fastenings of the gown. He then untied the laces of her corset, loosening the restrictive garment, allowing her to breath easier. "That's heaven," she murmured through a deep breath.

Devon heard her and leaned forward to whisper against the soft skin at the nape of her neck. "I hope you say that again very soon."

Laly warmed visibly at the suggestion in his words. "I'm sure I will, Devon."

"Now off with this." Devon reached for the bottom of her gown, searching through the folds of fabric for the hem.

Laly felt him begin to lift the gown and tried to assist in the process by tugging the fabric from the front. In moments she was lost in turquoise satin. "Wait a minute, something's caught," she said through a face full of cloth. She could tell Devon was pulling fabric from the front of the gown up between her legs, not from the back and over her head. "Devon, wait, please," she tried again.

Devon heard her speaking, but couldn't make out her words as she was muffled by the yards of satin over her head. He tugged harder.

"Wait," Laly nearly shouted. Trying to stand, she thought she might be able to pull the front of the gown back down away from her face, but when she struggled to an almost standing position, Devon pulled mightily on the dress, tumbling her forward into the rope coil. Before she knew what was happening, the lamp she'd balanced on the rope fell with a crash into the center of the coil and exploded into flames. "Devon!" she screamed. "Fire!"

Devon heard the lamp break and saw the flames licking up from the inside of the coil. "Damn!" he cursed. Jerking Laly back out of danger, he leaped to his feet and ran for a bucket on a rope, kept for just this purpose. "Fire!" he shouted loudly to the crew. "Fire, men. Jump to!" Swinging the bucket over the side, he let it fall to the ocean, then hoisted it back up full. Throwing the water over the fire, he cursed loudly when it did little good, then repeated the process.

Laly watched in horror as the rope coil seemed to come to life in the flames. Twisting onto itself, it writhed like a giant serpent on the deck, sending sparks and flames out like tiny monsters, skittering dangerously over the wooden planks. Many of the crewmen had run to assist the captain in his fight. Buckets of water flew from every direction, but the stubborn flames refused to be put out. She could see that the hungry blaze was attempting to make its way up the mast.

Devon fought the flames like a most hated enemy. Fire on a ship was one of the most dangerous things that could happen. "More water, men. Move faster!" he shouted.

Laly backed away from the horrible sight of the fire. She wanted to help but knew in her present state of undress she'd only be in the way. Her gown hung loosely around her shoulders, the back open to the night breeze and prying eyes. Then it occurred to her. This was the opportunity she'd been waiting for. Turning quickly, she ran for the stairs that led to the cabins.

Moments later, Laly was in Wainwright's cabin. She

looked frantically around the small room, wondering where she should begin looking, not knowing how long she'd have for her search before the captain came looking for her. If only she could find the medallion and get back to her own cabin before she was discovered missing! Starting with the hammock strung across one corner of the room, she dug through the blankets folded at its middle. She then shook out the clothing nestled beside the blankets.

"Where would he have put it?" she asked herself. Going to a small armoire against one wall, she opened the doors and began to pull the drawers along its bottom. Rummaging through another person's belongings wasn't something she was used to doing, and it made her very uncomfortable and nervous. She jumped at several sounds, nearly having heart failure twice when she heart footsteps in the companionway outside the door of the cabin. "I'd definitely make a terrible Bond girl," she whispered, after the second set of footsteps passed innocently.

Sighing heavily, she went back to her task. After searching the clothes hanging in the armoire, she proceeded to the drawer beneath the bed. Wainwright kept his guns and ammunition in this drawer, also his sword and daggers of assorted sizes. Laly shivered as the memory of the Frenchman was brought vividly to mind. Closing her eyes briefly, she prayed for the strength to get through this adventure alive and sane.

"I'm afraid it's not here," Devon spoke softly from the door.

"Oh!" Laly jumped at the sound of his voice. "How did you get in here without . . . I, ah . . . what's not in here? I don't know what you're talking about," she stammered.

"The medallion, Laly. It's not in here." He leaned against the doorjamb, disappointment evident on his handsome face.

Laly pondered for a moment the wisdom of arguing with him, then thought better of it. "I guess I've got my hand in the cookie jar," she said sheepishly. "But you can't blame me for trying."

"No. I knew you'd try something. I just never thought you'd go so far as to attempt to burn my ship."

Laly's eyes opened wide at his accusation. "I never tried to burn the ship. How could you think such a thing?"

Devon raised one brow. "The evidence, Laly."

"Devon, the fire was an accident. I'll admit I used the opportunity when it arose, but I didn't start the fire on purpose. I couldn't do such a thing." Her heart beat defiantly in her chest and she had to swallow to hide the hurt she felt at his allegation. Letting her eyes meet his, she hoped he'd read the sincerity in her expression.

Devon straightened and entered the cabin completely, kicking the door shut behind him. He advanced on her slowly, all the time watching her eyes, those damnable turquoise eyes. "You know something? When I came down here I was going to wring your pretty neck. Now I can't make up my mind whether I want to kill you or kiss you."

Laly felt her pulse race through her body as he stalked her. "You believe me, don't you?"

Devon shrugged. "I believe you. I may be damned for it later, but I do believe you." He let his eyes roam over her state of undress. The loose bodice of her gown barely concealed the tightly pouting buds of her breasts, their smooth curves swelling from the shining fabric. Her long, moon-gold hair fell softly about her shoulders, creating an aura around her as though she stood in moonlight. Raising his left hand, he picked up a lock of her hair and brought it to his nose. Inhaling its fragrance, he brushed the soft wisp across his lips, lowering his lids as he watched her. "Now what?" he asked. "Do we pick up where the fire caused us to leave off, or was your ardent response to me part of your ploy to get the medallion?"

Laly glanced guiltily toward the floor. She needed the medallion, but she also felt pretty sheepish about the way she'd been ready to have sex with a man she barely knew.

"I'll take that as my answer," Devon spoke plainly, dropping her hair.

"No, Devon. I don't want you to misunderstand."

"Don't worry, my dear. I can handle rejection."

"But I'm not . . ."

Devon held up a hand to silence her. "Let's leave it be, Laly."

"You're hurt," Laly blurted, when she saw the back of his right hand.

"It's nothing."

"Like hell it's nothing. Let me see it," she ordered, grasping his fingers and tugging his hand closer. "Here, under this lamp." She pulled him with her nearer the source of light. "You need ice on this."

"Ice? I think not. Where would I get ice on a ship?"

Laly thought for a moment. He was right, of course, but his burn was serious enough to cause her concern. "Does Dr. Wells have any medicinal salves or lotions in his quarters?"

"Dr. Wells may have some ointment, but this injury isn't worth bothering him about."

"Damn it, Devon. This could get infected, and I know you don't have antibiotics yet."

"Antibio. . . . what?"

She bit her lower lip as she thought. "Never mind." She examined the back of his hand again. The skin had started to blister in several spots and the rest of the tissue was fiery red and swollen. "At least let me put a dry dressing over it."

Devon shook his head. "It isn't necessary."

"It is necessary. Now, sit down." She pulled him down to the bed beside her and lifted her skirt. Ignoring his raised eyebrows, she tore fabric from the hem of her slip to make a bandage. Several minutes later she had his hand wrapped in a passable dressing. "I guess that will have to do," she said. "I still wish you'd let me see what the doctor has in the way of ointments and salves. He may have something I might recognized as being helpful to burns."

"This is more than enough," Devon assured her, holding his hand up to inspect the bandage.

Laly watched him examining his hand and grew silent. Earlier he'd asked, "Now what?" And that was the question that kept going through her mind now. She still didn't have the medallion and she needed it before morning. She wondered if she should try to reason with him, although her reasoning made no sense to him. She'd tried the truth. She'd tried letting him believe she and Sugar were mermaids. She'd tried to find the medallion on her own. Nothing had brought her one step closer to it. "Captain?" she ventured.

"Yes, Laly?" Devon's defenses went up at her use of his title.

"Captain," she repeated. "I need to talk to you."

"Yes?"

"It's difficult." She stopped there, not knowing how to continue.

Devon waited. He knew she was going to try and talk him out of the medallion, and he couldn't help the curiosity that flowed through him wondering what her next story would be.

"Devon, Sugar and I really *are* from the future," she started. "I know it sounds crazy. It sounds crazy to me, too. People don't just travel through time every day. At least, not real people. I mean, you can read about time travel, and aliens, and monster babies, and Elvis being sighted at K-Mart in the *Enquirer* while standing in line at the 7-Eleven, but things like that don't happen to real people. I can't explain it. I don't understand why or how it happened. I just know it did. For some very crazy reason Sugar and I were sent back in time over three hundred years." Frustrated tears began to fill her eyes.

Devon watched her tell her story. He had no idea what she was talking about when she mentioned monsters and aliens and something called an "elvis" being sighted somewhere, but he listened.

"We were diving off the coast of New Providence. I found the mast of a ship, and under it the medallion. Sugar came down to warn me that the storm was closing in on us. Then, before we could surface, the storm hit." She looked pleadingly up into his eyes. "It was like nothing I've ever experienced before, Devon. A bright light shot through the water and held us for what seemed like forever. Then it was gone. When we surfaced, it was between your ship and Rodriquez's. At first we thought your battle was staged for the benefit of tourists. You can imagine how horrified we were when we realized what had happened to us, that your battle was real, that the men we saw die were truly dead, not actors playing a part.'' The tears that filled her eyes began to fall and she brushed at them. ''I know this is hard for you to believe. Just think how hard it is for Sugar and me to believe. But it's true. All of it. And I know the medallion had something to do with us being delivered to this time and place. Don't you see? It makes sense, doesn't it?''

''And you think the medallion can take you home,'' he stated.

''Yes, oh yes. You believe me now?'' She clutched his arm tightly with her fingers.

Devon looked sadly at her. ''I believe that you believe what you've told me is true. Either that, or you're the best actress I've ever seen.''

Laly's hands fell to her lap and she let her head lower in defeat. She sighed heavily before she spoke. ''I suppose I wouldn't believe you, either, if you appeared on my doorstep and announced you were from another time.''

''No, you wouldn't.''

She thought for a moment and felt a tiny spark of anger begin growing in her breast. Damn it, maybe she would believe him. She'd at least allow the possibility that it might be true. ''Isn't there even one tiny part of you that wants to believe?'' she asked, raising her head and meeting his gaze once more.

Devon saw her defiance. ''Yes, but common sense must prevail, Laly.''

''Why? It wasn't common sense that brought me here. It wasn't common sense that had me in your arms last night, nor again tonight. It isn't common sense that you'd be attracted to someone you believe to be either a mermaid or affiliated with a murderer, now, is it?'' she demanded. ''Nothing that's happened since yesterday has anything to do with any kind of sense, common or otherwise. So why should common sense prevail now?''

Devon heaved a deep breath. ''Laly, I am attracted to you. This I cannot deny. The fact that I want to push you backward onto this bed and bury myself within you does not denote that I am using much common sense, but where the medallion is concerned, there is a definite course of action to be taken and it is my duty to take it.''

Laly looked directly into his dark eyes. She, too, wanted him to bury himself within her and the visual picture his words brought to mind had her burning with desire. But the medallion was between them. ''What do I have to do to get the medallion? What can I bargain with?'' she asked bluntly.

Devon knew exactly what she was asking. ''You would sleep with me to obtain the medallion?'' He'd assumed so earlier, but for her to put it in such blatant terms caused a twist of pain to spear his heart.

''I would do a lot of things with you to obtain the medallion, the least of which would be to sleep with you. I guarantee you wouldn't be sorry,'' she stated boldly, inwardly unsure she could fulfill her boast.

Devon's eyes closed slightly and the blood heated in his loins. ''You speak as though from experience,'' he challenged. Her gaze faltered slightly and he was pleased to see her weakness. She was bluffing. ''Perhaps I'll consider your 'bargain.' ''

Laly's eyes flew to meet his again. ''You mean you'd really give me the medallion for one night of sex?''

''Perhaps.'' He leaned toward her, softly placing his hand over her breast.

Laly's breath caught in her throat as the warmth

of his palm heated her skin through the fabric of her dress. She felt her nipple harden at his gentle teasing and couldn't help but sway toward the fire of his touch.

Devon slipped his arm around her and pulled her closer still, bending to steal a kiss from her sweet lips. "And perhaps not," he murmured against her mouth.

"What?" Laly asked, not sure she'd heard him correctly.

"I said, perhaps not." Devon raised his head only inches and stared down into the turquoise whirlpools of her eyes. "I don't bargain against doing my duty, Laly. There is nothing I would enjoy more than to spend the night sating my passions with your lovely body, but I won't sacrifice my honor or my duty to do so. So, unless you want to stay with me of your own free will, no bargain attached to our actions, I suggest you return to your own quarters. You'll not get the medallion from me this way."

Laly seethed at his words. "You bastard!" she hissed. "Let go of me," she demanded, even as she pulled away from him. Standing quickly, pulling her dress around her, she headed for the door. "I may not get the medallion this way, but I will get it! I give you my word on it." Slamming her way through the door, she heard him chuckle as she left. "You bastard," she ground silently between clenched teeth. "You knew what I was up to from the start."

Nine

"Where have you been?" Laly demanded as Sugar tiptoed through their cabin door just after dawn.

Sugar straightened. "I've been keeping Wainwright busy so you could get the medallion. Did you?"

Laly looked down at the bed where she sat. "No."

"Why not? What happened? Didn't you get the chance?"

Laly looked back up at her friend. "I tried. I managed to search Wainwright's cabin, but it wasn't there. Then Devon found me searching, and I didn't know where else to look after that. I was certain it'd be somewhere in that cabin."

Sugar raised a speculative brow. "Devon?" she inquired.

"He asked me to call him Devon, though I think he just did it to throw me off guard. That man is a bastard of the first order."

"You don't say. What exactly happened to make

you feel that way about him?'' Sugar sat on the bed next to Laly.

"He just . . ." She heaved a heavy sigh. "He just knew what I was up to and called my bluff, if you must know."

"Ha! You've finally met your match," Sugar announced.

Laly glowered at Sugar for a moment. "You can make ridiculous remarks if you want to, but we don't have the medallion, and we're being put ashore this morning."

Sugar sat briefly silent, then touched Laly's arm. "Couldn't you give it one last-ditch effort? Maybe if explained . . ."

"I explained last night," Laly interrupted. "I explained. I snuck off to search their cabin. I even offered to have sex with him to get the medallion. Nothing worked. And now, this morning, he's sending the medallion back to the governor."

"Then I guess we're stuck here," whispered Sugar, her eyes clouding with disappointed tears.

"Not necessarily," Laly offered.

Sugar looked up curiously at her best friend. "What do you mean?"

"I mean, just because we couldn't get the medallion from the captain, doesn't mean we can't get it from the governor."

"Laly, I doubt the governor is going to be any more willing to hand over the medallion than the captain was."

"Who said I'm going to ask him to hand it over. Who said anything about approaching the governor at all?"

"But I thought . . ."

"I've already got one man thinking I'm crazy, or

a liar, for telling him the truth. Do you think I'm going to waste our time trying to convince another man that we're from the future? Not me. I've learned my lesson."

"Then how do you propose we get it?"

"In the middle of the night, when everyone's asleep, I think."

"We're going to steal it?" Sugar squealed.

"Shhh. Keep your voice down. You don't know who could be in the companionway right now. And yes, we're going to steal it."

"But what if we get caught? I seem to recall something about floggings and hangings and being sent to the stocks in this time period."

"And what if we never get the medallion, and we never get back home? Do you want to live the rest of your life here? Just what do you think you could do for a living here? I don't think there's a great big demand for female professors of anthropology."

Sugar shook her head. "I guess not, but what if we do get caught, Laly?"

"Then we deal with the consequences. I think it's worth the risk."

"I know you're right," Sugar acquiesced.

"Good. Now let's get a few hours' sleep. I have a feeling we're going to need it."

Bradley lay in his hammock with his eyes glued to the ceiling. He'd given up trying to sleep hours earlier and wondered what Laly was doing at this moment. Was she sleeping? Or plotting? He had a feeling it was the latter.

After she'd left the cabin the night before, he'd nudged open the secret compartment along the baseboards of the wall near the bed. The medallion was still safely hidden within the recess. "Just a few more hours and you'll be home in the governor's mansion," he'd whispered over the piece.

Now, with morning well establishing its reign over the day, he was ready to send the damned medallion on its way and be done with it. He would then be free to follow Laly and Sugar and see where their loyalties really lay.

"Wainwright," he called across the small room. "Wainwright, are you awake yet?" The groan he heard from the bed caused him to smile. "Drank a bit too much last night, did you?" he asked.

"Aye, Sir. That lovely Sugar had me drinking rum 'til it was coming out my ears."

"I daresay it was part of their plan," Bradley informed him.

"Plan, Sir?"

"To get the medallion."

"But she never said anything about the medallion, Sir."

"No. That was Laly's job. Sugar's was to keep you busy."

Wainwright groaned again. "And that she did, Captain. That she did."

Bradley raised his brows with curiosity. Laly had been willing to sleep with him last night to secure the medallion. Had Sugar been willing to do the same to keep Wainwright occupied? "Just what did you do?" he couldn't help asking.

"Well, Sir, after we finished the bottle of rum, she wanted to play a game."

"A game?"

"Yes, Sir. A card game. Very interesting it was, too." He smiled in memory.

"You do say?"

"Aye, Captain. She called it 'strip poker'."

Bradley rolled to his side to see Wainwright's face. "Strip poker? I've never heard of it."

"Neither had I, Sir, but I'm sure you'd enjoy it."

"Did you win?"

Wainwright chuckled. "That depends on how you look at it."

Bradley sat up in the hammock. "You're not making sense, man. Either you won or you didn't."

Wainwright laughed out loud. "Sir, would you call it winning to see a beautiful woman undress slowly before you? Right down to her pantaloons and chemise? I could see through the fabric, it was so delicate."

"She undressed for you?"

"Yes, Sir. It's part of the game."

"So you won."

"No, Sir. Actually, I lost."

Bradley was truly confused. "But she undressed for you. Down to her underthings."

"Aye, Sir. But I was wearing even less before the game was through." Wainwright blushed a deep crimson at confessing such a thing to his captain. "It was all in good fun, Sir."

Bradley rubbed his whiskered jaw as he thought. "Sounds like good fun, Wainwright. Good fun, indeed."

"Do you think all mermaids ... or women like them, play such games where they come from?"

Bradley raised one dark brow. "I don't know, but I'd like to play this game with one mermaid I know," he said, under his breath." Then, louder, "I don't know, man. Let's heave to. We're docking this morning."

* * *

Laly felt the bump of the ship nudging the dock and woke from a fitful sleep. "Sugar, wake up. We're here," she said, shaking her friend's shoulder vigorously.

Sugar sat bolt upright and rubbed the sleep from her tired eyes. "Lord, what are we going to do in Charles Towne in 1678?"

"We're going to find the governor's mansion," Laly said with conviction.

Sugar swallowed her apprehension. "You're right. Do we change into the captain's trousers, or keep these on?" She indicated the dresses they still wore.

Laly looked down at the crumpled satin of her gown. "As much as I'd like to be wearing pants when we go ashore, I think we'll be less conspicuous in these. Damn, this thing is uncomfortable," she grumbled.

"Stand up and I'll fasten you back up," Sugar offered. "Then you can do me."

Laly stood and turned her back toward Sugar. "If you can manage to leave it a little less tight than before, I'd be eternally grateful," she said.

"I'll do my best, but this dress doesn't leave much room for adjustments."

A few minutes passed and Laly was securely fastened into her gown once more. She then turned to refasten Sugar. "Hey, I just realized something. I didn't undo your dress for you, so who did?" she asked, with a busybody tone to her voice.

"Wainwright managed the task quite well," Sugar offered haughtily.

"Wainwright? You're kidding."

"No, I'm not. And I didn't do what you're think-ing," she defended.

Laly smirked. "Yeah, right."

"I didn't. I taught him how to play strip poker."

Laly began to giggle. "And you lost?" she asked incredulously.

"Of course not, but I had to let him win a few hands to keep him interested."

Laly laughed openly. "The poor guy never knew what hit him."

"Laly, it wasn't that bad."

"I should tell him you're the world's greatest card shark."

"You'll tell him no such thing. He wouldn't believe you anyway. He thinks I'm sweet."

"That's just the point. You are sweet. You're just a terrible cheat at cards." Laly had to sit on the bed to catch her breath in the tight dress. "So, what does he look like naked?"

"Laly!" Sugar hissed.

"Don't act so pious. I've seen you strip enough men playing poker to know you have no mercy."

"But they were twentieth-century men with low morals and a death wish. Wainwright is different. I left him with his dignity."

"How much dignity?"

"Enough to know he doesn't wear a stuffed cod-piece," she giggled.

"I knew it! Now 'fess up."

"Really, I left him his shirt, and it was long enough to hide his . . . you know."

"Nice?"

"Very."

"You peeked."

"Of course."

Laly tossed her head back and laughed some more. "I wish I'd been there. And I wish you'd cheat the captain out of his pants, too."

"I'm sure you don't need my card tricks to get the captain out of his pants."

"And you didn't need tricks to get Wainwright out of his, but it was an innocent way to have some not-so-innocent fun."

"Laly, Sugar, it's time to go!" Bradley called through the door.

Both women stopped dead, their mirth forgotten.

"Laly, I'm frightened," Sugar confided, her eyes suddenly filling with tears.

Laly stood and clutched her dear friend's arm. "Don't worry. I'm with you, and what ever happens, we'll be okay."

"I wish I could believe that," Sugar sniffed.

Opening the door slowly, Laly gazed defiantly up into the captain's eyes. "Good morning, Captain," she said formally.

"Good morn, Laly," he acknowledged. "Good morning, Sugar," he added.

"Captain," Sugar nodded at him.

"Are you ladies ready to go ashore?"

Laly raised her chin. "Yes. We have . . . business to attend to."

Bradley narrowed his eyes at her. "Business? What kind of business, Laly?"

"None of your nevermind, Captain. You seem in a hurry to wash your hands of us, so I won't burden you with my plans. Come, Sugar." She tugged Sugar's arm to get her started. "Let's be on our way."

Bradley watched Laly's back as he followed the women along the corridor and up the stairs to the deck. He saw her stiffen when she looked toward the city, and noticed that her grip on Sugar's arm became tighter. "Do you have people here?" he couldn't help asking, as they neared the gangplank.

Laly jerked around to face him. "Yes. There is one man here we plan on visiting this very evening, so don't bother yourself worrying about us. Now, goodbye, Captain Bradley." She whirled back around to the gangplank and tugged Sugar along after her. She could feel Devon's eyes on her back as she descended the plank and pulled Sugar into the mire of humanity that swarmed along the pier.

Bradley felt a twinge of guilt as he watched them depart. They looked like two lost butterflies in the dark rabble that visited the waterfront, their brightly colored dresses visible for a great distance. "Lawson, Spears," he called his men.

"Aye, Sir," Lawson answered first.

"Take this to the governor, and guard it with your lives. Tell him I'll report to him later." Bradley handed Lawson the medallion wrapped in oilcloth. "See you're not distracted."

"Aye, Sir," the men answered in unison, then turned to leave the ship.

Bradley followed their progress as they left the ship and waited until they'd secured a carriage. He then let his eyes seek out Laly and Sugar, still making their way slowly along the waterfront. "They act as though they've never been here before," he said quietly to himself.

"Sir?" Wainwright asked as he neared.

"Nothing," Bradley answered. "Can you see to the cargo and the transfer of the French prisoners for me? I have something I need to do."

"Of course, Sir. But you usually like to do the final tally on the cargo yourself. Should I wait for you?"

"No. I don't know how long I'll be," he said, his eyes still following the turquoise of Laly's dress through the crowd. It was becoming more and more difficult to keep his eye on her as she moved away from him. "I have to go. I'll see you . . . well, I'll see you whenever I get back."

"Aye, Sir," Wainwright acknowledged with confusion. Captain Bradley's distracted attitude was something new, and he didn't know quite how to take it. Shrugging, he watched him leave the ship and begin pushing his way quickly through the crowd.

Laly grasped Sugar's hand tightly as she pushed and bullied their way through the smelly, sweating throng of ruffians who seemed intent on creating a wall of bodies just ahead of them. "Out of my way," she ordered a particularly foul-smelling man as he blocked her passage and offered her a shilling to feel her teats.

"My God," groaned Sugar. "We'll never get out of here alive."

"Oh yes, we will. I've killed one man so far during this nightmare, and I'm about to kill another."

"That toothless pig who just propositioned you?"

"No. Captain Devon Bradley for putting us through this."

"But we'll probably never see him again," Sugar moaned, then screeched when a strange hand grabbed her buttocks.

Laly's heart took a defiant dip at the thought of never seeing Devon again, but she refused to give in to the melancholy emotion as it threatened to grip her. "It doesn't matter. We'll find another way back out to sea. We've got to in order to find the storm.

Besides, if I saw him right now I would kill him. I'd shoot him with his own gun. I'd run him through with his own sword. I'd . . . I'd . . ."

"I get the picture," Sugar said, turning quickly to avoid another hand groping toward her.

Laly knocked a man's arm from her path and looked overhead at the street signs hanging from the buildings on either side of them. "I have no idea which of these establishments is respectable, but we've got to get off this street." Seeing a sign just a few feet ahead of them, she guided Sugar along behind her and managed to make it to the door. Peering in through the open doors, she noticed men sitting at a large carved wood bar, and others seated at rough-hewn tables. Many were eating. "This must be a lounge. Let's duck in here for a while."

Sugar looked past Laly and grimaced. "I wouldn't call this a lounge. All the customers are men, and they look pretty rough," she whispered into Laly's ear.

"We *are* on the waterfront. Haven't you ever seen the longshoremen who frequent the lounges along the piers back home?"

"I don't usually frequent the waterfront," Sugar hissed.

Laly rolled her eyes. "Neither do I, but I do watch TV. Besides, we don't have much choice. It's here or the street. At least, in here we might be able to find out where the governor's mansion is."

"All right." Sugar let herself be led through the door and to an empty table. She couldn't help but notice the stir they caused when they entered, nor the leering stares they were receiving as they sat down. "Laly," she begged.

"We'll be fine. Just ignore them and they'll get the idea," Laly said, with more bravado than she felt. She, too, had noticed how out-of-place they were. Their idea of blending in by wearing the dresses the captain had given them had turned out to be ridiculous. They'd have fit in better in trousers. At least then they'd have been able to tie their hair up and pass as young men. Now they looked like two streetwalkers with insomnia.

Sugar squeezed Laly's arm as the barkeep walked toward their table.

"You ladies want somethin'?" he asked gruffly.

"Just water, please," Laly asked, realizing too late the folly of not asking the captain for some money.

"Ha! If it's water ye want, the trough's outside. If it's business ye're after, I gets 'alf o' what ever ye take."

Laly and Sugar gaped open-mouthed at the surly man.

"Do ye understand me, or are ye addle-brained?"

"We understand," Laly found her tongue.

"And if'n ye need a room, ye can use the one at the top o' the stairs, only I git paid in advance, see?"

Laly just nodded. This was worse than anything she could have imagined, but she couldn't let Sugar see how frightened she was.

Nodding in return, the barkeep went back to the bar.

"Laly, let's get out of here," Sugar pleaded. "At least in the street we didn't have a pimp watching us."

"No, we're staying here for now. At least here we know what we're up against. He can't make us have sex with someone, and as long as we sit quietly, he'll probably leave us alone. Out there," she tilted her head toward the door, "we don't really have any defense."

Sighing, Sugar let her eyes fall in agreement. "How long will we be here? I'm getting awfully hungry."

"Don't let yourself think about food. We have no money, and we'll probably be here until tonight, that is if the bartender lets us stay."

Bradley followed Laly and Sugar until he saw them duck into the Blue Parrot. His heart burned with the realization of Laly's betrayal. The Blue Parrot was where he'd had his run-in with Rodriguez, and it made sense she'd meet the blackguard in his usual hang out. Standing to the side of the door, he could keep out of sight and still see Laly's profile as she sat with Sugar and waited for their meeting with Rodriquez. "I'll catch you with him and confront you with your lies, woman," he rasped through clenched teeth.

Hours went by slowly and Laly could hear her and Sugar's stomachs growling loudly with hunger. "Maybe we'll be able to steal some food from the governor, too," she hoped out loud.

Sugar grinned weakly. "I've been meaning to lose a few pounds anyway. Besides, it won't kill us to miss a few meals."

Laly smiled at her friend and nodded. Just at that moment a man wandered to their table.

"The barkeep says ye're not doing a very good business today," the man spoke softly while leering down at Laly's exposed cleavage. "He says I should come over ta ask ye why."

Laly looked up at the filthy creature wavering on his feet before them. He stood no more than five feet two, if that, and his narrow shoulders and slightly bent legs gave him a puny, rather sickly appearance. Two teeth were all she could see as he spoke, and the thinning whiskers that waggled as he moved showed several streaks of gray. They also held several chunks of unidentifiable food particles.

"Tell the barkeep it's none of his business," Laly answered.

"He won't like that answer none. Ye're working his fine establishment, aren't ye?"

Sugar squeezed Laly's arm under the table. "Tell him it's just been a slow day," she offered.

The man let his attention transfer to Sugar. "Ye're a pretty one. How much fer a tumble wi' ye?"

Sugar's eyes opened wide in surprise. They'd been approached by several men since entering the bar, but all had been interested in Laly's voluptuous figure, and she'd gotten rid of them; now, this reprobate was asking for her. "I'm not for sale," she huffed.

"Then what ye been sittin' here all day fer?"

"Well, I . . ."

"She's one hundred pounds," interrupted Laly.

"One hundred pounds, ye say!" the man sputtered. "I wouldn't pay one hundred pounds to stick it in the governor's wife herself! No wonder ye're makin' no money. Ye're daft!" He shook his shoulders and headed back to report to the barkeep.

"Oh, hell, we're probably going to have to leave now," complained Laly. "I should have kept my big mouth shut."

Sugar couldn't help but giggle. "Even if we get kicked out of here, it was worth it. Did you see the look on his stupid face?"

"Damn, here he comes." Laly indicated the barkeep stomping toward them.

"What's the meaning o' askin' such a ridiculous price for yer services?" he demanded.

Laly raised her chin to the man. "We're worth it," she announced.

The barkeep stopped short. He couldn't imagine a woman being worth one-tenth what these two were asking, but the fact the blond one thought they were worth the money gave him reason to question. "What makes ye different than any other wench?"

"What we do," Laly answered.

The barkeep leaned over the table toward them. "And just what is it ye do that's worth so much?" he whispered, his dirty imagination taking a tailspin.

"I won't even tell you without being paid. Your poor body couldn't take it. Now, if you'll be so kind as to leave us alone to our business?"

The barkeep licked his lips and looked as far down Laly's bodice as he could. "But I'm yer partner, so to speak, since I'm lettin ye work here."

Laly glance toward Sugar as though she were thinking about telling the man her secret. "No. I really can't say anything about what we do." She leaned closer and allowed him a deeper look. "Let me just say that if you laid even one hand on me I'd send you to heaven," she whispered seductively, pinching Sugar under the table to keep her silent.

The barkeep jerked back as though burned, his eyes, and other parts, bulging with desire. Swallowing repeatedly, he gulped as he asked, "And ye've done this before?"

Laly closed her eyes slightly and thought about the Frenchman. "I sent a man to heaven just yesterday," she assured.

"Well, I guess I'll let ye stay then. Just remember, I get half of whatever ye make here."

"Believe me, any money we make whoring here today we'll gladly share."

"Right then," he said, satisfied that he'd get his fair share when the time came. He was only sad he didn't have enough money to "go to heaven," like the woman said. But that didn't mean he had to go entirely without. He indiscreetly rubbed the front of his trousers. "Magda!" he bellowed as he went behind the bar. "Magda, get over here, girl!" he yelled, as he passed beneath a dirty carpet hung over a door in the back of the room. He'd enjoy the little wench he had washing dishes for him. He might even give her an extra pence or two if she'd shut up long enough to let him imagine he was sticking it in the blond whore.

"Whew, that was close," remarked Sugar. "You had him ready to wet himself. What would you have done if he'd offered to pay you the hundred pounds?"

"No chance. Have you seen how little he's paid for ale and that greasy stew he keeps serving everyone? It'd take him three years even to have a hundred pounds pass through this place, let alone to save that much."

"I still think you took a big chance." Here Sugar stopped and started to grin. Her grin quickly turned into a giggle. "I almost died when you told him you'd send him to heaven if he touched you."

"I was just being honest," defended Laly, smiling. "And we don't have to leave."

A screech, then a loud growl, from beyond the door where the barkeep had gone suddenly quieted the conversation all around them. Looking up, the they saw the barkeep coming back under the carpet over the door. He was quickly fastening his trousers and sported a bright red mark over his left cheek.

"Apparently, the barkeep got turned down," Laly whispered.

"He doesn't look too happy. And he's headed this way."

"I just lost me dishwasher, thanks to ye!" he accused, as he neared their table.

"Thanks to me? How is losing your dishwasher my responsibility?" Laly demanded.

" 'Coz ye're the one what got me hot, and she'd have none o' me. Run outta here like a scalded cat, she did. Now what am I gonna do?"

"I'll do it," blurted Sugar.

Both Laly and the barkeep turned their attention on her the same moment. "You?" Laly gasped.

"What do ye know about washing dishes? Ye ever been a scullery maid?" asked the barkeep.

Sugar rolled her eyes. "It's certainly easier to wash dishes than it is to send a man to heaven," she answered.

"Sugar, what are you doing?" whispered Laly.

Sugar just nudged her in the ribs. "So, what do you say?" she asked the barkeep.

He rubbed his stubbled jaw. "I don't know. It was her what lost me my dishwasher." He pointed his thumb at Laly.

"She'll help," Sugar offered before Laly could protest.

"I guess ye'll do," agreed the barkeep. "But I don't pay no one hundred pounds fer dishwashin'."

"Of course not," smiled Sugar. "We'll work for food."

The bar keep looked puzzled.

"You just send us back the dirty dishes. When we're

through we get to eat our fill of your delicious-looking stew,'' explained Sugar, shushing Laly with her hand.

"It's a deal.'' The barkeep slapped the table with finality. "Come git to work. I got a whole pile of dishes already waitin'.''

Laly groaned as Sugar pulled her to her feet. "Do you know what you've done?'' she hissed as she was being led toward the bar.

"Yes,'' answered Sugar. "I've kept us from starving.''

Ten

"My back is killing me," complained Laly. "I've never seen so many dirty dishes in my whole life."

"At least we got to eat," said Sugar.

"I'm not so sure that was a good thing. My stomach's been a little woozy since I ate that stew. I'm still not sure what kind of meat that was."

"Don't think about it. You'll only make yourself sick."

Laly and Sugar wiped their hands and faces on a dingy rectangle of cloth used to dry the dishes. "At least Hodges isn't too particular about how clean the dishes are when we get through with them. A few of those dried-on stains just wouldn't come off," Laly explained.

"Mmmm," Sugar moaned in agreement, as she arched her back and rubbed her neck. "I think that's probably as clean as they've been since they were new."

"Ye two gonna stand around gawkin all day, or are

ye gonna git to work?'' the barkeep, Hodges, groused, as he stuck his head under the hanging carpet.

"We're finished," Laly declared.

"Not bloody likely," the man argued. "I've got a whole slew of dishes here under the bar."

"Well, you can just wash them yourself. It certainly wouldn't hurt those filthy hands of yours to see a little soapy water," issued Laly. She then turned to Sugar. "Come on, I'm getting out of here now. It's nearly dark and we should be on our way."

Sugar nodded in agreement and started toward the door.

"Now, wait just a minute," interrupted Hodges. "Ye ate plenty of stew, and washed it down with a good bit of ale, I might add. Ye haven't washed enough dishes yet to pay me for what ye ate."

Laly glowered at the rude man. "Listen to me, you miserable excuse for a human being, that stew was barely edible, I'm sure you use rat meat in it, and the ale was stale and warm. You're lucky I don't file charges with the local authorities about the poor standards you keep here. Now, get out of our way!" She'd had enough. Her back and neck ached, her feet were sore, and her stomach roiled each time she thought about the greasy food she'd consumed. Passing Sugar, she pushed her way through the door, lifting the carpet as she went, and forcing the barkeep to back up.

"Listen here, Missy . . ." Hodges attempted to interrupt their departure.

"Listen, nothing! We're leaving, and if you, or anyone else, tries to stop us, I'll sue you!" Laly stomped toward the door, Sugar, wide-eyed, following close behind.

* * *

Bradley heard a commotion of raised voices within the Blue Parrot and was certain one of them was Laly. Peering around the doorjamb, he watched as she bullied her way past the barkeep and made her way toward the door. Backing up and flattening himself against the outside wall, he hid from view behind passersby as she burst through the door.

He'd waited outside all day, sure that at any moment Rodriguez would show up for his rendezvous with the women. Impatiently pacing the street, eyeing each man that entered the foul establishment, and becoming more and more angry with every passing hour, he'd nearly decided to go in and confront Laly with what he knew to be true, that she was working for the despicable pirate. But without actually catching them together, Laly could laugh in his face—something he wouldn't let happen. No, when he confronted Laly, it would be with a full arsenal of evidence.

Right now, he needed to keep his temper in check and to continue to follow where Laly led. As she stepped out onto the street and began walking away from the Blue Parrot, he waited until she was far enough in the distance to allow him to follow discreetly.

Rodriguez couldn't believe his luck. Just when he thought this trip into port would prove to be less than profitable, he spied the mermaids coming out of the Blue Parrot. Evil glee filled his heart when he noticed them being followed by the hated Captain Bradley. "*Mira*, Carlos, Juan!" he ordered his mates. "Look there, the mermaids!" He pointed in the direction of the women making their way through the crowd on the street. "I'll make a fortune from them," he hissed.

"Captain?"

"I'll sell them in the slave market," Rodriguez murmured, closing his eyes briefly as he counted the gold he'd receive for their sale. Then his eyes flew open. "Go! Follow them. See where they go, then come tell me. And keep your eyes on the British bastard that follows them also. Him I will kill."

"*Sí*, Captain. We go," Carlos agreed, turning to leave with Juan at his side.

Rodriguez watched his men depart. "And don't lose them, if you value your lives," he called to their backs.

Entering the Blue Parrot moments later, Rodriguez went directly to his regular table at the back of the room and signaled the barkeep to come over. "Hodges, I saw two women leaving here. What were they doing here?"

"Being more trouble than they were worth," grumbled Hodges. "They ate like a couple o' starved kittens, then wouldn't pay me."

"And you let them leave?" Rodriguez asked, his dark brows raised in question.

Hodges looked sheepishly at the floor. "They done a few dishes for me. And the blond one got right nasty."

Rodriguez rubbed his chin in thought. "How long were they here?"

"All day."

"Did they say what they were doing?"

"They were whorin'. Said they could send a man to heaven, they did."

Rodriguez listened with interest. "Did they do much business?"

"None, now that ye mention it," Hodges answered.

Rodriguez pondered the information. Two women as beautiful as these should have made a small fortune whoring. If that's really what they were up to. Perhaps the mermaids had been waiting for him. Hadn't they made it possible for him to escape the clutches of the English bastard? "Did they say where they were going?"

Hodges pulled his chin back indignantly. "No. They left in a huff, and the one said she would soo me if I tried to stop her. What does soo mean?"

Rodriguez waved an irritated hand at the barkeep. He didn't care about what the mermaids had said to Hodges, now that he was sure their presence at the Blue Parrot had something to do with him. "Bring me rum. A bottle," he ordered.

Hodges put his hands on his hips in disgust. No one ever cared about his troubles. "All right," he answered, as he turned to fetch the bottle. "And I hope ye get a heavin' bloody hangover," he whispered when out of earshot.

Laly pulled Sugar along behind her up the cobbled streets that led away from the waterfront.

"Do you have any idea where you're going?" asked Sugar, as she stumbled over a break in the street.

"No, but I can bet you the governor's mansion is somewhere far inland." She looked around them at the unshaven faces of the rough characters that still crowded the street. "And I haven't yet seen anyone I'd feel safe asking."

Sugar let herself glance from side to side, examining the men that passed them. "No, I haven't either, but we'd better do something quick, it's nearly pitch dark.''

Laly sighed as she checked their surroundings. Bars seemed to be the only establishments taking up space on either side of the street. "We're bound to get to a better-class area if we keep going away from the waterfront.''

Sugar just nodded. She was tired, and though the stew still sat in her stomach like a heavy weight, she was thirsty.

"Come on,'' Laly urged, taking Sugar's arm to guide her along.

Bradley saw the women stop in the street and wondered if this were another location where they were hoping to run into Rodriguez. Ducking behind a lamp post, he waited, then saw them continue their journey. "I've got all the time it takes to catch you, Laly,'' he whispered. "All the time it takes.''

"The top of the hill?'' Laly confirmed. They'd finally reached a residential area and had managed to get the attention of a maid throwing out the garbage.

"Yes'm,'' answered the young woman, bobbing a curtsy as she spoke.

"This hill?'' Laly pointed further up the street.

"Yes'm,'' the woman assured.

Laly smiled at the servant and turned to Sugar. "Can you believe our luck? This street leads to the governor's mansion.''

Sugar smiled weakly. "Oh boy,'' she said, with little enthusiasm.

"Thank you," Laly addressed the young woman, freeing her to continue her tasks, then nudged Sugar into continuing their walk. "I can't believe it. We could have been walking the opposite direction from the governor's mansion, and yet we were walking right toward it. It's fate," she said.

Sugar closed her eyes for a second. "I'm worried, Laly. I just know we're going to get caught. We're not professional burglars. We're not even *amateur* burglars," she moaned.

"No, but we'll be fine. I can feel it."

Sugar shook her head. All she could feel were the blisters on her feet, the ache in her back, and the nausea in her stomach. But she followed Laly up the hill, knowing this was probably their only chance of getting home.

The mansion loomed in the darkness like a giant white ghost. Laly stopped beneath some trees that formed a thick barrier around the property. "We're here," she whispered.

"I can see that. Now what?" Sugar whispered back.

Laly searched the outside of the mansion with her eyes. It was two stories high, with a deep gallery all around. Thick white pillars circled the gallery and held up the high roof. Every few feet a window stood open to the night breezes. Candlelight illuminated some of the rooms and soft laughter wafted out on the warm night air. "Our luck is holding," she murmured. "We just have to peek in some of those windows and hope the medallion is in plain sight."

Sugar shuddered with apprehension.

"Follow me," whispered Laly. She bent at the waist and ran quickly to the side of the mansion. Climbing the stairs very slowly, she was soon making her way to one of the open windows. Peering behind her, she

saw Sugar making her way reluctantly across the vast
lawn that separated the treed area from the house.

"Okay, now what?" mouthed Sugar, when she'd
reached Laly's side.

Laly pointed silently into the window. "We watch,"
she breathed.

The evening moved slowly by as Laly and Sugar
began their vigil. The window they had chosen for
their espionage had a good view of the entrance hall
and beyond into the parlor, where several people sat
drinking brandy and listening to each other speak.

Laly nudged Sugar after a while. "I can't make out
what they're saying, but they seem to find themselves
quite witty. Listen to all the laughter," she whispered.

Sugar nodded, then twisted her stiff neck, letting
her eyes scan the parlor for the millionth time. "Oh,
my God," she hissed suddenly, grabbing Laly's arm.
"Look, on the mantel, over the fireplace. The medallion!"

Laly searched the area Sugar indicated. "Yes, yes,
yes," she whispered, grinning excitedly. Leaning on
its side against a pewter picture frame was the medallion. "If they'll only leave it there, this will be easy,"
she muttered hopefully.

"So we wait until everyone goes to bed?" Sugar
speculated.

Laly nodded. "Yeah. We keep our eyes on that
hunk of gold and pray that someone doesn't move
it."

Bradley crept along the line of trees at the perime-
ter of the governor's grounds. He'd lost Laly and
Sugar in the crowds once and spent precious time
headed down the wrong street. Then it hit him: Laly

was still after the medallion. He'd changed his course and arrived at the mansion in time to see Laly and Sugar crouched outside one of the open windows. "I've got you now, Laly," he murmured. The next second he lost consciousness when blinding pain crashed through his skull as he was struck from behind.

"So, Captain Bradley, we meet again," Rodriguez gloated over Bradley's fallen body.

"What will we do with him?" asked Carlos, still holding the club he'd used on the English captain.

"I will have the pleasure of watching him die," explained Rodriguez. "But first we will take the mermaids." He looked toward the house where Laly and Sugar still waited by the window.

"What are they doing, Captain?" Juan asked.

Rodriguez pondered the man's question. The mermaids looked as though they were getting ready to enter the mansion, and without benefit of invitation. "What ever they do must be important or they would not risk hanging. It might be valuable to us to wait and see what it is they're after." His greedy heart beat rapidly at the thought of more treasure, especially a treasure he did not have to steal for himself.

"Damn it!" hissed Laly, as she watched a heavyset man with muttonchop whiskers pick up the medallion and wrap it in oilcloth. "What is he doing with it?" she whispered.

Sugar watched the man make his way toward the entrance hall. "I hope he doesn't have a safe," she wished out loud.

Laly looked at her wide-eyed. She hadn't even thought about the possibility of the medallion ending up in a safe. Watching the man as he slowly made his way through the entrance hall, she crossed her fingers, childishly hoping it would do some good. She breathed a sigh of relief when he started up the stairs. "It looks like he's taking it to bed with him," she whispered.

Sugar smiled hopefully at Laly. They might actually be able to pull this off.

Waiting about half an hour for the other people in the house to retire, then another hour to be sure everyone was asleep, Laly finally crept through the window and stood breathlessly inside the house. Signaling Sugar to follow, she started tiptoeing toward the stairs.

Sugar stepped over the window sill and stopped as a feeling of dread slipped over her. "Laly?" she whispered.

Laly heard Sugar behind her and turned, placing her finger across her lips in a signal of silence. She was about to climb the first step of the huge staircase that the man had taken and her nerves were raw. Waggling her finger at Sugar, she urged her to follow.

Sugar sighed and started after Laly. There was no point in letting her own fears get the better of her. They had to get the medallion, and if this was the way they had to go about it . . . she shrugged her shoulders at her own thoughts. Reaching the stairs, she saw that Laly was halfway up them already.

Laly grimaced each time her foot caused the wooden stairs to creak. She winced at each sound of the massive house settling. Closing her eyes briefly, she said a prayer that she'd be successful at finding the medallion without getting caught. Checking to see if Sugar followed, she finally reached the top of the stairs.

The uppermost level of the mansion was a mezzanine with double sets of doors along the wall at about fifteen-foot intervals. Laly bit her lower lip as she wondered which room the man had entered. As Sugar caught up with her, she pointed toward the doors and looked at her friend with puzzlement. "Which ones?" she mouthed.

Sugar looked up one side of the mezzanine, then the other. Shaking her head, she nearly started to cry. They'd come so close. Then a thought struck her. She mimicked the shape of the man with the medallion by puffing out her cheeks and making a big belly with her hands.

Laly watched Sugar and couldn't figure out what she was doing. They both saw that the man was heavy. What did that have to do with anything?

Sugar continued her act, miming the way the man had climbed the stairs. She then acted out going to bed. Here's where her pantomime took on new meaning. She pointed at her nose and took deep breaths, pushing out her lips and making faces.

Laly's face lit up when she realized what Sugar was doing. She was snoring! The man probably snored! Grasping Sugar by the arms, she squeezed her hard. She then gave her the thumbs-up sign and started toward the far end of the mezzanine, signaling Sugar to go to the opposite end.

Minutes later, they were standing outside the doors of a very loud snorer. Laly carefully pushed open the door and peered around the jam at the man in his bed. Pulling Sugar after her, she crept into the room and looked around. The room was bathed in moonlight, making the search relatively easy, but her heart sank when she spotted the medallion. The man must have admired it before he went to sleep and left it lying beside him . . . in his bed!

Sugar saw the medallion lying next to the man and began to back out of the room. They couldn't do this. He was sure to wake up. They were going to have to think of another way to get the thing.

Laly saw Sugar faltering and grabbed her arm. Shaking her head in defiance, she pointed at the medallion, then at herself, indicating she was going after it.

"No," Sugar implored silently. She knew this was a mistake.

Laly shook her head again. She released Sugar's arm and crept toward the man's bed. Inching slowly closer, she felt her heart beating a wild pace in her chest. Saying a little prayer, she reached across the man's great bulk toward the medallion lying halfway beneath his coverlet. Carefully slipping it from the covers, she grasped it tightly, lifting it slowly and bringing it away from the bed. Stepping back, she realized she'd been holding her breath and released it quietly.

Sugar nearly squealed when the man suddenly snorted and rolled over. Covering her mouth, she dived for the floor.

Laly saw the man's eyes open as he turned, and she, too, fell to the floor.

Seconds passed like hours as the women stared at each other across the gleaming wood floor. Had he awakened? If so, why hadn't he sounded the alarm? Why hadn't he risen and grabbed them? Laly raised her head slightly and listened. The man's breathing was even and deep. Apparently he'd merely turned over in his sleep. She pushed herself up on all fours and peered over the edge of the bed. Her heart lurched when she saw him looking directly at her. Falling back to the floor, she waited for his large hands to jerk her upward.

Sugar knew they were going to be hanged. She knew she'd never see home again. Never watch TV or go to the movies. Never eat breakfast at her favorite restaurant, or mix up a batch of brownies at midnight. She let her head fall forward between her hands, her forehead resting against the cool wood floor.

Laly continued to await her doom, but it didn't come. Was the man used to having women sneaking around his room at night? Did he think she was a dream? Waiting and wondering was killing her. Better to face the trouble head-on than to lie here and have heart failure while he decided if he was going to choke her with his own hands or turn her over to the authorities. Rising once more, she peered at the man who continued to stare at her. Her heart nearly stopped as she stared back and waited for him to acknowledge her presence.

Moments passed. Laly waited. Nothing happened. Lifting one hand, she waved it in front of his face. Still nothing happened. It finally struck her: he slept with his eyes open. Nearly crying with relief, she sat back on her heels and breathed a little easier. But they weren't out of danger yet. Creeping to where Sugar lay with her face to the floor, she touched her on the shoulder. "Let's go," she mouthed when Sugar looked up at her.

Sugar couldn't believe they hadn't been caught. She'd been certain her life was over. A flood of relief washed over her as she followed Laly from the room and down the stairs. Once outside the house, she grabbed her friend and hugged her tightly. "We made it," she whispered, giggling. "We made it."

Laly hugged Sugar and nodded her joy and relief. Then, taking her by the arm, she pulled her toward the trees once more. They had the medallion, but now they had to find a way back out to sea where they hoped they'd find the mysterious storm again.

As they ran through the trees, Laly was plotting the next steps in their attempt to return to their own time. The hard, steel-like arm that grabbed her nearly slammed the wind from her chest. She heard Sugar gasp behind her as she, too, was stopped by an unknown assailant.

"So, my little mermaids, you have found me," Rodriguez announced, when the women were brought fighting to him. "I will not harm you. You saved me from my most accursed foe, see?" He pointed toward the crumpled body of Captain Bradley.

Laly nearly screamed when she recognized Devon lying in a pool of blood on the ground at Rodriguez's feet. "What have you done to him, you bastard?" she demanded.

Rodriguez raised one brow. "You care for the captain?" he asked. This might prove to his advantage.

Laly saw the speculation on the evil man's face. "No," she lied. "I just don't like to see anyone hurt." She tried to see if Devon was still breathing and was grateful when she saw a slight stirring of his chest. She wanted to go to him, to see to his injuries. She ached with concern at the amount of blood that had spilled around him.

"Look, Captain. See what she carried?" The sailor tossed the medallion to his captain.

Rodriguez caught what was thrown to him and his eyes widened with disbelief. "The King's Medallion? You've brought me the King's Medallion?" he said incredulously. Smiling at the blond mermaid, he bowed slightly. "I knew you were good for me."

Laly tried to jerk free of the man that held her. "Give me that back," she demanded. "We need it."

Rodriguez laughed. "No, little mermaid. I think it was meant for you to bring it to me. You see, our lives have been destined to cross." He turned the medallion over in his hands. He couldn't believe his good fortune.

Laly continued to struggle against the grip on her arms.

Sugar glanced at the wounded English captain and then at Rodriguez. Her heart sank as she watched him handling the medallion, but she had a feeling that losing the medallion was the least of their worries. "What do you intend to do with us?" she asked.

Rodriguez tore his attention from the medallion. "I intend to sell you at the slave market, of course. Mermaids should sell high and fill my pockets with gold," he explained.

"But we're not . . ." Laly began.

Sugar kicked at her, stopping her sentence. "What do you intend to do with him?" she asked, looking down at the lifeless form of Bradley.

Rodriguez raised a dark brow. "I am going to kill him," he said bluntly.

"No!" cried Laly, wrenching violently against the man who held her. "Please don't harm him any further," she begged.

Rodriguez leaned toward her until only inches separated them. "I have waited a long time to end this man's life. Your pleading will not save him," he breathed into her face.

"I would not be happy if you killed this man," said Sugar calmly.

Laly looked startled at her friend.

"What?" asked Rodriguez.

"I said, I would not be happy if you killed this man," Sugar repeated.

Rodriguez threw back his head and laughed. "Do you think I care whether or not you are happy?" he asked.

Sugar raised her chin and stared at him defiantly. She then let her gaze swing around to take in the men that surrounded them. "Would you care if a mighty tidal wave swallowed your ship the next time you sailed?"

"What?" Rodriguez asked quietly.

"I want to know if your crew will sail on a doomed ship."

Laly listened to Sugar and realized what she was doing. Straightening her shoulders, she, too, let her gaze take in Rodriguez's crew. She was rewarded by the frightened murmurs she heard in the dark.

"How many men will sail into the jaws of death, Rodriguez?" Sugar asked louder.

"Stop it," demanded Rodriguez. "You cannot do these things," he said.

"Do you want to take the chance? Will your men take the chance?" Laly asked.

Sugar smiled inwardly, grateful Laly had picked up on what she was trying to do. "If you let Captain Bradley live, we won't sink your ship," she challenged.

Rodriguez heard the fear in the mumbled voices of his crew. Damn these mermaids. He'd been certain they were good luck for him, but now they interfered with his revenge on the English bastard. "You will not harm my ship," he blustered. "And I will kill the Englishman as I planned."

Laly's heart nearly stopped as Rodriguez drew his sword. "No!" she begged.

"I call on Neptune, King of the Sea!" Sugar wailed. "Father, hear me!"

Rodriguez took a step toward her. "Stop this!" he threatened.

Sugar threw back her head and continued to cry. "Father Neptune, this man is evil," she called toward the sky.

The sailor that held Laly released his grip on her and fell to his knees praying. Laly quickly knelt beside Devon and felt for a pulse. It was there, but it was weak.

"Get up, you fools," Rodriguez yelled at the men who prayed on their knees.

"Neptune, take his ship if he harms Captain Bradley," Sugar cried.

More men dropped to their knees.

"All right! I'll let him live," bellowed Rodriguez. "I'll let him live! Now, stop your threats."

Sugar looked to Laly and smiled.

"But I'll not let you go," Rodriguez warned. "You I am taking to the slave market if I have to drag you there myself," he ground out between clenched teeth. "Even if my entire crew shakes with fear," he added, staring accusingly at his men.

Several of the men stood with their heads bowed in shame and Rodriguez seized the moment. "Take them and tie their hands," he ordered, pointing toward Laly and Sugar.

Laly found herself being jerked to her feet once more.

"And gag them," Rodriguez added. He wanted no more threats or prayers to Neptune from them.

"But what about him?" Laly asked, before a filthy handkerchief was shoved in her mouth.

Rodriguez looked at Bradley. "We'll leave him here. If he dies, it will be God's doing. If he lives . . ." I will kill him the next chance I get, he finished silently to himself.

Eleven

Twice during the walk back through town, Laly stumbled and fell. And twice Rodriguez pulled her to her feet with a threat that if she did it again, he'd run her through. She glared at him in answer to his feeble threats. She knew he expected to receive high payment for her and Sugar in the slave market. If only she could get rid of the foul rag stuffed in her mouth, she'd call for help. But since that rag was secured by another, she could do no more than stumble and try to look as though she needed assistance.

As they neared the waterfront, she noticed the crowds were thinner, now that it was late in the evening, and the men that remained were the worst-looking rabble she'd ever seen. She began to doubt the wisdom of getting their attention. Comparing Rodriguez to a group of drunks standing outside a bar, she couldn't have chosen one over the other if she'd had to.

Passing several ships, it suddenly occurred to Laly

that they might pass the *Vengeance*, and so she began looking for it. If someone noticed her and Sugar being taken against their will, they might come to their aid. And then she could tell them where Devon was.

Her heart ached with worry each time she thought of him lying bleeding near the governor's mansion. Why had he followed her? If only he'd stayed near his ship, Rodriguez wouldn't have been able to assault him. Dear Lord, please let him be all right, she prayed.

"Here we are," announced Rodriguez.

Laly and Sugar both looked around them. They could see they'd arrived at no great or impressive destination. A tall fence circled a small stucco building and was fronted by a tiny shack. They watched Rodriguez as he went to the door of the shack and began to bang loudly.

"Wake up! I have slaves for the market," Rodriguez called, as he knocked on the door.

Laly began to struggle against her bonds. If they were ever going to make an escape, it would have to be now.

"Stop her," ordered Rodriguez. "You are causing me much trouble, mermaid. If you cause me too much, I might forget how much you are worth to me," he threatened.

Laly still tugged against the rope that bound her wrists, but the sailor who held her arms squeezed down painfully, bringing stinging tears to her eyes.

The shack door opened and a sleepy man wearing only his nightshirt stepped out into the moonlight. "Rodriguez, you scoundrel. What have you brought me this time?" the man asked jovially.

"Mermaids," Rodriguez answered proudly.

The man guffawed loudly. "You are such a joker," he chuckled.

"I am not joking, Gaspar. These two came up from the bottom of the ocean. I have seen this with my own eyes," Rodriguez insisted.

Gaspar continued to laugh. "Yes, yes. And I suppose you want a fortune for them."

"Mermaids are worth a fortune."

Gaspar stepped down from the low porch of the shack and proceeded to walk around the women. "So, if they are mermaids, where are their tails?" he asked.

"They are able to take the form of women when they are out of the sea," Rodriguez explained.

Laly caught the attention of Gaspar and rolled her eyes.

"This one seems to find fault with your words, Rodriguez," Gaspar commented.

"They are troublesome creatures," Rodriguez said, and then added, "Do you think they would admit to being mermaids?"

Laly grunted behind the gag.

"Take that rag out of her mouth," ordered Gaspar, his eyes turning cold.

Rodriguez didn't try to alter Gaspar's request. Instead, he nodded at his crewman to remove the gag.

"So, Rodriguez claims you and your friend are mermaids. Is this true?" Gaspar asked, while leering over Laly's décolleté.

"Of course not," Laly answered. "There are no such things as mermaids."

Gaspar walked slowly around Laly, looking her up and down. "No such thing? Then where did he get the idea?"

"I haven't a clue," lied Laly. "Can you please take

the gag out of her mouth, too?" she asked, pointing toward Sugar.

Sugar smiled with her eyes. The gag was filthy, and if she let herself think about what might be on it, she knew she'd vomit and probably end up choking to death.

Gaspar waved a hand at Sugar without saying a word, but his action was enough. Quickly, Carlos untied the band that held her gag in place.

Laly noticed how the men jumped to do Gaspar's bidding. Even Rodriguez didn't balk at his orders. She began to think that if she could sway him in her favor, she might be able to win their release. "You seem like an intelligent man, Mr. Gaspar. You don't believe in mermaids, do you?" she asked in a condescending tone.

Gaspar narrowed his eyes at the blond. "I have never said that I believed in them," he answered noncommittally.

"I could tell you had more sense than that." She smiled at him.

"Don't listen to her," interrupted Rodriguez. "She is a troublemaker."

Gaspar raised a hand toward Rodriguez, silencing him. "If you are no mermaid, why does Rodriguez believe you to be one? Is he trying to cheat me?"

Rodriguez took a threatening step forward, but was stopped by a lethal glance from Gaspar.

"I don't know that he's trying to cheat you, although I wouldn't put it past him," Laly said conspiratorially, "but I can assure you we are not mermaids." She glanced toward Sugar, including her in the reference.

"What are you?" Gaspar questioned, his shoulders raised in curiosity.

"Just women, of course."

Sugar listened to the exchange and worried that Gaspar was setting Laly up for something. She was afraid the man's shape and demeanor weren't indicative of his true personality. "Laly?" she whispered. "Be careful."

Laly heard Sugar and smiled at her friend.

Gaspar turned to Rodriguez. "I'm afraid I don't believe these women are mermaids, Rodriguez, but . . ."

"They are . . ." Rodriguez interrupted.

Gaspar scowled darkly. "If you will let me finish," he threatened. "Where did you find these women?"

Rodriguez clenched his jaw tightly and fought the urge to defy the trader. "Outside the governor's mansion," he answered stiffly.

"You took women from the governor's mansion? Are you daft?" demanded Gaspar. "The governor will send out search parties."

"They were not guests of the governor's. They were burglarizing his home," explained Rodriguez.

Gaspar's eyes darted to the two women. Stealing, he wondered? "What were you doing at the governor's mansion, Rodriguez? If he'd caught you there, you'd hang."

"I followed them there." He nodded toward Laly and Sugar.

"Followed them from where?"

"From the Blue Parrot."

Gaspar smiled. "And what were they doing at the Blue Parrot?"

Rodriguez looked Laly and Sugar over one time. "Hodges said they were whoring," he offered.

Gaspar grinned and began a slow walk around Laly

again. "You see, Rodriguez, I knew we'd get to the truth. These women are not mermaids—they are *whores*."

"I beg your pardon!" gasped Laly. "We are *not* whores."

Sugar shook her head. She knew Gaspar was trouble.

"The townsfolk would laugh me out of business if I tried to sell these women as mermaids. Really, Rodriguez, you should have thought of that. But when I sell them as . . . sex slaves, professionals of a sort, I think I can get a high price. Especially for the blonde. Her body would give any man pleasure." His eyes dropped to her cleavage once more. "Perhaps I will sell them as a pair. Many men would enjoy having two such lovely women service them."

"You'll do no such thing!" Laly protested loudly. "You have no right to sell us. We're free adult women. This whole thing is ludicrous." She looked at Sugar. "Can you believe this?" She looked back toward Gaspar and a grinning Rodriguez. "You can't sell us!"

Gaspar rubbed his chin. "Do you have husbands?" he asked.

Laly shook her head.

"Do you own property? Can you tell me where you live so I can check Rodriguez's story with your families?"

Laly didn't know what to say. She just stared bewildered as Gaspar.

Sugar felt them slipping deeper into trouble.

"You see? They have no one," Rodriguez gloated.

"Then I think they will fetch a good price on the dock tomorrow," announced Gaspar. "Put them in the pen," he told Rodriguez's men. "The usual split, my friend?" he asked Rodriguez, putting his arm across the pirate's shoulders.

"*Sí*, that would be suitable," Rodriguez agreed. He would have liked more than the usual thirty percent, but men who haggled with Gaspar ended up headless and floating under the pier.

"Good, good," murmured Gaspar. "Let's drink on it." He led Rodriguez toward his shack.

Laly felt someone grasp her hands behind her and start to pull her toward the tall fence. "No! You can't do this!" she shouted. "Release us, or I'll tell the authorities!" She heard Gaspar laugh as he and Rodriguez disappeared into the shack.

Sugar watched Laly fighting against the man who jerked her along. She heard her words and knew she was right; these men had no right to sell them. But in the year 1678, it seemed that rights weren't an issue. The person with the rights was the person with the upper hand. "Laly, don't fight it now. You might end up getting hurt. Wait. Just wait until later," she implored.

Laly couldn't see Sugar behind her, but she could hear her. Why on earth would she not want to fight this injustice? Why wasn't she fighting, too? "Sugar, we've got to get away," she called over her shoulder.

"I know that, but wait until later. We have no chance right now," Sugar called back.

Laly looked around her. Sugar was right; there were at least ten of Rodriguez's men around them. They were all armed, and though she doubted any one of them would risk punishment for killing her, they would not fear retribution for injuring her. How perfect did she have to be to sell? Giving up her struggle, she walked silently between the posts that flanked the gate.

Once inside the pen, Laly watched Sugar being untied while she felt her own bonds being released. Seconds later they were left alone in the fenced yard.

"What are we going to do?" Laly asked, not expecting an answer.

Sugar shrugged. "We're going to be sold." She paused. "As sex slaves," she added. It was the most horribly ridiculous thing she'd ever heard, and she felt herself very near hysteria. A low giggle escaped her lips. "Sex slaves," she repeated, giggling more.

"Sugar?" Laly touched her friend on the shoulder.

Sugar giggled louder, tears welling up in her eyes.

"We'll think of a way out of this," Laly tried to assure her.

Sugar's laughter grew louder and harder. She had to hold her sides as she bent over and released the hysterical laughter that had a hold on her. "Oh, God, Laly . . ." she hiccupped, "we're being sold as whores." She felt her legs giving out and was soon sitting in the dirt of the compound. "Sex slaves . . . it sounds like a B movie. *Laly and Sugar . . . Sex Slaves of 1678 . . .*" Tears rolled down her cheeks as she let her head fall forward.

Laly knelt beside Sugar. "Please," she pleaded. "We'll be okay. We'll think of something." She wrapped her arm around Sugar's shoulders. "Really, Sugar. Please be all right." She was frightened Sugar had snapped under the pressure they were having to endure.

Sugar heard the fear in Laly's voice and looked up through tearfilled eyes. "I'm okay . . ." she sobbed. Her laugher was quickly turning into all-out crying.

"I wish this was just a bad dream. I wish I could pinch myself and wake up," she cried.

Laly held onto Sugar and lowered herself to sit beside her. "I wish so, too, but it's real."

"And in the morning, we'll be sold as slaves," Sugar whispered through her tears.

Bradley felt the pounding in his head like a hammer across his temples. Nausea gripped him like a vise, bringing up the contents of his stomach in a wrenching upheaval. Over and over he shuddered as his muscles contracted and his head throbbed in response. What had hit him? What had happened? And why wasn't he dead? Whoever had done this to him should have finished him off. He felt near death anyway.

Feeling a tiny bit of relief as his stomach calmed, he rolled onto his side. Looking up through the leaves of the trees, he wondered where he was. He couldn't remember what he'd been doing before he was struck. Closing his eyes against the early morning sun, he tried to bring back the details of the day. "What was I doing?" he muttered.

Raising a hand to his head, he winced when his fingers found a bump and a deep gash across the back right side of his scalp. Whoever had hit him had done a good job of it.

Noises nearby caught his attention. He didn't want to open his eyes but decided if he wanted to figure out this puzzle he was going to have to know at least where he was.

Opening his right eye first, he lay there on the ground, staring at the leaves overhead. Nearly a full minute later, he opened his left eye. The sky seemed too bright and made his head pound more fiercly, but he had to go on. Rolling over onto his stomach made him feel as though his brains were going to explode through his eyes and brought on another fit of nausea. Fighting the spasms that rocked him, he raised up on one arm and looked in the direction of the sounds he'd heard minutes earlier.

The governor's mansion! Laly! It all came back to him in a rush. He'd been about to catch Laly entering the mansion when someone had hit him from behind. Looking up, he saw the sun high in the sky. How late in the day was it? Where was Laly? Damn it, what had happened?

Pushing himself up, he winced at the intense pain in his head. Who had struck him? Blinking hard and trying to relieve the agony behind his eyes, he eased into a sitting position and looked toward the mansion. Again he asked himself, what had happened?

Going over the events in his mind, he tried to figure out who might have been following him . . . or Laly and Sugar. Rodriguez? He hadn't shown up to meet with the women, but that didn't mean he wasn't in port. He mentally shook himself. He remembered the *Puta* wasn't docked in the bay, but she might be anchored around the point. And Rodriguez was the only person he could think of who might have reason to follow him. But if Rodriguez had struck him, why wasn't he dead? Rodriguez would surely have finished him off. Some of the pieces didn't fit, but enough evidence was there to make him believe that Rodriguez was involved. Perhaps it had been Laly's plan all along to meet Rodriguez at the governor's mansion. His heart sank at the thought. All his suspicions about her seemed to be coming true.

Then he was struck by another thought: maybe it

had been Laly who'd stopped Rodriguez from killing
him. He tried not to let his hopes soar. It was foolish
of him to hope anything where Laly was concerned.
But the memory of how she'd responded to his kisses
kept burning through him, sending his pulse racing
and causing a thickening of his manhood. "I will get
to the bottom of this, Laly. I will find you out, and
if you are working with Rodriguez, I will kill you
myself. If you are not . . ." He let his imagination
finish his thought.

Forcing himself to stand, he half walked, half stumbled toward the mansion. He needed to find out if
anything had happened during the night. It took all
his strength to climb the stairs and cross to the huge
double doors at the front of the mansion. His knocking sent pain bolting through his temples. He was
grateful he had to wait only seconds before the doors
swung open.

"Goodness gracious, Sir," Harvey the butler
exclaimed, when he recognized the man at the door.
"Governor, Sir!" he shouted, as he bent to assist the
young man falling into his arms.

"Ask the governor . . ." was all Bradley got out
before he lost consciousness once more.

Laly and Sugar watched the sun come up with
dread. "What time do you think they sell slaves?"
Sugar asked.

Laly glanced at the sky for the hundredth time in
ten minutes. "I don't know," she murmured.

Sugar let her head fall forward to rest on her knees.
She'd come out of her hysteria but felt as though she
were living in a haze.

Laly looked at her friend and worried that she

wasn't able to cope with what they were going through. She patted her shoulder affectionately, not knowing what to say.

"You ladies fer sale?" an old man asked.

Laly looked up at the toothless creature. "What did you say?"

"I want to know if you ladies are fer sale? They don't usually sell sech pretty wenches," he rasped wickedly.

Laly raised her chin. "We are for sale, but it's a mistake. We're being sold illegally."

The old man just cackled as he started away from them. "I heared that a'fore." Then he called over his back. "If'n ye're hungry, you better git yourselves up and inta' the house."

Laly watched him as he walked with a limping gait toward the building in the center of the fenced compound. Several other people had gone in and out of the house, but Laly and Sugar had kept to themselves. The others were to be sold also, and it didn't seem appropriate to make small talk with strangers whose lives were held in limbo while they waited to see who would own them, and therefore hold their destinies. Now, with her stomach grumbling loudly, she thought it might be a good idea to investigate the house.

"Come on, Sugar. We're going to get some breakfast . . . I think."

Sugar raised her head. She wasn't hungry. In fact, she felt nothing at all anymore. "You go on. I'll wait here."

"I'm not leaving you alone out here. Besides, it'll do you some good to get up and look around."

"What would I want to look at?" she asked, her voice a monotone. "Other slaves?"

"Come on, Sugar. We'll get out of this. I'm sure

we weren't meant to live out the rest of our lives as some pervert's slaves." She stood and tugged on Sugar's arm.

Sugar slowly stood and let herself be led toward the building that was referred to as the house. It was a squat structure of stucco with a narrow paneless window in each of its four walls. One door was carved in its side and stood without benefit of a step or covering of any kind. As she neared it, the stench of human excrement met her nose and raised her senses. "I'm not going in there," she told Laly.

"But the old man said there was breakfast inside. I think we should eat whenever we get the chance. We need to keep up our strength."

Sugar pulled back on Laly's grip slightly, but she continued toward the house, knowing Laly was right about the need to eat whenever possible. She just couldn't imagine that there could be anything edible inside the filthy structure.

Laly stepped into the house first and stopped, letting her eyes get used to the shadowed interior before she walked further. She could hear bits of muffled conversation and what sounded like metal clicking against metal and stone. Stepping deeper into the interior, she began to scan the room.

To her immediate left stood a low table. On this was a huge iron pot with the handle of a ladle just showing over its edge. Next to the pot were shallow wooden bowls and dull wooden spoons. No aroma issued from the pot, or if one did, it was overpowered by the horrendous odor of human urine. "Maybe I'm not hungry, either," she murmured.

Continuing her perusal of the room, she saw ten to fifteen men and women sitting on the dirt floor and leaning against the walls. Most were wolfing down some sort of gray gruel as though it were their last meal. She shuddered to think in some cases it might be, and was reminded of her own plight. "Come on, we'd better try to eat something," she said, indicating the pot.

Sugar didn't want to eat. She didn't want to so much as think about eating, but she followed Laly toward the table.

"Here." Laly handed Sugar a bowl and spoon and took a set for herself. Leaning over the pot, she picked up the ladle and stirred the thick gruel that coagulated at the bottom. "Not very appetizing," she remarked. "But we don't know when we'll get to eat again," she added, sighing. Bringing up the ladle, she dropped a glob of the gruel in Sugar's bowl and served herself the same. "Let's go back outside and eat. I can't stand the smell in here."

Turning around, Laly heard the clank of metal on metal again and her attention was drawn to a corner of the room that was darkened by shadow. Squinting to discern the people seated against the wall, she was horrified by the sight that met her eyes. "Oh, my God, Sugar," she gasped, gripping her friend's arm.

Sugar looked where Laly indicated and was outraged by what she saw, her own problems instantly forgotten. Against the wall sat a large black man, his wrists and ankles chained. These chains were attached by more chains to heavy iron rings embedded in the wall. "We've got to help him," she announced.

Laly led the way toward the man. Kneeling beside him, her heart wrenched with compassion when he opened his eyes and looked at her. "Are you hungry?" she asked.

The man looked at her with glazed eyes. No one cared whether he was hungry or not.

Laly repeated. "Are you hungry?" She held her bowl of gruel up for him to see.

"Maybe he doesn't speak English," ventured Sugar.

Laly held up the bowl once more. "Food?" she tried again.

Samuel looked up at the white lady kneeling beside him. Was she serious? Was she really offering him something to eat? Or was she playing games with him, like other white people? He clamped his mouth tightly and raised his jaw in defiance.

"He speaks English," Laly said. "He's just stubborn."

"Try to feed him," Sugar suggested. "He may not answer you, but he won't turn down food if he's hungry."

Laly glanced up at Sugar and smiled a smile of relief. She seemed to be nearly her old self again. She'd just needed something to take her mind off her own troubles for a while, and this man's problems were, at least for the time being, a whole lot worse than theirs.

Laly scooped a small dollop of gruel onto her spoon and aimed it toward the man's mouth. She wasn't sure he would take it, but at the last second he opened his mouth and accepted her offer.

Samuel took the gruel the white lady held out to him on her spoon. He'd expected her to pull it back at the last moment, then laugh at his gullibility, but she'd actually fed him. He opened his mouth for another bite and felt the gruel filling the empty pit that was his stomach.

Laly smiled when she saw him eating and realized the poor creature, for all his size and apparent strength, was nearly starved. "Why did they do this to you?" she asked him softly.

Samuel met the lady's eyes a moment longer than was proper for a black man. He knew that would explain it. He knew she'd be offended and quit feeding him. He was just grateful to the Lord for the few bites she'd already given him.

Laly waited for the man to speak. He didn't. He looked at her for a moment, making her believe he was about to tell her his story, then he just looked away. She wondered if he was a criminal and too ashamed to admit it. She held up another spoonful of gruel and let her eyes roam over him as he leaned forward to take it. Even sitting, she could see he was of a great height, passing six feet by several inches. The muscles of his shoulders, arms, legs, and chest were thick and well defined. His hands were rough, with thick calluses and many scars. Looking back to his face as he accepted another bite, she decided he was no criminal. This man was used to hard, honest work. "What's your name?" she inquired gently.

Samuel was still surprised that she'd continued feeding him after he'd looked at her so disrespectfully, and now she wanted his name. Turning his head curiously, he tried to size her up. She was definitely a lady, but then, so had his former mistress been a lady, and she was the reason he was here at the slave market. But this woman seemed different. She looked him over, true, but she didn't make him feel dirty when she did it. She seemed genuinely concerned for him. He glanced at her friend still standing next to her. She, too, was obviously a lady. A thought occurred to him. Why were these women being sold in a slave auction? "My name is Samuel," he spoke quietly, his throat still sore from the bruising rope around his neck that had dragged him here from the plantation.

Laly's face lit up at his words. "I'm glad to meet you, Samuel, although I wish it could be under better circumstances. My name is Laly, and this is Sugar."

Samuel nodded at Sugar, then looked back at Laly. "Water?" he ventured.

Laly looked quickly around the room. "Of course, Samuel. I don't know . . ."

"Outside," he rasped.

"I'll get it," offered Sugar.

"Don't . . ." urged Samuel. He looked at Laly. "Don't let her go alone," he said.

Laly smiled warmly at the giant man. "We'll be right back." She stood and headed with Sugar for the door. Stopping briefly to grab a clean bowl, they were soon outside, looking for a water source. Behind the house was a water trough and a pump. Mud and muck surrounded the pump. Mosquitoes and bees swarmed over the brackish water in the trough.

"I think we'd better pump fresh," suggested Sugar.

"I think you're right," agreed Laly. "And let's hurry." She'd noticed several men start walking their way when they'd left the house.

Sugar pumped the handle five or six times before water started to flow. Then it was warm and tinged with brown. "I guess this is as good as it gets," she said.

Laly nodded, quickly filling the bowl. The men who watched them had come even closer, and some of the ribald remarks they were making made warning bells ring in her head. Samuel had been right not to let Sugar fetch the water alone. "Let's get back inside," Laly whispered.

Sugar nodded, and taking Laly's upper arm, they walked together back toward the front of the house.

"You made it." Samuel seemed genuinely relieved.

"Of course we made it. Here, drink this," Laly offered, holding the bowl where he could reach it.

Samuel let the water soothe his parched lips and throat and wash down the horrible concoction that passed as gruel. At least it was nourishment. "Thank you, ma'am," he said.

"Please, call me Laly."

Samuel was bewildered. Where did this fine woman come from? "Why are you being sold?" he asked, before he thought about the propriety of such a question. "I'm sorry," he hurriedly amended.

"We were kidnapped by a despicable pirate named Rodriguez. Have you heard of him?" she asked.

Samuel's eyes widened. "Yes, there's not a soul in the islands who hasn't heard of Rodriguez. But why would he bring you here? Why didn't he ransom you to your families?" Samuel's voice was getting stronger, now that he'd eaten and had some water.

Laly glanced nervously to Sugar, then back at Samuel. How could she explain? She couldn't. "We have no families, Samuel. No families and no property, so Rodriguez turned us over to Gaspar."

"But anyone can see you're not servants," Samuel commented.

Laly felt herself blushing. "He's not selling us as ordinary servants. He's going to sell us as a pair, and promise our buyer that we'll do certain things that we don't do."

Samuel suddenly understood. His chest heaved with anger at what was being done to these kind women. "You will not be sold that way," he growled.

Laly was startled by his reaction. "Samuel, there's

nothing you can do about it. If you try, you'll only get yourself in worse trouble than you already are in. And looking at the chains that hold you, I don't think you can stand any more trouble.''

Samuel looked from Laly to Sugar. His wrists and ankles were raw from the bite of the rough metal against his skin. His back ached from being forced to remain in a bent position, and he knew he smelled atrocious from having to lie in dirt soaked for years by the urine of others. Yet he couldn't abide the thought of what would happen to his new friends once they were sold.

"It's time!" a voice bellowed from outside the fence.

Samuel jerked violently against the chains that held him.

Laly felt her heart lurch with fear as she stood and took Sugar's hand. "At least we're being sold together," she breathed feebly.

Twelve

Bradley sat in the parlor of the governor's mansion and fought the continuing nausea that twisted through him. His head had been tended by the governor's doctor, but it still pounded like the devil himself was banging around inside. "I've got to get back to my ship," he insisted. "I want to start a search for the medallion." He closed his eyes and let his head fall back against the cushion of the sofa.

"Really, Captain Bradley, I commend your tenacity, but the constable is searching even as we speak," Governor Madison assured him.

"But I know what she looks like," Bradley whispered.

"You've given a detailed description. I'm sure there aren't that many female thieves running around with moon-colored hair and turquoise eyes."

Bradley's own eyes flew open. Had he really told the constable she had moon-colored hair? Didn't he just say light blond? Obviously not. "The medallion is probably in Rodriquez's hands by now. If so, I'm sure he's sailed. He wouldn't chance staying near port with so valuable an article in his possession."

"Whether it's in Rodriguez's possession or in the hands of the female thief, you need to rest and recover, and not go running around the island with a search party or sailing off to do battle with a pirate. My doctor says you're lucky to be alive."

"I know that, Sir. But I can't rest until the mystery is solved," he murmured.

"Mystery?" asked the governor.

Bradley blinked several times. "The mystery of the location of the medallion." He couldn't very well tell the governor he was referring to the mystery named Laly.

"Yes, yes." The governor nodded his head. "I do insist, though, you recover some before you join the search. I won't have you dropping dead on my account. Harvey!" he called.

Bradley watched the butler appear like magic. "Sir?"

"See to a carriage for the captain, will you?"

"Yes, Sir," Harvey answered.

"Really, Governor Madison, I can walk," Bradley offered.

"Nonsense, boy. I wouldn't let you walk in this heat if you were a hundred percent well."

Bradley had to allow he was grateful he didn't have to walk back to the *Vengeance*, but as soon as he returned he would sail. Rodriguez already had one tide's head-start.

* * *

"Can you see anything?" Laly asked Sugar.

"No. There are too many people standing in the way."

"Damn it," she hissed. The slave auction had been proceeding for over an hour and so far only four slaves had been sold. Unfortunately, one of those had been Samuel. He'd been led out second, and from the sound of the cheering, he'd brought a nice sum. Laly and Sugar prayed he'd been purchased by a kind person.

"I wonder when we'll be put up," Sugar speculated.

Laly shrugged. This whole course of events was so ridiculous she couldn't imagine what turn they'd take next. Then, as if someone had heard Sugar speak, one of Gaspar's guards came toward them.

"You two. Come now," the guard ordered.

Laly glanced frantically around, hoping for a last-ditch chance of escape. "Where's Indiana Jones when you need him?" she whispered to Sugar.

Sugar smiled weakly. "Obviously, saving some *other* damsels in distress."

The block where the slaves were sold was little more than a five-foot-square raised platform. Laly and Sugar stood in the center, holding hands and staring out at the leering faces of the people in the crowd. Few women attended, and those who did waited in their carriages under the watchful eyes of their menfolk.

"Look there, it's Samuel," Laly pointed out.

Sugar looked where she indicated and saw Samuel sitting in the shade in the back of a carriage that was attended by a footman. "Looks like he may have a decent master," she commented.

"Here we have two lovelies!" shouted Gaspar.

Laly and Sugar both jumped at the sound of his voice.

"These two will be sold as a pair, and I'm firm on that, so don't none of you be tryin' to buy them separately," he continued. "I'd like to draw your attention to their many attributes. As you can see, they both have their own hair and teeth."

Laly watched as he climbed onto the block and approached them. When he tugged roughly on her hair, she let out a yelp that sent a ripple of laughter through the crowd. "Ouch! Damn you!" she hissed.

"Watch it, Missy. I don't mind selling damaged goods," Gaspar threatened. "Now, open your mouth so they can see your teeth."

Laly stepped back defiantly. "I will not!"

"I said, open your mouth," he ground out between clenched jaws.

"Do what he says, Laly," Sugar advised. Gaspar still frightened her. There was something cold about him that she couldn't quite put her finger on, but the fact that he traded in human souls should have given Laly a clue to the man's vicious character.

"He wants me to show these . . . these pigs my teeth. I'm not some horse for sale," she argued.

Gaspar advanced on her. Reaching out with one beefy hand, he grasped her jaw with his fingers and pulled her forward. "I said, open your mouth," he ordered again.

Laly's neck and face ached from the brutality of his grip, but a stubborn streak in her kept her fighting him. "No!" she hissed.

Gaspar reached the end of his patience. Raising his free arm, he swung and connected with the side of her head.

Laly saw stars and heard Sugar scream. Fighting to

remain standing, she felt her mouth opened and filthy fingers probing its interior. Without caring about the consequences, she bit down as hard as she could.

It was Gaspar's turn to cry out in pain, and the laughter of the crowd behind him chilled his blood. No one laughed at Gaspar, no one.

Sugar tried to step between Laly and Gaspar. She could see the rage on the man's face and knew Laly was still reeling from his blow. She'd never remain conscious through another.

"Get this wench away from me," Gaspar yelled to his men.

Before Sugar could do anything, she was grabbed and pulled away from Laly's side. "Don't hurt her, please, Mr. Gaspar. She doesn't know any better. She's always been a troublemaker," Sugar begged.

"It's time she learned to do as she's told," he responded.

Laly wasn't sure what he meant. She only knew she was dizzy from the man's brutality. His second blow sent her to her knees. Another scream from Sugar and a disapproving groan from the crowd was all but drowned out by the blood pounding in her temples. Focusing her eyes became difficult, and she was suddenly very cold. "Go to hell, you bastard," she rasped.

Gaspar heard her curse and raised his arm to strike her again.

"Here, here, man. I'm thinking about purchasing the wench, but I'll not pay top dollar for her if she's all broken up. In fact, I may not purchase her at all. If she looks too bad, she won't serve my purpose."

Gaspar stopped his hand in midswing. "You wish to purchase these women?" He swung around to see who was making his intentions known.

"I may . . . if you can convince me of their worth," the voice called through the crowd.

Sugar searched wildly for the face that belonged to the voice.

Laly could hear, but was still having trouble seeing. "Sugar?" she croaked.

"Let me go to her!" demanded Sugar. Gaspar waved his hand in her direction and she felt herself released. Kneeling at Laly's side, she helped steady her while she tried to stand.

"Who wants to buy us?" asked Laly.

"I don't know. Oh, your face!" Sugar moaned.

"Do I look awful?"

"Just your left cheek and temple. You're beginning to swell, and you may get a black eye out of the deal."

"Good. Maybe no one will want us as sex slaves if we're looking ugly. Want me to punch you once or twice?"

"How can you joke about this?" Sugar wanted to know.

"Maybe I'm just punchy," Laly grinned. "Ouch, it hurts to smile."

Gaspar searched the crowd for the man who'd stopped him from teaching the blonde a lesson. "Shall we start the bidding?" he called loudly.

"Not yet, Gaspar. I want to know more about them," the voice called back.

Gaspar still couldn't see who was speaking. "As you can see, these two women could give any man many nights of pleasure."

A low murmur of approval went through the crowd.

"They are not only beautiful, they are used to working as a pair," he said lasciviously.

"We are not!" rebutted Laly loudly.

Tittering laughter traveled through the crowd.

"It seems the blonde doesn't agree with your statements, Gaspar," the voice remarked.

"She's a feisty one, all right," Gaspar tried to joke. "How do I know she'll perform?"

"How you discipline your slaves once you purchase them is no one's business but your own," Gaspar said to the voice.

"I quite agree, Gaspar." The man stepped around several people and made himself visible. "I would like to inspect them more closely."

Gaspar grinned from ear to ear. "Yes, of course, Mr. Devereaux, Sir."

Laly and Sugar watched as people stepped aside to make a path for Mr. Devereaux. "He must be someone important," observed Sugar.

Laly nodded, and winced with the pain her movement caused. "Mmmm," she agreed.

"Maybe he just wants house servants," Sugar hoped out loud.

Laly watched the man's eyes as he came forward. He wanted no house servants. He wanted what they were being sold as—whores. Raising her jaw, she refused to let herself be intimidated by his lecherous stare. She allowed herself to inspect him in an equally insulting way.

Mr. Devereaux was no more than five foot three or four, and he was nearly as wide as he was tall. His clothes seemed to be of an excellent quality, but no amount of money could hide his many flaws. His face was as round as his body, his jowls hanging below his collar. His pale blue eyes were nearly lost beneath heavy lids, and his lower lip protruded as though he'd filled it with a plug of tobacco and forgotten to remove it. "What a horrid little man," she whispered to Sugar.

Devereaux stepped up on the block and crossed the few feet to where the women stood. He frowned at the bruises Gaspar had put on the blonde's face, but he was satisfied no permanent damage had been done. Walking around them slowly, he was pleased to see straight backs and strong shoulders. Coming back around to stand in front of them, he turned to Gaspar. "May I?" he inquired.

"Be my guest," Gaspar offered.

Before Laly and Sugar knew what he was up to, he reached out and grasped each one of them by one breast and squeezed.

"Hey!" "Ouch!" they screeched in unison. "You dirty old man!" added Laly.

The crowd howled at her remark. Even Devereaux himself chuckled at her observation. "Oh, my dear, you will indeed give me many hours of pleasure before I turn you over to Hattie."

"Who's Hattie?" Laly asked.

"The madam of Dove's Nest Plantation, of course."

"They will give you pleasure only if you pay for them, Mr. Devereaux," Gaspar interrupted.

Devereaux turned to the slaver. "Yes, yes, Gaspar. And what price to you want for them?" he said in a bored tone.

Gaspar looked at Devereaux and wondered how far he could push the wealthy man. "They are up for bid, you know."

Devereaux nodded.

"We'll start the bidding at ... five thousand pounds," Gaspar called across the compound.

Several gasps were heard, and a few people even laughed.

"Really, Gaspar. You don't think anyone is going

to pay you that kind of money for them, do you?" Devereaux asked.

"It's an open auction," Gaspar defended.

"But no one here will pay you that much for two whores."

Gaspar looked around at the faces of the people in the crowd. There were several who could afford to pay, but would they bid against Devereaux? The women he purchased always ended up for sale to the public anyway. Damn it, Gaspar fumed. He'd been happy to see Devereaux's interest in the women at first, certain he'd get a high price from the wealthy man, but now he felt himself loosing out. "What will you pay for them?" he asked grumpily.

"Don't be disappointed, Gaspar. You will be able to enjoy them, too, someday," Devereaux offered.

"Just tell me what you'll pay," he demanded.

"Nine hundred pounds," Devereaux stated with finality.

"Nine hundred pounds!" stuttered Gaspar, appalled.

"But someone will pay me more than that."

Devereaux glanced over the crowd, a superior glaze to his eyes. "I think I can safely say no one here will outbid me."

Gaspar saw his dreams of a quick fortune slipping through his hands and he wondered how he could cheat Rodriguez out of his share. "Very well," he spat. "Give me my money, and take them."

Laly and Sugar watched the exchange and weren't sure what to think. They had been sold as sex slaves to this little pig of a man. "I won't go," announced Laly.

Devereaux heard her statement and turned. "My girls don't defy me, Miss . . .?"

"Laly."

"Miss Laly—hmmm, I like it. And you are?" He turned to Sugar with raised brows.

"Sugar."

"Indeed? I think my luck was good today. Now, back to what I was saying. Laly, Sugar, my girls don't defy me in any way. Those who have have barely lived to regret it. Oh, well, you'll see for yourselves, once we're at the plantation." He turned back toward Gaspar to complete their business.

A cold chill of fear coursed up Laly's back. Something about the way Devereaux had spoken frightened her as Rodriguez's threats and Gaspar's cruelty hadn't.

In minutes they were being led toward the trees and the waiting carriages. A kind of joy leapt in Laly's heart when she saw they were riding in the same carriage as Samuel.

"I didn't know Devereaux bought you, too," Laly whispered as she climbed into the back of the carriage.

"His manservant did the bidding on me. I guess he didn't want anyone to know he was here until he was ready to buy you."

"He wanted us?"

Samuel nodded.

"How did he know we were here?"

He shrugged. "News travels fast on a small island."

The carriage began to roll from under the trees and swung in a wide circle before heading along a street that led away from the waterfront. Laly adjusted her seat for the ride to the plantation, pulling her long skirt under her to form a softer cushion. When she looked up, she saw two familiar faces receding into the distance. "Lawson, Spears!" she called, but she wasn't sure they'd heard her.

"Quiet, Laly," Devereaux ordered sternly. "My girls behave like ladies in public. They don't bellow like fishwives."

Laly glanced at Sugar and bit her lower lip with worry. Seeing Lawson and Spears had renewed her concern over Devon. Was he all right? Had his men found him yet? She whispered a prayer that he was recovering, and another that she would see him again.

Bradley paced the deck of the *Vengeance*. His head was splitting and his stomach refused to hold food. "So where were they being taken?" he demanded.

"We don't know, Sir. They were sitting in the back of a carriage with a black man. The carriage was heading away from the waterfront," Lawson explained for the tenth time. His captain had come aboard ship wounded and in a foul mood, ranting and raving about the mermaids and the governor's mansion. He'd given no one any rest since he and Spears had said they'd seen them leaving town.

Bradley paced again and rubbed his aching head. He was certain Laly had more sense than to stay in Charles Towne visiting people when she'd just stolen the King's Medallion. He'd have been willing to bet his commission she'd be on board the *Puta* with Rodriguez, sailing to another port. "Did you recognize the carriage?" he demanded.

"No, Sir," answered Spears.

"There's got to be an answer," he muttered. "I'm going ashore to find it."

"Do you want us to come with you, Sir?" Lawson asked.

"No, this is my quest," Bradley answered.

Laly and Sugar marveled at the fine furnishings of the room they were to occupy. Watered silk covered the walls, ecru lace adorned the windows and the huge double bed, sculpted carpets covered the hardwood floor, and ornate tapestries and oil paintings hung tastefully around the room.

They'd been given a hearty meal as soon as they'd been shown to their quarters and had been promised baths.

"Do you get the feeling we're being fattened for the slaughter?" Laly asked Sugar.

"Sort of, but I couldn't help eating. We never did eat any of the wonderful gruel we'd been served for breakfast," she answered sarcastically.

A knock at the door took their attention. When the door opened, a beautiful black woman entered pulling a huge brass tub. "Mr. Devereaux says you are to bathe and be ready for him," she said softly.

"He did, did he?" Laly asked indignantly.

"Yes, ma'am. And I am to give you anything you desire."

"How about our freedom?"

The woman cast her eyes down.

"All right. How about some rum?"

"This I can do. I will bring it when I bring your new garments."

"New garments?" Sugar asked.

"Yes, ma'am. Mr. Devereaux said to give you the best in the house." She then backed quietly from the room.

"Rum? You want rum?" Sugar asked incredulously.

"I have an idea," Laly told her.

Sugar closed her eyes for a moment. "Do I want to hear it?"

Laly raised her shoulders. "Maybe."

"Does it include making Devereaux mad?"

"Probably."

Sighing, she asked, "But does it also include getting the hell out of here?"

Laly nodded.

"Okay, then tell me."

A brief knock ended their conversation and preceded the entrance of a servant with two buckets of hot water. Before the woman was through pouring, another servant entered with two more buckets. This process continued for the next several minutes until the tub was full. As the last water carrier left the room, the woman who'd brought the tub arrived with two bundles of clothes and a bottle of rum.

"Thank you," said Laly. "I was wondering if you might bring me one more thing?"

The woman nodded. "If I am able," she answered.

"I have a terrible headache," Laly pointed to the swollen side of her face, "and I have been having trouble sleeping lately. Can you bring me something for my pain and to help me sleep?" she asked innocently.

"You cannot take a sleeping powder before Mr. Devereaux arrives," the woman said.

"Of course not," assured Laly. "I won't even need it until later, but it would be nice to have now so I won't have to disturb you. I don't know how late it will be when we're finished with Mr. Devereaux."

Sugar nearly choked on the laughter she held in check. Laly's plan was obvious now; she just hoped the woman wouldn't get suspicious.

Laly chose that moment to reach for the side of her head as though it throbbed horribly. She moaned softly. "I'm sorry, it's just so painful," she said convincingly.

The woman's eyes softened. "I will bring you the things you ask for. I have had bruises, too."

Laly looked at the woman and couldn't imagine anyone having reason to harm such a quiet, elegant person. "Devereaux?" she asked.

"Yes. Mr. Devereaux sometimes has reasons to punish," she explained softly.

"No human being has the right to harm another," Laly argued.

Sugar touched her on the arm to stop the speech she felt was coming. "You can't change this woman's life, Laly. Don't make it worse."

Laly looked at Sugar. "How can you accept what's going on here?"

"I don't accept it . . . for us. It may be unfair, unjust, brutal, archaic, but it's the acceptable way of life for this time period, and all you'll do ranting about equal rights is cause more harm."

Laly sighed heavily and nodded. "You're right," she acquiesced. Turning back to the woman, she spoke softly. "Please bring me what I need. I'll be very grateful."

The woman bowed slightly and left the room.

Laly walked to the bed and lowered to sit on its edge. "You bathe first. I'm going to lie down for a while."

"Are you all right?" Sugar asked, concerned.

Laly smiled weakly at her friend. "I'm fine. Things around here are just getting to me a little, I think. Wake me when you're through with the tub." She pushed herself further onto the bed and leaned back against the pillows. She was asleep even before she heard Sugar answer.

Bradley walked along the waterfront looking at faces, trying to recognize someone, anyone. He'd been searching for over an hour but hadn't found anyone who knew Laly or Sugar. "Damn it," he mused. "It's as if they didn't exist until recently." He abruptly stopped walking and went back over his thoughts. "No, it isn't possible," he told himself. "They just aren't from this island," he said out loud. But each time he thought about Laly's remarkable looks, he realized that if she'd been anywhere in the area for any length of time, someone would have seen her. Shaking himself mentally, he decided to go to the Blue Parrot. Perhaps the barkeep would be able to tell him something.

The crowd at the Blue Parrot was the usual group of wharf rats and scoundrels. Bradley surveyed the room as he entered and seated himself with his back against the wall.

"What can I get ye, Sir?" Hodges asked.

"Just the answer to a question, if you've a mind to tell."

"Tell what?"

"Where the two women you had working in here yesterday might have gone off to."

"How would I know that?" asked Hodges.

"They spent the whole day here. Surely they've been here before? You might remember who some of their friends are, if you try," he said, as he placed a coin on the table.

Hodges eyed the money. "Is that for me?" he inquired.

"If you answer my question."

Hodges picked up the coin. "All I have to do is answer your question?"

Bradley nodded.

Hodges made a tight fist around the coin. "I never saw 'em before in me life. They come in and sat themselves down at that table over there," he waggled his bar towel toward the other side of the room, "and they asked fer water."

"You've never seen them before? Are you sure? They may have been with a pirate named Rodriguez."

"They ain't been in here before," he insisted. "Ye think I don't know who's been in my place and who hasn't? I'd especially remember that blond one. She was right nasty. Besides, Rodriguez don't like grown women. He likes 'em young."

Bradley remembered his run-in with Rodriguez over the child he'd later murdered. "Yes, I'd forgotten," he said in a clipped tone.

"I get to keep this?" Hodges asked holding out his fist.

"Yes," Bradley scowled. "Bring me an ale," he ordered.

Hodges nodded and hurried away.

Bradley watched him go behind the bar. The man was a fool. He himself had been in the Blue Parrot before and had not been recognized. Of course, he had been disguised. And he had a point about Laly's looks. She wasn't easily forgotten. But if Laly and Sugar had never been in the Blue Parrot before, why had they chosen it as their destination the day before? And why had they remained there all day, if not waiting to meet someone, that someone logically being Rodriguez?

When Hodges set a mug of ale in front of him, he

tossed down payment and grabbed the mug, bringing it to his lips.

"Ye know, someone else was askin' about those women," Hodges ventured, hoping to increase his purse.

Bradley set the mug down hard in front of him. "Who?"

"Let's see, now." Hodges rubbed his chin as though trying to recall.

"Maybe this will help you remember," Bradley remarked, dropping a heavy coin on the table.

Hodges hurriedly picked it up. "Rodriguez asked about the ladies, too."

"Rodriguez was here yesterday?"

"Right after the ladies left. He wanted to know what they'd been doing here all day."

"Did he act as though he'd expected to meet them here?" Bradley demanded, his eyes narrow slits.

Hodges took a step back from the threatening look of the captain. "No, Sir. He just wanted to know what they'd been doing and where they went."

"Did you tell him?"

"Only that they'd been whoring and washed a few dishes for me—and not very well, I might add. I didn't know where they went."

"They aren't whores," said Bradley, certain he was correct.

"Ye may be right. They didn't do no business. 'Course, they wanted more for themselves than any sane man would pay." complained Hodges.

"Really?"

"They was askin' one hundred pounds, they was."

Bradley nearly laughed out loud, understanding Laly's ploy for what it was. But his mood quickly shifted. He stood and looked down on the barkeep.

"Are you sure you didn't tell Rodriguez where they'd gone?" he asked in a menacing tone.

"I'm sure," Hodges answered, a twinge of fear running through him at the implied threat of the captain's stance.

Bradley studied the barkeep's eyes. After a few seconds, he decided the man was telling the truth. Sitting back down, he raised the mug and swallowed a gulp of the stale brew. "You can go," he directed Hodges, when he noticed the man still standing next to the table. He watched him scurry away nervously.

Bradley finished his ale and tried to decide what course to take next. He knew he should be sailing in search of Rodriguez and the medallion, but the knowledge that Laly was still in Charles Towne somewhere kept him from leaving. He needed to settle things with her once and for all. He needed to catch her in her deceit, making her suffer the punishment for her crimes, and hopefully get her out of his system. Or he would prove her innocence and complete what he'd started with her in the moonlight.

Thirteen

Bradley finished several more mugs of ale before he was ready to leave the Blue Parrot. The weak brew had finally started to dull his nerves, taking away a little of the pain that throbbed in his head. Standing, he surveyed the room one last time before he headed toward the door. He'd had no luck here. Perhaps he'd be more fortunate back on the waterfront.

Stepping out onto the street, he'd begun his trip toward the docks when Rodriguez's name, spoken in the crowd, caught his attention. Turning to see who was speaking, he recognized several of the *Puta*'s crew.

Ducking into a narrow alleyway, he watched the men go into the Blue Parrot. Was the *Puta* still anchored near the island? Why hadn't Rodriguez sailed yet? Did Laly still have the medallion? Was he waiting for her to deliver it? Or perhaps she wasn't working with the pirate after all? No, he wouldn't let himself hope.

Bradley stepped back out onto the street once the

Puta's crewmen were out of sight. Nearing the Blue Parrot's door, he peered in to see the men seated at a table ordering ale and a meal. "I've got to know," he murmured. He wanted to rush in and demand they tell him what they knew about Laly, but he knew they'd tell him nothing. Then an idea occurred to him. Backing away from the door, he made his way around to the rear of the building. Pushing open a weathered door, he entered a small workroom where a young woman stood washing dishes.

"Don't be alarmed," he spoke softly when she looked up. "I only want to speak to the barkeep, Mr. . . . ?"

"Hodges," she supplied.

"Yes, Hodges. Will you call him for me, please?"

The woman looked wary, but she walked over to the door between the washroom and the bar. "Hodges, there's . . ."

"Don't tell him I'm here," Bradley quickly interrupted.

She shrugged her shoulders. "Can ye come back 'ere a moment?"

"What do you want, wench?" Hodges called back.

"I just need ye for a moment," she tried again.

Hodges slung his bar towel over his shoulder and started toward the back. Magda had shown up for work this morning, but the first thing she'd said was that she'd stand for no funny business. He raised one brow. Maybe she'd changed her mind. He was grinning hopefully when he lifted the carpet between the rooms. "What do you want?" he demanded when he saw Bradley.

"I want you to keep your voice down, for starters," Bradley threatened quietly.

Hodges clamped his jaws tightly. "What are you doing back here?" he asked through clenched teeth.

Bradley walked to the door and pulled back the carpet so he could peek at Rodriguez's men. "Come here," he told Hodges. "See those men? The ones who just came in?"

"Yes."

"Those are Rodriguez's men," Bradley explained.

"Yes," Hodges said suspiciously. He wanted no part of anything that involved the pirate.

"I want you to ask them something for me. Can you do that without making them wonder why you're asking?"

"That depends on what ye're havin' me ask 'em."

"I want you to find out if they know where the women went that were in here yesterday."

"The ones ye were askin' me about?"

"Yes."

Hodges remembered the money he'd been paid for answering a question. "It'll cost ye," he said greedily.

Bradley looked the man over. "I've got twenty pounds here. If you find out where they are, it's yours. If you find out nothing, I'll give you two pounds for your trouble."

Hodges looked the captain over. "How will ye know if I tell ye the truth?"

Bradley stood to his full height. "Because I'll be checking out what ever you tell me. If I find out you've lied to me, I'll come back and take the money out of your hide."

Hodges sighed. "All right, I'll see what I can find out," he murmured, as he pushed his way past the hanging carpet.

Bradley waited and waited. He peered through the opening at the crewmen and Hodges talking. He waited some more. "Come on," he hissed impatiently. Finally, he saw Hodges walk away from their table and start back around the bar.

"What did you learn?" Bradley demanded, as soon as Hodges was through the door. "Where are they?"

"The money first," Hodges announced.

"Do you know where they are?" Bradley asked, one brow raised skeptically.

"I do. The money."

Bradley dug for the twenty pounds, then held it out without releasing it. "Where are they?"

Hodges lowered one lid slightly, sizing up whether he could trust the captain or not. "They were sold at the slave market this morning."

Bradley was certain he'd heard wrong. "They *what?* You must be mistaken."

"I know what they told me. Rodriguez himself delivered 'em to Gaspar."

Bradley couldn't believe this. Rodriguez had double-crossed Laly and Sugar! Which meant he *did* have the medallion. "Why, then, is he still anchored nearby?" he wondered out loud.

"The men say Rodriguez is waiting for his share of the sale from Gaspar," Hodges offered.

Bradley dropped the twenty pounds into Hodges' waiting hand. "You did well. Thank you." He turned toward the door. Just before leaving, he asked over his shoulder, "Who were they sold to?"

Hodges shrugged. "They didn't know."

"Don't worry, I'll find out," seethed Bradley, as he left the Blue Parrot.

* * *

Sugar held up the garments Devereaux expected them to wear. "He's got to be kidding," she commented incredulously.

"What?" Laly asked waking up.

"Oh, I'm sorry. I didn't mean to wake you," apologized Sugar.

Laly pushed herself up on the bed. "It's okay. What were you talking about?"

"This." Sugar showed her the costumes Devereaux had sent for them. "He thinks he's some kind of sheik and we're the harem."

Laly climbed off the bed and reached for the costume Sugar held in front of her. The top was a cap-sleeved bra covered with beads and colorful embroidery. The bottom was little more than a bikini with see-through pantaloons to wear over it. "The dirty old pervert. He doesn't even know how ahead of his time he is," she remarked.

"I wouldn't even wear this in the twentieth century, let alone now," said Sugar.

Laly looked at her through the fabric of the pantaloons. "Oh, yes you will," she said.

"You can't be serious!"

Laly pursed her lips while she pondered her plan. "We've got to convince him he's irresistible."

"Nooo," moaned Sugar.

"Yesss," mimicked Laly. "Did my headache and sleeping powders arrive?"

"Yes. I put them on the table."

"Good." Laly grinned. She felt better, now that she'd slept for a while. "Did you bathe?"

Sugar nodded.

"Then I'll jump in quickly and be ready to try on my costume."

Sugar shook her head. "I can't believe we're doing this."

"Don't worry. If all goes well, we'll be out of here before morning."

"Then all we'll have to do is steal the medallion back from a bloodthirsty pirate, steal a boat, and head out to sea in search of a storm no one saw the last time it blew through," Sugar complained under her breath.

"What's that?" Laly asked, as she stepped into the tub.

"Nothing, just take your bath. I'll try on this lovely outfit."

Laly giggled at her friend's sarcasm. "We'll be fine, Sugar."

Sugar just nodded as she held up the tiny costume.

Bradley banged on Gaspar's door loudly. He'd found no one who knew, or would tell him, who'd bought Laly and Sugar. "Gaspar, open up. I know you're in there."

"Go away, Rodriguez. I told you I don't have the money yet," Gaspar yelled through the bolted door.

Bradley's brows rose in speculation. So Gaspar owes Rodriguez money, he thought. That would explain Rodriguez's still being in town. "This isn't Rodriguez, and I want nothing from you but information . . . information I may be willing to pay for," Bradley yelled through the door.

Gaspar peered out through a tiny crack. The man standing outside looked formidable, but he'd said he wanted nothing but information. And he was willing to pay. But maybe this was a trap set by Rodriguez. "How do I know you weren't sent by Rodriguez?" he called.

"Because I'll kill the bloody bastard with my bare hands when I find him," Bradley promised.

Gaspar could hear the truth in the man's words. "Very well." He raised the wooden barrier across the door and opened it slowly. "What information do you require?"

"I want to know who bought the women Rodriguez brought to you."

Gaspar took a step back. "Rodriguez promised me they belonged to no one. Even the women could tell me of no one who would miss them. I swear I wouldn't have sold them if . . ."

"Shut up, Gaspar," Bradley threatened. "I only want to know where they are now."

Gaspar closed his mouth for a moment. He hadn't made as much money on the two as he'd have liked. Perhaps this was his opportunity to make up the difference. "You said you'd be willing to pay?"

"Yes," said Bradley, his brows lowering.

"Well, the gentleman who bought them is very discreet," Gaspar remarked, his hands together as though in prayer.

"Yes?"

"Yes. He's instructed me to keep his purchases a secret. You can't expect me to disclose information about a regular customer?"

"Hmmm."

"I'm sure you understand I must be trustworthy where my customers' wishes are concerned."

"How much will it cost to make you less trustworthy?" Bradley questioned.

"Well, a thousand pounds, perhaps?"

Bradley raised one brow and clenched his jaw in anger. He took a step toward Gaspar. "I think you place too high a price on your loyalty. In fact, I think your price would be next to nothing if any other sort of inducement were added."

"Oh?" Gaspar said nervously.

"Yes. I believe you'd divulge all you know, with the right encouragement." Bradley placed his hand over the butt of his pistol resting in his belt.

Gaspar laughed weakly. "I suppose the gentlemen wouldn't mind terribly if I mentioned his most recent purchase."

Bradley waited for him to continue.

"I should still be compensated for the information."

Bradley merely nodded.

"They were sold to Devereaux."

"Devereaux?"

"Yes, of the Dove's Nest Plantation."

"That place is a brothel," Bradley ground from between his teeth.

"They were whores. Where did you think they'd end up?" Gaspar asked.

"Did they tell you they were whores?"

"No. They said they weren't, but I didn't believe them."

Bradley backed away from Gaspar's shack. "Here's your payment, little man. If they've been harmed, I'll be back to teach you to listen to women when they tell you something." He tossed several small coins in the dirt in front of Gaspar.

"If this weren't so serious, I'd be laughing like an idiot," said Laly, as she looked at her and Sugar's reflections in the mirror in their room. "We look like we belong in a rerun of *I Dream of Jeannie*."

"I just wish we could blink our way out of here," said Sugar.

Laly turned from side to side and viewed her costume. The bra was pale blue with white beads sewn in intricate circles and curls. The bottom was of the same blue, but the pantaloons were a white see-through fabric. It had taken them several tries to decide that the bikini-like bottom was to be worn over the pantaloons, and they still weren't sure they were wearing the outfits properly. Sugar's costume was similar in design, but it was a deep red.

"How much longer do you think we'll have to wait until the 'sheik' gets here?" Sugar wondered.

Laly shrugged. "Who knows? I only wonder how long it'll take for him to pass out after we give him the sleeping and headache powders."

"You don't think it's dangerous, do you?"

"Giving him the powders?"

Sugar nodded.

"I don't really care. He didn't have us dressed like this to have us read him Scheherazade's *Thousand and One Nights*."

"I know," murmured Sugar.

Laly understood her friend's concern. "Don't worry, I'm sure he'll be fine. He'll just get a good night's sleep."

Two hours later a soft knock on their door announced Devereaux's arrival.

"Ah, ladies, you look lovely," he cooed, as his pale blue eyes ogled them.

"Do you like what we're wearing?" Laly asked coyly.

"Yes, my dear Laly. I had these clothes made espe-

cially for my most beautiful guests. Do you approve?"
Devereaux circled Laly, then Sugar, as he spoke.

"Sugar and I could speak of little else since we saw
them," said Laly, hoping he wouldn't hear the slightly
sarcastic note she couldn't force from her voice. She
was relieved to see him smile at her words.

"Would you care for some rum?" Sugar offered.

"No, thank you, my dear. Maybe later," he
answered. "I don't want anything to numb my . . .
senses."

"Oh . . . of course," stammered Sugar, giving Laly
a panicked look behind Devereaux's back.

"You don't mind if we enjoy a drink, do you? We've
found in our . . . shall we call them adventures . . .
that rum actually enhances the pleasure."

"Really?" Devereaux asked. "I've never heard that
before."

"What a pity, you've missed so much."

"Well, maybe I'll have just a little," he agreed.

Sugar could barely keep a straight face as Laly
picked up the rum bottle. "Here, Mr. Devereaux.
Come sit beside me," she invited, diverting his attention from what Laly was doing.

"Yes, my dear. You're called Sugar—correct?"

"That's right, Mr. Devereaux."

"Because you're of a sweet disposition?"

"No, for another reason entirely," she said sugges-
tively.

Devereaux practically started drooling at her
remark. He took the glass of rum from Laly and raised
it high. "I'd like to toast my good fortune in finding
you two wonderful creatures."

"Thank you, Mr. Devereaux," simpered Laly. She
watched Devereaux swallow the entire contents of his
glass and winked at Sugar over the rim of hers while

she sipped gingerly of the potent liquid. "And here's to you. We had no idea how fortunate we were when you purchased us until we arrived at your lovely home. Why, Mr. Devereaux, your glass is empty. Let me fill it for you."

"I'll pour this round, Laly," offered Sugar.

"Thank you, Sugar. I'll keep Mr. Devereaux company. Would you like a back rub?" she offered.

"My goodness, that would be nice," Devereaux beamed. He'd been afraid the two new girls were going to give him trouble. Instead, they were being more than accommodating.

"Let me help you out of your coat." Laly grimaced as she removed Devereaux's coat. Body odor wafted from the fabric and the heat of damp perspiration clung to the garment. He obviously didn't practice the same bathing habits that he expected of his slaves.

"Here we are," offered Sugar. "A full glass of rum. This will make you feel . . . wonderful," she purred.

Devereaux's beady little eyes nearly popped from his head as Sugar bent to hand him his drink. She wasn't as voluptuous as Laly, but her breasts were firm and full, and he'd just been given a very good view of them in the low-cut top she wore. "My, my, we are having fun, aren't we?"

Laly grinned and put her finger on the bottom of his glass as he drank, making him finish every drop. "We certainly are." She winked at him. "And it's only going to get better. Now, lie down and I'll give you that back rub."

Devereaux climbed onto the bed and lay facedown. He had some very specific ideas about what he wanted them to do later, but if they wanted to start the evening off by massaging him, he'd certainly oblige them.

Laly let her lip curl in disgust as she gripped Devereaux's shoulders. The oils from his body had soaked the fine fabric of his shirt. Rolling her eyes at Sugar, she shuddered with revulsion. "My, I'm thirsty. Sugar, dear, would you please get us all another drink?" she asked.

Devereaux smiled into the bedclothes. He was beginning to feel warm all over, and his lower parts were swollen with desire from Laly's gentle touch on his back. He decided he'd have her massage him all over before the night was through.

Sugar filled their glasses once more, carefully putting the sleeping and headache powders into Devereaux's rum. She had to be careful to put enough in to do the job, but not so much that he'd notice the white stuff in his drink. "Here we are again. Too bad we don't have a straw. You wouldn't even have to sit up then," she said as she approached the bed.

"A what, Sugar, dear?"

Sugar realized straws probably hadn't been invented yet and looked to Laly for advice.

Laly shrugged her shoulders. "My goodness, Mr. Devereaux, you seem to be very tense," she said while increasing the pressure with her fingers.

"Mmmm, that feels good," groaned Devereaux. "Laly, I believe I'll keep you around a while. Your hands are divine."

Making a gagging face behind his back, she crossed her eyes and stuck out her tongue. "Mr. Devereaux, Sir, I can't tell you how that makes me feel," she crooned.

Sugar bit her lip to stifle the giggles that threatened to erupt over Laly's behavior. "Let's have our drinks, shall we?" she just barely managed to say.

"Yes, let's," agreed Devereaux, pushing his weight

up off the bed. "I'll let you massage me some more in a minute, all right, Laly?"

Laly just smiled and took her drink. She couldn't have forced a pleasant answer for all the money in the world. Devereaux was a pompous pig. The very idea, that he'd "let" her massage him! As if she couldn't think of anything she'd rather do than rub his greasy body. Sipping her rum, she watched him down his in one gulp. She knew he'd be easy to drug. A man of his girth probably never tasted his food, just gobbled it down like the porker he was.

Devereaux watched the two women before him and decided it was time to make things more interesting. "I'm getting very warm. Perhaps you ladies would be so kind as to help me remove my clothing, slowly," he told them.

Sugar gulped with surprise, her eyes opening wide.

Laly, in contrast, lowered her lids in challenge. "Really, Mr. Devereaux, it's quite comfortable in here."

"I'm warm," he repeated, wondering if he was going to have trouble with the women after all.

Laly opened her mouth to argue, but Sugar interrupted. "Do you have a deck of cards, Mr. Devereaux?"

"Cards? What?"

"Yes, cards. You indicated you'd like us to remove your clothing. Wouldn't it be more exciting to turn it into a game?"

"Well, I don't know."

Laly smiled sideways at her friend. Leave it to Sugar to come up with cheating at cards to save a bad situation. "What a good idea," she exclaimed. "I'm sure you'll enjoy the game, Mr. Devereaux."

"I don't know," he answered skeptically.

"Please, Mr. Devereaux? Try just one game. If you don't like it, we'll stop," Sugar pouted.

Devereaux pursed his thick lips. "I suppose it wouldn't hurt to play one game. As long as it doesn't take too long."

"Good. Where are the cards?"

Devereaux pointed toward a small desk near the door. "I think there are some in there."

Sugar crossed to the desk and opened the top drawer. Bringing the deck back to the bed, she smiled at Laly. "Why don't you refresh our drinks while I shuffle and explain the rules to our host?"

"What a good idea."

Minutes later, after they'd played the first hand, Devereaux chuckled as he removed his shirt.

"You know, you can remove any item you chose. It doesn't have to be a main article of clothing," instructed Sugar.

"I know, but I really am getting very warm. Aren't you ladies finding it stifling in here?"

Laly and Sugar exchanged glances. Perhaps the powders were taking effect and causing him to feel excessively warm. "It *is* a bit hot in here," agreed Laly, not wanting him to become suspicious. "May I open a window?"

"Yes, yes," said Devereaux, waving a hand toward the one beside the bed.

Laly nearly jumped at the chance to open the window. She and Sugar had looked out earlier, but opening it while Devereaux was still conscious would alleviate any suspicion, should someone come to question it. "Are we ready for our next hand?" she asked, as she returned to the bed.

Sugar nodded and began to deal.

Devereaux laughed again when he lost, but only removed his shoes. "It seems you two have tremendous luck," he observed.

Sugar smiled innocently. "It does seem the cards are running in our favor, doesn't it?"

The next hand Laly lost. Sugar grinned and raised her shoulders as Laly tried to decide which tiny piece of clothing she'd remove.

"I need a moment of privacy, anyway. I'll just think about it while I'm in the next room," she said, as she headed toward the water closet.

"Yes, my dear." Devereaux waved her away and tried to focus on the cards Sugar had just dealt him. "Opening the window didn't seem to help much. I'm still very warm," he said, his words slurring slightly.

"Maybe you need another drink," suggested Sugar.

"No, I definitely don't need another drink," he answered. "If I didn't know better, I'd think you were trying to get me drunk," he remarked. "But it takes a lot more than a few glasses of rum to do me in," he said, winking.

Sugar's pulse leapt with concern. She didn't want him becoming suspicious and calling for help. Laughing weakly, she assured him, "Mr. Devereaux, there's no way a fine figure of man like you could be affected by a few little glasses of rum. Laly and I know that."

Devereaux smiled in satisfaction and nodded. "Just so you know."

Laly returned then. She'd had a hard time removing her pantaloons in the confines of the tiny water closet, but she'd decided they were the only things she could take off without ending up nearly naked. "As long as I was in there, I decided to leave these off. Do you approve?" she asked Devereaux.

Devereaux nodded sleepily. "Mmmm, you look . . . lovely," he stammered.

It was obvious the sleeping and headache powders were beginning to work. "One more drink should do it," she said out loud without thinking.

"Should do what?" Devereaux asked, his brows lowered in a scowl.

"Why . . . ah . . . put us in the mood, of course," she tried to cover her error.

"I am already in the mood," he stated. "In fact, I've been in the mood since I arrived. You two have been stalling, and you've done it well. Until now I really wasn't aware of your deceit." He reached a hand out toward Laly. "Come here, wench," he ordered.

"Mr. Devereaux," she said hurriedly. "I don't know what you're talking about. We've just been enjoying our evening with you."

"I didn't come here to play card games, or even to receive a massage, although you can massage something else right now."

Laly gulped with concern. How was she going to get out of this?

"Really, Mr. Devereaux," Sugar joined the conversation. "We don't know what you mean. We've been doing what we always do with our clients. All the men we've serviced before have liked to start the evening this way," she lied.

"Well, I've had enough." His eyelids drooped as he spoke.

Please, Lord, let the powders take effect, Laly prayed.

"Come here," Devereaux ordered. "We'll just lie back here on the bed together and you can show me what else you do for your clients."

Laly dropped the pantaloons on the floor and slowly started walking toward the bed. Sugar was sitting as far from Devereaux as possible, but he reached out and took her hand, pulling her closer. "We'll have a good time," she said weakly.

Devereaux leaned back against the pillows and adjusted himself in the middle of the bed. He wanted them on either side of him so he could enjoy them equally.

Sugar let herself be pulled only so far toward Devereaux. "Laly?" she groaned.

Laly crossed the room and sat on the edge of the bed. "Are you sure you don't want me to finish your back rub?" she tried.

"No, I want . . . I want you," Devereaux was suddenly getting so drowsy he could barely keep his eyes open. What was wrong with him? He was never affected by rum this badly. Shaking his head and blinking, he tried to focus his eyes on the blonde. "I want you to do what I bought you for," he finished.

Laly's heart leapt when she saw him having trouble finishing his thoughts and focusing his eyes. "Are you feeling all right, Mr. Devereaux? You look a little pale," she told him.

Sugar glared at Laly. All they needed was for her to make him think there was something wrong with him.

"I'm fine," Devereaux grumbled, blinking again. "I'm just a little sleepy. Suddenly his eyes opened wide. "You did this," he hissed at Laly. "Gaspar *said* you were troublesome. You did this to me. What did you put in my drinks?" he demanded.

Sugar winced when he squeezed down on her hand in anger. "We didn't do anything to you," she complained.

Laly tried to smile at him although her heart pounded with the fear that he was going to yell for help at any moment. "Mr. Devereaux, I can assure you, we did nothing to your drinks. Sugar and I drank from the same bottle. Maybe you're coming down with a virus."

"Maybe I'm what?"

"Maybe you're becoming ill. Should I get a cool cloth for your head?"

"I don't need ... you ... to do anything ... for me." Devereaux's head sagged as he spoke. "I'll kill you ... for this," he threatened, as he lost consciousness.

"Yes!" Laly nearly shouted. "Let's get the hell out of here!"

"I'm right behind you," Sugar laughed, relieved Devereaux had fallen asleep. "Are you going to get dressed?"

"I'm not taking the time to do anything but run. We don't know how long he'll be out. Just grab your dress and let's go."

Fourteen

Bradley rode toward the Dove's Nest at breakneck speed. He'd managed to pay a stablehand to let him use the horse beneath him, and he was pushing the poor animal to its limits. Ever since he'd learned from Gaspar that Laly and Sugar had been sold to a brothel owner, he'd been frantic with worry. Laly might be many things, but he knew she was no whore. "I'm coming, Laly," he breathed into the night. "Come on, you nag!" he berated the horse.

Laly and Sugar tried to climb from the window, but upon looking closer, realized rosebushes grew around the outside of the house. Neither of them wanted to land in the prickly plants.

"What do we do now?" whispered Sugar.

"We go through the house."

"We'll get caught," she worried.

"It's the house or the roses," Laly told her.

"None of this is going to be easy, is it?" Sugar breathed.

"I don't think it's supposed to be," said Laly.

"What do you mean?"

"I'm not really sure. I just sort of feel like I'm being tested."

"Great. And I'm just along for the ride," sighed Sugar.

Laly tugged on her arm. "Quit complaining. How many other history professors get to have an adventure like this?"

"I prefer my history in books, thank you very much."

Laly rolled her eyes and shook her head. "Come on." She slowly opened the door and peered out and down the hall. Opening the door further, she stepped out and pulled Sugar after her, closing the door silently behind them. "I hope that old goat sleeps for a week," she whispered.

Making their way down the hall, they passed several doors that were probably bedrooms. "Should we try another window?" suggested Sugar.

Laly shook her head. "The roses looked like they go all around the house. Besides, we don't know who might be in these rooms. I think we'd better head for the front door."

The wing of the house that was made up of bedrooms opened off a hallway that led to the main part of the house. As they neared the center of the building, they realized it might be easier to get out unnoticed through one of the back entrances. "I think the kitchen is this way," whispered Laly.

Sugar followed silently behind, praying with every step.

Soon they were standing in the doorway to a huge

kitchen. Laly pointed toward the door at the far end of the room. Tiptoeing into the kitchen, she glanced nervously around her in the moonlight at the hanging pots, cupboards, cutting boards, two stone ovens, and the table and benches that filled the room. She stopped, breathless for a moment, when she heard the soft mewing of a cat. "Just a cat," she mouthed to Sugar, and continued to lead the way.

As she neared the end of a long cupboard, she heard the cat again. Turning toward the noise, she froze in terror at the sight of a deformed creature staring at her in the semidarkness.

Sugar grabbed Laly's arm in fear and clutched her hand over her mouth to keep from screaming.

It took Laly several seconds to gain the strength to try and speak, but she was unable to find the words.

Quietly, in a rasping voice, the creature spoke. "You are leaving?"

Laly just nodded. Her horror was subsiding and being replaced by anger and pity. The creature was a woman, or had been a woman, her face horribly disfigured. One eye was missing, the lid hanging loosely over the empty socket. Scars pulled and puckered the skin over her face in several places. Half her nose was missing as though sliced in two, exposing one nostril nearly up to the empty eye socket. Her mouth was twisted downward by a massive scar that deformed her jaw and distorted her speech.

"I left once, too," the woman mumbled. "This is what he did when he caught me."

Laly caught her breath in her throat. "He? Devereaux did this to you?" she asked, unable to believe one human being could do something like this to another.

The woman nodded. "I don't try to leave now. No

one would want me anymore." She lowered to sit on a pile of blankets and rags near the cupboard. A cat curled next to her. "You'd better run far, so he doesn't find you," she said, rubbing the cat's fur.

Laly looked to the horror-stricken Sugar. "Are you ready?"

Sugar just nodded. She didn't trust herself to speak. She was afraid she'd start to cry. Glancing back at the poor creature as they passed, she noticed how she lovingly held the cat, whispering softly into its fur. She shuddered with emotion, and followed closely behind Laly. Devereaux was a worse demon than either one of them had guessed. It had become imperative that they get away quickly and find their way back to their own time.

Once outside, Laly led the way across the lawn to the trees that skirted the yard. Under their protective shadow, she began to run, listening for Sugar's footsteps behind her. She kept remembering the woman in the kitchen, and her fear increased with each step.

Only a short distance from the house, she heard a man's voice calling her name. Her heart lurched to her throat in fear it might be Devereaux, but a moment later she realized it was Samuel.

"Samuel, where are you?" she whispered.

"Here, I'm over here," Samuel tried to guide her.

Laly followed the sound of his voice and soon found him tied to a tree. "What are you doing out here?" she questioned.

Samuel looked to the ground, embarrassed to tell his white friend what Devereaux had planned for him.

"Samuel?" Sugar asked softly.

Samuel looked into the compassionate eyes of Sugar. "Devereaux said he would have me castrated

in the morning. When I tried to fight, he had me
tied here. He said it would do me good to spend the
night on the ground. It would make me appreciate
the bed I would be given later.''

"That monster," Laly hissed, the memory of the
poor woman in the kitchen still haunting her. She
quickly knelt beside Samuel and began to untie the
knots that held him.

"You have to hurry, Miss Laly. I have a guard. He
went to the pump behind the house to get a drink.
He'll be back any second.''

Fear clutched Laly's heart. If they were discovered,
they'd all be punished in ways too horrible to contem-
plate. "Sugar, help me.''

Sugar knelt down and began tugging at the knots,
too. "Damn it, they're so tight," she cursed.

"Just keep working, we don't have much time.''
Laly pulled against the ropes with all her strength.
Finally, one of the knots gave way. After a few more
seconds, another, then another, but before they
could totally free Samuel, they heard the guard
returning.

"Get back," warned Samuel. His hands were free
and he knew what he had to do.

Laly and Sugar ducked behind some trees not far
away and waited. They hoped the guard would find
another reason to leave so they could finish untying
Samuel.

"So, Samuel. That water was mighty good. Too bad
Mr. Devereaux didn't tell me you could have any,"
taunted the guard.

Samuel's black eyes narrowed as he looked at the
hated guard. "I don't need anything from you," he
responded.

"You ain't thirsty?" the guard asked.

Samuel just shook his head. "I wouldn't tell you if I was," he answered. "And I wouldn't drink after the likes of you, anyway."

"Why, you uppity . . ." The guard stepped toward Samuel with his musket held high. He'd teach this slave a thing or two.

Before the guard could strike, Samuel reached up and jerked him downward. Wrapping a piece of rope around his neck, he choked him to unconsciousness, then signaled Laly and Sugar to come help him tie him up. In a matter of minutes Samuel was free and the guard was tied to the tree in his place.

"We can't let him yell for help if he wakes up," observed Laly. Ripping a piece of fabric from the dress she carried, she stuffed it in the guard's mouth and secured it with another strip. "That should buy us a little more time," she said.

Following the road that led toward town, they ran as fast as they could from Dove's Nest.

Bradley keep his mount to the center of the road, the moonlight illuminating only small areas of ground where the trees broke for short intervals. He didn't want to take a fall and end up on foot. He had to get to Laly as soon as possible. There was no telling what atrocities she was being subjected to.

Sugar needed to stop and rest. "Wait!" she called breathlessly after Laly and Samuel.

Laly stopped and looked back. "Are you all right?" she asked.

"I just need to catch my breath for a second."

Samuel walked back to where she stood leaning against a tree. "We need to keep moving," he said.

"You go on ahead, Samuel."

He looked around them into the dark night. "No, I won't leave you here."

Laly smiled up at the big man. "You're very special, Samuel. Thank you," she said.

Samuel looked down at the small blond woman. She was so different from any other white woman he'd ever known. He glanced at Sugar and realized they both were. Neither one talked down to him in any way. They treated him as an equal, even putting themselves in more danger to help him. And they wanted nothing in return. The woman he'd worked for before the slave market had granted him condescending favors, but she'd wanted plenty in return. He remembered with disgust the many times he'd had to service her. It probably would have continued forever if she hadn't given birth to a mulatto child, his child. His dead child.

He closed his eyes against the memory. She'd drowned his baby and sent him to the slave market. He opened his eyes again and looked at Laly. There was no deceit in her face, only friendly concern. He'd protect these women with his last breath.

"Are you about ready, Sugar?" Laly asked.

Sugar took a deep breath. "I think so."

"We can wait another minute, if you need to."

Sugar pushed herself away from the tree. "No, we can go on."

"Shhh," Samuel held up a warning hand. "Someone's coming."

"Devereaux?" Laly whispered in terror.

"No, the other direction. It's someone from town. Get down."

Laly and Sugar clasped one another and crouched in fear beneath the tree Sugar had just rested against. "Dear God, help us get away from here," Laly prayed.

Hoofbeats grew closer and louder. Whoever rode toward them seemed to be in a hurry. In an instant they could see the rider as he passed through the patches of moonlight on the road.

"Devon!" Laly shouted, startling Sugar and Samuel as she jumped up and ran for the road.

Devon nearly unseated himself, jerking hard on the reins so as not to run over the apparition that jumped to the road in front of him. "Whoa!" he ordered his frightened mount. "Whoa. Who goes there?" he demanded.

Laly hadn't thought about the danger of dashing in front of a running horse, she'd only known she had to get to Devon before he rode past her. "Devon, it's me," she said weakly, shaking with fright at the side of the road.

"Laly? Is it really you?"

Samuel stepped behind Laly and glared at the man on horseback. "Do you know him, Miss Laly?" he asked.

"Yes," she murmured, not sure of the greeting she'd receive from the captain. They hadn't parted under the best of circumstances.

Devon jumped from the saddle and tried to calm the excited horse as he made his way to Laly. He couldn't believe she was standing in front of him. Letting himself take in her appearance, he saw she was barely dressed, only covered by two tiny bits of cloth. "Laly?" he queried.

"Yes," she said, taking a step toward him.

Bradley could see a giant black man behind her

and wondered if her hesitancy was due to him. "Are you all right?" he asked firmly, looking at Samuel.

"I'm fine, Devon. I just . . ." She couldn't tell him her heart was beating so hard she feared it would leave her chest. She couldn't tell him she wanted to run into his arms and have him kiss her until she couldn't think or see. "I'm fine," she repeated.

Devon stepped forward and touched her hair, her moon-colored hair. Suddenly it didn't matter whether she worked for Rodriguez or not. It didn't matter whether she claimed to be a mermaid or a woman from the future. It didn't matter if any or none of it were true. It only mattered that he'd found her again. Slowly he lowered his head and touched her lips with his.

Laly's soul burned with joy as he kissed her gently.

"Captain Bradley?" Sugar stepped from the trees to the road.

"Yes, Sugar. It's me," Bradley answered while staring into the turquoise depths of Laly's eyes.

"I'm so glad to see you're all right. We've been worried about you," Sugar told him.

"How did you get here?" Laly asked.

"I found out you'd been sold to Devereaux. I was on my way to get you back."

Laly's heart soared at his words. "Let's get off the road. Devereaux might be looking for us," she said, taking Devon's hand to lead him into the trees. "Oh, Devon, this is Samuel. He's a good friend of ours. Samuel, this is Captain Devon Bradley."

Samuel let his eyes fall in the expected manner.

"I'm pleased to meet you, Samuel," Devon said, offering his hand.

Samuel looked up surprised. He tentatively held

out his hand and felt his first handshake as an equal man. "Yes, Sir," he responded.

A few minutes later, as they stood in a small clearing, it was decided they should rest a bit longer. The trees and underbrush were going to thicken and be more difficult to traverse the closer they got to the waterfront, and they couldn't chance traveling on the road.

"Captain, Sir, you could take both ladies on the horse with you. I'll be all right," Samuel offered.

Laly grasped Devon's arm. "We're not leaving him. We've seen what Devereaux does to runaway slaves, and I won't take the chance of him getting caught while we escape."

"But . . ." Samuel tried to argue.

"I agree with Laly. We won't leave you, Samuel," Sugar piped up. "So just drop it."

Bradley grinned at the black man. "Stubborn, aren't they?" he commented.

"Yes, Sir," answered Samuel, but his heart swelled with affection for the women who'd accepted him as their friend.

Sugar settled herself beside a log in the moonlight. "I think I'll rest here for a few minutes. If I fall asleep, just wake me when it's time to go."

Samuel sat beside her, ready to defend her from the devil himself. He watched as the captain led Laly off into the dark. He'd seen the captain's love for her, so he knew she'd be safe.

"That's quite an outfit your wearing, Laly," Devon whispered softly.

"My dress is back at the clearing. I could go put it on. It was just easier running through the brush like this."

"No, don't put on the dress yet. You'll have to soon

enough when we reach town. I like you this way. You look like a mermaid again," his voice dropped to a sultry groan.

"I'm not a mermaid," Laly whispered back, her nerves tingling from the timbre of his voice.

"I know that."

"I . . ."

"Don't talk now, Laly. I've been waiting too long for this." He bent to take her in his arms, his mouth claiming hers in a passionate mating.

Laly let herself get lost in Devon's kiss. She opened her mouth to his exploring tongue and met his probing with aggression of her own. "Oh, Devon," she breathed into his kiss.

Devon devoured Laly with his mouth. He thrust his tongue deeply into the sweet recesses of her kiss and felt himself growing with desire at her response. Over and over he let himself taste her. Again and again he claimed her with his mouth, pulling her more tightly against him, letting her feel the need she'd caused in him.

Laly accepted all that Devon had to offer. She was on fire with a desire only he could satisfy.

Devon kissed her eyes, her smooth cheeks, the tip of her nose. When he kissed her temples, he felt her flinch. Pulling back slightly, he looked more closely at her in the moonlight. "Your face is swollen. Who did this to you?" he demanded. "Devereaux?"

Laly could feel the rage coursing through Devon's body. "No. It doesn't matter now."

"It matters to me. Whoever did this to you will pay," he promised.

"I don't want anyone else hurt."

"Who did this, Laly?" he insisted.

"Promise me you won't kill him," she pleaded.

Devon knew he wouldn't kill the bastard who'd injured her. He would make him beg for death, but he wouldn't kill him. "I promise," he answered her.

"It was Gaspar," she said quietly.

"Gaspar," he breathed his name like an oath.

"You promised you wouldn't kill him," she urged.

"And I'll keep my promise," he told her, gently kissing the tender flesh of her bruised temple.

Laly felt a tingling of her nerves from the teasing touch of his lips on her skin. She reveled in the sensation of his light kisses over her hairline. Leaning into him, she wound her arms around his strong shoulders and pulled him even closer.

There was nothing and no one more beautiful than Laly in the moonlight. He watched her expression as he kissed her, feeling his excitement grow when he saw the passion she was feeling register on her beautiful face. Clasping her bottom in both hands, he moved her more snugly against him and watched her full lips part in surprise at the size of his manhood pressed wholly against her abdomen. He began a slow, tantalizing motion with his hips, promising her the fulfillment they both desired.

Laly matched Devon's rhythm. She moved her hips against his, rocking with the motion he'd begun, loving the feel of his erection, so large and firm against her.

Devon kissed Laly again, delving deeply with his tongue, matching the motion of his hips to the mating kiss. He brought her lower lip into his mouth and bit gently, hearing a sensual moan in reward. "Laly, I need you," he groaned against the softness of her lips.

He kissed her again and again, teasing her with nipping bites as he explored the soft curve of her jaw, the hollow below her ear. He licked her lightly with the tip of his tongue, tasting the sweet, heady fragrance that was hers alone. Following the soft arch of her neck, he held his mouth still over her pulse point, feeling the rapid flutter of her heartbeat.

Laly wound her fingers in the thick mass of Devon's hair and allowed her head to fall back, giving him freer access for his bold exploration. She shivered with excitement at each kiss and waited expectantly for what she knew would follow.

Devon brought one hand up to Laly's neck. He brushed her long hair from her shoulder and caressed the soft flesh there. Then, sliding his fingers lower, he molded his hand to fit the swell of her breast.

Laly gasped as Devon's hand closed over her breast. Pushing herself deeper into his palm, she waited for him to tease the throbbing bud of her nipple.

Bradley rubbed his hand over Laly's breast, holding its weight gently, molding it to fit his palm. Releasing it slowly, he let his fingers tickle the hard passion bud of her fruit.

The fabric of her top had to go. He pulled the obstructive garment upward, releasing her beautiful breasts to his view. "Laly, let me remove it completely," he whispered hoarsely.

Laly nodded and felt him tug the top over her head. She then leaned forward into him, pushing her breasts upward to receive his attention.

Devon clasped both her breasts in his hands, moving them together, massaging the hard nipples, feeling their weight and size. "Laly, you're so beautiful," he groaned, as he lowered his head to taste her.

Laly could barely breath as Devon took one of her nipples deeply within his mouth and suckled her strongly. Shooting spasms of ecstasy flew through her body, centering in the sensitive bud of passion between her legs. Pushing her hips forward, she rocked against his huge arousal, moving up and down its length.

Devon groaned against Laly's breast. He suckled one nipple and then the other, pressing his face into the soft globes. He tilted his hips into her motion, allowing her to move deeper against his manhood, arousing him even further.

Laly brought her hands from his shoulders, feeling the muscles of his chest contract under her touch. Finding his nipples hard under his shirt, she pinched them gently through the fabric. "Take this off," she instructed.

She watched as he pulled the shirt over his head. The moonlight glistened over the swells of his muscles. His chest was broad with a dark patch of soft hair over his breastbone, narrowing as it trailed downward, only to widen again as it disappeared beneath his trousers. Swaying into him, she moaned as flesh touched flesh.

Devon shuddered when Laly's breasts were flush with his body. He could feel their hard peaks pushing their fiery message into his skin. "Oh, God, Laly," he groaned.

Laly raised a hand to find Devon's nipple now that no shirt blocked her path. The hardened bud puckered even more at her touch. Lowering her head, she followed her fingers with her tongue, flicking the bud swiftly, then tantalizing him with her teeth.

Devon's head fell forward as he watched Laly torture him. "I can't take much more," he rasped.

Laly looked up for a moment. "You will," she promised. Lowering herself even further, she followed the path of dark hair over his stomach, stopping only to let her tongue circle his navel briefly before continuing on her course. When she reached his pants, she let her eyes caress the huge bulge beneath the fabric. "Oh, Devon," she breathed, laying her cheek against the throbbing shaft.

"Laly," hissed Devon.

She didn't know if he wanted her to stop or keep going. It didn't matter. She would have this no matter what. Reaching for his belt, she unfastened it and dropped it to the ground, along with his pistol. Then, unfastening his trousers, she pulled them downward slightly, instantly exposing the head of his passion. Leaning forward, she flicked her tongue over the sensitive tip and heard him groan deep within his chest. Pulling his trousers further down, she released the entire length of him. Taking him in her hand, she touched him with her tongue.

Devon groaned and shook with ecstasy. He couldn't believe the sensations he was feeling at Laly's touch. The sight of her moon hair between his legs while she suckled him was almost more than he could stand. "Laly, stop . . ." he begged, afraid he'd lose himself in her mouth and not be able to take her as he wished.

Laly suckled gently, massaging between his legs as she stroked his passion to a frenzy. "I want you, Devon," she breathed against his molten flesh.

Devon dropped to his knees, freeing his manhood from her touch. "I can take no more," he ground between clenched teeth. Pushing her backward, holding her as she lay down, he tugged at the tiny briefs she wore. In seconds she was naked to his view. Quickly removing his boots and pulling his trousers the rest of the way off, he, too, was totally naked in the moonlight.

Laly admired Devon's male beauty. She'd never

known a man so perfect in her life and knew deep in her heart what she'd suspected since she first met him. He was her soulmate, the other half of herself. Tears came to her eyes at the realization. Why did I have to cross time to meet him? she wondered. Seconds later, all thought left her head as Devon lowered to kiss her once more.

Devon kissed her lips, her throat, her breasts. He trailed his kisses lower, nipping playfully over her stomach as he descended. Her abdomen was a smooth plain he made tantalizing circles over with his tongue. When he reached the soft, golden hair that protected the apex of her thighs, he nuzzled her softly. Finding her most sensitive spot with his fingertips first, he followed with the tip of his tongue.

Laly arched to meet Devon's touch. She opened to him as a flower to the early morning sun. His tongue flicked over her swollen bud of passion and sent electric spasms coursing through her body. "Devon, Devon," she moaned his name. "Please."

Devon let his tongue dance over Laly's womanhood. She was moist and ready for his sex. He plunged his fingers deeply within her in promise of what was to follow. He heard her moaning his name and his manhood throbbed in response. Rising above her, he poised himself to enter her all at once. "Laly, look at me," he urged. "I want to see your eyes when I fill you."

Laly's eyes flew open as she waited for him. She wanted him deeply within her. She wanted him to explode inside her. "Yes," she breathed.

Devon lay the head of his manhood against Laly's heated core. With one swift stroke he buried himself completely inside her. Shuddering with emotion, he watched the sheer pleasure in her turquoise eyes.

"I'll never let you leave me, Laly," he whispered, as he began the deep, probing rhythm that would bring them both to heaven.

Laly was filled, physically and emotionally. Never in her life had she felt so complete, so whole. This man, her lover, was doing something no one had ever done before. He was making love to her soul. Over and over he plunged deeply into her body, bringing her closer to the brink of a great chasm. She could feel his muscles rocking against her as she arched to meet his thrusts, their rhythm perfect. She wrapped her legs around him, holding him closer to her as he loved her. She grasped his thick shoulders as he labored over her. She climbed ever higher with him and lost all ability to think.

Devon thrust deeper and deeper into Laly's tight core and felt her responding motion against his thighs and hips. Her long legs wrapped around him in possession and her nails dug deeply into his shoulders. Each second that passed brought him closer to the release he so desperately needed. "Laly," he rasped. "I can't . . ."

Laly gripped Devon's shoulders even tighter as she began to lose control. "Devon," she gasped, the spasmodic waves of completion washing over her.

Devon felt his muscles begin to tighten. He was nearing release. He could tell Laly was with him as he moved them toward their shared ecstasy. Thrusting deeper, he fell forward and grasped her closely to him. His rhythmic spasms began as he rocked against her.

Laly could feel the tremendous contractions of Devon's release as he poured himself within her. Her own body exploded into a million pinpoints of light that seemed to whorl around the huge man who filled her. She fluttered and floated for what felt like an eternity before she began the slow descent back to reality.

Devon had never experienced such an explosive coupling before in his life. Again and again he felt his fluid rushing to fill Laly's body. Over and over he shuddered with the spasms of completion. As he lay above her he was wracked by the continued rhythm of their lovemaking, his manhood still throbbing as he released every drop of his desire into the woman he loved. "I meant what I said, Laly. I'll never let you leave me.

Fifteen

Laly lay cradled in Devon's strong arms and let his words wash over her. He didn't realize what he was saying. She didn't belong here. This wasn't her time. But, what if . . .? She shook her head. No, they didn't belong here. She and Sugar had to return to their own time.

Devon felt the slight movement of Laly's head. "You don't want to stay with me?" he asked.

"Yes, I want to stay. I can't."

Devon raised to look into her eyes. "Why can't you? Will someone try and stop you? Is it Devereaux? I'll kill him if he tries to harm you."

"No, it isn't Devereaux. It isn't as easy as that." She felt tears filling her eyes and she didn't know how to stop them. They spilled over and ran down her temples into her hair.

"Laly, don't cry, please. I'll fix whatever's troubling you," he offered.

She almost laughed at his words. He couldn't fight

what was meant to be. "I don't belong here," she stated.

Devon looked down at her body beneath him. "I can think of noplace you belong more."

"That's not what I mean." She closed her eyes again. "Damn, this is useless," she muttered.

Devon felt a cool hand touch his heart. "Our love is useless? I do love you, you know."

Laly looked up into his dark eyes. "And I love you more than I ever thought it was possible to love a man."

"Then there's . . ."

She put her fingers to his lips to silence him. "There are obstacles between us you could never understand."

"What kinds of obstacles?" he demanded.

Laly tried to think of a way to explain the truth to him so he'd believe her. She'd already told him the truth twice and he'd thought her crazy and a liar. Pushing from beneath him she sat up, pulling his shirt from the ground and wrapping it around her. "Devon, you claim to love me." She saw him nod. "If you love me, you must believe me."

Devon sat up opposite her and saw the fear in her eyes and heard the urgency in her voice. "Yes," he said tentatively.

"I mean, you have to really believe me. No matter how ridiculous I sound."

"All right," he agreed.

Laly bit her lower lip while trying to decide how to begin. "I was born September twenty-fifth, nineteen sixty-seven," she said carefully. "When I was born, you'd already been dead for about three hundred years. I know this sounds crazy, and I know I can't prove it, but it's true, Devon. Please believe me," she asked, tears falling once more.

Devon's eyes narrowed as she spoke. She'd told him this story about traveling back through time before, and he'd all but called her a liar to her face. Somehow, now, he wasn't so determined to find fault with her tale. Was it because he'd fallen in love with her? he wondered. "I must be losing my mind," he muttered.

"Why? You believe me?" she asked hopefully.

"I don't know, Laly. Traveling through time is impossible."

"I thought so, too. Great scientists have been studying the possibility for centuries, and no one has been able to do it. The closest thing to it is the theory about traveling out into space to hear the sounds that have moved away from the earth. Supposedly, if you could go far enough out, you'd be able to hear sounds from ancient Egypt and the Pharaohs. That kind of space travel would be, in a sense, going back in time."

"Space?" Bradley asked.

"Yes. Oh, dear. Space, the sky." She waved her hand toward the heavens. "In my time, men travel in space quite often, although only a select few astronauts get to go. It's still considered very dangerous. A few years ago, one of the shuttles blew up while taking off, killing everyone on board. Of course, the whole thing was shown on TV. The entire country and parts of the world mourned the loss."

Devon shook his head. "Space travel? Astro . . . astro . . ."

"Astronauts. They're scientists who travel through space."

"Laly, I don't understand anything you're saying,"

he admitted. "You expect me to believe that men can fly through space in your time, yet man can't fly."

"Not yet. It won't happen for centuries, but man will fly in machines. I've flown myself. It's really quite an everyday occurrence, where I come from."

"You've flown?"

"Yes. Several times."

"Where did you fly?" he wanted to know.

Laly thought about it. He wouldn't know any of the places she'd been to. They didn't exist yet. Then her face lit up. "I flew to this island," she announced.

"But we found you in the water," he reminded her.

"That was several days later. In the twentieth century, there will be an airport here. 'Airport' is what we call the place the flying machines land. The machines are called airplanes, or jets, or helicopters. There are several different kinds."

"And these machines fly people wherever they want to go?"

"For a price. Companies own most of the planes and charge a fee for their services, just like some ships here take on passengers for a fare."

"This is all so hard for me to believe, Laly," he stated. "Men flying through space. Airplanes and airports."

"But you do believe me, don't you?" she asked, reaching to take his hand in hers.

He looked down into her beautiful eyes. It was clear she believed what she said. And how could she make up such incredible things? "I'm beginning to believe you," he said guardedly.

She squeezed his hand. "Thank you, Devon. Oh,

Devon, there are so many wonderful things that are going to happen in the future, your future. I don't even know where to begin to tell you. I don't even know if I should." Her eyes clouded over briefly. "There are terrible things, too," she murmured. "Wars and attempted genocide. Crime and senseless killing. But the good outweighs the bad, I think." She looked deeply into his eyes. "*Now* do you understand why I can't be with you? I have to try and get back to my own time. I don't belong here."

Devon felt her words like a sharp blow. "I can't believe you were sent here only to be ripped away from me now that I've found you," he said.

Laly's heart wept with despair. "I don't know how or why Sugar and I were sent here either, but I have to try and go home."

Devon tugged her hand, bringing her closer to him. Folding her in his arms, he kissed the top of her head. "I won't let you go," he threatened.

Laly wound her arms around his torso. She didn't say anything, but her tears fell freely to wet his chest as he held her.

"If you could stay with me, would you?" he whispered.

Laly's mind raced with the possibility. Would she? Could she? She didn't belong in this time, but would her continued presence here mess up history in any way? "I would," she finally answered.

Devon crushed her to him. "I love you," he groaned over her.

"I love you, too," she murmured against the warmth of his chest. "But I have to try to go back. I have to try to get Sugar back. Do you understand?"

"Yes. I understand," he sighed. "How can I help?"

Laly's chin quivered at his words. He believed her, and though he wanted her to stay, he was willing to help her. "The medallion," she stated.

"You really believe the medallion had something to do with bringing you here?"

She nodded, leaning back to see his eyes. "Remember the monster you cut from my back when you found me?"

"Yes."

"It wasn't a monster, it was a machine designed to allow a person to breath underwater. It's not magic, and I'm no mermaid. I'm just a diver. That's a person who's qualified to use the underwater breathing machine. Sugar is also qualified. We were diving when a strange storm hit. I'd just found the medallion. When we surfaced, it was here, in your time. The medallion had to have something to do with it."

Devon sighed deeply. "And Rodriguez has the medallion. By now he's probably far out to sea."

Laly lowered her eyes. "Then it's lost to us."

"Not necessarily. The *Vengeance* is a fast ship. We should be able to catch the *Puta* for you within a few days."

"You'd do that for me?" she asked surprised.

"I'd do anything for you," he confirmed.

"I feel the same about you," she offered.

"I already know this. You killed a man to protect me," he said solemnly.

Laly wrapped her arms around his neck and brought his head down to kiss him gently. Softly, she let her tongue slip between his lips. "Make love to me again," she whispered.

Devon smiled against her kiss. "Gladly, my sweet mermaid," he answered. Slowly, he lowered her to the ground and covered her body with his own. The softly yielding curves of her sensual form brought his senses to life instantly.

Laly cradled Devon between her legs, letting him rest against her. She kissed him again and again, feeling she might never get enough of him. When he lowered his head to suckle her breasts she felt as though it were the first time, and wondered, if she spent a lifetime with him would it always be so?

Devon rocked gently against Laly's abdomen, letting himself enjoy the pleasure of being with her. His blood raced in his veins and his heart pounded with a fury, but he wanted to go slower this time. Nipping at the rosy buds of her breasts, he tantalized each in turn and listened to the rapturous sigh that escaped her lips.

Laly explored his back with her hands. His muscles rippled beneath her fingers and she felt him quiver with desire when she raked her nails along his flesh. "Take me, Devon," she begged. "I need you."

Devon could refuse her nothing. Entering her tight body, he nearly lost himself and had to lie still for a moment. "Laly, you've bewitched me. I feel like a gauche schoolboy in your arms, ready to embarrass myself with my lack of self control."

"You, my lover, are no schoolboy," she answered huskily, laughing deeply with pleasure.

"Ah, Laly, you undo me with your laughter," he groaned. Slowly, he pulled from her body, then quickly thrust deep within her again.

Laly gasped as he became rougher in his lovemaking. She smiled in delight as he drove into her, holding her hips tightly to him. Taking him inside her deeper and deeper with each thrust, she felt as though they'd become one entity, and she reveled in the sensation.

Devon slowed his rhythm and began to pull her upward. Her beautiful eyes opened and she looked at him with blatant passion. "I'm going to turn over," he whispered.

Laly smiled her approval. Moments later she was sitting astride him, feeling his manhood pushing even deeper within her. Stars began to explode before her eyes as she fought to hold onto reality a little longer.

"Let it go, Laly," he hissed. "Let it go." He thrust upward again and again, feeling the shuddering, shocking spasms begin low within him. He clenched his jaw and groaned as he felt himself shooting upward like a volcano, hot and wet. "Laly!" he cried out at the eruption.

Laly rode him as she would a mighty stallion bucking beneath her. His every pulse brought more stars to her eyes and every gasping breath another shiver of joy coursing through her. When the wild storm of passion finally started to abate, she lay forward and rested her head against his chest, sated.

"We were made for each other," he murmured.

Laly nodded her answer even though her heart was breaking.

Minutes passed, each of them lost in their own thoughts. Then Devon touched her shoulder. "Are you sleeping?" he asked.

"No."

"We'd better be moving."

"Yes, I suppose so," she agreed. She didn't want to move yet. She never wanted to move. She wanted to stay cradled in his arms forever. But she stirred, rising up and parting their bodies. "Where are my clothes?"

Devon looked around them and found the tiny bits

of cloth she'd been wearing. "This is all Devereaux would let you wear?" he grumbled.

"There were some pantaloons, but I took them off while we played cards."

"You what?"

She giggled. "Don't worry. Sugar had everything under control."

"Sugar had . . . were you playing 'strip poker'?" he asked.

"How did you know? Wainwright told you," she answered her own question.

"He told me about the game. What if you'd lost?"

Laly grinned up at him as she pulled her bottom up over her hips. "No chance. Sugar is a card shark."

"A what?"

"Well, to be blunt, she's a cheat. The best damn card cheat I ever saw. She can bottom-deal better than any riverboat gambler I've ever heard of."

Devon shook his head. She was talking in riddles again, but he understood the part about Sugar cheating. "Did she cheat Wainwright?"

"A little. She left him his dignity," she said, smiling to herself, remembering she'd peeked.

Devon tugged on his pants and reached for his shirt. While watching Laly adjust her top, he wished he could watch her dress everyday for the rest of their lives. If there was anyway to make it happen, he would. "Are you ready?" he asked a moment later.

Laly nodded. "As ready as I'll ever be," she said.

Devon led Laly back to the clearing where Sugar slept with her head against Samuel's shoulder.

Laly crossed to Sugar and nudged her softly. "Wake up. It's time to go."

Sugar opened her eyes and blinked several times. "Did I fall asleep?"

Laly grinned at her friend. "You were sawing logs like the devil."

"I don't snore, Laly Lawrence, and you know it," she said indignantly.

"Samuel, she was snoring, wasn't she?" Laly asked, winking at him.

Samuel just laughed softly.

"I don't snore," repeated Sugar. "Laly, you're just a troublemaker."

Laly laughed out loud. "Not me?" she said innocently.

Devon watched the silly exchange between the women and realized it would be difficult for Laly to let Sugar leave without her. He only hoped when the time came she'd decide to try and stay with him. "Let's go, ladies, Samuel. We have a long walk yet ahead of us."

The walk back to town was long and hard. Since they were avoiding the road, they had to fight their way through thick underbrush. Devon had shooed the horse he'd rented back toward town, hoping the animal would make it safely, and that he wouldn't have to pay for a lost horse when he got back. And even though he and Samuel tried to break a trail for Laly and Sugar, the going was slow. It was nearly dawn when they reached the outskirts of town.

"It's time to put on your dresses," said Devon.

Laly was sweating from the exerting walk through the junglelike terrain and didn't want to put on the stifling satin gown, but she knew she had to in order to pass through town. "We didn't bring the corsets," she mentioned. "I hope we can get these fastened."

Sugar pulled her dress over her head and let it

drop around her. Tugging the back together, she turned toward Laly. "Doesn't look like it," she said, the edges of the open back missing each other by two inches.

Laly stepped into her dress and found the same problem with hers. "What are we going to do?"

"Samuel and I will walk close behind you. At this early hour, maybe no one will notice."

Laly lifted her shoulders. "Fine by me," she agreed. As they left the shelter of the trees and started into town, she felt Devon right behind her. But as they started seeing people on the street, she became concerned about Devereaux and less worried what people might think about her state of partial undress. She feared he was searching for her, Sugar, and Samuel at that very moment. He'd surely awakened by now. And if he hadn't, Samuel's guard had probably been found. "Let's hurry," she urged.

"We'll be aboard the *Vengeance* very soon," Devon assured her.

As he'd said, they spotted the masts of the ship in minutes, and within half an hour they were walking up the gangplank.

"Captain, we were getting worried about you," exclaimed Wainwright as they boarded.

"I'm fine. Laly and Sugar will be sailing with us again on tomorrow's tide," he informed his officer.

"Aye, Captain. Hello, Miss Sugar, Miss Laly." He bowed in greeting.

"Hello," Laly answered.

Sugar smiled her greeting.

Wainwright waited for the captain to explain the black man who accompanied them. "Sir?"

Devon raised his hand to silence Wainwright. "Samuel, do you have any plans?" he asked.

"No, Sir," Samuel answered. He only knew he didn't want to be caught.

"Have you ever thought about working on a ship?"

Samuel's eyes opened wider. "No, Sir, but it sounds like a good idea."

"Then you can consider yourself employed. Wainwright, this is Samuel. Find him a bunk."

"Yes, Sir," Wainwright accepted his captain's order. "Hello, Samuel. I'm Charles Wainwright. Follow me, please."

Samuel looked from Wainwright to the Captain, then to Laly and Sugar. He couldn't believe his good fortune. "Thank you," he said softly.

"I told you I want you to wait here," Devon grumbled.

"Tell me what you're going to do," insisted Laly.

They'd been arguing for nearly half an hour, ever since Devon had told her he was going ashore to take care of business but was evasive about what kind of business.

"You're just being stubborn, Devon Bradley. I know your trip ashore has something to do with me."

Devon rolled his head back and let out an exasperated breath. "All right. I'm going to see Gaspar," he finally confessed.

"No, Devon. You promised me you wouldn't kill him."

"And I won't break the promise," he told her. "But I am going to teach him a lesson." He started for the door. "Wait here," he told her.

Laly watched him leave, closing the door tightly behind him. As soon as she was certain he was gone, she dug through his clothing and began to change.

She was going to follow him, but she was going in disguise.

Sugar knocked softly on the cabin door. "Laly, it's me. Can I come in?"

"Yes, hurry."

Sugar stepped through the door speaking. "I saw Captain Bradley leaving the . . . what are you doing?"

"I'm going after him," Laly said, tucking her long hair up under a cap. "He's going to see Gaspar, and I'm afraid he means to kill him for what he did to me." She pointed to the bruised side of her face.

"He wouldn't kill a man just for that," Sugar assured her.

"You didn't see how angry he was when he noticed it. He still gets tense every time he looks at me."

"But surely . . ."

"I can't take the chance of having another man s blood on my hands, Sugar. Even a bastard like Gaspar has a right to live."

Sugar shook her head. "You're just going to get yourself into more trouble."

"Not if I stay close enough to him. If I need help I can yell for it."

"What if you need more help than one man can provide?" Sugar asked.

"I have to take that chance. I can't let him kill Gaspar." She turned completely around for her friend. "How do I look?" she asked.

"Like a woman dressed as a man," Sugar answered sarcastically.

Laly sighed. "It'll have to do."

Bradley walked the waterfront until he reached the turnoff to the slave market. As he neared the site, he was stunned to see nothing but a few burned timbers leaning precariously at odd angles where Gaspar's shack had once been. The fence around the slave quarters was torn down and the building and yard were empty. He stood in front of the charred remains for several minutes while he decided his next course of action.

After a few minutes a boy walked nearby, veering close enough to the timbers to grab a piece of charcoal.

"Can you tell me what happened here?" Bradley asked, getting the boy's attention.

"What's 'at? Didn't ye see the flames?" the boy asked incredulously, his eyes wide with surprise. "It were a monstrous sight, it were."

"I was out of the city last night," Bradley offered. "Perhaps you would fill me in?"

"I'll say. Gaspar got his throat slit clean open, he did. I'd swear his head was hangin' by a thread, it were."

"Gaspar's dead?"

"Dead as a month-old corpse, he is. Never have I see'd so much blood. It were a horrible sight." The boy shivered with glee in telling the gruesome tale. "After Gaspar were killed, whoever done it set fire to his place."

"You don't know who did it?" Bradley asked.

"No, Sir. And I can't say as I want to know. A body what'd do such to old Gaspar wouldn't be afeared of doin' it again. I'd just as soon not be the one he done it to. I got to go now, Sir. Me friends are waitin'."

Bradley nodded as the boy walked away, joining a group of boys not far away. It seemed they wanted the charcoal to write on walls with. He shook his head as they took off to do their vandalism.

Remaining in front of the burned shack a moment longer, he wondered who'd done the crime. "Probably one of the people you sold illegally, Gaspar," he mused. "Or Rodriguez!" he hissed, suddenly remembering Gaspar had owed the pirate money. The murder and fire had occurred the night before. That still gave Rodriguez time to sail on the morning tide. But had he? Was there a chance he was still in Charles Towne?

Leaving the scene, he headed for the Blue Parrot. If Rodriguez was in town, that's where he'd be.

Laly followed Devon to the slave market and stood behind a vendor's wagon while he inspected the burned-out ruins. She listened to the men around her talking about the murder of Gaspar and the fire. Swallowing the bile that rose in her throat as they went over the gory details, she couldn't help but be a little relieved that Devon would have no chance to kill the man himself. She still wasn't sure he meant to keep his promise.

When Devon took off at a quick pace, she had to run to catch up with him. "Where are you going in such a hurry?" she wondered out loud.

As Devon neared the Blue Parrot, he decided it might be wise to keep out of sight. If Rodriguez was inside, he probably wasn't alone. Sidestepping into the alley, he made his way to the back door of the bar as he had the day before. Slipping inside, he found the washroom empty. "Good," he whispered to himself. The fewer people who knew of his interest in Rodriguez, the better.

He quietly went to the door covered by the carpet and pulled it aside a fraction of an inch. Surveying the room with one eye squinting through the crack, he nearly shouted in triumph when he saw Rodriguez sitting at a table with some of his crew. The pirate hadn't sailed. That meant the medallion was also still in port.

"What are you doing in here?" Laly asked.

Bradley straightened instantly at the sound of Laly's voice. He jumped across the room and put his hand roughly over her mouth. "Do you want to get us both killed?" he hissed.

Laly stiffened at his treatment and tried to turn her head away from his hand. "What are you doing?" she said into his fingers.

"Damn, Laly, be quiet. Rodriguez is in the next room," he warned.

Laly's eyes widened. She nodded to let him know she understood. When he took his hand away, she tiptoed toward the door.

Devon reached out and grabbed her by the coat she wore. "Stay away from there. We don't need him seeing either one of us."

"You just looked," she pointed out.

"Only long enough to see if he was here."

Laly crossed her arms defiantly in front of her. "You're certainly one way about things," she accused.

"One way?"

"Your way," she whispered.

"Laly, I had a hunch he might still be in port. I had to check it out."

Laly grew suspicious. "Why would you think he'd be in port? You told me he'd probably sailed for sure."

"I remembered Gaspar owed him money." He watched her eyes for a reaction.

Laly put her hand over her mouth to stifle the scream she felt boiling in her chest. "Gaspar? You think he . . . you think Rodriguez killed Gaspar?"

"It makes sense, doesn't it?"

Laly closed her eyes and leaned forward, letting Devon wrap his arms around her. "Gaspar was murdered so horribly," she murmured.

"Yes, he was," he agreed quietly. After a few moments, he looked down. "What are you doing here?" he asked. "And why are you dressed like this?"

Laly leaned her head back and grinned sheepishly at him. "I followed you. And I didn't want to be conspicuous."

Devon rolled his eyes. "Do you ever do what you're supposed to do?"

"Rarely," she answered honestly.

"Come on," sighed Devon. "Let's get out of here."

"But what about Rodriguez? He has the medallion."

"From the looks of the money he's spending on drinks in there, he probably stole all Gaspar's money before he torched the shack. He'll be drinking for some time to come, and I doubt he's carrying the medallion on his person. It's probably aboard the *Puta*. That's where I have to go to get it."

"That's where *we* have to go," she argued.

"Laly . . ."

"Devon . . ."

Rodriguez toasted Gaspar again. He'd done so many times and would continue to do so many times more. The man had turned out to have a huge stash of coins under his bed. "To my good friend Gaspar. May he rest in peace," he laughed.

It had been so easy to kill Gaspar. And to think he'd let the man make him nervous for so many years. When it came to dying, Gaspar had done it like anyone else. "Gaspar!" he shouted as he raised his mug, watching while his crew did the same.

How could his life get any better? Rodriguez wondered. In the past two days, he'd killed the English captain, sold the mermaids, gotten rid of Gaspar and found his loot, and stolen the King's Medallion. He teetered in his chair as he drank to his good fortune. "Life is good, my friends," he said, raising his mug again.

Devon led Laly through town and back to the ship. "I can't believe you thought you'd be inconspicuous dressed like this," he told her. "You look as much like a boy as I do a woman."

"I wanted to follow you, and this was the only way I knew how to get away with it," she said.

"You're lucky someone didn't see you were a woman and decide you were a waterfront doxy."

"Really, Devon. You're so dramatic." She pulled the cap from her hair and scratched her scalp. "This thing is itchy," she complained.

He looked down at her and couldn't stay angry. "It's wool," he explained. "People don't usually wear wool caps in the West Indies."

"Oh," she said, trying not to smile.

"You really look ridiculous," he chuckled.

"Then you'd better help me find a more convinc-

ing disguise to use when we go after the medallion,"
she said coyly.

"You're not going."

"I am going."

Devereaux sat astride his horse and watched the
English captain pulling his property toward a ship.
He saw Laly stop and throw her arms around his waist
and reach up to kiss him. "It seems, my dear, you've
found someone else to make a patsy of. Pity you won't
live long enough to enjoy it," he promised under his
breath.

Sixteen

"Are you sure you don't want to come with me?" Devon asked, looking down into Laly's eyes as he held her close. "I'm sure. I've already seen the governor's mansion. Remember?" She grinned sheepishly up at him.

Devon chuckled deep within his chest. "Yes, I remember."

"What does he want?" she asked.

"The note doesn't say. It just summons me to the mansion at once. So, my sweet mermaid, I'll see you later." He bent and placed a kiss on the tip of her nose.

"Hurry," she prodded.

"Don't worry, I will. I have an appointment with the *Puta* this evening."

Laly smiled up at Devon and nodded. She hadn't yet convinced him to let her go along on the quest for the medallion, but she was going, come hell or high water. "What if he asks you about the medallion?"

"The medallion is yours, my sweet."

Laly rose on tiptoe and pulled him down for a kiss.

Devon deepened the kiss that Laly started, groaning against her when he felt the sure rush of blood to his manhood. "I must be going," he whispered.

"I'll be waiting for you," Laly murmured seductively.

Devon released her and shook himself, blowing his breath out in one quick puff. As he left the cabin, he turned and winked at her.

Laly felt Devon's kiss long after he left the cabin, and she had to fight the melancholy that tried to settle over her. He was being so wonderful about helping her get the medallion back, but his assistance would help her leave him. Needing to talk to Sugar, she left the cabin she now shared with Devon and headed down the companionway to a smaller cabin Sugar occupied alone.

Devereaux watched the captain leave the ship and felt a swell of satisfaction that his plan was working so far. It would take well over an hour for Captain Bradley to return from his wild-goose chase, and by then he would have the women back in his possession at Dove's Nest. His fingers itched in anticipation of teaching Laly and Sugar not to run from him again. It would be a pity to destroy such beauty, but they must be taught. He felt a growing stiffness in his trousers at the thought of the pain he'd inflict. "Soon, ladies. Soon," he crooned.

Laly was sitting on Sugar's bunk when a knock sounded at the door. "Come in," she called.

"I have a note for you, Miss," the young sailor said as he held out a small piece of paper tied with a blue ribbon.

"Thank you," she said, waiting for him to leave before opening the note. Turning toward Sugar, she raised her brows. "Who could be sending me notes?"

"Probably the captain," Sugar answered.

Laly untied the ribbon and unrolled the paper. Seconds later all color left her face as her heart stopped beating.

"What is it?" rushed Sugar, alarmed by Laly's expression.

Laly couldn't speak as terror filled her soul. She held out the note to Sugar.

Sugar held up the paper and read out loud: *"I have your captain. Bring Sugar with you. Tell no one. Devereaux."* She paled as her arm fell to her side. "What do we do?" she whispered.

"Exactly what the note says," Laly answered in a daze. "He'll kill Devon if we don't."

"But we could tell the crew. They'd fight for Captain Bradley."

"Devereaux would kill him before they got the chance. I'm going. I won't ask you to do the same. Maybe he'll be satisfied with just me."

Sugar squared her shoulders. "As if I'd let you go to that devil alone," she huffed.

Laly looked down at the dress she wore. It was one of many Devon had given her and Sugar upon their return to the ship. It was a much more serviceable style and fabric than the satins had been, but it was still cumbersome, with a long, full skirt that got in the way everytime she took a step. "I'm changing back into the pants I had on earlier today. I want to be able to fight or run if I need to."

"Good idea. Let's find me some, too," Sugar agreed.

Minutes later the two women were making their way across the deck of the *Vengeance* wearing men's clothing.

"Where are you going?" asked Wainwright when he saw them.

"We . . . ah . . . we have some errands to run," lied Laly.

"Pardon me, Miss Laly, but . . . dressed like that?"

"Yes. We didn't want to soil the pretty things Devon gave us."

"Well, I don't know." Wainwright paused. This didn't feel right. The captain had explained that he believed their story about time travel. He'd had a hard time accepting it at first, but if his captain believed, so would he. He now understood why Laly and Sugar were so different from other women, but he still didn't think they should go into town unescorted, not even dressed as they were. "If you'll wait just a minute, I'll have one of the men accompany you."

"No!" Then, quieter, "No, thank you. We're in a hurry, and . . . we'll be fine," said Laly nervously. She pushed Sugar into action, leaving the ship as quickly as they could.

Samuel saw Laly and Sugar leaving from atop the mainmast, where he was learning to check the rigging. From his vantage point he saw them enter a carriage that seemed to be waiting for them. Frowning, he wondered where they could be going dressed as they were. "Look lively there, man. Ye nearly got yer foot caught in the riggin'," his teacher yelled at him, taking his attention from Laly and Sugar. He straight-ened himself, and when he looked back to where he'd seen the carriage, it was gone. Shrugging, he went back to his work in earnest.

Devon was about to leave the city when he noticed the governor's carriage waiting outside a local eatery. An alarm went off in his head and he crossed the street to check out his hunch. Once inside, he found the governor just finishing his meal.

"Hello, Captain Bradley," boomed the large man when he looked up from his dessert. "You look like you're doing better than the last time I saw you. Any luck with the medallion?"

"No, Sir. I'm sorry . . ."

"No need for apologies. That hunk of metal is turning out to be more trouble than it's worth. I don't . . ." he grumbled.

"Excuse me, Sir," interrupted Bradley. "Did you send for me?" he asked urgently.

The governor blinked several times. "Why, no, Captain."

"Damn!" cursed Bradley, punching his open hand with a fist. "Sorry, Sir, I have to go," he called over his shoulder as he ran for the door.

As he raced for the ship, he prayed Laly was all right. He'd been gone only a half hour or so. Whoever had lured him away expected him to be gone much longer. "Please don't let it be too late," he breathed.

Laly and Sugar sat in the closed carriage, staring at the horrible face of Devereaux. "You see, my dears, I keep what I buy."

"You'll never get away with this," threatened Laly.

"I already have," laughed Devereaux. "You belong to me, and you'll stay with me."

"But what of the captain?"

"You'll see him soon enough," he lied. As they rode toward Dove's Nest, he enjoyed the frightened expressions on the women's faces. He particularly enjoyed the defiant facade Laly attempted to maintain. It excited him to think of how he'd make her beg before he used the whip on her pretty face.

Devon reached the *Vengeance* at a dead run. He mounted the gangplank in two huge strides and pushed his way passed several crewmen in his haste to get to his quarters. "Laly!" he yelled, as he burst through the cabin door.

"She's gone, Sir," Wainwright said behind him.

Bradley turned and grabbed his first officer by the coat. "Where is she? Where did she go?" he demanded.

"She and Miss Sugar left only minutes ago," answered a startled Wainwright.

"Minutes? Did you see where they went?"

"No, Sir. I'm sorry." He watched as the Captain released his coat. "But they were wearing men's clothing, Sir—if that means anything to you."

Bradley looked frantically around the room. The last time Laly had worn men's clothing was that very morning, and she'd done it to blend in, to be inconspicuous. She'd failed miserably, but her reasons were sound. Why had she felt the need to dress as a man again?

Samuel knocked on the open doorjamb. "Excuse me, Sir."

Bradley looked wild-eyed at the black man. "Yes, Samuel?"

"I was just checking." He feared he was stepping beyond his bounds.

"Yes, Samuel?" Devon repeated.

"Well, Sir. I was just wondering if you knew where Miss Laly and Miss Sugar took off to in that carriage?"

"Carriage?" Bradley's heart leapt.

"Yes, Sir. I was in the rigging when they left in a black carriage. I don't know, Sir, it just seemed odd."

"Did you see who was in the carriage?" Bradley questioned hopefully.

"No, Sir. It was a closed carriage. Is everything all right, Sir?"

"No, Samuel, everything is not all right. I was sent on an unnecessary mission, to get me out of the way, I think."

"That might explain the note," offered Wainwright.

"Note?" Bradley charged.

"Yes, Sir. It arrived almost as you left."

"Who delivered it?"

"Just a boy, Sir."

"You don't know what it said?" he asked.

"It was sealed. I'm sorry, Sir," Wainwright apologized.

Bradley began to look around the room for the note. Perhaps they didn't bring it with them. "Help me look for it," he instructed.

"I think they were in Miss Sugar's room when it was delivered.

Bradley ran for the door. In seconds he was pushing his way into Sugar's cabin. There, crumpled on the bed, was a slip of paper. Grabbing it with frantic fingers, he read. "Dear, God, no!" he groaned.

"Sir?" Wainwright took the note from Bradley. "I'll get the men together and we'll come with you, Sir."

"I can't wait," he answered, rising and heading for the door. When he reached it, Samuel was standing to the side. "Samuel, Devereaux has them."

Samuel's heart instantly burned with rage. "I'm coming with you."

"You know what he'll do to you if he catches you."

"Better than you, Sir."

Bradley looked on the man with even more respect. "Let's go."

"But, Sir?" called Wainwright. "You shouldn't try to do this alone. Sir?" he called to his Captain's back.

Laly and Sugar fought the ropes that held them tied to the wooden posts in the basement of Dove's Nest. They'd been stripped to their undergarments and shivered in the cool, damp air that filled the dark.

"Laly?" whispered Sugar.

"What?"

"Can you loosen your ropes at all?"

"No." Laly's heart beat a guilty tempo for having gotten Sugar into this mess. She burned with anger when she thought about how Devereaux had tricked her with the note into thinking he had the captain. Why didn't she do as Sugar asked and alert the crew? Why did she always have to go off half-cocked, running headlong into trouble before she thought about the consequences? She shuddered. This time the consequences were life-threatening. "I'm sorry, Sugar," she whispered, tears in her voice.

"It's not your fault, Laly," Sugar offered.

"We both know you're a liar," Laly muttered.

A few more minutes passed before either of them spoke again. Then it was Sugar's voice breaking the silence. "Do you think it was a whip that did . . . you know, the woman in the kitchen?"

"I don't know," Laly murmured, knowing for certain Devereaux's hand had wielded the whip that had destroyed the woman's face. She heard Sugar's sniffs as she tried not to cry. "Dear, Lord, please get us out of here," she prayed.

Bradley and Samuel spurred the horses they'd gotten from the stable—after arguing with the man because Bradley had sent the last horse back alone. Bradley's fierce countenance had finally shut him up and they'd gotten under way.

"Faster," Bradley growled, kicking the poor animal unmercifully.

Devereaux sipped wine and watched as one of his servants fondled him. He was excited about the beating he was to give Laly and Sugar. He'd found through years of experience that it was best to relieve himself at least once before he began the punishment, or he'd get *too* excited and have to stop and use one of his girls, putting off the real fun of the beating. As he neared his climax, he rested his head back against the wall above the headboard of his bed and thought about what the whip would do to the soft skin of the women. *"Yesss,"* he groaned in pleasure, never seeing the look of revulsion on the face of the woman forced to service him.

Devon and Samuel reached Dove's Nest and pulled their horses to a stop in the seclusion of the trees.

"Where do you think he might be holding them?" Devon asked.

"I don't know, Sir. I was never in the main part of the house."

Devon surveyed the house and tried to make a plan. "We'll go around back." He nodded in the direction of the rear of the house. "Let's tie the horses here."

Seconds later, they were running, crouched, under the protection of the trees that skirted the property. "There's not much cover by the house," observed Devon. "Do you know if there are any guards?"

"I know of three. They left only one to watch me after I was tied to a tree, but it took three of them to tie me there," Samuel said, angry at the memory.

"Well, I haven't seen any yet. I hope they're busy elsewhere."

Running quickly across the open yard between the trees and the house, Devon led the way to the kitchen door. Raising slightly, he praised their good luck at finding the room empty. "Come on," he whispered, signaling Samuel to follow.

The kitchen was large and surprisingly cool. Apparently, the ovens weren't being used today in deference to the heat. Devon peered around the table and benches as he half crawled along the floor toward the interior door. He could feel Samuel behind him and was grateful for the big man's help.

"What are you doing?" a soft, mumbled voice asked from out of nowhere.

Devon jumped in surprise, then heard Samuel gasp. "Damn," he cursed as he turned, ready to fight. The sight that met him caused his stomach to turn. The poor woman was horribly deformed beyond anything he'd ever seen before.

"What are you doing?" she asked again.

Devon didn't know what to say. His mind raced, trying to find a lie that would keep her from screaming an alarm. Then her heard Samuel's quiet voice.

"We've come to rescue Laly and Sugar, the two women Devereaux just bought at the slave market. This man is in love with one of them," he explained.

The men watched as tears formed in the pitiful woman's one eye. "Someone loved me once. But no more." She picked up a cat that purred at her ankles. "Your women are in the basement," she said calmly. "It's the small door at the end of the hall." She pointed toward the door.

Devon couldn't believe his ears. She wasn't going to call for help. She'd actually given them assistance. Then it hit him like a cannon ball in the gut. Devereaux had disfigured her. "The bloody, fucking bastard," he groaned, terror gripping his heart that they'd be too late to stop a similar fate for Laly and Sugar.

Samuel grabbed Devon's arm. "Let's go," he said.

Devon nodded, looking back briefly at the poor woman and her cat. If Devereaux had put one mark on Laly's body he'd kill him. He might kill him anyway. No one deserved to die more.

The door to the basement wasn't locked, and Devon said a grateful prayer as he pushed it open. The basement was dark, with rickety wooden stairs leading down into the abyss. Taking the steps slowly, he cringed when he heard them creak under his weight. Stopping, he waited for an alert call from below. Hearing none, he breathed a sigh of relief and started his descent once more.

* * *

Laly and Sugar heard the basement door open
and someone start to come down the stairs. "Please,
God," Laly whispered, fear and remorse clutching
her soul.

Sugar closed her eyes and laid her head against
the cool wood of the post she was tied to. Smelling
dried blood, she gagged and pulled her head up once
more. She wouldn't give Devereaux the satisfaction
of seeing her vomit.

Laly heard the footsteps getting closer. Devereaux
was nearly at the bottom step. It wouldn't be too
much longer and their punishment would begin.

Devon could hear breathing in the dark, but he
couldn't make out where it was coming from. Afraid
of ambush, he kept quiet and listened as he pro-
gressed further into the basement.

Laly could take no more. "Devereaux, punish me,
but let Sugar go. This is all my fault . . ."

"You'll do no such thing," interrupted Sugar. "It's
no more your fault than it is mine," she argued.

Devon was startled by the voices he heard. "Laly?
Sugar?"

"Devon?" Laly cried. "You came! How did you
know where to find me?"

Devon and Samuel rushed toward their voices.
"You left the note on Sugar's bed." He reached Laly
and bent to kiss her urgently. "Now, let's get you out
of here." He began to feel for the knots that secured
her to the post while Samuel untied Sugar. In minutes
they were heading toward the stairs and the light of
the open door.

"Isn't this touching," said Devereaux, as he
stepped into the light.

Samuel started to lunge for him, but stopped when

a loaded musket appeared over Devereaux's shoulder.

"You didn't think I'd be without protection, did you?" asked Devereaux, stepping aside so his guard would have a better shot. "Come on, finish coming up the stairs," he directed. "I can't very well kill you in the basement. I must make it look as though you were shot while trying to break into my lovely home."

Devon climbed the stairs in front of Laly, shielding her from the guard. Sugar and Samuel followed. "You're going to murder the women, too, Devereaux?" he asked.

"Oh no, my dear captain. The women will get what they deserve after you've been dispatched. This way please. I think we'll do this at the back of the house. It makes sense you'd try to break into my home from the back."

Laly followed Devon into the kitchen. She wondered frantically what she could do to stop this, but she knew Devereaux was a madman. "Please, Mr. Devereaux." She turned abruptly toward him. "I'll do anything you say; just let them go."

Devereaux laughed at her attempt to save the captain. "You'll do anything I say anyway, my dear." He then turned to Samuel. "I'm disappointed to have to kill you, too, Samuel. I paid a lot of money for you, and I had a wonderful life planned out for you. I know you'd have enjoyed it, once you got used to it."

"As half a man?" Samuel growled.

"It's better than being dead," Devereaux said. "But I can see you're too much of a troublemaker to have around." He glanced at Laly again. "Step aside, ladies."

"No!" defied Laly.

"Oh, dear. You are being difficult." Just then, another guard entered the room. "What perfect timing," cooed Devereaux. "Get these women out of the way."

Laly and Sugar were grabbed by the wrists and pulled across the room.

"Let go of her!" ordered Bradley, his fists clenched uselessly at his sides.

"You're in no position to tell anyone what to do, Captain," said Devereaux. He smiled and nodded at the guard aiming the musket at Devon. He pulled a pistol from his belt to use for his second shot at Samuel.

Laly and Sugar clutched each other's hands and stood helplessly while the guard took careful aim. "This can't be happening," cried Laly. "He can't die."

Sugar pulled Laly against her, shielding her from seeing the man she loved shot before her eyes. "Devereaux, you'll burn in hell for this," she hissed.

"This is already hell, my dear," Devereaux answered. "As you will soon . . ."

"Now!" shouted Devon, as he jumped for the guard.

Sugar gasped and Laly looked up in time to see Devereaux grasping a huge knife handle that protruded from his neck. His eyes were bulging and his tongue hung from his mouth dripping blood. The woman he'd disfigured stood over his body smiling a hideous, twisted smile.

Devon fought the guard with the musket and struggled for control of the weapon. Samuel lunged for the other guard, but the man ran before he could be caught.

A violent explosion shook the room as the musket went off.

"Oh, my God," cried Laly, as the musket shot ripped into the woman's chest. "Sugar, help me." She knelt beside the poor, disfigured creature and cradled her head in her lap. "Find something to stop the blood!" she pleaded.

Sugar looked quickly around the room but could find nothing to staunch the river of blood that flowed from the woman's chest. Tears filled her eyes as she knelt beside Laly. "It's no use," she said.

The remaining guard fled the room quickly, now that his employer was dead.

Laly looked down into the woman's distorted face. "I'm sorry," she whispered.

The woman opened her eye and sanity had returned. "Is he dead?" she asked.

Laly looked to Devereaux's grotesque figure and nodded.

"Good, then I can rest," the woman whispered weakly. She looked up at Laly. "I was beautiful once, too."

"I'm sure you were," Laly sobbed.

"See that I'm buried decent," the woman asked.

"Of course," Laly promised.

"My name is Margaret Tra . . ."

Laly leaned over Margaret's body and cried freely.

Devon knelt beside Laly and touched her on the shoulder. "She's better off," he said quietly.

Laly nodded. It was true. The woman was so horribly disfigured, she'd have had no life outside this house. "We will see to her burial?" she asked.

Devon nodded. "I'll see to it personally."

"I wish she could have told us her last name."

"It might be better we don't know it," he said.

"But for her tombstone?"

"She saved my life. We'll use Bradley," he stated with conviction.

Laly swung part way around to hug him. "No wonder I love you," she whispered.

Sugar heard what Laly had said to the captain. She knew Laly and the captain were having an affair, they were sharing the same cabin on the *Vengeance*, but Laly had said "love." Was it that serious?

"We'd better be going. We've got to get the constable back here to Dove's Nest, and I still have to find the *Puta* tonight," said Devon.

Laly looked up into his dark eyes. "I'm going with you," she said calmly. "And no argument from you will change my mind."

Devon saw the determination in her turquoise eyes and realized she'd just follow him again like she did that morning if he didn't agree to let her go. Besides, with everything that had happened that day, he didn't want her out of his sight. "Very well. You may come." He held up his hand when she would speak. "But you will do exactly as I say, understood?"

Laly nodded.

"Humph," Sugar spouted. "*That* I'd like to see."

Two hours later, Margaret's body was being prepared for a Christian burial. Devereaux had been pronounced the evil bastard that he was, and his body was to be buried in an unidentified grave in the debtors' graveyard. It seemed a fitting end.

And Laly was readying herself to accompany Devon on his search for the *Puta*.

"Lower the boat!" Devon yelled to his crewmen. It had been decided that Samuel and two others would go along on the quest for the medallion. And only Samuel was told what they were looking for. Samuel, and, of course, Wainwright.

"Sir, are you sure this is such a good idea?" Wainwright asked.

Devon smiled at his first officer. "No, I'm not. But I know of no other way to secure the medallion."

"And you're really going to turn it over to the women when you get it?"

"They need it," he stated plainly.

"But what if it does no good? I mean, what if they do find a storm and nothing happens?" Wainwright argued.

"Then we'll turn it over to the governor once more. But I have to let them try," he said.

"But, Sir. If they're telling the truth . . . they'll leave. She'll leave."

Devon's eyes cast downward. "Perhaps," he said quietly.

Seventeen

Laly listened to the oars slicing the water as they made their way round the point in search of the *Puta*. "You're sure Rodriguez is still ashore?" she asked for the third time.

"Yes. I told you, Spears checked to see that he was still in the Blue Parrot. He was," Devon assured her.

Laly couldn't help but be nervous. Every day since she and Sugar had traveled through time had become more harrowing. She was beginning to wonder if their presence wasn't causing some horrible chain reaction. "Do you see it? Is it there?"

Devon stared hard into the night. So far they hadn't found the *Puta*, but she had to be anchored somewhere nearby. "No, not yet," he answered.

Laly watched Devon at the bow of the boat. Her heart ached with love for him, for his stalwart ways, his strong exterior and tender emotions. He was the perfect man, and he loved her. He loved her enough to let her go. She sighed and saw him glance in her direction. She smiled reassuringly at him and kept on with her thoughts. How can I leave him? she wondered. I'll never find anyone like him back home. Yet what would happen if she stayed behind? Was it even possible? She and Sugar had come through the time warp together; could one of them get back alone? She closed her eyes wearily. There were so many questions she couldn't answer.

Devon glanced at Laly, her eyes closed in thought. Could he convince her to stay with him? He only knew he was going to try. He had to. She was everything he wanted and needed in a woman. She was intelligent and high-spirited. She was funny and daring. She was beautiful. And she understood his love for the sea. He had to convince her to stay. Turning back around to search through the darkness, he suddenly saw it. "The *Puta*!" he rasped.

"Where, Captain?" one of the crew asked.

"There, look in that bay. Why, you sly fox, Rodriguez," he mused. "No wonder we didn't see him anchored near the point. He's found a deep channel. Look, you can barely see the masts against the background of trees."

Laly could see the *Puta* floating where Devon indicated. Her heart began a quicker pace in nervous anticipation. "What do we do?" she asked.

Devon put his finger over his lips to bring them to silence. "Sound travels over water great distances," he breathed. He then signaled the oarsmen to muffle their oars.

Laly watched in fascination while the men took rags they'd brought with them and wrapped them around the oarlocks. They then preceded to row silently toward the *Puta*.

When they were finally along side the ship Devon signaled the oarsmen to wait while he, Laly, and Samuel went on board to search. "If we get into trouble, get out of here," he barely breathed.

Laly climbed the rope ladder which dangled over the side of the *Puta*. Devon and Samuel had already boarded and were waiting for her, watching out for any crewmen that might still be on board. So far, they'd gone unnoticed.

As she peered over the rail, she could see cannon and muskets standing at the ready along the casemate. She shivered remembering that this ship and the *Vengeance* had been in battle the day she and Sugar had arrived from the future. They'd nearly swum toward the *Puta* to be rescued, and she shuddered to think how things might have turned out if they had. Rodriguez would probably have turned them over to his crew, after he was done with them himself.

Devon helped Laly over the side, ducking when he heard a noise.

Laly knelt behind Devon and waited. A crewman walked along the port side of the ship, looking out to sea. He stopped finally, and stepping up to the rail, he opened his trousers and released his bladder into the sea. Laly breathed a sigh of relief that he wasn't on guard duty. A few moments later, the man sauntered back below deck.

Looking around, Laly wondered why there weren't guards posted. Raising her brows at Devon, he merely shrugged his answer.

Devon signaled Laly and Samuel to follow. He headed toward the stairs leading below. Slowly, he descended, watching every second so they wouldn't be discovered. In minutes they were outside the captain's cabin. Touching the door handle, he turned it gently and pushed. They were in!

Sugar paced the deck of the *Vengeance* and looked out to the dark sea. Her hands ached from wringing them together, and her jaw hurt from clenching her teeth.

"Miss Sugar?" Wainwright addressed her.

"Yes?" She took her eyes from the sea only long enough to acknowledge his presence.

"Are you all right? I noticed you've been out here since Miss Laly left."

"I . . . I could kick myself for letting Laly go off on this hare brained scheme to steal the medallion from that bloodthirsty pirate. She could be killed, and here I am, helpless to do anything about it."

"I'm sure she'll be fine. Captain Bradley won't let anything happen to her. He loves her."

Sugar turned and met his eyes. "He does, doesn't he?" she said softly.

"Very much."

"And she loves him."

"I hope so. The captain is a good man. He deserves to be happy."

Sugar pondered his words as she stood once again looking out to sea. "Laly has to go back," she finally said.

"Why?"

"She doesn't belong here."

"Doesn't she?" Wainwright studied the beautiful woman before him. "Doesn't she belong wherever, or whenever, she's happy?"

Sugar felt a light breeze begin to tilt the ship. She

tipped her head to move the hair that blew across her face. "You're a philosopher, Wainwright," she said.

He shrugged. "I just believe in love," he said.

"You do? That seems a strange admission for a man to make."

"Really? A man of my time, or yours?"

"A man of any time, I think."

Wainwright reached out and brushed aside the tendril of curling black hair that insisted on blowing in her eyes. He tucked it behind her ear. "What do you know of men, Sugar?"

"I'm not going to get into this with you, Wainwright."

"Call me Charles," he urged. He'd been attracted to Sugar from the start, and now that there was a possibility Laly would stay with the captain, he thought it a good time to approach her.

Sugar took a step back, surprised at what she heard in the tone of his voice. "Wainwright ... Okay, Charles. I'm not in the mood for love." She dropped her head and laughed. "God, I sound like a bad song," she said. "But all I want to do is get Laly safely back to this ship and then home."

"Without even giving this place a chance?" He meant without giving him a chance.

Sugar knew exactly what he meant, but she chose to take his words at face value. "Since we got here, Laly has killed a man, Gaspar has been murdered, Devereaux was justly killed, and Margaret died accidentally. I think this place has had more than a fair chance. I want to go home," she stated flatly.

Wainwright felt his heart sink a little at her appraisal of the events. "Yes, I guess you would." He looked out to sea. "They should be back before long. Then you can be on your way."

"If we can find the storm," she murmured.

"Yes, the storm," he agreed.

Laly dropped piles of smelly clothes on Rodriguez's bed. Didn't the filthy man ever bathe, she wondered? They'd been searching for over half and hour and still hadn't found the medallion. "Where could it be?" she whispered.

Devon shrugged as he continued to push against every board in the walls. He'd already checked the molding, the bottom of the sea chest, and inside and outside the closet. Somewhere in this room there had to be a secret compartment, and he was determined to find it. Every minute or so he'd glance to where Samuel was keeping watch by the door. So far, they'd been very lucky.

Rodriguez grumbled as his men walked along the beach with him. He was angry with himself for spending all of Gaspar's money, and he was angry with Gaspar for leaving so little behind, forgetting that earlier that day he'd toasted his good fortune at finding such a large sum of money under Gaspar's bed. "I am ready to leave this place. I feel my good luck has changed," he said.

"We are ready to go, too, Sir," one of the men agreed.

"Who asked you?" demanded Rodriguez. He was also angry the little whore he'd been buying drinks for all night had suddenly disappeared. He had been ready to stick his thing in her, and now he would have to go to sleep without relief. "Damn the gods," he mumbled.

They had one rocky hill to climb before they dropped down into his private bay, his hiding place. And he needed to rest before he started to climb. "You go on ahead. I will rest for only a moment, then I will follow you."

The men knew they'd have to come back for him in the morning. Many nights he slept at the foot of this hill, but none were going to argue with him. "*Sí,*" they agreed. When they reached the top of the hill, though, they raced back down to their captain. "There's a boat beside the *Puta!*" they shouted.

Rodriguez had already started to doze off when he heard their shouts. "What do you say?"

"There is a boat beside the *Puta,*" they repeated excitedly.

Rodriguez stood up, instantly sober. He climbed the hill quickly and stared down over its crest at his ship. There was, indeed, a boat where it didn't belong. "Whoever it is will be sorry," he rasped.

Laly sat on the bed, then quickly stood back up, remembering the dirty state of the sheets. She wouldn't have been surprised to learn it was infested with lice. "I don't know where else to look," she whispered. She'd gone through every piece of dirty clothing in the room. She'd torn the bed apart and put it back together, she'd even searched the water closet, gagging over the chamberpot that hadn't been emptied in days.

Devon had to admit he was stumped. "I don't know, either." He'd finally found a secret compartment in the wall behind the bed, but it held nothing more than a small money pouch and some charts. "He must have put it in another room, though I can't believe he'd trust anyone else with it," he said.

"What do we do now?" Laly asked. "Samuel, can you think of anything?"

Samuel turned his head from watching the companionway for only a second to answer Laly, but it was long enough for Rodriguez to fire a shot that hit him in the shoulder.

Laly screamed as Samuel slumped to the floor.

"Laly, get down!" yelled Devon, pulling his pistol.

Laly rushed to Samuel's side, feeling for his pulse, grateful it was strong.

"Laly, get out of the way!" ordered Devon, but it was too late. Rodriguez jumped to the doorway and placed a pistol to her head.

"Captain Bradley, how nice to see you again. I thought you were dead. And my little mermaid. I thought you were enjoying your new life with Devereaux." He glared at Bradley. "Captain, you may put your pistol on the floor. Unless you want the mermaid's brains all over this room."

Devon gritted his teeth and put down his pistol. "Let her go, Rodriguez. She came with me only because I forced her."

"How gallant of you, Captain. And how stupid. You don't think I'll believe your lies, do you?"

Laly hadn't moved since she'd felt the barrel of the pistol touch her head. She'd seen firsthand the kind of damage the ancient weapon could do, and she knew how unpredictable the triggers were. "May I do something for Samuel?" she asked quietly.

Rodriguez looked down at the black man on the floor. "No, I will do something for him. Carlos, take this man topside and throw him overboard," he ordered.

"No!" Laly cried.

"He can join the other two already floating face down in the sea," he laughed.

Devon's gut wrenched at the news of the men he'd left below. "You killed them?" he hissed.

"Of course, Captain. You would do the same if you found dirty, thieving pirates trying to steal from your ship, would you not?"

"My men weren't pirates."

"They were to me," Rodriguez spat. "Carlos, get this garbage out of here," he said of Samuel. "And hand me the captain's pistol."

Carlos entered the room and picked up the weapon, all the time keeping his eyes on the big English captain. Once he handed Rodriguez the pistol, he backed up, grasping the black man's arm. He started to pull him from the room. A groan from the man's chest stopped him for a moment, but he soon had him in the companionway. "He lives," he said to Rodriguez.

"Not for long," the pirate answered.

Laly backed away from Rodriguez after Samuel was gone. She couldn't believe they'd come to this end. Not after everything else they'd survived.

"Get up," ordered Rodriguez. He had a headache and looking down was making it worse. Watching the woman stand and lean into the captain's arms, he was filled with joy at the idea that flashed through his mind. He even laughed out loud.

"What's so funny, Rodriguez?" Devon asked.

"I am a genius," he answered.

"I find that funny, too," agreed Devon.

"Shut up!" ordered Rodriguez. "You will think nothing is so very funny in a little while."

Laly tightened her grip on Devon's torso. At least if she was going to die, she was glad it was with the man she loved. Raising her chin defiantly, she waited for Rodriguez to pull the trigger. She was surprised when he laughed again and backed out of the room, closing the door behind him.

"I will leave two guards outside this door, Captain, so don't try anything too stupid," he yelled through the door.

Laly looked blankly at Devon. "What's going on?" she asked. "I thought he was going to kill us."

"He is. He just has something special in mind."

Laly let her head fall forward to rest on his chest. She listened to the sound of his strong heartbeat and prayed.

"The ship is moving," Devon whispered minutes later.

Laly raised her tearfilled eyes to his.

"We've set sail."

Sugar was dreaming of pizza. Her mouth watered and her stomach growled. She could even smell the stuff. What a lovely dream, she thought. Then she was suddenly awake. What time was it? How long had she been asleep? Where was Laly?

Unfolding from the uncomfortable position she'd dozed of in, she stood on shaky legs and looked toward the sea. "Oh my God," she whispered. The sun was turning the eastern horizon a brilliant orange. It was morning and Laly and the captain weren't back yet. "Wainwright!" she called. "Wainwright!" She headed for the stairs.

Half way down the companionway she met a sleepy Wainwright. He'd obviously slept in his clothes and was rubbing the sleep from his eyes. "Are they back?"

"No. We've got to go find them," she insisted.

"We don't know where to look," he said sadly.

"Well, if you think I'm going to just sit here on this bloody ship and wait for their bodies to wash ashore, you've got another thing coming, sailor. So think of something!"

Wainwright was taken aback by her aggression. "I don't know what to do, Miss Sugar."

"Send out search parties. Go looking yourself! I don't care what, just do something!" Sugar yelled, her voice getting louder with every word.

"Wainwright!" called Lawson. "Come quick!"

Sugar and Wainwright exchanged glances. "Laly," Sugar whisper.

Running up the stairs and back out on deck, she was shocked to see Samuel lying on an oilcloth. "Samuel? Where are they?" she asked. Rushing to his side, she knelt beside him. "Oh no, you're injured." Her heart broke as she thought the worst.

"They were alive when Rodriguez had me thrown overboard," whispered Samuel weakly. "I saw them sail." His eyes rolled back then, and he lost consciousness.

Sugar felt for his pulse. "Take him to my cabin," she told the crewmen standing nearby. As she watched him being lifted, she turned to Wainwright. "Do you know what to do now?" she demanded.

"Yes, Miss Sugar." He turned to the crew. "Get ready to sail!" he yelled loudly.

Satisfied that at last something was being done, Sugar went below to tend to Samuel's wound.

Laly and Devon sat on the wooden floor of Rodriguez's cabin. The bed was too filthy to use and the chairs that skirted his table were too small to hold them both. That left the floor. Laly didn't mind. She only wanted to be near Devon as long as she could. "What do you think he's going to do with us?" she asked.

"I don't know," Devon answered. He couldn't believe he'd come to this. Two of his crewmen were dead—three, if he counted Samuel—and he and Laly were going to die in some horrible fashion at the hands of his most hated enemy.

"Make love to me, Devon," Laly whispered.

"What?" he asked incredulously. She couldn't have surprised him more if she'd suddenly sprouted wings and flown around the room.

"I want you to make love to me," she repeated.

"Here? Now?"

"This may be the last here and now we have. I want to love you once more before I die." Laly's eyes filled with tears.

Devon looked down into the magical turquoise eyes he loved so much and leaned to kiss her. The second his lips touched hers he felt himself begin the ascent to that place only she could take him. Somehow it seemed fitting they should make love one last time. Reaching beneath her hair, he pulled her more closely to his kiss, delving deeply with his tongue into the sweet recesses of her mouth.

Laly felt the desperation in Devon's kiss and knew

their lovemaking would have new meaning. This was their last time. Her tears fell and mingled with the moistness of their mouths, giving their kiss a salty flavor.

"I love you, Laly," Devon moaned, as he licked the tears from her cheeks. He then kissed her eyes, drying the moisture that twinkled on her lashes.

Laly lay back, leading Devon to lay on the floor with her. She loved the feel of his hard body over hers, molding to fit her perfectly.

"Is the floor too hard?" he asked, cradling her head in his hands.

"No. Just love me," she pleaded huskily.

Devon obliged her, lowering his head to kiss her in the open V of the shirt she wore, letting his tongue trace the soft mounds of her breasts under the fabric.

Laly arched to his kisses, her nipples growing hard to his touch. Tangling her fingers in his hair, she pulled his head down and clasped him tightly to her breasts.

Devon lay against the softness that was Laly. He listened to her heartbeat and heard the tempo racing wildly in her chest. Rubbing his hands along her sides and down her hips, he let himself enjoy the feeling of her body under his fingers. He pressed himself to her, moving his hips in a rhythmic pattern over her abdomen.

Laly moaned with passion as Devon's manhood branded her through their clothes. She felt marked by his desire, forever his possession. Rotating her hips to match the rhythm he played over her, she put her hands down over the tight muscles of his buttocks, forcing him even closer to her.

Devon raised his head slightly and pushed Laly's shirt up to expose her breasts. Leaning down, he took the tight bud of her nipple wholly into his mouth and let his tongue rough it playfully.

Laly arched under Devon and sighed with pleasure. He could make her feel all things at once. She continued to hold him to her, mirroring his movements to perfection.

Devon cupped the fullness of her breasts in the palms of his large hands. He suckled her and rubbed his thumbs over the rosy pouting crests that jutted up for his attention. "You're so beautiful, Laly," he murmured.

Laly reached to remove his shirt. She wanted to see his magnificent body once more. She pulled the shirt over his head, then tried to unfasten his belt. Her fingers fumbled and he had to help her, but in seconds he was naked before her. "You are perfect," she told him adoringly.

Devon smiled at her. It was so strange to hear a woman speak as she did. It was time to finish removing her clothing. Tugging her shirt off, he tossed it aside. His fingers wandered over her body from her shoulders to her waist. He grasped the waistband of her trousers and began to pull them slowly down. As he inched the fabric lower, he kissed the newly exposed skin, licking her lightly, then blowing on the moist skin, sending chills running through her.

"You make me cold?" she giggled.

"Only to warm you again," he answered.

When his lips and tongue found Laly's most secret place she arched her back and gave him easy access to her body. She wanted him to devour her completely, to make her disappear with him into oblivion.

Devon finished pulling off Laly's pants and rose to cover her with his body. He was hot and ready. Probing her softness with the head of his passion, he entered her slowly at first, torturing himself with his patience.

Laly raised to meet him, only to have him pull out again. She groaned with desire. "Please, Devon."

"Not yet, my sweet mermaid." Again and again he drove himself into her only inches, then pulled himself free. He could see the glazed passion in her eyes and could feel the need in her grasping fingers where she clutched his skin.

"Devon, pleased," she begged again.

Finally he plunged deeply within her loving sheath. Pulling back, he thrust again. Over and over he repeated the depth at a desperate pace, rocking her with him in his need for fulfillment.

Laly accepted and matched the urgency of Devon's lovemaking. This was their last time, their last moment of passion together. They had to have this.

Devon looked down at Laly's face and saw pain there. "Do I hurt you?" he asked.

Laly opened her eyes. "No, it isn't you. Don't stop," she begged.

Suddenly he realized she was accepting the full weight of their bodies against the hard wooden floor. "Let me," he urged. Lifting her from the floor, he stood up, taking her with him.

Laly wrapped her legs tightly around his waist and smiled at his concern for her. She waited for him to begin their rhythm again.

Devon swung his hips slightly and reveled in the sensation of burying himself deeply within Laly's core. Holding her by the waist, he was able to lift her as he thrust, magnifying each movement and pulling them closer to their moment of ecstasy together.

Laly closed her eyes and let Devon lead her in their lovemaking. She raised when he gently lifted. She fell against him when he impaled her. She was merely an extension of his passion, a part of his already incredible body.

Devon soon felt himself nearing the precipice of release. Bending slightly, he made his thrusts more powerful, bringing Laly with him in perfect harmony. As the shuddering eruption began, he felt her gripping him more tightly, heard her gasping for air as she lost control.

Laly felt herself explode into a million pieces. Each piece fluttered like spring leaves before falling to unite once more over Devon's strong body. "I love you," she whispered.

Devon suffered the agony of perfection. He couldn't have known such exquisite pain existed. His body erupted again and again in a powerful release. He felt himself filling Laly with his seed and wished they had a future to see that seed growing within her. Holding her tightly in his arms, he crushed her to him in desperation. How could he have found her only to lose her now?

Laly lay against Devon's chest. She unwrapped her legs and slid down his body to stand in the circle of his arms. "We'd better get dressed," she murmured.

Devon nodded, but didn't move.

Laly raised her head and looked up. "Did you hear me?" she whispered, smiling.

"Yes. I just wondered what Rodriguez would do if he knew what we were doing down here."

"I don't want to even think about it," she grimaced. "Now, hand me my clothes."

Devon released her and bent to reach their clothes. In a matter of minutes, they were dressed and sitting together as they had been before Laly's request.

"Isn't there something we can do to escape?" she asked. "What about the porthole?"

Devon glanced back. "Too small," he stated.

"Oh. I guess I don't really want to try and swim to shore, anyway. We're probably pretty far out by now."

Devon nodded.

"Could we bribe the guards?" she asked.

"With what?"

"Your charm?" she teased.

"I don't think so," he said dryly.

"Really. Do you think we could talk the guards into helping us? You could promise them amnesty or something."

"The only thing those men understand is money or death; neither one can we provide or cause."

Laly lay back against Devon's shoulder. "I'm not giving up," she said.

"I never thought you would." He grinned.

Sugar remained on deck all morning, searching the horizon for a sign of the *Puta*. "How could they have gotten so far?" she complained.

"It's not that far to the horizon," Wainwright said.

Sugar jumped with a start. "I didn't know you were there," she said.

"Then who were you talking to?"

"Myself."

"Oh. Sorry to interrupt your conversation."

Sugar laughed softly. "It's okay. You didn't interrupt, you just startled me."

Wainwright smiled and sat next to her. "We could see them anytime," he said.

"I hope so," she said, her hand shielding her eyes as she scanned the horizon again. "I just wish I knew we were headed in the right direction."

"I'm pretty sure we are," answered Wainwright.

Sugar turned to look at him. "Why do you say that? We don't know which way they went."

"Rodriguez usually sticks close to a tiny island called, coincidentally, Pirates' Cove."

"You're kidding. Why didn't you tell me this sooner?"

"I didn't want to get your hopes up."

"Then why tell me now?"

"Because we've been sailing for hours with no sign of him. That in itself is a pretty good indication he's making a beeline for someplace. It's logical he'd head for a place he thinks of as home."

"Wainwright, you surprise me," she offered.

"Charles," he told her.

"Okay. Charles, you surprise me," she repeated, smiling. Then, more solemnly, "Do you think they're still all right?" she asked.

"Yes, I do," he answered firmly. He could see the doubt in her eyes. "Again, I'm being logical. If Rodriguez didn't have some grandiose plan for their deaths, he'd have killed them when he shot Samuel." He looked toward the horizon. "No, he has something special planned for them, and since we haven't caught up with him, he hasn't stopped to carry it out. Yes, I believe they've still alive," he said bluntly.

Sugar felt some relief, albeit small. Part of what

he'd said scared her to death. If the *Vengeance* didn't catch up with Rodriguez soon, he was going to do something hideous to Laly and Devon. She closed her eyes and shuddered with fear. She couldn't let them die at the hands of that madman.

Eighteen

Laly stretched and felt the strong muscles of Devon's arm under her head. Sometime during the early morning hours, she'd dozed off. Looking up, she saw Devon smiling down at her.

"Sleep well?" he asked.

"I think so," she answered. "Did you sleep at all?"

He shook his head.

She reached up at touched the dark circles under his eyes with her fingertip.

Devon took Laly's hand and kissed her fingers one at a time. "I love you," he whispered.

A cloud descended over the usually brilliant turquoise of Laly's eyes. "It's almost time, isn't it?"

Devon heaved a deep sigh. "I don't know. I don't know what he has planned."

Laly pulled away from his embrace and went to the porthole. "Do you know where we are?"

Devon stood and joined her at the porthole. "I have a pretty good idea. I think we're nearing Pirate's Cove."

"What?" Laly asked frowning.

"It's an island, and Rodriguez's most frequent port," he answered.

"But if you know where he usually is, why hasn't he been arrested before now?" she asked incredulously.

Devon turned her to face him. "Because we can arrest him only if we catch him with stolen goods."

"And you haven't yet."

"We did once," he said.

"Then why didn't you stop him?" she questioned.

"We were interrupted . . . by the surprising arrival of two mermaids," he explained, grinning.

"Oh, no," breathed Laly. "If it weren't for us, you'd have caught him."

Devon shrugged. "Things happen. And I won't say I'm sorry you showed up." He leaned to place a gentle kiss over her lips.

Laly extended the kiss, loving every second of the contact, but pulled away when an exciting thought occurred to her. "Devon, do you think Wainwright might figure out where we are?"

Devon looked out the porthole once more. "I hope so." He shook his head. "But he won't know we've sailed."

"But he'll figure it out, won't he? I mean, when we didn't come back to the *Vengeance*, he'd have known something was wrong. Sugar would have made him do something."

"I don't want you to get your hopes up, but yes, I've begun hoping the *Vengeance* isn't too far behind us." He looked down into her eyes. "All we can do is try to stall."

Laly glanced around her. "I'll stall, all right." She searched her brain for an idea that would gain them some time. Letting her eyes roam Rodriguez's filthy room, she suddenly focused on his bedding. Stepping up to his bunk, she picked up the edge of one of his blankets. Grimacing at the odor that clung to the sheets, she wrinkled her nose as she pulled the blanket up to smell it. It wasn't as bad as the sheets, but it still had an odor. "Oh, well, it will have to do," she said.

"Do what?" Devon asked.

Laly looked pointedly at Devon. "Help me look like a mermaid," she answered.

"What? You're crazy," Devon spewed.

"No, I'm not. What I am is desperate. And I'm going to try and buy us some time. Now, help me get ready."

Devon squinted in rebellion as he watched her pull the blanket from the bed. "What do I have to do?" he reluctantly asked.

"Help me tear this blanket into strips."

"What for?"

"My costume, of course. It's blue. That should help."

Devon didn't know how Laly wanted to look. He had no clue what she had in mind, but she was right about them being desperate. It would be ridiculous of him to argue with her when she had an idea. No matter how strange the idea sounded.

An hour later he couldn't believe his eyes when he looked at her. She'd wound strips of the blue cloth around her nearly nude body in a tantalizing fashion. Bits of the fabric covered her breasts and wrapped around her hips and between her legs. She'd taken thinner pieces and hung them, overlapping, from the strip at her hips to form a wild kind of skirt. Other long pieces she'd braided in her hair and left hanging nearly to the floor. She'd tied still others from her upper arms, elbows, and wrists, leaving them trailing to her ankles. Bits of a broken bottle found under the table became a kind of jewelry, the small pieces of green glass tied along a thin strip as a necklace.

"What do you think?" she asked, turning before him.

"I think you're amazing," he told her.

Rolling her eyes, she grinned at him. "Do I look like a mermaid?" she asked.

"I don't know about a mermaid, but you definitely look like something from the sea. Maybe a sea goddess?" he suggested.

"I hope that's good enough," she murmured. At that moment the door burst open.

"Good morning, my friends," Rodriguez announced, as he entered the cabin. "What's this?" He gaped at Laly's costume.

Stepping forward, Laly raised her jaw to stare defiantly at the pirate. Her heart pounded with fear, but she fought the sensation. "I have decided to admit what I am," she stated.

Rodriguez raised a brow. "And that is?"

Laly turned slowly before him. "What do I look like?" she asked.

Rodriguez glanced back at the guards still standing in the open door. Their eyes were wide with fear and surprise. "You look like a woman dressed in some sort of costume," he said loudly, to dispel their fears.

"It's a pity you don't believe in mermaids," she said strongly. "Those that don't believe are the ones who suffer most."

"Are you threatening me?" He took a step closer to her.

Devon moved swiftly between Laly and Rodriguez. "She made no threats, Rodriguez. She only made an observation."

Rodriguez frowned at Devon. "Tell her to keep her mouth shut or she'll lose her tongue," he threatened quietly.

Laly swallowed with fear at his words.

Devon looked down at the pirate. "You'll have to kill me before I'll allow you to lay a hand on her," he promised.

Rodriguez took a step back and began to laugh. "Don't worry, Captain. I plan to."

Laly shuddered as Rodriguez continued to laugh.

"I have such an end planned for you both," Rodriguez chuckled. "Even you will have to admit it's brilliant."

Devon just stared hard at the pirate. He knew the Vengeance would never get here in time to save them, and he only wished Rodriguez's plan included a quick end for Laly. He couldn't bare the thought of her suffering. "Let's get on with it, Rodriguez. I'm tired of your foolish talk," he challenged. "And so is Laly. She thinks you're an idiot."

Laly's eyes opened wide at Devon's words. Did he want Rodriguez to shoot them now? Then she realized that's exactly what he was hoping so as to spare them the diabolical end he'd planned for them. Her heart swelled with love for him. "Yes, Rodriguez. You bore me," she added.

Rodriguez stood still for a moment, his blood boiling with rage, then he smiled again. "You almost fooled me," he said. "I see what you try to do." He shook his head. "It won't work." He started for the door. "You will die within the hour," he told them.

"An hour?" Laly murmured.

"*Sí*, mermaid, an hour. That gives you time to make your peace with God."

"I'm at peace with God," said Laly. "But how does it feel to know you'll burn in hell for eternity, Rodriguez?" she asked.

Rodriguez only laughed some more. "Me and the devil, we're best friends," he told her.

Devon stepped forward. "You don't mean to kill us on empty stomachs, do you?"

Rodriguez looked puzzled.

"I mean, you're going to give us a last meal, aren't you?"

"I have never given a 'last meal' to anyone I've killed," answered Rodriguez.

"Then you should start with us."

Laly didn't know what Devon was up to. She certainly didn't think she could eat anything right now, but she trusted his judgment. "I'm starving," she lied.

Rodriguez contemplated their request. "I suppose it would hurt nothing to let you eat," he said.

"You could even join us," Devon added.

"Why would I want to eat with you?" asked Rodriguez, disgusted.

"We have much in common. We are both captains. We have been adversaries. The better man has won. I think it would be fitting for us to have one meal together." He bowed slightly.

Rodriguez's ego swelled at Devon's words. He didn't trust the Englishman, but he spoke the truth. "I will eat with you," he agreed.

Devon nodded. "Then we'll see you shortly."

Rodriguez left them, making sure the guards were posted by the door.

"What are you thinking?" Laly asked. "You sounded positively cordial with that animal, as if you were inviting him to tea?"

Devon looked down at her confused face. "Buying time, my sweet mermaid. Buying time."

An hour later they were still alive. Laly listened while Devon and Rodriguez told each other tales of their adventures at sea. Each tried to outdo the other and they laughed jovially like old friends. Only the guards, standing with muskets ready to fire, gave the scene any realism.

Laly forced herself to laugh as Rodriguez told how he'd had one of his crew keel-hauled for stealing a bottle of rum. "Justice served," she commented, while thinking he should be skinned alive for the many crimes he'd committed in his wretched life. Pushing her nearly full plate aside, she looked to Rodriguez.

"*Sí,* mermaid. When one is in charge of a ship, one must be firm. Don't you agree, Captain?" He turned to Devon.

"Yes, of course. I myself have had to punish men for less than stealing," he agreed.

"What have you done?" asked Rodriguez, leaning forward to hear a ruthless tale.

Devon had to think fast. He looked to Laly and winked slightly so only she would see. "I had a man's legs broken," he lied.

"I am proud of you, Captain. For what crime?"

"For dancing while on watch."

Rodriguez lowered his lids suspiciously. "For this you had his legs broken?"

Devon leveled him with a challenging stare. "Yes. He was pulling double duty for returning late from his leave. Some of the men were dancing and celebrating another's upcoming wedding. The man decided he should join the fun. I saw to it he didn't dance again for quite some time."

Rodriguez decided his story had the ring of truth. "Yes, I am proud of you, Captain."

Laly was amazed Devon could lie so efficiently. She smiled at him over the rim of her mug and brushed his leg with her toe under the table.

"And what do mermaids do all day?" Rodriguez asked, looking in Laly's direction.

Laly swallowed her drink quickly. "What?"

"What do you do?"

Laly decided she'd tell him the truth. "I'm a college professor."

"A coll . . ."

"I'm a teacher," she simplified.

"You teach other mermaids?" Rodriguez asked.

"I teach others, yes."

"What do you teach them?"

Laly looked around the room at her surroundings. "I teach them current history," she said smiling, enjoying her private joke.

"Current history? Sounds very boring," shrugged Rodriguez.

"Current events can be quite interesting," interjected Devon, looking at Laly with a suggestive tilt to his head.

"Enough about this. I want to talk about something else," complained Rodriguez.

"Yes, of course," agreed Devon. "But first, do you have any cigars, Captain?"

Rodriguez thought about turning down his request, then decided he would enjoy a cigar also. "I will get them," he said, nodding. Crossing to the closet, he pulled out a small box and brought it back to the table. Offering Captain Bradley one, he took one for himself and set the box on the table.

Laly cleared her throat to get his attention. "Don't you offer cigars to all your guests?" she asked.

Rodriguez raised his brows. Pushing the cigar box toward her, he watched in amazement when she took one, biting the end off and rolling it between her fingers.

Devon caught Laly's eye and raised on brow. He hoped she knew what she was doing.

"A light, please?" she asked.

Rodriguez lit the cigars and continued to watch Laly. "Mermaid, do you smoke often?" he asked.

"Only when I can get a good cigar, which isn't often at the bottom of the ocean. They don't burn well underwater, either," she added seriously.

Devon clamped his jaws tight so as not to laugh at her ridiculous statements. Sucking hard on his cigar, he began to choke when his laughter got the better of him.

"You could take lessons from the mermaid," Rodriguez told him.

Laly continued to puff on the cigar and smile at Rodriguez when she'd rather spit on him. She didn't know how much longer she could keep up the facade.

"Captain Rodriguez, I have one more request of your most generous hospitality," said Devon, when he'd gotten his wind back.

"Yes, Captain?"

"Just to satisfy my curiosity, since we're your prisoners anyway, might you tell us where you've hidden the King's Medallion? We searched everywhere and couldn't find it."

Laly stopped her cigar in midair. She couldn't

believe Devon had the nerve to come out and ask where the medallion was.

Rodriguez narrowed his eyes. His crewmen standing guard took a threatening step forward, but he waved them back. "You still think you will escape and take the medallion with you?" he asked.

"Not at all, Captain. I realize we are doomed. That is why I asked. I knew you wouldn't show us your hiding place if there was any chance of escape," explained Devon.

Rodriguez banged on fist on the table. "You are correct. You are doomed. So I will show it to you."

Laly was startled by Rodriguez's violent action, but she was shocked when he agreed to show them where he'd hidden the medallion. She watched wide-eyed as he walked toward the water closet.

"I looked in there," she murmured, remembering the disgusting chamberpot. Her eyes opened even wider when he knelt in front of the filthy commode. He hadn't put the medallion inside, had he, she wondered?

Rodriguez reached for the rim of the chamberpot and tilted the whole thing backward slightly. Then, reaching beneath it, he pulled the medallion from a hollow spot in the floor.

Devon watched with fascination. No wonder they couldn't find it, and no one else would have either. No one would be brave enough to tilt the chamberpot. It looked ready to overflow at any minute. "I stand corrected, Rodriguez," he murmured.

"Captain?" Rodriguez inquired.

"You are a genius."

Rodriguez threw his head back and laughed. "Would you like to hold it before you die?" he asked.

Laly's heart did a terrified flip when he mentioned their deaths again, but she managed to keep smiling, and nodded that she'd like to hold the medallion.

Rodriguez brought the medallion to the table. Handing it to Laly, he smiled as he thought about the money he'd get when he sold it. For now, though, he just liked having it.

Laly turned the medallion over in her hands. "You have no idea what this means to me," she whispered. If only Sugar could obtain it one day, perhaps she could still get back home.

"May I?" Devon held out his hand and watched as Laly placed it carefully on his palm. "It's quite heavy," he remarked, as though he'd never touched it before.

"Solid gold," crooned Rodriguez.

"What do you plan to do with it?" Devon asked.

"Do with it? I will sell it, of course," answered Rodriguez. "After a while," he added.

"It's a famous piece. You may have trouble finding a buyer," Devon told him.

"I will find a buyer when I am ready. I may even ransom it back to the governor," said Rodriguez.

Devon raised his brows. "If he wants it back. He told me himself it was becoming more trouble that it's worth," he said.

"As are you, Captain. I grow tired of our conversation," said Rodriguez. Snatching the medallion from Devon's hand, he went back to the water closet and placed it carefully under the chamberpot.

Laly looked at Devon with panic in her eyes.

Devon glanced around the room. "Aren't you worried your guards will try to steal the medallion, now that they know where it is?" he asked hurriedly.

Rodriguez stood and looked as his men. "No. They know I would kill them if they did."

"But if they ran?"

"I would find them. Then I would make them beg for me to kill them. Much as you will soon do, Captain."

Laly stood abruptly from the table. "Please, Captain, let Devon go. He was just doing his duty. I'm the one you have the quarrel with," she pleaded.

"This is why your deaths are going to be so much fun," Rodriguez said. "You care for each other. What a pity." He started from the room. "Bring them," he ordered his guards.

When the guards waved the muskets at them, Devon refused to move. Instead, he stood defiantly in front of Laly and stared hard at the two men, daring them to shoot him.

"Captain!" one of the men called.

Rodriguez stuck his head back through the door. "Why must you be difficult? Did I not give you a last meal? Did I not sit with you? Did I not show you where the medallion was hidden, and even let you hold it? All of these things I did for you and you will not do one thing for me?"

"We won't make our deaths easier for you," growled Devon.

"Very well. Pedro! Manuel! Esteban!" he called loudly.

Seconds later crewmen rushed through the door.

"Hold him!" ordered Rodriguez. "And Carlos, keep your weapon on the woman. If she moves, shoot her."

Devon fought their attack, swinging wildly with his

punches, even knocking one man out cold, but there were too many of them. Soon he was being held to the floor.

Laly watched in agony as Devon suffered blows at the hands of Rodriguez's crew. Once they had him down, they punched and kicked him for spite. "Rodriguez, call off your men," she pleaded.

"My men have suffered bruises, too. They only pay him back for what he did to them."

"You are a low, stinking, filthy, cowardly bastard, Rodriguez. If I could get my bare hands on you, I'd rip your eyes from their sockets and feed them to the fish," she hissed.

"What a lovely idea you have given me, mermaid," Rodriguez chuckled. "Bring them," he ordered.

Laly was led up to the deck with Devon being hauled behind. The warm tropical breeze, sparkling blue water, and beautiful blue sky made a ludicrous setting for what was about to happen. As she was pulled toward the railing, she began to fight in earnest. It took two men grabbing her arms to subdue her, and she was soon tied to the railing, her hands bound at her back.

She watched as Devon was tied to two oars that had been lashed together, and she wondered, terrified, what they were going to do with him. She didn't have to wonder for long. Rodriguez himself walked to where Devon lay helpless and began to slash shallow cuts across his stomach and thighs.

"Noooo!" Laly screamed as she watched. *"Noooo, Rodriguez!* Please, I'll do anything you say. *Please!"* she begged.

Rodriguez only laughed and made another cut slowly while she watched.

Devon flinched under each cut, but he refused to

cry out. He could feel his blood running in rivulets from the wounds, soaking his clothing with the sticky stuff. He'd begun to guess what Rodriguez had planned for him, and his greatest worry was that Laly was going to be forced to watch. He knew she'd never bear it.

Laly's eyes burned with the tears that flowed in rivers down her cheeks. She felt each wound on Devon's body as if it were her own, and she'd have gladly traded places with him if she could have. When she saw Rodriguez's crewmen begin to lift him, she realized with horror what they were going to do. "No, Rodriguez. Not even you could be so cruel. If you're going to murder us, just do it and get it over with!" she shouted.

Rodriguez laughed. "It is truly touching to see such devotion," he called to her. "Be sure to watch carefully, mermaid. We will see if the little fishes," he turned his head toward his crew, "and some not so little, listen to you. Over the side with him! Put him under once so he feels his wounds," he ordered.

Laly watched as Devon was raised over the rail and lowered toward the water. *"Nooo!"* she screamed, though she knew it did no good. Fighting her bonds, she pulled so hard against the ropes she felt her wrists begin to bleed. She didn't care. If she had to take the flesh off from the wrists down, she'd escape, she vowed.

Devon tried to take a deep breath before he hit the water, but the shock of the salt water burning his wounds was more than he could stand and he gasped, choking on the salty brine. Sputtering and gagging as he was pulled back up, he heard Laly sobbing at the rail. "Please, God, don't make her see this," he prayed.

"Dunk him again!" laughed Rodriguez. This was more fun that he'd hoped for. The captain's wounds were bleeding well, the mermaid was suffering to see her lover's pain, and soon the sharks would come. Yes, things were going wonderfully.

Devon managed to hold his breath this time when they dunked him, though it took all his will to fight the agonizing pain that burned through his legs and stomach. Once more suspended over the water, he waited for what was coming.

Laly could feel her own blood dripping from her fingertips. She couldn't see if she'd made any progress with the knots, but she kept pulling, trying to escape, to get to Devon.

"I think once more!" shouted Rodriguez to his men. "And hold him under a little longer!"

Again, Devon managed to hold his breath, but his lungs were ready to burst by the time they brought him up. He was getting weaker by the minute from loss of blood, and he knew it wouldn't be long before the sharks arrived. The vicious maneaters would finish him off much quicker than Rodriguez's dunkings would, but he knew that was the pirate's plan all along.

Laly saw the dark shadow under water before Rodriguez did, and she shook with fear to her very soul. The next time Rodriguez ordered Devon put underwater the shark could strike. If not then, the next, or the next. It was only a matter of time. And many more sharks would soon arrive, making Devon's odds worse with every passing second. She tugged harder on her ropes.

"Again!" Rodriguez shouted. He was so enjoying his sport.

Devon saw the water rising up to meet him. He

also saw the large gray form of the shark circling beneath and wondered if this was the one that would do him in. He'd often thought about dying at sea, but he always thought he'd be killed in battle, or drown. He'd never once thought he'd die in the jaws of one of the ocean's monsters. He gasped for air as he hit the water.

Laly closed her eyes, too terrified to watch, then she opened them again, hoping to see Devon surface unharmed. She shuddered with relief when he was pulled up whole. "Devon," she sobbed. "I love you so," she cried though she knew he couldn't hear her.

Devon sputtered for air. He was very near to losing consciousness and prayed he'd be unconscious when the shark struck. At least he should be granted that small favor. His head fell back against the oars in exhaustion.

"He is passing out. Keep him above the water until he wakes up!" ordered Rodriguez. He didn't want to torture someone who didn't know what was happening to him. "We'll wait a moment." He scanned the water below Devon to see if he was dripping enough blood or if he needed to be cut some more. "Sharks!" he shouted happily. "See, pretty mermaid? The ocean will kill him."

Laly glared at Rodriguez. "You are not even human," she hissed, pulling with all her strength against her ropes. She was startled when she felt them slip and loosen a little. She was making headway.

Devon rolled his head to the side. Breathing deeply, he fought to remain unconscious, but his eyes opened against his will. The pain in his legs and stomach was nearly unbearable, and he shook violently, shock running through his system.

"No, Devon," whispered Laly. "Keep your eyes

closed," she prayed. She cried anew when she saw him raise his head slightly.

"He's awake!" shouted Rodriguez. "Send him under!"

Laly watched in horror as Devon was put under the surface in the direct path of a huge shark. She held her breath as the animal veered off at the last second, not yet ready to strike. Devon was pulled up and she heard the disappointed moans of the crew as they watched Devon escape the first attack.

Looking at the ignorant faces of the men that waited like vultures to see death, she suddenly remembered Sugar's trick. There was nothing she could do about the sharks, but she might be able to do something about the human animals on the ship. Throwing her head back, she shook her long hair behind her and began a crooning wail.

Watching from the corner of her eye, she saw many heads turn in her direction. Wailing louder, she began a prayer. "Oh, Neptune, Father of the Sea, hear me, please. Reach up from the bottom of the ocean and destroy this ship and the evil men on it!" she screamed. She heard murmured concern from the crew.

"Shut up, mermaid!" bellowed Rodriguez.

Laly looked directly at him and opened her eyes wide, making herself look crazy. "Smite this man, Neptune! Rip him from this ship and take him down to the depths of hell!" she growled.

Several of the crew stepped back from her, wanting to be farther away from her wrath.

"I told you to shut up, mermaid!" warned Rodriguez. He looked to his crew. "She can do nothing. Did she stop me from cutting the English bastard?

Did she stop us from putting him in the ocean? I tell you, she can do nothing. Ignore her."

"I stopped that shark from attacking the captain!" she shouted in a powerful, booming voice.

The crew stepped back further, cold fear in their eyes.

"She did nothing!" Rodriguez roared.

The crew continued to watch Laly twisting her long hair in the wind and letting her eyes roll wildly in her head.

"I will prove to you she is nothing. Put the captain under again. This time the sharks will have him and you will see!" ordered Rodriguez.

The crew stood very still.

"Do it!" bellowed Rodriguez, pulling his pistol from his belt.

The crew moved forward to the oars once more.

Devon had heard yelling from the ship above, but he couldn't tell what was happening. Then he felt himself being lowered again. The dark shadows under the water had grown to too many to count. He knew this was the last time he'd go under, and he wished with all his heart he could see Laly one last time and tell her he loved her. The water swirled up around him as he took his final breath.

Laly stopped her wailing as Devon was plunged under the water. She saw the sharks circling for the kill and closed her eyes. "I love you, Devon," she whispered, and waited for the crew to cheer his death.

Moments passed. She heard nothing. Then a quiet murmur of fear passed through the crew. Laly opened her eyes to see them bringing Devon's body up from the water once more. He was alive! The sharks hadn't attacked! Laly swung her turquoise eyes to the crew.

"Bring him up, or I destroy this ship!" she threatened.

Crewmen hurried to obey her command, pulling the oars that held Devon's body. A shot rang above their heads, stopping their actions.

"I'm still captain of this ship," growled Rodríguez, "and you'll obey my orders or die!" he promised.

"You're no longer in command, Rodriguez. These men know I'll destroy them if they harm Captain Bradley."

"You can do nothing!" he shouted. "You did nothing to the sharks. They are not hungry," he tried frantically to explain.

"Sharks, not hungry?" she made fun of him.

Rodriguez could take no more. Rushing to where Laly was tied, he took out his knife. "You will join the captain. We will see if the sharks like your blood better." Slicing her across the thigh, he left a trail of blood coursing down her leg.

Laly winced as Rodriguez dragged the knife across her flesh. Using the pain to give her strength, she pulled against her ropes with all her might. Her arms flew wide as the knots gave way. With her arms wide, blood dripping from her wrists and flowing down her thigh, her long hair blowing wildly in the breeze and her strange costume wrapping her body indiscreetly, she did indeed look like a mighty creature from the sea. "You're through, Rodriguez," she hissed, grabbing the knife he held aloft. Turning to his crew, she ordered, "Get Captain Bradley on board, now!"

Crewmen scrambled to do her bidding.

"No!" shouted Rodriguez. "This is my ship!" He grabbed for the knife, knocking it from her hand. "I'll kill you with my bare hands," he hissed. Reaching for her throat, he was startled when he was grabbed from behind by some of his crew. "Let me go, you fools!"

"Sir, you cannot hurt the mermaid. She will kill us all," they begged.

Rodriguez struggled against them, fighting with all his strength, but he couldn't free himself.

Laly untied the ropes that held her legs and ran to where Devon now lay on the deck. "My darling," she whispered against his temple. "You'll be all right now. I promise."

The explosion of cannon fire across the deck sent men flying in every direction. Laly screamed and covered Devon's body with her own.

Rodriguez jerked free of the last fool who held him. Looking across the open water, he saw the ship. "Battle stations!" he yelled. "It's the *Vengeance*!"

Nineteen

Sugar stood at the rail of the *Vengeance* and saw the cannon balls flying over the deck of the *Puta*. "You hit her!" she shouted. "One of the masts is falling!"

Wainwright stood at the head of the line of cannon and ordered another round. "Fire!" he shouted.

Sugar saw the volley hit the side of the *Puta* with violent force. Closing her eyes, she prayed, "Please let them be all right."

Laly pulled Devon to the side of the ship and covered his body with her own again. Masts were falling and fires had broken out across the ship. Men screamed in agony as limbs were torn from their bodies by cannon fire, and others shouted orders and readied their cannon to return fire.

Devon moaned as he became conscious. He felt a weight upon him and instantly thought of the sharks.

Fighting with all his strength, he pushed the weight off him.

"Devon, it's me," Laly soothed, as he shoved her aside. "Please, Devon. Open your eyes."

Devon heard Laly's voice and couldn't believe he was alive. Raising on one elbow, he took in the scene around them. "What's going on?" he asked weakly.

"It's the *Vengeance.* They've found us," she told him. "We're going to be all right," she whispered.

"Not if they don't win this battle." He tried to sit up and realized he was still very weak. "I've got to get up," he told her.

"But what can you do?"

"I can find Rodriguez," he said.

"And do what? You're as weak as a kitten."

He pushed himself up. "But I've got to do something."

"You've got to sit here. You've lost a lot of blood. Some of these wounds are still bleeding." She grimaced as she inspected the gashes across his thighs, ribs, and stomach. One in particular had her concerned as she could see muscle and bone, as well as blood. "I think you need some bandages," she said.

"I'm fine," he told her.

"Be quiet. I'm going to take care of you whether you like it or not." She tried to tear some strips of cloth from her skirt, hoping to tie them around his upper thigh. She looked around for something to use to cut the thick material. Seeing Rodriguez's knife still lying on the deck, she quickly crawled to get it. Bringing it back, she slipped it beneath her skirt and began to slash at her clothing. She immediately swathed the worst of Devon's wounds in pressure bandages. It took only seconds for the blood flow to slow, so she felt relatively certain he'd be all right.

Another crash of cannon fire blew across the deck and Devon grabbed Laly to hold her down. "If they're not careful, they're going to blow us up with this ship," he said.

Sugar was worrying the same thing. "Wainwright!" she yelled, over the din of the cannon. "If you sink the *Puta*, Laly and Devon will go down with it," she told him.

"We're only shooting across the deck and into the upper level of the ship. We're not striking any sinking blows," he explained.

Sugar didn't feel much better. She was afraid a cannon ball would land smack on top of Laly and there'd be nothing she could do about it. If she's still alive, she thought, then shook herself. "She *is* alive," she said out loud. But she couldn't help feeling doubt. The *Puta* had been dead in the water when they'd come upon her. And the crew had been staring off the far side of the ship, which was why they'd been able to sneak up on them. They'd been watching something, and Sugar prayed it wasn't Laly's death.

Rodriguez burned with hatred as the *Vengeance* swung round to fire again. "Fire!" he shouted, his crew finally ready to fight back. He watched the volley of cannon balls land far short of their mark. "Reload!" he ordered. "Raise the angle!" He hadn't lost this battle, yet. He was going to win, and then he'd finish what he started and kill the English captain and the mermaid. Oh, how the mermaid would suffer. He would do things to her he couldn't even imagine yet.

* * *

Devon felt himself getting stronger. He still shook with chills, and his body burned from the salt water soaking his clothes and running into his wounds, but he was feeling stronger. "We've got to get below," he told Laly.

"Why?"

"It's the safest place."

"But if the ship sinks, we'll be trapped," she said.

"Wainwright won't sink the *Puta*, he'll board her. We've got to get below."

Laly nodded and started to stand.

Devon pulled her back down. "Stay low," he warned.

"Okay. Let me help you." She put her arm under Devon's and half lifted him. She could feel the tremors that shook his body and looked deeply into his dark eyes. "Can you make it?"

"I can," he said.

Crossing the deck, they reached the stairs just as another volley of cannon fire grazed the ship.

Rodriguez saw the captain and Laly heading down the stairs to the lower deck. He would follow them soon and finish them off. "Fire!" he shouted.

The *Vengeance* suffered the damage of one cannon ball blowing a hole in the casemate and taking out a single cannon.

"Fire!" ordered Wainwright. The explosion of the cannon rocked the ship and he watched as more of the *Puta*'s masts were damaged and a hole the size of a wagon was blown in her side above the waterline. "Good job, men!" he shouted. "We've about got her where we want her! Come about to fire again!"

Sugar crouched at the bow behind Wainwright.

She covered her ears with her hands and prayed. She'd never said so many prayers in her life as she had the last several days and she hoped she wasn't using up more than her share of divine grace.

Rodriguez raised his arm to signal another round. His ship was badly damaged, but she could still fight, and fight she would. "Fire!"

Wainwright saw the volley coming, but he couldn't move fast enough. The ball took the jib, sending pieces of sail and wood splinters flying like bullets. One of these caught him in his left arm, nearly taking it off.

Sugar looked up in horror as he stood there, staring down at his useless limb and the ripped tissue that hung from it. "Wainwright, get down!" she screamed. "Oh, my God." Jumping from her crouched position, she pulled him down and saw he'd instantly gone into shock. She looked at the damaged arm and nearly vomited at the sight of torn flesh. She knew there was no doctor, no treatment, no medicine in this century that would restore his arm. It would have to come off, and soon, if they were going to save him. "Dr. Wells!" she shouted. "Someone, get me Dr. Wells!"

Lawson heard Sugar screaming from the bow and looked to see what was the matter. "Reload, men," he ordered. "I'll be right back."

Spears stopped him as he passed. "What's going on? Where's Wainwright?"

"I don't know. I'm going to find out." As he climbed the steps to the bow, he knew there was trouble. Sugar was bent over a very pale Wainwright whose left arm looked bad. Turning around again, he called to Spears. "Get up here, now! And bring help."

Minutes later, Sugar watched Wainwright being carried to sick bay. His left arm dangled at an odd angle to his body. She didn't know if Dr. Wells knew what he was doing, but she was going to see to it he did *something*.

As Lawson and Spears placed Wainwright on a table, Sugar heard them discussing what their next course of action should be. Turning to face them, she announced in a belligerent tone, "Take that bloody ship and throw that bastard pirate to the sharks!"

"Aye, aye, Miss," Lawson said.

Spears saluted her. "We've got our orders, Lawson. Let's go."

Shortly after they left, she felt another shudder of satisfying cannon fire.

Immediately she turned her attention to Wainwright and his injury. "Dr. Wells?" she called, expecting to see him enter from his quarters beyond the sick bay. "Doctor?" She waited a moment, then knocked at the door. When she didn't hear anything, she opened the door. What met her eyes filled her with fury and fear. Dr. Wells was passed out drunk on his bed, the rum bottle still in his hand. "You disgusting old reprobate," she hissed.

Crossing to the bed, she shook the doctor by the shoulder. When that didn't rouse him, she picked up a basin of water and threw it in his face. He didn't even sputter. "*Now* what am I going to do?" she murmured. A groan from Wainwright had her hurrying back to his side in the next room. Already a pool of blood had formed on the floor under his arm. She was going to have to do something, but what? Her meager first-aid knowledge wouldn't get her through an amputation. But did she have a choice? Without it, he'd bleed to death.

Digging through the doctor's medical supplies, she

realized how primitive his medicine really was. It didn't seem the doctor knew much more about amputation than she did. She could certainly tie off major veins and arteries. She could sew muscles together, and skin. Tears filling her eyes, she decided she might as well try. She was his only hope.

Sugar knew infection was her biggest worry, something the doctor probably didn't know, so she looked for something to sterilize the wound and the primitive instruments with. It wasn't hard to find more rum in the doctor's quarters. She just wasn't sure how potent a sterilizer rum would be. "It's better than nothing," she said out loud.

As the battle continued to rage overhead, Sugar began the most difficult thing she'd ever attempted.

Rodriguez raised his arm for another round of cannon fire. The battle was not going well, but he knew the tide would turn in his favor at any moment. It only took one good volley to change the odds. "Fire!" he shouted, and watched as the cannon balls hit their mark. "Yes, men! That's the way!" He nearly danced with joy as one of the *Vengeance*'s masts crashed to her deck. "I think I will dance," he said, jumping a little jig. His dance reminded him of the English captain. "I would bet you never broke a man's legs for dancing," he muttered. "But maybe I'll break yours for you," he said.

Laly and Devon sat in the companionway below deck. "It looks like the bleeding has about stopped," she said.

"You can probably take this thing off now." Devon touched the bandage.

"No, I'll leave them on a while longer. I want to be sure you're all right first."

"What happened to your wrists?" he asked. He'd seen the cut on her thigh right away, but he just noticed the deep scratches and tears in the flesh at her wrists.

"I did it myself," she said. "Trying to free myself from the ropes I was tied with."

Devon's heart beat with rage at Rodriguez. He was going to enjoy killing that man. "I think I should go up and see how the battle goes," he said as an excuse to find Rodriguez. "Wainwright should have my crew nearly ready to board the *Puta*."

"You're going nowhere. We're staying right here where it's safe until the battle is over. I almost lost you once today. I'm not letting you take any unnecessary chances."

"But I feel useless sitting here. I am the captain of the *Vengeance*," he said stubbornly.

"And I'm the mermaid, remember? Today proved I'm pretty powerful, so I wouldn't argue with me if I were you," she teased.

"What did happen?" he asked. "The last thing I remember was going underwater into a swarm of sharks."

Laly shuddered at the memory. "It turns out I am a mermaid, after all."

"You're what?"

"I called on Neptune to help . . . and I guess he did. The sharks ignored you."

"There has to be some logical reason," he said.

Laly raised her brows and shoulders in question.

A huge explosion as several cannon balls struck at once brought Devon to his knees. "I have to go up,

Laly. There might be something I can do from this end."

"If you go up, I go up," she said stubbornly.

"I guess that's one thing I've learned about you. Where I go, you go," he sighed. "Come on, then. Let's go see what's going on."

Rodriguez shouted orders faster than his crew could carry them out. The deck was on fire in several spots, the masts were all blown to hell, and many of the cannon had been destroyed. He could see the *Vengeance* was nearing to board, and he relished the chance to kill some English with his bare hands. "Stand to, men!" he roared. "We'll slit their throats for them!"

Lawson and Spears had their crew ready to board the *Puta*. Each man had his musket, pistol, and sword at the ready, and many carried small daggers in their boots. It would be a battle to the death. As the *Vengeance* floated into position, Lawson ordered the grappling hooks thrown to catch the other ship. In seconds the two ships collided. "Now, men! Now!" he shouted.

Spears swung to the *Puta* with the first wave, shooting a man while he boarded, and another before his feet were firmly planted on the deck. He never saw the blow coming that sent him to the boards.

"They're aboard, Laly!" Devon shouted. "They're aboard. Now to find Rodriguez."

"You're still too weak," she argued.

Devon turned and took her upper arms in his hands. "I know you won't stay here if I tell you to, so I'm asking you to. Promise me, because I love you, that you'll stay here, where it's relatively safe."

Laly stared up into the dark eyes she loved. "You bastard," she whispered.

Devon smiled. "Does that mean yes?" he asked.

"Yes," she murmured. "But your tactics aren't fair."

"Maybe not, but I got my way," he grinned. He bent to her, parting her lips in a possessive kiss. Then he left her to find Rodriguez.

Laly watched Devon's back as long as she could. Too soon he became lost in a sea of writhing, fighting bodies. Chewing her knuckles nervously, she tried to judge the tide of the battle, but from where she stood, it looked as though no one was winning. Everywhere she looked, she saw blood and gore. How could anyone truly call himself a winner when this was the price?

Rodriguez saw Captain Bradley fighting his way across the deck. He hadn't spied him yet, and that gave him the advantage. Shoving his sword through an English crewman, he smiled as he pulled the bloodied blade from the body. "You will not die so easily, Captain."

Sugar heard the screaming overhead, and knew they'd boarded the *Puta*. She didn't pray for Laly's safe return, nor the captain's. All her prayers were for Charles Wainwright.

She'd cut away his clothing first, and the sight of his mangled arm terrified her, almost making her abandon her plan to try and save him. Only a moan from deep within his chest, and the steady flow of blood filling the basin she'd placed on the floor under his arm, had caused her to pick up the knife and approach him. If she didn't do this, he would die.

Her first cut into human flesh brought hot bile to her throat. The second and third only caused her skin to crawl. By the time she circled his arm with the knife, she only shivered slightly at the sight of the loose flesh.

Pulling down on the lower arm, she could see where she had to cut through the muscles. As ridiculous as it would sound if she told someone, she thought about the way she cut up a chicken before frying it. "The tendons and muscles must be similar in all animals," she reasoned. Carefully cutting through the muscle tissue, she exposed the tendons. Some had been blown away by the wood shrapnel. Others were still attached to the bone below the injury. These she cut, leaving as much length as possible.

When the last of the tissue was cut, she jumped back in revulsion as his forearm and hand fell to the floor. "Oh, my God. I can do this. I can do this," she chanted.

Covering the arm with a piece of cloth, she moved it out of the way. She then went quickly back to finish the job she'd started. Blood flowed more freely, now that the arm had been amputated, and she knew she'd only have a few minutes to stop the bleeding or lose him. Grabbing the needle and thread she'd found in the doctor's things, she poured rum over the stump, then looked for the veins and arteries. As nimbly as possible she fought to tie off the slippery vessels. One by one she accomplished the task and was able to breath a little easier while she finished the long process of sewing up the stump.

Rodriguez made his way toward the captain's back. He wanted to make him suffer, but mostly he wanted him dead. If he had to run him through from behind, so be it.

Devon fought violently with one of Rodriguez's men. So far, he'd seen no sign of the pirate devil, and he anticipated with relish their sure meeting.

"Captain, Sir. Behind you!" shouted a young English sailor coming to join the fight.

Devon turned in time to see Rodriguez lunge for him. He deflected the sword he had pointed at his back and managed to catch him across the arm with the tip of the sword he'd taken from a dead Spanish officer. He loved the irony of killing Rodriguez with one of his own swords. "Fighting a coward's battle, Rodriguez? I should have known you'd try to stab me in the back."

Rodriguez bellowed with rage and lunged again. "I am going to kill you, Englishman. From the front or behind, it matters not to me. As long as you are dead, I will be happy."

"Then you are not going to be happy, Rodriguez. Because I am going to kill you." Devon parried Rodriguez's attack and lunged forward in an attack of his own, this time catching his shoulder with the sharp edge of his blade. "You see, Rodriguez? I will cut you into tiny pieces and feed you to the sharks, as you were going to do with me."

Rodriguez growled deep in his throat. His fury was blinding him. "You will not live long enough to do me damage, Captain. You are merely lucky. My luck is about to change." He swung his sword in a wide arch, nicking Devon's cheek before he could deflect the blow. "You see?" he laughed.

"Laugh all you want, Rodriguez. Soon you die," promised Devon, slicing the back of Rodriguez's hand. "You see?" he mimicked.

Laly could stand it no longer. Promise or no promise, she had to make sure Devon was all right. She was afraid in his weakened condition he wouldn't be able to defend himself.

Stepping out onto the deck, she had to dodge fighting everywhere. Men fought with swords, with daggers, even with their fists, and it looked, from the number of uniforms still standing, that the English were winning. Sighing with some relief, she looked around for Devon. Her heart lurched to her throat when she saw him and Rodriguez locked in a fierce sword battle. "No," she cried, clutching her hands to her chest.

Rodriguez had started to tire. He'd been cut several times without being able to give answering wounds, and his palms were sweating nervously, ruining his grip on his weapon. Hearing Laly behind him was a godsend.

Jumping back, he grabbed her around the waist and placed the edge of his sword against her throat. "Tell your men to surrender, Captain, or I'll cut her head off right in front of you," he said.

Devon took a step forward.

"Do it!" screamed Rodriguez.

"No, Devon. He'll kill us anyway," Laly cried.

Devon knew she was right and kept coming.

Rodriguez began backing up with her. "You know I'll do it, Captain," he threatened. Pulling her along with him, he started down the stairs, using Laly as a shield. "You know I'll kill her," he warned.

"And then I'll kill you, Rodriguez. Very slowly," Devon rasped.

Rodriguez continued down the stairs and along the companionway. "Get back, Englishman," his threats becoming less impressive.

"Let her go and I might let you die quickly," offered Devon.

Rodriguez kept Laly in front of him as he backed along the companionway. "I'll kill her," he repeated.

"Let her go," ordered Devon, his voice a barely audible threat.

As they near his cabin, Rodriguez could see the door stood open. It gave him an idea. "I'm going to cut off her head," he said again.

Devon was deadly silent. He just followed, waiting for his chance to kill the man he hated.

Rodriguez saw his opportunity. Shoving Laly aside through the open door, he lunged to kill the Englishman.

Devon was ready for Rodriguez's assault and answered with one of his own. It was then the bandage around his leg loosened and fell to the floor around his ankle. Devon glanced down.

Rodriguez smiled as he knocked the captain's sword from his hand.

Laly saw what was happening. She grabbed Devon's sword and slid it back to him. *"Devon . . .!"* she screamed.

Rodriguez dived for the kill. He aimed for Bradley's heart and put all his weight into the blow.

Devon fell to the floor as Rodriguez began his lunge. Grabbing the sword, he drove it upward through the pirate's diaphragm, twisting it as he pushed. Blood poured down over his hand as Rodriguez slid to the ground.

"You have killed me, Englishman," rasped Rodriguez in surprise.

Laly fell into Devon's arms. "I thought . . ." she sobbed. "I thought . . ."

Devon turned her away from the sight of Rodriguez's unseeing eyes. "I know," he said quietly. "Let's get out of here." Rising up, he brought Laly with him. Seconds later, as they climbed the stairs together, he felt her shivering. "I'll have you back aboard the *Vengeance* soon. We'll sleep," he told her.

Laly nodded, too shaken to say anything.

Sugar finished bandaging Wainwright's stump and could think of nothing else to do for him. She covered him and decided to go topside. "Everything's so quiet," she whispered, as she left the sick bay. "The battle must be over." Stopping in the companionway, she found another prayer for Laly. "Please, Lord?"

On deck, she watched as the wounded were helped back onto the *Vengeance.* She grimaced as she thought of the doctor passed out below. "Laly wonders what I'd do if we were stuck here. I'm a better doctor than that drunken fool," she said. "And I've already got a full waiting room." Kneeling beside the first man, she saw a minor cut over his left eye. "You can wait," she said, and went on to the more seriously injured.

Laly walked out onto the deck of the *Puta* with Devon. The fighting had ended; the English had won. She looked around her as though in a daze. "So much violence," she murmured.

"What? I didn't hear you," said Devon.

Laly looked up into his eyes. "There's so much violence here," she said.

"And there's not in your time?" he asked.

Laly thought for a moment. She thought about the wars and the street crime. "There's violence everywhere," she answered. "I'm just not usually involved."

"I'm sorry," whispered Devon.

"It wasn't your fault. As Sugar has told me and told me, I'm my own worst enemy, always looking for trouble. I guess this time I really found it." She almost laughed. Almost. The sight of so much destruction and death around her was very sobering, indeed. "I guess we'd better get back to the *Vengeance*. Sugar is probably worried sick about me," She scanned the side of the ship. "Although I don't see her anywhere. I'd have thought she'd be waiting for . . . there she is. What's she doing?"

"Looks like she's helping the wounded," observed Devon.

Laly smiled. "That's Sugar." She began walking to where a gangplank had been placed between the ships. She stopped when Devon didn't follow.

"Aren't you forgetting something?" he asked.

"What?"

"What you've risked your life several times for?" he prodded.

"The medallion!" she gasped. "How could I have forgotten?" She began to run toward the stairs again, then stopped. "Rodriguez is still down there," she said.

"Do you want me to get it for you?" he offered.

Laly looked at him with tears in her eyes. "Would you?"

Devon nodded. "Wait here," he said.

Minutes later, Laly held the medallion in her hands. "I can't believe I really have it," she said.

"Let's get back to the *Vengeance*," Devon said solemnly.

Laly could see the sadness in his eyes. "Okay."

*   *   *

Two hours later, Sugar, Laly, and Devon stood together with the crew on the deck of the Vengeance, watching the *Puta* burn.

"Will she sink?" asked Sugar.

"Eventually," answered Devon.

"How long will it take?"

"Maybe several hours."

Laly listened to the melancholy note in his voice and wrapped her arm around his waist. She was careful not to touch the cuts on his stomach.

"I'm not going to stand here and watch that horrible ship for hours. I've got patients to take care of," said Sugar, as she walked away.

Laly shook her head. She still couldn't believe what Sugar had done to save Wainwright. He certainly wasn't out of the woods yet, and he had a long recovery ahead of him if infection didn't set in, but Sugar had done a remarkable job. "I guess people can do some pretty difficult things, if they have to," she remarked.

"Yes, I guess they can," Devon agreed. The difficult thing he had to do was convince Laly to stay with him forever.

An explosion on board the *Puta* took their attention. The hull of the ship heaved outward, then sucked in. Water started to rush into her sides. "She's going down," whispered Laly.

Devon nodded. He was relieved to see the *Puta* sink. It had been an evil ship, captained by a disciple of the devil himself. "Good riddance," he whispered.

Twenty

In the days that followed, Devon kept the *Vengeance* circling the area where he'd found Sugar and Laly. Each day when he rose, he searched the sky for clouds from an impending storm, and each day his heart filled with relief when he saw none.

"What if the storm never appears?" he asked, on the fourth day of their search.

"Then I'll believe it was meant for us to remain here," answered Laly.

Devon turned his back to her and crossed the cabin to stand and stare out the porthole. "Would you be sad if you had to remain here . . . with me?" His voice was low. He hadn't asked her this question before, directly, and he was leading up to asking her to stay with him forever.

"I would never be sad with you," she told him. Laly stood from the table where she'd been eating her breakfast, and walked to put her arms around him. "I love you," she whispered against the broad muscles of his back.

Devon swung around to face her. "Then let's forget this search for a storm that probably doesn't exist. Let's head the *Vengeance* back to England. I want you to see my home, to meet my family."

Laly's expression sank. "I can't," she said quietly.

Devon stiffened. "I understand," he said.

Laly could see he didn't understand at all. He was hurt and angry, and he didn't understand. He wouldn't even see what this was doing to her. Everytime she thought about a life without him, her heart felt as though it was being ripped from her body. Everytime she thought about returning to her life in the future, she saw only empty days and even emptier nights. But she had to try and go back. It was where she belonged. And it was all Sugar talked about. Going home.

"I have work to do," Devon said quietly, unfolding her arms around him. He crossed to the door and opened it. "I'll be back later."

As he left, Laly sank to the bed.

"Can I come in?" asked Sugar, pushing the door open. "I saw the captain leave. Are you all right? You look like you've just lost your best friend." She sat next to Laly. "Which you haven't, because here I am," she teased.

Laly smiled weakly. "I'm fine," she lied. "How are Charles and Samuel?" she asked.

Sugar grinned. "Very well. Samuel is insisting on going on deck today. And Charles sat up to eat breakfast this morning."

"That's good," said Laly, her voice lacking the enthusiasm she attempted to show.

Sugar looked at her friend sympathetically. "Maybe you would like to come visit them?" she offered.

Laly nodded. "I'd like that. When?"

"How about now?"

Laly looked to her half-eaten breakfast. She wouldn't be able to finish now, anyway. "All right. Just let me get dressed."

Sugar nodded. She watched as Laly pulled a dress from the armoire and shook out the wrinkles. She pulled the garment over her head and preceded to fasten it herself. "No corset?" Sugar asked.

"Never again," said Laly, smiling.

"You're getting pretty good at dressing yourself in those get-ups."

Laly thought about it for a second. Raising her eyebrows, she answered. "Yeah, I guess so."

Sugar looked around the cabin and saw all the little things Laly had done to make the room nicer. Curtains at the porthole, a matching bedspread on the bed, the woodwork polished, the armoire neatly arranged with her things and Devon's hanging side by side. "If a person didn't know you, they'd think you belonged here. Except for the corset, of course," she teased.

Laly swallowed her surprise at Sugar's words. Her friend was only teasing, making conversation. "Except for the corset," she repeated. "I'm ready. Let's go."

Sugar led the way from the cabin toward sick bay.

As Laly followed her, she thought about her words. She was beginning to feel like she belonged here. But it was only because of Devon. If she hadn't met him she'd be chomping at the bit to get away from this primitive, violent time. She'd be barely able to wait to get back to her modern conveniences. Her TV, her car, her microwave, her radio, and, good God, her flushing toilet.

But she had met Devon, and she'd fallen in love with him. She'd fallen deeply, hopelessly, madly in love with him. Tears filled her eyes at her dilemma. Realistically, she didn't belong here, but when she left, she'd leave her heart behind.

"Here we are. Doesn't my patient look wonderful?" exclaimed Sugar, as they entered sick bay.

Laly stepped from behind Sugar and smiled at Charles. He was pale, and obviously in a great deal of pain, but he did look wonderful. He was alive. She crossed to the bunk he rested in. "Sugar's right. It won't be long before you're up playing strip poker again," she teased.

"I'm ready whenever Sugar is," he teased back, his voice weak and shaky. "But I think I'll have *you* deal next time. I'd like a fighting chance," he added.

Sugar tilted her head back and laughed. "I play only if *I* can deal," she told him.

Lawson stuck his head through the door then. "Miss Sugar, one of the crewmen just slipped up on deck. He's yelling bloody murder about his foot being broke. Can you come look at him before someone shoots him to put him out of his misery?"

Sugar laughed. "I'll be right there." She turned to Laly. "Do you want to come with me?"

"Would you stay with me a while?" asked Charles.

Laly smiled at the officer. "I'll stay. Sugar, you go on ahead. I'll be on deck later," she said. Much later, she thought.

Once Sugar and Lawson were gone Charles patted the bunk beside him. "Sit with me," he offered.

Laly carefully lowered herself to the bunk. "Are

you sure you feel up to a visit? Shouldn't you be resting?'' she asked.

"All I've done since this happened is rest," he said, looking briefly at his stump. "I've been wanting to talk to you, but I haven't had the chance.''

"You've been wanting to talk to me?" Laly smiled curiously at him.

"Yes, Miss Laly. About the captain. I know it's none of my business, and he'd skin me alive if he knew I did this, but I have to ask you to stay with him. Don't go back, please.''

Laly's heart wrenched at his request. It seemed she was being bombarded from every side to remain here. "It's not that simple, Charles.''

"Why not? He loves you. And you love him. How much more simple does it have to be?" Charles asked, his voice becoming thready.

"You're getting weak. You should sleep," Laly changed the subject.

"But if you go . . . I don't know what he'll do, Miss Laly," Charles whispered.

"Devon's a big boy. I'm sure he'll be fine," she said, raising from the bunk. Tucking the covers around him, making sure his stump was elevated, she brushed a stray curl from his forehead. "He's lucky to have you as his friend," she told him. "Now, go to sleep." She put her finger gently over his lips when he tried to speak again. "Sleep," she whispered. She turned from the bed. He was already breathing slowly when she reached the door.

Devon watched the horizon without seeing it. The sun reflected brilliantly off the water. A cloudless blue sky stretched endlessly overhead. A warm sea breeze billowed the sails of the *Vengeance*. He saw none of these things. All he could see were Laly's turquoise eyes as she'd sadly watched him leave their cabin that morning.

"Damn it," he hissed. He hadn't meant to act the way he had. He wanted her to have only good memories of him when she left. His eyes closed as he fought the stinging tears that threatened to spill from his lashes. How could he have fallen so deeply in love with her?

Clenching his fists, he opened his eyes again with a resolution firmly in mind. He would do nothing to spoil the time they had left together. If it was to be an hour, a day, a month, or the rest of their lives. He'd make the most of each moment. He'd make her as happy as he possibly could. But make no mistake, he would still try to talk her into staying.

Laly lay on Devon's bed, staring at the ceiling. Her mind was in a turmoil and her heart twisted painfully in her chest. She turned her head into his pillow to smell the essence of him, and pictured his handsome face. Tears slipped silently from her eyes to spot the pillowcase. She squinted tightly, trying to stop the flow, but gave up after a moment. Why should she not cry? Her heart was breaking.

Devon heard Laly's sobs as he stood outside their door. He felt tremendous guilt at having been the cause of her sadness. "Laly?" he whispered as he opened the door. "Forgive me?" he pleaded.

Laly sat up in the bed, her tear swollen eyes feasting on the sight of him. "There's nothing to forgive you for. You aren't to blame for the predicament I'm in."

"No, but I don't have to make it worse by acting like a spoiled child."

Laly held her arms out to him, clutching him tightly when he knelt at her side. "I'll love you forever," she promised.

"And I you," he murmured against her ear, nibbling softly on the lobe.

Laly felt chills of excitement course through her at Devon's playful bites. "That feels good," she whispered huskily.

"I can make you feel better," Devon growled softly, biting her gently along the curve of her jaw.

"Prove it," she challenged.

"Ah, my sweet mermaid, you put me to the test?" He pushed her down into the softness of their bed, covering her pliant body with his strong one. "You see? I am ready to prove it," he purred, rubbing the huge length of his arousal over her abdomen.

Laly's deep laugh turned into a moan as she raised her hips to feel even more clearly the shape of his manhood.

Devon drove himself against her, beginning a rhythm that would carry them through to fulfillment. Sliding his hands along her sides, he reached to cup the fullness of her breasts beneath the soft fabric of her dress. Massaging her gently, he found her passion-hardened nipples thrusting upward to meet his touch. Stroking them with his thumb, he covered one with his mouth, wetting the fabric in a circle over the throbbing crest of her breast.

Laly leaned into Devon's loving assault. She reached to the neckline of her dress and pulled the fabric down, exposing her breasts to him, encouraging him to suckle her, flesh to flesh.

Devon loved the glazed look in Laly's eyes. He pressed his face deeply into the cleavage between her breasts, pressing them together with his hands and kissing the inside curve of each. He then went back to the dark pink buds at their tips, kissing each in turn.

Laly matched Devon's rhythm with her hips as she enjoyed the attention he paid her breasts. She arched against him and pulled him ever closer. Reaching to twine her fingers in his thick, dark hair, she held him to her, groaning as he bit tenderly on the sensitive pink tissue of her nipples.

Devon kept up his onslaught of Laly's breasts but wanted more. Reaching with one hand down her side, he began to pull up her dress, bunching it around her waist as he went. Soon he felt the soft cloth of her pantaloons, and then their waistband. Untying them quickly, he slipped his hand inside, finding the soft mound of her womanhood. Delving between her legs with his fingers, he entered her quickly, feeling the rush of moistness his invasion caused.

Laly saw stars at Devon's touch. She swallowed and took gulps of air to calm her sensitive nerves. The deep, plunging rhythm he began with his fingers he matched in the motion of his hips. "Devon, let me," she breathed, sliding her hand along his broad back. Reaching his waistband, she felt him rise slightly to give her easier access to his body. Slipping her hand into the front of his pants, she was immediately rewarded with the feel of his hot, throbbing manhood against her hand. Grasping it firmly in her fingers, she slid her hand downward, then back.

Devon ground his teeth together as Laly stroked him. He arched his hips and pushed himself into her hand again and again as she repeated the motion.

He matched her action by delving deeply within her with his fingers.

Laly felt herself losing reality. The stars started to explode behind her eyes and she felt herself beginning to shatter. "Devon, stop," she breathed. "I want you inside me," she panted.

Devon, too, was near the brink of his release. He was too close. He couldn't stop. "Laly," he rasped as he felt the familiar shuddering beginning deeply within him.

Laly cried out Devon's name as she arched against his hand. "Devon, Devon," she moaned again and again. She felt the spasms of release in her body and the matching spasms of his organ as it jerked against her fingers, sending fluid upward. When she felt his passion dwindling, she stroked him gently, draining the last of his desire.

Devon rotated his hips, moving his manhood between her loving fingers. "I want more," he groaned.

"So do I," she answered.

He pulled her dress upward, stopping only briefly when she needed to unfasten it.

"You too," she said.

He stood up and finished removing his clothing. By the time he was through, she lay naked before him. Lying next to her once more, he took her in his arms, he kissed her gently. First her eyes, then her lips. He was almost startled by how quickly his body began its recovery and was ready to possess her completely.

Laly smiled up into Devon's eyes when she felt the heated shaft of his passion pressing into her hip. "Remarkable," she whispered, teasing.

"Only with you," he answered, grinning back. Rising above her, he entered her slowly, pushing himself deeply inside her. "Only with you," he repeated in a rasping breath.

Laly took him again and again. She rode the wave of their passion and felt as though she soared above the ocean on a high, keening breeze. When she fell, crashing to the surf, Devon was there to catch her. Tears slipped easily from her eyes as her passion cooled.

Devon exhilarated in the explosive passion he felt with Laly. He lost himself in her, in her eyes and her fire. He gave all he had to give, shuddering violently as he filled her. Finally, he was spent. Clasping her to him, he let his head rest over hers, his tears falling unashamedly across his cheeks.

When Laly woke it took her a few seconds to realize where she was, then the feeling of Devon's body next to hers reminded her. Smiling, she snuggled more deeply against him.

"Are you awake?" Devon whispered.

"No," Laly answered.

"Then how do you know what I just said?"

"I'm talking in my sleep, so shut up," she teased.

Devon grinned at her playfulness. "I wish I could wake up like this for the rest of my life," he said without guile.

"Me, too," she answered. She didn't add that it was impossible.

Devon heard what she thought in the tone of her voice. His heart skipped a saddened beat, but he kept his resolution. "I'm starving," he said, biting her on the shoulder.

"Well, you can't eat me!" she squealed.

Devon lowered his brows evilly. "Sounds like a good idea to me," he said lecherously.

"You're a monster," she accused.

"Not me?" He acted hurt.

"Yes, you. You're a . . . a . . . sexy beast."

Devon laughed out loud. "That doesn't sound so bad," he said.

"Well, it is."

"And what do sexy beasts do that is so terrible?" he wanted to know.

Laly had to think quickly. "They take advantage of innocent mermaids."

"I guess that's pretty bad, huh?"

"Yup. That's what they do."

"And did I take advantage of you? Or did you bewitch me, mermaid?" he demanded, biting her again.

Laly laughed deep in her throat. "I bewitched you," she said. "I saw you standing in the bow of this ship, and I said to myself, I want him."

"Well, mermaid, you got me. But I'm still starving."

"How long did we sleep?"

Devon shrugged. "It doesn't matter."

"What if we slept through lunch?"

"Then we'll go raid the kitchen. I happen to know the chef," he said, with his nose in the air.

"Aren't we snooty today?" Laly said with a fake British accent.

"Quite," Devon replied. "Come on, let's get dressed. My stomach is growling."

"A man with a one-track mind," she said.

"Absolutely."

Laly pushed herself up and reached for her clothing strewn across the bed. "Goodness, these are wrinkled," she observed. "Oh well, they'll have to do."

She tugged on her pantaloons, then stood to pull her dress over her head. Fastening it behind her, she watched Devon dress. She frowned at the sight of the still angry-looking cuts Rodriguez had inflicted, but she sighed with the knowledge that Devon would heal and that the pirate would never hurt anyone again. "Ready?" she asked.

"Do I look ready?" he asked, still shirtless, the front of his pants hanging open.

"I don't know. You claimed to be starving. A starving man wouldn't care if he were stark naked," she said coyly.

"Sugar's right about you. You *are* a troublemaker."

"So you want to be rid of me, then?" she teased, walking toward the porthole.

He watched the way the light from the porthole reflected off her hair and made her eyes sparkle. He loved the teasing tone in her voice and the way she stood up to him. He got hot just thinking about making love to her again, and he died a little every time he remembered she was leaving him. "No," he said, the playful tone gone.

"What?"

"No," he repeated softly. "I never want to be rid of you."

Laly lowered her eyes. It always came back to this. "Please stay, Laly. Stay with me forever."

Laly didn't know what to say to him. Her heart was once again being torn from her body. Leaning forward, she rested her hand on the edge of the porthole, her head against her hand.

"Please, Laly," he begged.

Raising her eyes, she looked out across the sea. Her heart stopped beating all together.

A frantic knock on their door was followed by Sugar's gleeful yell. "The storm, Laly! It's the storm!"

Laly turned from the port hole. The look on Devon's face was one of ravaged pain. "I'll let her in," she said. She crossed the room, brushing past Devon as she went.

"Can you believe it! It's finally, really out there!" Sugar squealed, as she burst through the open door. "We're going home!" She grabbed Laly by the shoulders and jumped up and down. It took her a second to realize Laly wasn't jumping with her. "Are you all right?" she asked.

"I'm okay," Laly said, her voice choked with emotion.

"Do you need some time alone?" Sugar asked, looking at Devon's pale face.

"No," he suddenly remarked. "We'd better get you two topside."

Laly heaved a tattered breath. "Yes, we'd better. I'll get the medallion." Crossing to the armoire, she took the medallion from the bottom drawer and carried it to the door. "Let's go."

Once on deck, they watched the storm approaching with uncanny speed. "Are you sure it's the same storm?" asked Laly.

Sugar nodded as she spoke. "It's the same." She'd watched the storm advance once before, when Laly had been under the surface.

"Keep the bow pointed into the wind!" shouted Devon to the crew.

"We're tryin', Captain. The wind seems to be coming from all directions at once."

"That's it," murmured Sugar, blinking as a bolt of lightning ripped open the sky.

Devon squinted into the fury of the storm. "You're going to swim out into that?" he asked.

"That's how we got here," Laly said, raising her voice above the ever-rising wind.

"You're crazy. You won't last five minutes in that water," he yelled back. The swells were getting higher every minute and whitecaps could be seen though they were still some distance from the storm.

"What can we do?" Sugar asked.

"What about a boat? One of your lifeboats might work," she suggested, looking up at Devon.

Devon thought about it for a moment. He'd feel better about them being in a boat. If the storm didn't take them back to their own time, they'd at least have a fighting chance of surviving. Even if the boat capsized, it would still float. "Yes. It might work."

"But we were in the water before," yelled Sugar, pulling a wildly blowing curl from her eyes.

"I don't think we have a choice," yelled Laly. "We don't have any diving equipment this time. If we got pulled under, we'd drown."

Sugar shrugged. "I guess you're right. Okay, Captain, a lifeboat it is."

Devon turned to his crew. "Lower a boat!" he shouted into the wind.

They watched as the crew of the *Vengeance* began to lower a lifeboat into the churning sea. Huge swells lifted the ship and dropped it again, making the timing of getting the lifeboat into the water precarious at best. At the last moment, a huge swell took the tiny boat and cracked it against the hull of the *Vengeance*, breaking its spine.

"Damn it," cursed Devon. "Release it!" he shouted.

The crew let go the ropes to the lifeboat and watched it sink beneath the waves.

Devon turned to Laly. "I can't let you try this," he shouted, his word almost lost on the wind.

"You have to. We've got to try," she shouted back.

Devon looked at Sugar's frantic expression. She wanted to go home. Turning toward the crew once more, he cupped his hands around his mouth. "Lower another!"

The crew exchanged nervous looks. "Are you sure, Sir?" one man asked.

"I'm sure," yelled Devon.

Grasping the ropes to another boat, the crew heaved it into position over the side. Lowering it slowly, they tried timing the waves, but the swells had no rhythm, striking upward without warning, dropping suddenly when the wave seemed to be nearing its peak. "Damn, Captain! The bloody ocean's bewitched!" one man yelled. "How're we going to get her in?"

Devon looked at the life boat dangling over the water. "Drop her!" he yelled.

"What?"

"Drop her!" he yelled again. "If she hits straight, she'll float."

The men exchanged glances again, but on a count, they released the ropes, rushing to the side to see if the little boat survived. "She made it, Sir!" they yelled.

"Pull her alongside and drop the rope ladders. You two," he pointed to some of the crew, "get down to her and hold her as steady as you can."

Laly leaned over the side and watched as the men climbed down the ladders to the waiting boat. It took all their expertise not to end up in the ocean. "I don't know if we can do that," she yelled to Sugar.

"We have to, it's our only hope of getting home," Sugar returned.

After what seemed like an hour, the two crewmen had the little boat somewhat secured at the side of the *Vengeance.*

Sugar closed her eyes to a flash of brilliant lightning. "It's time," she shouted.

Laly felt her throat closing in dread. Looking to Devon, she saw tears in his beautiful eyes. Walking toward him, she wrapped her arms around his waist and put her cheek against his chest. "I love you," she said, though she knew he couldn't hear her over the wailing of the storm.

Devon held Laly tightly to him. The time had come that he'd been dreading for days. Tears slipped from his eyes, and he saw his crewmen looking away as though they didn't notice. Leaning down, he brushed his lips across the top of her hair. He'd asked—no, begged—her to stay with him in their cabin, and she hadn't answered him. She was determined to go home. He supposed he shouldn't blame her. "It's time," he shouted.

Laly walked to the ship's rail in Devon's arms. "Sugar, you go down first," she yelled against the wind.

Sugar nodded. She understood Laly wanted to spend these last few seconds with the captain. Swinging her leg over the rail, she found the rope ladder and began to climb down. The wild movement of the ship swung the ladder from side to side, and she had to hang on tightly or fall. Each step she took lowered her closer to the lifeboat. Stopping to rest, she looked down. The lifeboat bounced crazily on the water below her, looking too much like a toy in comparison to the ship she clung to. She took a deep breath and continued. She had to get home.

Laly watched Sugar climbing down the ladder, and her heart jumped to her throat as she swung back and forth with the rocking of the ship. When she neared the lifeboat, she saw the crewmen help her to find a safe seat on one of the cross benches. It was her turn.

Devon knew his life would never be the same without her. Tilting her chin up with his fingers, he looked down into her turquoise eyes for the last time. Tears streamed down her cheeks. "I love you!" he shouted.

"I love you, too!"

"Don't go, Miss Laly!" shouted Charles, clinging to the railing for support.

Laly swung around. No one had seem him come up on deck. "Some one help him!" she shouted.

Several men ran to his side. "Don't go, Miss Laly!" he shouted again.

She took a step toward him.

"It's that simple!" he yelled.

She turned back to Devon and saw the tears in his eyes. She felt her own heart breaking so thoroughly it would never be whole again. It was simple; Charles was right. Why did it take her until this moment to realize it? Leaning over the rail, she waved down at Sugar. "I'm staying!" she screamed, tears of joy racing down her cheeks. "I was meant to be here. That's why it happened!"

Sugar shook her head. "No, Laly! You've got to go back!"

Laly smiled at her friend. "I'm going to miss you!" In one smooth motion she threw the medallion to land perfectly in Sugar's lap. "Take care. I love you!"

She turned back to face Devon. "And I love you!"

The crewmen jumped from the life boat and clung to the ladders as they pushed the tiny boat away from the *Vengeance*. Sugar watched Laly and Devon embracing on the deck overhead. "Laly!" she yelled into the wind. "I'll miss you, too!" She felt her face becoming wet with her own tears. "But maybe you're right," she whispered. Clutching the medallion tightly, she let the storm take her into its heart.

Laly watched the tiny lifeboat disappear before her eyes. A cloud seemed to envelop it for a moment, then it was gone. Just as suddenly, the storm blew over and the sea was calm. A murmur of uncertainty passed through the crew. She turned to face them. "It's all right. Everything's as it should be." She turned to where Charles stood weakly, held up by two of his crew mates. "Put that man to bed," she ordered.

She then looked up into Devon's surprised, happy face. "And I'll put this one to bed," she whispered.

He leaned down to kiss her. Just before his lips touched her's he murmured, "I'm still hungry."

"You beast!" she squealed, laughing.

"Sexy beast, remember?"

"And what do sexy beasts do?" she asked playfully.

"They take advantage of sweet mermaids."

She swung her arms wide. "We've got a long lifetime ahead of us, so you'd better start taking advantage."

Epilogue

Sugar lay in the bottom of the boat and shivered. Her clothes were wet. Her hair was wet. She felt like she hadn't eaten in days, and she was dehydrated. Every time she rose up she expected to see the *Vengeance* floating nearby. How long had she been here, she wondered?

"Ahoy! Anyone in the boat?" a voice yelled.

Sugar shivered and remained lying down. She'd heard voices before. They weren't real.

"Ahoy! Anyone in the boat!"

This voice was persistent. She decided to be gullible one more time and sat up. Her heart nearly quit beating when she saw a beautiful, sleek yacht floating close by. She weakly raised her hand in greeting.

"Oh my God, Chuck. It's a woman. Quick, call the Coast Guard."

Sugar was transported by helicopter to the hospital on Nassau. She was put to bed, given fluids intravenously, and told it was a miracle she was alive.

She'd been missing nearly two weeks. She cried for hours.

The second night in the hospital a reporter came to see her.

"My name's Hank Thomas," he introduced himself.

"I don't know what you want to hear," said Sugar.

"Anything you think of, Miss Stephens. You've been through a harrowing experience. People like to hear about things like that. Remember that couple that got stranded in the snow a while back? They made a movie about them. Wouldn't you like a movie made about you?" the reporter asked.

"No, Hank, I wouldn't."

Not in the least chagrined, Hank tried another approach. "Well, I understand you had a friend with you." He looked down at his notes. "A Miss Lorraine Lawrence. Would you like to tell her story?"

"Laly," whispered Sugar, her eyes filling with tears.

"I'm sorry. I guess that wasn't such a good idea. Just tell me what happened to you."

Sugar looked him in the eye. This fresh kid needed to be put in his place. "Laly and I went back in time to the year 1678. We fought pirates, were sold into slavery, escaped a madman, and I amputated a man's arm," she said in a level tone. "Laly decided to remain there."

Hank raised his eyebrows. "Really? All that in two weeks, eh?" He laughed a nervous little laugh. Either she was putting him on, or her brain had been affected by her ordeal. "So, what are your plans for the future?" he asked, putting his notepad away.

Sugar saw the skepticism and started to laugh. If she lived to be a hundred, no one was going to believe her. "Please leave," she asked. She had no other visitors while in Nassau.

Her first night back in her apartment, a friend of hers and Laly's stopped by. After the initial hugs and offered condolences, they sat down to talk.

"How are things going in your summer session, Mary?" asked Sugar.

"Fine, fine," she said.

"Good. How are Larry and the kids?" Sugar asked.

"Fine," Mary answered.

Sugar was puzzled. Mary was usually very talkative. "What's up?" she finally asked.

"Well, I hate to bring up a painful subject."

"But?"

"A crazy story has surfaced."

"About me?"

Mary nodded. "The dean wanted me to ask you about it."

Sugar just waited.

"There's a story in one of the tabloids stating you said you'd gone back in time and fought pirates, or something like that?"

Sugar let her head fall forward. "That little shit," she said. "A reported came to see me while I was in the hospital in Nassau. I wouldn't give him the story he wanted . . ."

"So he made this one up?" Mary interrupted relieved.

"No, I said it. But it was only to get rid of him."

Mary stood up. "I'm so glad to hear that. The dean will be, too. I've got to run. It was good seeing you."

"You have to leave so soon?"

Mary shrugged. "Larry and the kids are waiting.

You really should find a nice guy and have some kids yourself, Sugar.'' Mary gave her advice, then left.

Alone once more, Sugar sat on her couch and thought. She'd told her story to that reporter and he'd sold it to a tabloid. Sighing, she stood and walked to the picture window of her living room.

Looking in the direction of the ocean, she thought of Laly. It was obvious anyone who heard her story doubted her sanity. She began to doubt it herself. Had she gone back in time, or had her mind made up the whole elaborate tale because she couldn't deal with the death of her best friend?

"I'm going to find out," she said.

Spending the next four days checking out books from the library, she finally felt she'd found all the ones she needed. Sitting in the center of the piles she'd created in her living room, she began her search.

Day after day she read. Frozen pizza crust and empty soda cans built up around her. Showering became unimportant as she searched. Her hair hung in limp curls around her face, and her bathrobe began to smell bad. Then, when she'd all but given up, she found it. "Laly!" she shouted.

Pulling her finger across the reference again, she began to cry as she read out loud. "Lord and Lady Cheswick had four children. Charles Osgood, William Lindsey, Thomas Gordon, and Elizabeth Laly, the daughter named for her eccentric great-grand-mother, Mrs. Laly Bradley, the wife of an English sea captain.''

Sugar jumped to her feet and began dancing around the room. "You made it, Laly. You were meant to be there. You had children and grandchildren.

You made it!'' She suddenly stopped dancing, ''And it's time I did, too.''

The doorbell chime brought her to the door. When she opened it, Mary stood outside.

''Hello, Sugar, I brought you . . . oh, dear.'' Mary stopped, shocked by Sugar's disheveled appearance and the odor coming from her filthy bathrobe. ''Are you all right, Sugar?''

Sugar grinned happily. ''I couldn't be better. And I'm taking your advice. I'm going to look for a husband and start having those kids.''

Mary looked her up and down. ''Right now?'' she asked.

Sugar looked down at her appearance and started to giggle. In moments she was howling. ''I think I'll take a shower first,'' she laughed.

Dear Readers,

I am, and have been, many things in my life. Wife, mother and writer are my present occupations. During the years I was standing behind a chair in the beauty salon I owned, I dreamed of making my writing a career. During the hours I spent singing and playing guitar in a band, I thought up stories to put down on paper. During my stint as the owner of an aerobic wear clothing store, I spent the quiet times writing down the many ideas I'd come up with. And as far back as grade school, when I'd been moved away from the window, yet again, for daydreaming, writing was a part of me.

If you are a writer, you will write, no matter what else you must do to survive. I can only encourage others out there with similar dreams to keep dreaming. Dreams do come true. I hope you all enjoyed reading *Mermaid's Dream*, and will look for my name, Alane Fay, on future book covers. I also write Western romances under the pseudonym Faye Adams. If you like tales of strong women who meet their matches in the old West, you might like to give Faye Adams a try.

Thank you!

HISTORICAL ROMANCE FROM PINNACLE BOOKS

LOVE'S RAGING TIDE (381, $4.50)
by Patricia Matthews

Melissa stood on the veranda and looked over the sweeping acres of Great Oaks that had been her family's home for two generations, and her eyes burned with anger and humiliation. Today her home would go beneath the auctioneer's hammer and be lost to her forever. Two men eagerly awaited the auction: Simon Crouse and Luke Devereaux. Both would try to have her, but they would have to contend with the anger and pride of girl turned woman . . .

CASTLE OF DREAMS (334, $4.50)
by Flora M. Speer

Meredith would never forget the moment she first saw the baron of Afoncaer, with his armor glistening and blue eyes shining honest and true. Though she knew she should hate this Norman intruder, she could only admire the lean strength of his body, the golden hue of his face. And the innocent Welsh maiden realized that she had lost her heart to one she could only call enemy.

LOVE'S DARING DREAM (372, $4.50)
by Patricia Matthews

Maggie's escape from the poverty of her family's bleak existence gives fire to her dream of happiness in the arms of a true, loving man. But the men she encounters on her tempestuous journey are men of wealth, greed, and lust. To survive in their world she must control her newly awakened desires, as her beautiful body threatens to betray her at every turn.

Available wherever paperbacks are sold, or order direct from the Publisher. Send cover price plus 50¢ per copy for mailing and handling to Penguin USA, P.O. Box 999, c/o Dept. 17109, Bergenfield, NJ 07621. Residents of New York and Tennessee must include sales tax. DO NOT SEND CASH.

FUN AND LOVE!